Caught Midstream

A NOVEL

Uta Christensen

To Ellen —
It was a pleasure meeting
you. Love, Uta

PublishAmerica
Baltimore

At the specific preference of the author, PublishAmerica allowed this work to remain exactly as the author intended, verbatim, without editorial input.

Rainer Maria Rilke. New Poems, A Bilingual Edition (page 83 "Experience of Death" and page 103 "Spanish Dancer"), translated from German by Stephen Cohn, Copyright 1997. Used by permission of Northwestern University Press, Evanston.

"Lament," copyright 1982 by Stephen Mitchell, from THE SELECTED POETRY OF RAINER MARIA RILKE by Rainer Maria Rilke, translated by Stephen Mitchell. Used by permission of Random House, Inc., New York.

"Autumn," from Rainer Maria Rilke Selected Poems, translated by J.B. Leishman, published by the Hogarth Press. Reprinted by permission of the Random House Group Ltd., London, UK, for throughout the UK and Commonwealth and by permission of the Suhrkamp Verlag, Frankfurt am Main, Germany, for throughout the USA, its Dependencies, and in all foreign countries.

ISBN: 1-4241-0967-1
PUBLISHED BY PUBLISHAMERICA, LLLP
www.publishamerica.com
Baltimore

Printed in the United States of America

In memory of my father,

to Bernhard

and

to my husband for his undying support

Author's Note

The harrowing, historical backdrop of this novel, *CAUGHT MIDSTREAM*, is the staggering numbers of prisoners of war taken by the Nazi German and Soviet militaries and the horrifying treatment of these POW's by both nations. The numbers of prisoners of war taken during World War II are unprecedented in world history.

It was in June 1941 that the Germans launched a four-million-man Blitzkrieg eastward into the Soviet Union on a front 1,500 miles wide, now known as the biggest military operation the world has ever seen. The goal was to establish German dominance by overthrowing the communist regime of Joseph Stalin. It is estimated that the German military killed 2.8 million Russian POW's through starvation, exposure, and summary executions during only eight months of the blitzkrieg operation. Since the Soviet army had been decimated through pre-war purges under Stalin, the Soviet forces caved in quickly under the initial Nazi onslaught. By the time the brutal Russian winter set in (the winter of 1941-42), Soviet POW's began dying in captivity in massive numbers. They were either penned behind barbed wire with no protection from the elements and were being starved; were executed en masse by the German army; or were transported to the rear to be exterminated by the hundreds of thousands.

Eventually the decimation of Soviet POW's was stopped, and the Germans began to use them as slave laborers. The total number of Soviet prisoners taken by the Germans during the entire war is estimated to be 5.5

million. One of the most tragic ironies at the end of the war was that the estimated 2 million Soviet POW's who survived German incarceration were arrested en masse by the Soviet authorities upon repatriation on suspicion of having collaborated with the Germans. Almost without exception, these returning Russian POW's were sentenced to long terms in Soviet death camps.

The Soviets stopped the Nazi blitzkrieg armies at Moscow in December 1941 and eventually gained the upper hand at the Battle of Stalingrad (1942-43) and the Battle of Kursk (July 1943). By April 1945, the Soviet forces had crushed all German resistance and occupied Berlin, the German capital.

The Soviets took terrible revenge on millions of German POW's and POW's of other nationalities who were captured by the Soviet armies. Some were executed, but most of them were sent to prisoner of war camps deep within the Soviet Union where many died of starvation, overwork, and exposure. Once in the camps, the POW's were treated as slave laborers. Of the estimated 3.2 million German prisoners of war, at least 1 million died in the Soviet camps.

None of the prisoners held by the Germans or the Soviets were treated even remotely in accordance with the Geneva Convention.

After the war international negotiations concerning German POW's held by the victorious forces (United States, Britain, France, and Soviet Union) resulted in an agreement that all German POW's should be released by the end of 1948, more than three and a half years after the end of the war. It became later known that the only nation ignoring the agreement was the Soviet Union. Many of their German POW's were held considerably longer.

CAUGHT MIDSTREAM is the moving story of a very young German conscript who survived incarceration in Soviet POW camps in an unusual way because of his youth, innocence, attitude, talents, and exceptional character.

Experience of Death

We know nothing of our departing, for
it refuses to confide in us.
Our wonder should not be required, nor
love nor hatred, faced with Death, whose

tragic mask of grief disfigures it.
The World is full of parts which we must play,
as long as we still wonder if we please
Death will perform its own unpleasing part.

But when you left us, a reality,
a ray of light, shone in upon our stage
through the same chink through which you'd slipped away:
real green, real sunshine on real foliage.

We still perform and anxiously recite
our hard-learned lines; from time to time we must
make actors' gestures. But your presence might,
though far from us, no longer in the cast,

descending like a breath of that reality
take hold of us sometimes and overcome us.
Then for a time we are transported: we
at last act life and look for no applause.

Rainer Maria Rilke

PART I
1959

1

Dancing With Gypsies

Rumors had it that he was an incorrigible eccentric though I refused to believe it and tried to pay no attention to the incessant chatter. But when it was time to go home at the end of the day, it not infrequently happened that he burst into our office with his booming presence. "Hey, my friends, I feel again like dancing with the gypsies tonight. Please join me. I implore you. The evening is going to be my treat." He sounded upbeat, and yet, I thought, I detected a faint desperation in his plea. As usual, he refused to take no for an answer. The more anyone resisted, the more persuasive he became. It never took too much persuasion for we, too, yearned for a release from the day's tensions of the fast work pace. We promised we would meet him at seven.

We were almost entirely a young staff, and we loved and admired him. By day he was a taxing boss, demanding top performance, speed, and efficiency. He exacted these qualities of himself more than of anyone else. When we spent the evenings with him it was different—he brought excitement, exuberance, and imagination into our lives. He treated us like his beloved, showering us with attentiveness and wooing us with drink, music, food, and dance.

Like this night, he most often took us to the Gypsy Baron, a favorite Hungarian restaurant of his in the old part of the city. It was located in a house built more than three hundred years ago, thick-walled, with deep-set, many-paned windows, and an ornate, hand-carved entrance door. On entering, the passionately exotic gypsy music, the guests' laughter and excited chatter, and the spice-laden wafts from the simmering goulash stew transported us into a world at once foreign and utterly inviting, full of sensuality and temperament. The center of the house had been opened up when it was converted into a restaurant so that one could see from the ground floor up to the third story ceiling. The two upper floors appeared more like enormous balconies braced from the ground floor up by heavy timbers. They were filled with diners and enchanted listeners. The place vibrated with sound and energy.

You could almost call us regulars at the restaurant. I wondered what pulled Janos back to the same place again and again, to the same ambiance with its wailing, weeping gypsy violins, at once passionate and yet also full of sadness and yearning. We were quickly seated at one of the most prominent tables near the band. The table was set and seemed to be waiting just for us. Maybe Janos had been planning this all day long behind a facade of business and efficiency. Maybe what appeared to be spontaneity was a well-planned outing, dictated from an inner need. We would never really know how he planned or arranged these events; but after we left the office, everyone had already voiced his or her own surmise. Though Janos appeared to be an open, communicative man, I was certain there was much within him we were not privy to.

We were barely seated when the first round of Slivovitz arrived, a delicately scented yet powerful plum schnapps. Everyone toasted at once and downed the little glasses bottoms up. Later in the evening Janos would crush each of his slender schnapps glasses in his bare hand with a kind of furious delight, and never once did his hand show any trace of blood.

He was a bear of a man in his early to middle thirties. I would not have called him handsome now, though I guessed he could have been handsome when he was younger and slimmer. He had that husky Germanic look with a trace of the Slavic—a rather broad, high cheek-boned face, blond wavy hair, not more than five foot ten, very broad shoulders, somewhat paunchy around the middle, sturdy thighs ill hidden in his trousers, and a pair of large, expressive hands. He had a powerful presence, tempered somewhat by his usual warm, broad smile. He loved people and was always surrounded by them. It was as if he magnetized them. He gave them what they needed and yearned for—a release from the every-day, the ordinary. I could never quite figure out from where his stamina and power emanated, certainly not from his intellect alone, which was one of the sharpest I had ever encountered in my young years. I suspected it was mainly an indomitable spirit that seemed to come from the depth of his being. To us he was, what we termed amongst ourselves, a golden man worthy of emulation, whose rumored early suffering and being tossed about had buffed his presence into a deep lustrous sheen, one that could not be overlooked. Though I had not been with the company for a long time, I had heard stories about Janos, but couldn't separate the truth from the myth even if I had wanted to.

We were all seated one minute and up again the next as we downed another round with clinking glasses. It was like a ritual. Presently, the waiters brought a mighty pot of pungent goulash stew, bowls and spoons, and then the feasting began. All through dinner, the gypsy band played its slow and most melodic strains that would become inevitably faster, more furious, and mesmerizing as the evening wore on.

Having downed a fair amount of the plum schnapps and a bowl of stew, Janos got up, chatted briefly with the musicians, and started dancing on the wooden floor in front of the band. It, too, was part of the ritual. He started hesitantly at first, not being the most graceful man anymore. But soon he fell into rhythm with the band or the band fell obligingly into rhythm with him. I don't know which. We clapped enthusiastically and hollered and spurred him on. His footwork became fast and fancy, while his body turned and swayed. It always ended up that he danced himself into a near trance-like state. Many of the guests had come forward to the railings of the 'balconies' on the upper floors and watched and clapped. Somewhere on the top 'balcony' someone began to stomp his feet. The stomping caught on, and soon the whole place became like a huge pulsating, throbbing organism. The blood soared in every one of us, and the excitement was at a fever pitch. It always was at a moment like that, when a state of ecstasy and delight had been reached, that the music abruptly stopped. The cessation came so shockingly sudden that we all fell back in our chairs, stunned. Then, after a short pause, the music began again, lovely, softly, as if it were intended to stroke us. And then came the release as we laughed and hugged each other.

Janos had one more treat in store for us on this particular evening. It was like his special encore. He walked over to the band and spoke to them, seemingly persuasively. Out came several balalaikas and the music turned Russian.

"This dance I dedicate to my friends in Russia, whom I love very dearly," Janos bellowed out with his booming voice and a sincere expression on his face.

Many guests clapped approval, but a great many booed. Only someone like Janos would dare to express love for the old archenemy. Apparently, he didn't give a damn what everybody thought.

He would give us one more dance performance, a Cossack number with fancy footwork and some impressive squats and leg work on the floor. Most guests who had by now become his standing audience loved every moment. I always wondered where he learned such dancing and where he mustered the stamina and agility. When he finally returned to the table, he was quite exhausted and perspiring profusely. Now that the ritual and show was over, he appeared spent but happy. He has purged himself, was the thought that suddenly entered my mind. But purged of what? I asked myself. Yet I knew, I had no answer and did not pursue the thought any further.

We soon left the restaurant as a group, but not before Janos had called on the flower lady to buy little bunches of violets or miniature roses for 'the girls' in his company. In the lobby, people walked up behind him, women mainly, who crowded around and begged him to stay. By then, however, he had gotten his fill physically and emotionally. He was determined to leave. In need to assure himself that we would get home safely, he asked the receptionist to phone for several taxis. He accompanied us out to the curb. As I walked by him, he unexpectedly turned towards me, causing me to hesitate momentarily. Bending close to my ear, he said in a low, barely audible, familiar sort of way, "Take care, Little Sparrow. See you tomorrow."

Another one of his unexpected and capricious moves I thought to myself.

"Good night, Mr. Jablonsky. Thank you for a very wonderful evening," I whispered respectfully.

"It's Janos in the evening," he whispered back.

The next moment I stepped into the back of the taxi and we sped away. As I turned my head and looked back, I thought he was standing there a bit forlorn and solitary, with shoulders bent forward and not nearly as big and powerful as I normally perceived him.

2

A Transitory State

Lately, the Chief Operations Officer of this large German conglomerate, Janos Jablonsky, had started to call me Sparrow. It meant to me that he had taken note of me, something I had not expected in the slightest considering his station in the company. I had no immediate working relationship with him. He was my boss's boss. In those years I had no particular ambition and did not even know why I worked for this company. Freedom to come and go whenever I pleased meant more than anything else to me. I just took the job when it was offered to me, thinking that I would buy some time to figure out what I really wanted to do. I was not even close to being in Janos's inner circle. His executive assistant was Miss Müller, several years my senior. A plainly elegant and polished young woman, Daisy Müller was perfectly suited to represent him. She knew seemingly instinctively how to put the importance of his position in the company into the right perspective. She was always highly visible but quite reserved at the same time and with a confidential air about her. Hans Gabriel was his right-hand man, an intensely ambitious man whose deference and loyalty to Janos was more than obvious; but towards the rest of us, he displayed an air of imperiousness and arrogance. Everyone was aware that he was courting Miss Müller, but we all questioned his motives. No one particularly liked him. I was working for Mr. Steiner, the youngest of Janos's circle of section managers.

Janos was the head of the company's import/export division. When he came on board he had rescued that division from a steady decline under his predecessor. Janos, it was confided to me, had come in ten years ago with fluency in four languages and connections in various countries, notably in the Eastern Block. Russia was his specialty.

With Steiner I worked relatively well. He and I saw things mostly the same way; though wanting to please Janos, he kept his and my nose to the grindstone. It was from Steiner I heard most of the stories about Janos. He told them in a more good-natured than gossipy way, seemingly glad to be able to impart a special inside knowledge to me. According to Steiner, Janos was married to a sweet, patient woman he had known many years ago and who had waited for him for years. He had two lovely little daughters, six and eight. He adored them, but he was not happy in his marriage. Steiner confided that Janos had had some rough experiences after the war that marked him for life. He added with a special confidential tone in his voice that some people had told him that Janos had lost his soul in Russia, though he hurriedly added that he thought that was a myth.

"He is great but sometimes a bit on the crazy side, you know," Steiner said one day. "The latest rumor is that he is still searching for someone in Russia he met years ago. That is maybe what is driving him crazy. Apparently, during each business trip he takes to Moscow, he hounds government officials to search for a certain person he has known in the past. They say he leaves no stone unturned. But so far, he does not seem to have had any luck. I got this confidentially from Gabriel who went with Janos on his last trip. At least Gabriel was pretty certain that this was what Janos was doing. He didn't actually go to the authorities with him."

I basically hated gossip to a point where I felt angry when I was listening to it. It was so hurtful, so destructive. There was too much of it in this society. Everyone knew stories about everybody else. Where was the truth in all of this? I paid as little attention as possible to what was said about Janos. I tried to keep an open mind and just tried to enjoy Janos for what he was to me--a great boss, a generous man, and a great entertainer.

One day Steiner said to me, "You have to hear this. Every morning when Janos takes a shower, he listens to a Beethoven symphony. That is how he starts his day, literally showered with music. He owns the finest sound system available. He showed it to me once. When he has listened to all nine symphonies, he starts again with number one. He never hears them out of sequence. It is said that he wants to follow Beethoven's development, that he wants to grasp his spiritual growth through his music or something like that."

Steiner went on, " I have asked myself why that heavyweight composer with his impenetrable music, especially that early in the morning? It's hard enough to hear him in the evening, at the symphony. I tell you, it's a bit weird."

I did not really know what to reply but I finally said, "Herbert, leave him alone and stop conjecturing. Janos is neither crazy nor odd. He is interesting; he is different; he is spontaneous; he follows his impulses. He is drawing his water most likely from a deeper well than we do. Maybe he is restless; maybe he feels confined; maybe he feels he belongs to a different time, to a different sphere. There are many, many maybe's."

One late afternoon, Steiner gave me the draft of a letter that needed to go to Janos that day. "Please polish and finish the letter before you go home today. You must get it to him, even if you have to stay late to finish it. If he is already gone by the time you finish, please place it on his desk. He will pick it up early in the morning. Please, don't screw up. It's important." I promised.

I worked on the letter, which was long and intricate, way past closing time. I hadn't even noticed that everybody had left. I finished up and was happy with the outcome. I just had to place it on Janos's desk. I was certain that he was already gone. I gently knocked on his door just to reassure myself that his office was empty. There was no answer. As I opened the door, I saw Janos sitting at his desk, facing me, in a very still upright sort of way. I had the feeling he was not seeing me. His eyes appeared focused on something in the distance, though they may also have been focused inward. Thinking back over this strange encounter, I can't really remember how his eyes were focused. For a few seconds, I stood hesitatingly in the doorway, expecting to be noticed and acknowledged. But Janos did not move, nor did he acknowledge my presence. The thought suddenly struck me that I was an intruder, that I was witnessing a very private moment. I stepped backwards, closed the door ever so gently, and pushed the letter under the door. He wouldn't fail to see it when he came out of his state. I was sure of that. As I walked home that evening after deciding to skip the bus, I reflected on that strange sight of Janos being present and yet not being present, like some ancient holy man practicing his state of mind emptiness. I knew I would not discuss this encounter with Steiner.

Janos was beginning to intrigue me more and more. I admired the different facets of his personality, the public and the private, the boisterous and the withdrawn, the gregarious and the serene, the showman and, through this latest encounter, the mystery man and the spiritual man.

3

Departures

Shortly after the letter incident—neither he nor I ever alluded to the encounter in his office—Janos was planning yet another business trip to Russia. The office was thrown into a flurry of activities. Proposals had to be readied; translations of documents made; telegrams were sent and received; last minute travel arrangements had to be confirmed and gone over. We were expected to work late. Janos made up for the inconvenience to us by ordering complete meals in and even provided late night snacks. There was no want. He spent his days almost entirely on the phone in shirtsleeves and loosened tie. His office door was permanently propped open during that time. He gave us the sense that these preparations were truly a joint venture. He had all of us hopping at his fingertips.

An important and, most likely, lucrative purchase agreement for rare raw materials was supposed to be negotiated on this trip. Janos was to travel with the president who was also the chief executive officer of the company. He would have to be ambassador and translator par excellence for the president who spoke neither Russian nor had ever been to that country.

We worked late the night before Janos's departure. Steiner, having been asked to put together the language for one of the agreements, had felt that it would show Janos the stuff he was really made of. He worked himself into a frenzy. He was still dictating parts of it to me at the time the office closed. We finished the agreement document by nine in the evening, both of us pleased because our product looked quite professionally done. Steiner asked me to drop it off at Janos's apartment early in the morning, for Janos was not scheduled to leave until mid morning.

"Tonight he is still with the president until late, going over last minute stuff," Steiner explained why the document couldn't be sent to Janos that evening.

Without any show of emotion, I said I would gladly do this. Inwardly, I experienced a rush of excitement, just by thinking that I would see how and where he lived, that I would get a glimpse of yet another part of his life. Though I hardly imagined that it would possibly lead me to the point of understanding Janos any better.

The next morning, I was up at five. It being summer time, a faint glow in the east already shed the first morning light. I had slept fitfully and had strange dreams, one of which kept recurring and seemed to persist till the early morning hours. It was with the images of that dream that I awoke. I was literally swallowed up by a giant cave, more like pulled magnetically into it. And just when I thought I would not be able to find my way back out of the underground labyrinth, I would suddenly, miraculously, reemerge into a beautiful sunlit landscape. Every time I came out I felt disappointed, for I knew there were mysteries in that cave, mysteries I had not been able to explore. I had groped around, touched on vaguely defined shapes, but could see nothing. Yet I knew something mysterious was there. The darkness prevented me from seeing it. That is why I was again and again drawn to the mouth of the cave, and, once there, I could not help entering even though I felt apprehension due to the darkness. Yet I also knew that some day I would penetrate the secret of the cave, that I would somehow acquire enough seeing power to take it in and to reemerge with knowledge.

I was glad the dawn had broken. I hurriedly, yet carefully, prepared myself for my mission. I couldn't shake the images of the dream--the dark secret and the light landscape. To calm my mind, I finally decided to see and embrace the dream in a positive spirit since I seemed not to have been overly frightened; actually, in a way, I was more curious than anything else about the things I could not see. With this inner resolve towards the positive, I set out on a brisk walk in the direction of Janos's place.

It was just after six, and although the walk would be an hour long, I decided to skip the bus and to take in the sights and sounds of the awakening city. I knew what kind of section Janos lived in, not the lower middle class quarters with its vast apartment complexes close to the outskirts from where

I emerged. He lived just off the main, tree-lined boulevard with its expensive and exclusive storefronts and its beautifully landscaped waterway flowing languidly down the center of that famous promenade. At every intersection the waterway was spanned by a graceful stone bridge on which the stone masons of old had practiced their artistry. Black and white swans floated on the water among the clumps of water lilies. This was the classiest part of this elegant city by the Rhine.

I had purposely taken a roundabout way to enter the boulevard at its southern end, so I could walk along the water. The Linden trees were in full bloom, and I walked in their shade and in their delicate, diffused scent that conjured up walks I had taken years ago in the palace gardens along the great river Rhine. The moment felt incredibly uplifting to me, and the world seemed pleasingly transformed into plays of early morning light and shade, sweet scent and color, freshness and newness as if it had just reborn itself. Noticing suddenly the clutched folder under my arm, I was brought back to the reality of my task. I needed to start looking for the street signs, needed to watch for Hohenzollernstrasse. I soon found it and turned off the boulevard.

This side street was lined with small, elegant apartment houses, bordered by low stonewalls topped by wrought iron fences behind which I saw lovely flower gardens and tiny, immaculately groomed lawns. The gardens were small, measuring maybe ten to twelve feet from the gate to the entrance door. I stepped through one of those gates and walked up the stone path to the front door. After ringing I heard a woman's voice asking through an intercom who was there. I had barely mentioned my name when I was buzzed in. Here she was, standing atop the stairs, smiling down at me. "Herbert called last night, informing us that you would be dropping off last-minute papers. Please come up, Miss Werner. I have some tea ready if you would like it. Janos is in the process of getting ready, but he is almost done."

"Thank you, Mrs. Jablonsky. You are very kind. I would love a cup of tea."

I had reached the top of the stairs and was ushered through a little entrance hall into the main living room, I assumed. Effie Jablonsky had walked ahead of me into the hall, then stepped aside to let me enter the living room first. She had a quiet, polite presence about her. She was rather small, dark haired with unusually dark green eyes that rested on me quite steadily, as if trying to read me. At this early hour, she was already carefully dressed in a simple pastel colored dress. Her hair was pulled back out of her face. She had clear, almost alabaster-like skin. She is quite a lovely woman, I thought to myself, she emanates kindness and understanding. Why did Janos never bring her to any of our functions or outings? He led a public life as if he were not attached to anyone; in fact, he often struck me as a solitary, self-contained figure, even in the midst of a crowd. My reflections were momentarily interrupted by Mrs. Jablonsky's saying, "I will get the tea then. Please sit down and make yourself comfortable, Miss Werner. Janos will be out soon."

She disappeared through the door at the far end of the room and left it standing open. Beautiful, symphonic music flooded into the room. It sounded as if an orchestra was playing right outside the door. Ah, Beethoven! I thought. The myth is becoming reality. I sat down in one of the comfortable easy chairs. All the couches and chairs were covered in a light beige fabric, very much in contrast with the beautifully sculpted Chinese rugs, delicate Chinese paintings and wall hangings, ornate Russian paintings with heavy gold frames, Russian icons on wall shelves, and an intricately crafted balalaika, no doubt a rare piece, on one of the tables. He is living with the objects and images he loves so much, I thought, though I was puzzled by the Chinese influence.

My reflections were again interrupted, this time by Janos bursting into the room straight towards me, smiling broadly, and obviously pleased to see me. "You brought the important papers. I am so pleased about everything. I consulted the stars last night. They have arrayed themselves in the most favorable manner. I believe good things will come of this trip for all of us, Little Sparrow. When I come back, I promise all of you a surprise."

"I am looking forward to that," I said, and, at the same time, I pointed to the door, "Beethoven, how wonderfully inspirational in the early morning." For a fleeting moment, he looked at me with surprise, his great blue eyes resting penetratingly on my face. I faintly blushed. He noticed and immediately averted his eyes, realizing no doubt his own power. In a light tone of voice he said, "I am very happy you noticed. You see, we do have something in common."

Effie came in carrying a tea and coffee tray with little biscuits. I took the tea gratefully and helped myself to a pastry. Janos was just about to take his coffee, but before he could do that and any of us could say anything, in burst the two little girls in nightgowns racing at top speed towards their dad. He spread his arms wide open, received them both at the same time, one in each arm, and swung them around. They both squealed with joy and excitement. It was obvious the love between them was mutual. As soon as Janos came to a halt, they hugged and kissed his head and he bear-hugged them back.

Probably another one of his nice rituals, to be repeated every morning, I thought. The two little girls, having finished their show of affection, started to glance over towards me. Janos set them down on the carpet.

"This is Miss Werner," he said. "She is a courier, delivering some very important documents for daddy to take on his trip. He could not do business without them."

He purposefully made me look important in their eyes. They looked at me with curiosity.

"Miss Werner," Janos said formally, "these are my daughters Erika and Theresa." He said it with enough importance in his voice that made them step forward, extending their little hands towards me. I was utterly surprised by the quick change in their demeanor from loving little girls to polite young ladies who carried themselves with an amazing amount of grace for their ages. In fact, they seemed to grow in stature in this serious, formal behavior.

I was still holding my teacup that I had half emptied when I glanced at the wall clock and indicated that I must be off to the office. That broke the spell of the moment. Effie, who had been staying in the background, came forward and gathered up the girls.

"Good bye," she said.

"Good bye, Miss Werner," the girls repeated and she whisked them out of the room. Beethoven was still playing in the background—a slow, melodic movement, an adagio I guessed it was.

"Thanks, again, Sparrow, for bringing these over," he said, holding the folder to his chest, "I appreciate your getting up this early. You and all the others will be rewarded for this. Wait till I come back. Let me take you down to the door. I'm sorry I can't drive you to the office."

"Oh, no, no! I love to walk. I had a most precious walk this morning coming here. It was delightful." He looked pleased. I sensed that he needed everything to go right and harmoniously at the threshold of his trip, and I was happy that I had done and said just the right things. Janos lightly touched my elbow, giving me a signal that it was time to go. He led me out of the room and down the stairs.

"Keep your good thoughts with me, Sparrow. I need the energy of purity."

"Oh, I will think of you and wish you good luck continuously while you are gone."

"Thank you, Little Sparrow. I will need that. You don't know what influence you can have."

He said all of this so sincerely and so genuinely that I found myself thinking, to my astonishment, he really believes in the power of the spirit, even that of the littlest of the spirits. It made me feel wonderful. We shook hands, and I hurried away for fear that the moment could not be sustained. Only once did I turn around and look back. Janos was still standing in the doorway. He lifted his arm and waved, and I waved in return.

The next moment I was out of sight. I walked on in a sort of daze trying to reflect on what had just happened. I thought, he is certainly a master of directing situations, but he is not doing it in an overpowering manner; he possesses the unusual ability to make people in his presence grasp their own worth. What a life he leads! Being that much in control and yet giving freely at the same time. It appeared he was always giving of himself and was yet never losing anything of himself.

4

Comings and Goings

Two weeks passed and Janos was about to return. We all had missed him very much. He was the division's life energy, the spirit that truly created cohesion among the staff and achieved excellent business results. As the day of his arrival drew close, our expectations soared. Preliminary communications from Moscow had indicated that everything was proceeding according to plan. No specifics were mentioned, however. But the day Janos walked through the door with all of our eyes on him, we knew the trip had been a great success. We knew it immediately from the expression on his face, his broad smile and laughing eyes. He walked up to every one of us and gave us a hug, something he very seldom did. Then he stepped back, "We made a fine deal; we made many connections; we made many friends and all that, at least in part, thanks to your great work up front. Thanks to all of you. It was good, very good. We even got some export contracts, something we hadn't expected. Tomorrow morning I want to get together with all of you. Then I will tell you what I have in mind for you." We all clapped and cheered, then chatted with Janos and amongst ourselves. We continued to talk animatedly even after Janos had left for home.

Most of the time, I had been lingering off to the side, thinking that I was the least important member of the staff, being the youngest and the least senior. When I received Janos's hug, I felt his immense, overpowering strength. He whispered in my ear, "Hi, Little Sparrow, good to see you. I am

24

looking forward to seeing you at the meeting tomorrow morning."

"Don't worry, I'll be there." I almost felt guilty saying that. While Janos was gone, I had done a lot of thinking for myself, even at work. Steiner had treated me humanely for once as far as work was concerned. I guessed he felt we both deserved a bit of a break.

During those fourteen days of Janos's absence, I looked very critically at my life and saw that I was not really heading anywhere. At least, I felt I could go overseas, perfect my language skills, meet new people, and, perhaps, embark on some adventure here and there. Just contemplating the many possibilities that might be opening up for me had me totally excited. I definitely felt called away. It was a strong powerful feeling that even withstood the temptation of putting everything on hold until I knew what Janos's promise would be that he had spoken of before his trip. In some ways I felt I was betraying him because he had made every effort to include me in the plans he had for his staff. I would have to tell him the day after tomorrow for I was going to sail in a little over two weeks. I had already made all the arrangements and there was no possibility of backing out unless I wanted to lose my slim savings.

We came together in the auditorium at 10 o'clock the next morning. A lavish brunch buffet was still being laid out by the catering staff of a fine inner city restaurant as we entered. Janos hadn't arrived yet. I sensed enormous expectations in all of my colleagues. I began to feel torn inside. How could I leave when so much is being done for us, when so much good will was being poured on us. Traitor! Traitor! It felt as if I was waiting for the last supper to begin. What in the world is wrong with me? Someone is extending himself, and I didn't even have the decency to at least consider the gift he had spoken of. My self-recriminations came to an end when Janos rushed in. I quickly glanced around. Everyone appeared very expectant, almost anxious. Janos appeared distant this morning, in stark contrast to the exuberance of yesterday afternoon. He was formally dressed, very businesslike. It fascinated me how he had the situation again fully under control, as if to mark the significance of the occasion. He gave an extensive report of the trip, the negotiations, the networking, the new people and companies they connected with, and, finally, described the agreements and contracts that were entered into. We were totally impressed.

After about an hour of talking, Janos switched gears. His tone became more casual than during the presentation. His face assumed once more his usual friendly, almost mischievous smile.

"My friends," he started, "contemplate for a moment what this latest involvement with Moscow and possibly other Russian cities means in the future." He deliberately paused for some moments while he gave us time to think. "It means that I cannot do the job alone. In the future, I will always need one or two support staff to accompany me. I therefore want to start teaching you Russian. I will commit myself to two three-hour sessions of instruction for a total of six hours per week. I will be fully committed and, if you sign up for my language course, I want total commitment from you. That is all it will cost you. I will teach you to read, write, and speak. It'll be intense I promise you, but you will greatly benefit. We must be able to speak the language. That will gain us trust, friendship, respect, admiration, and, above all, the best business connections."

He paused again. An intense murmur went through our group. He gave us time to digest his offer, at least somewhat. When he spoke again, he did so very simply.

"This is my offer, my gift to you for your future. Don't decide now. When you go home today, reflect on it. However, I would like you to commit very soon, for the sign-ups will start in two days. I don't want to say any more. Just reflect on it in your leisure time. But now, please join me for lunch."

We all broke out in a thunderous applause. Janos stood there in a simple, humble sort of way with slightly bowed head. He waited until we were done showing our gratitude. Then we all mingled and chatted and indulged in the good food.

5

The Disclosure

After closing his door behind me, I momentarily leaned against it to steady myself and to take a deep breath before going back to my desk. My mind was overwhelmed by what had just happened. After telling him of my decision, I had expected Janos to treat me impersonally, perhaps even coldly. After all, I was the least significant member on his team. What loss would there be for him if I refused to be a dedicated player, if I deserted his team? Surely, if need be, I could be replaced the same day I left.

Even though my resolve had been absolutely firm, I was quite reluctant to talk to Janos of my plans. I hated to be considered ungrateful. I hated him to think that my experience under his leadership and his offer to teach me meant nothing to me. I wanted him to know that my experience under him was very important to me, but I also wanted him to understand my need and drive to venture forth. I had feared going into his office because some of the people I had admired most had turned on me in the past; and I felt I could not trust the favorable impressions I had gathered of Janos during my short time in his division, those of being compassionate, sensitive, and caring. Too many times, my impressions had proven me wrong in the past. I was expecting the worst.

As I had opened his office door and peeked in hesitantly, he had looked up from his paperwork and a broad smile had flashed across his face.

"Come in, come in, Little Sparrow. Sit down. I was expecting you but not so soon."

"I am sorry, I am a little early. I don't want to disturb you in your work," I had said with as firm a voice as I could muster.

"Don't even mention an apology. I am glad you are here, and we are going to have a nice chat that I wanted to have with you for quite some time. No one has taken me up on my offer so far, so you are the first and I am happy for it. It shows me that you are eager to learn."

Hearing him say that, I decided to jump right into the fray in the most straightforward manner I could think of. "Mr. Jablonsky, I am not here to sign up but to tell you that I will be leaving soon. I am sorry that you expected something different. Believe me, I appreciate your offer very much, but I must go--must be moving on. It's the thing I am most sure about."

I was surprised to hear myself say that. It had not been my intention to make the announcement in quite that stark and abrupt a manner. The whole time I spoke I tried to focus on Janos's face, but it kept on slipping out of focus. Now that I had stopped, his face came back into focus. His broad smile had vanished. And instead of the disappointment or disapproval I had expected, his face was serious but his eyes had taken on a sad expression.

"Why, Little Sparrow, do you want to leave us? I am…, we are happy you are here. Everyone likes you--your bright smile and your happy, helpful demeanor. Even though you think of yourself as being insignificant, you are not. I know your value better than anyone else; believe me. I know what is inside you because I have known it before." Suddenly he hesitated, as if he had caught himself, and continued in a different vein, "How sure are you about your plans? There is no give, no leeway?" He had composed himself completely. He suddenly emanated kindness but no emotions.

"I am very certain about my plans and they can't be changed. I am going overseas, and I am booked to leave in two weeks. All my savings are invested. There is no turning back. I feel a strong drive to get away and experience the world." I replied quite determinedly with my eyes focused on his enormous desk in front of me.

"I see," he simply said, and, after a slight pause, added, "And I think I understand."

The slightest quiver in his otherwise strong voice made me look up and meet his gaze. With surprise, I detected an unexplainable emotion in his expression. What could it be? Why the emotion? Why the kindness, the understanding? Now I did not understand. I could not be anything to him, except an insignificant worker.

He interrupted my thoughts and said simply and with incredible sincerity, "Little Sparrow, I want to be completely honest and I want to emphasize that I do understand. You are very young; you have, I believe, a pure heart; you are an innocent, but you also need experience. Though I would have loved to teach you, I, too, believe now that you must go. It's not up to me to teach you or for me to learn from you, I see that now. I have grown very fond of you and if I still had my youth, I would have loved to get to know you better. You bring back memories. I am glad you are leaving me to fulfill your needs and desires. You have my full blessing, but I do hope that we will some time meet again."

Now I was close to tears. What had he really been saying? A haze had settled over my thinking process, preventing me from assessing things clearly. He seemed supportive and understanding, but he was cryptic at the same time. I was surprised that he had said all of that. He had no problems expressing his feelings in a most sensitive manner. I was fond of him too, but I would not have admitted openly to that. I would not allow myself to be that vulnerable in such an unequal relationship. It would have scared me to be in that kind of state.

Again, he interrupted my thoughts, by saying firmly and quite cheerfully this time, "Little Sparrow, I wish you very well. But before you leave, we will have to have a farewell party for you. Let me arrange it for this Friday night if that is all right with you."

"Please don't go to all this trouble for me, Mr. Jablonsky." Then I hastened to add, "But, of course, I would love it, and Friday night is fine."

"All right then. We'll have to move fast. I will think of some unusual gift for you, and I hope everyone will be there. We need to give you the best send-off possible."

With these words he rose from his chair. I rose too and we shook hands. He held mine in his large, strong hand for a few moments longer than was customary, and he held it quite tightly. As soon as he released my hand, I turned to the door because I was suddenly overcome with emotions that I did not want him to see.

6

The Party

Friday came around quickly. Even with all the excitement and expectation for the evening party, we still managed to complete our work. Throughout the week, colleagues had come up to my desk, one by one, out of curiosity mainly. Like some reluctant birds of prey, they hovered around me. Everyone wanted to know about my plans whether they approved of them or not. I received more attention than I cared for. I did not know much about the arrangements for the party but had heard that Joachim Breitner, one of Janos's junior assistants, had offered his parents' home, for his parents were away on vacation. Actually, Joachim was more of an intern than an assistant. Part of the time, he attended university and was engaged in pre-law studies. I was surprised that he was involved in the party arrangements to such an extent. He had never paid much attention to me. From his action and the interest shown by the others, I suspected that Janos was behind all that attention giving, that he was the driving force in everything connected with the party.

We were let go early on Friday. Most of us went home to freshen up and to pick up items we had been asked to bring. Of course, I was not supposed to bring a thing and was not to worry about anything. Even at the risk of being overdressed, I went home to change into my favorite red satin dress. I thought it suited my personality and my body perfectly and was bound to make a bit of a splash. Though I was never one to steal the show, I was thinking that I might steal just a little bit of it that night.

I arrived by taxi at the Breitner house. The address I had handed to the driver had meant nothing to me. I had not been in that part of the city before. As we were speeding through the suburban streets, I noticed that the apartment houses gradually changed into villas with lovely front gardens. This is unbelievable! They must have gone all out, but why? I am not important enough for this I thought to myself, feeling slightly uncomfortable. Realizing the senselessness of my questioning and the discomfort I felt, I suddenly decided to lean back and close my eyes. What if you let it all just happen tonight? nudged an inner voice. What if you do not question the why's and what for's for once? To my astonishment, I felt myself promising as if by solemn oath, tonight I will live every moment as it will present itself. I was surprised at myself that I could have such an internal dialogue, muster this kind of calmness and detachment. I had the impression, now that I knew where I was heading, that this may be the evening that will truly open the door to a new life.

As the taxi came to a halt, I opened my eyes. I glanced out the backseat window and saw before me a beautiful villa from the early years of the century--formidable in its heavy construction with wooden beams, window bays, and a little tower resembling something like a turret. Set back from the street, half hidden, the villa was surrounded by massive old trees, a beautiful garden and lawns, and an intricately fashioned wrought iron fence. The driver had stopped at the gate, had opened the door for me; and as I set foot on the pavement, I experienced a sudden floating feeling such as the princess must have felt on her way to the ball.

Janos and Joachim formed the reception line by the door. I was a little late and the house reverberated already with music and laughter. Joachim hugged me first, "Welcome to your party," he said in his usual formal and reserved way. Now I was not surprised anymore about Joachim's reserve and formality, considering his familial background. As Joachim released me, I turned towards Janos. He stood there with his usual beaming smile and arms outstretched. Just before he hugged me tightly I caught a glimpse of his eyes and was certain I detected a glimmer of mischievousness in them, something I had only once seen before. He appeared years younger with that look in his eyes. He is holding me just a bit too long, I thought. I felt slightly dizzy as I waited for the release from his powerful arms. "This is your evening, your night, Little Sparrow. Besides you look beautiful. Enjoy!" He whispered close to my ear. Then I was set free.

Joachim, Janos, and I walked down the hall and entered the great main living room. Its furniture had been placed against the walls. The small gypsy band that had been playing fell silent, and all talk and laughter subsided as we entered.

"Here she is, the little deserter," Janos blurted out. "Let's celebrate her breaking away."

Everyone clapped and hooted while I was led to the buffet table and was handed a glass of champagne. Everyone crowded around to get a glass. We all clinked glasses at the same time, and everyone shouted in chorus three times, "Leb wohl! Leb wohl! Leb wohl!"

Later on I moved from person to person. There they were--Steiner and his girlfriend whom I had never seen before and had never even known that he had one; Hans Gabriel with his latest lady friend who turned out to be the president's private secretary, a secret he had apparently kept until tonight (and I thought he was courting Daisy); elegant Daisy Müller alone, as always; and everyone else. I looked around to see whether Mrs. Jablonsky was present, but could not find her in this room filled with all these familiar faces. So, he has come again alone and seemingly unattached, I noticed. A strange but exceedingly kind man! Why? As soon as this question crossed my mind, I checked myself so that I would go no further. I reminded myself of the oath I had taken in the taxi--to let things happen without questioning.

We danced and laughed and talked all evening as the band played its passionate, melodic strains. The food had been richly laid out; there was no end to the flow of wine and champagne. There had never been more lightheartedness and more good will than I experienced that evening in the company of my co-workers. Surprisingly, I thought, I have come closer to all of them tonight than ever before. But Janos, who had created this opulence and abundance, had also achieved, intentionally or unintentionally—I could never figure out which—a kind of overindulgence for everyone but himself. I noticed that he had purposely stayed in the background all evening. He did not dance and made no speeches. I hardly even saw him drink which he normally did almost to a point of excess on occasions like these without ever getting really drunk though. I wondered what caused him to change that evening; but, again, refrained from pursuing this thought. I immediately remembered the oath, and I also was having too much fun to be bothered with questioning thoughts.

By midnight almost everyone had overindulged. Some had slipped away quietly by taxi. I assume Janos had seen to that. Others, like Steiner, had gone upstairs to sleep it off. I saw him go up the stairs, dragging his girlfriend behind him. Even Joachim, reserved Joachim, was weaving a little as I watched him shuffle down the hall. I had tried to drink as little as possible. All evening, I pretended that I drank, but really did not. I did not want to make a fool of myself.

I had had very little contact with Janos all evening except at my arrival. Whenever I saw him, he was in animated conversation with someone. He did not even once make an attempt to talk to me or dance with me. Every time I tried to interpret this situation, I reminded myself of the oath, and resisted all questioning thoughts.

As soon as I had noticed the thinning out of the guests, I decided that I would leave soon. Before making efforts to call for a taxi, I slipped unnoticed, I thought, into the Breitner's small cozy breakfast room to rest awhile. The evening had been demanding with all the talking and dancing. The room was empty. What a relief! No more people! But as soon as I had sat down, Janos walked in. Oh, no! What's up with him? I thought. He approached gently and addressed me politely.

"Dear Sparrow," he said, "I know that you are ready to go home, and I know you are resting right now. But please, don't go yet. Be so kind and let me talk to you before leaving. But you must excuse me for now. I must first see to it that everyone is safe, either in a taxi or here in the house. Please, wait for me. I will return soon."

He had a pleading look in his eyes as if to say, "Do me that one favor tonight."

Even though I felt tired and spent, I could do no other than promise to stay. As so many times in the past, I distinctly felt Janos's hand and will in everything that had happened this evening. Even now he was still directing, he was still in charge, even of me.

He left as gently as he had come in and I sat and waited.

PART II
November 1944

7

The Induction

I leaned back in the high, upholstered chair in this small, intimate room as soon as Janos had left. I closed my eyes and found myself lapsing into a state between sleep and wakefulness. A vision appeared before me of a beautiful, sunlit landscape where I stood all alone. Though its beauty seemed inviting and attractive, I yearned desperately for a darker, shadier place. As I was contemplating a way out of the light, I saw a shadow suddenly floating over the sunlit plane and heading straight towards me. At that moment, someone's hand, I could have sworn, was touching my shoulder ever so lightly from behind. Wondering who it might be, I slowly turned around opening my eyes wide the better to see. It was Janos's large, kindly face bending over me. It took me several seconds to realize that I had emerged from a half dream into reality, and that the dream and the reality had fused. In a voice full of sensitivity, he said softly, "Can you listen to me now?"

I replied, still as if in a trance, "Sure, I am ready to listen."

Sitting down on the chair opposite mine on the other side of the oak table, he reached across and cupped my hands lying on the table with his ever so gently. A sensation like a lightening flash ran through my body that seemed to invigorate my mind and senses. Momentarily, he removed his hands. I sat still and alert for I suddenly knew something important was about to happen.

It began emotionally. His eyes were focused on me and yet not on me, focused outward and seemingly inward at the same time as though watching some disturbing inner and outer drama. How strange, it came to my mind, that a man of his incredible vitality, often bordering on the boisterous, could lapse into such reflective, pensive moods. One moment he was in the full enjoyment of the present; the next moment reliving, perhaps, another time that may forever hold him in its grip. Even though he was there with me, there was for him, I suddenly realized, no escape from another experience. And then he began:

Imagine a stormy autumn night early in November of 1944. I had gone up to my room, had slipped behind the heavy drapes in the darkness, and stood for awhile between them and the window panes watching the large snowflakes being driven past my window furiously, like someone wildly shaking feathers from a torn pillow. The naked tree to the right of the window was swaying violently in the night's storm as if engaged in a frenzied dance. It was as if all nature was alive and bound together in a macabre ritual. At that moment, Rilke popped into my mind, the poet we had studied last, just before the schools closed down for good. I loved him more than any other.

The leaves are falling, falling as from far,
As though above were withering farthest gardens;
They fall with a denying attitude.

And night by night, down into solitude,
The heavy earth falls far from every star.

We are all falling. This hand's falling too—
All have this falling sickness none withstands.

And yet there's One whose gently-holding hands
This universal falling can't fall through.

Mankind, I could not help thinking, was engaged in its own fall, in its own diabolical dance of assault and counter-assault, of bombs falling out of the air, destroying all in its path; of air raid sirens howling by day and night; of people, driven by fear, rushing by the thousands into shelters. And in the aftermath, they were tending their wounds, mourning their dead, and grieving their losses. Where were those gently-holding hands that could have stopped this universal falling? I was utterly confused at my young age about human

38

actions. I was only sixteen then. My seventeenth birthday was still three weeks away. I saw people's, my parents' fear as they were huddled over their radios, listening to this damned, devastating news, day in and day out.

Though it was now quite late in the evening, I felt reasonably safe in our house on the outskirts of the city. They were always trying to hit the hearts of the cities, the centers of business and commerce. I was bundled up in three woolen sweaters and a woolen winter coat. There was no heat in my room. The only heat we could afford was that from a pot-bellied stove in our living room. My parents, my sister, and I had just said good night and gone off into our rooms. The mood was somber and, as always lately, I saw in their eyes that poorly concealed glimmer of fear. It was the same fear I saw in everyone's eyes in the streets and in the long breadlines.

As I stood there contemplating the fury of this stormy autumn night and man's violence, I thought I heard a faint knocking at the back door just below my window. For a moment I thought my mind was playing a trick on me. Though I had been certain that fear had not yet overcome me, the thought crossed my mind that it might be insidiously closing in on me, too. But then I heard the knock again. Since it was at the back door, I rationalized, it couldn't be anything threatening. Any assault on our home or on anyone of us would come from the air or from the front door. So I tried to steal my way as silently as possible down the steps to see who would be knocking at such late an hour. Quietly and slowly, I undid the two safety locks and peered through a small opening into the swirling darkness. A woman, wrapped in a fringed shawl stood shivering outside. I opened the door completely and recognized Annemarie, our neighbor's daughter. What could have happened? I stretched out my arm towards her, grabbed hold of her elbow, and pulled her into the house.

"What's wrong Annie? Anyone taken ill?"

No answer. Even in the darkness of this back hallway, I could sense her terror. I touched her face lightly and felt it was wet from crying. She was crying silently.

"Annie, please, tell me what has happened. I want to know."

"It's Jonah," she finally managed to whisper, "They have come to get him. Six uniformed men forced him to dress himself and to follow them. They abducted him. He is only a few months older than you, Janos. What is going to happen to him? The fighting is desperate now. He may never return to us."

She was now openly weeping, and her body began to shake violently.

"I ... am ... so ... scared ... Janos," she managed to stutter.

I put my arms around Annie and held her tight for a while. Slowly I led her down the hall into our living room that still had not lost its warmth from the evening fire.

"I will wake Ida and my parents. We must all sit together and talk about it." I did not know what else to say.

At that moment, Ida, Mother, and Father came in. Everyone's hearing was so sensitive in those days. They must have heard Annie's crying and my talking to her.

"Annie, what happened? What brings you here so late at night?" Father inquired gently.

"They came tonight and took Jonah. He is forced to serve in the army, even though he is under age. It was terrifying … my poor parents!"

"Janos go over and get Herr and Frau Weidner to come here. We must try to find comfort with each other."

I rushed over to their house and found them both still in a state of shock. They looked at me with empty eyes and ashen faces. They have even gone beyond fear, I thought, and I felt an enormous rush of pity for them welling up in me.

"Herr and Frau Weidner, Annie is at our place. Please come over. Come with me. My parents want you to be with us."

Though their expressions did not change, they got up and fetched their coats and hats. Like robots they came over to me and like robots they followed me through gale and whirling snow over to our house.

My parents received them silently and embraced them warmly, a gesture I had hardly ever seen before. Though my parents were always friendly, they were not normally demonstrative in a physical way in their feelings for others. It was Mrs. Weidner who broke down first. Her tears started rolling down her face without a change of expression at first, but then she started sobbing uncontrollably, and I felt glad for the release of her emotions. Eventually Mr. Weidner followed. My parents were loving and gentle with them. In those moments, I gained more respect and love for my parents than I ever had before, just seeing their compassion. I then vowed to myself to always honor them as our belief dictated.

Finally, the ice was broken. Father revived the fire and the Weidners were able to tell us about the events of their son's departure. The uniformed men had demanded their entry and had said with stern authority that nothing was going to happen to anyone except that Jonah must serve his country and follow them here and now. He will be trained at first and then may be used to do duty on the front or in the supply lines. They said the army lacks men and the high command considers it to be an honor for him to serve like others before him. "We need to save this country; it is imperative!" they had said with as much conviction, it seemed, as they could muster. The Weidners apparently had endured it all silently and had signed the papers without objection. Only as they led Jonah out of the house had they fallen into this state of utter despair.

"Everyone," they now said to us in a whisper, for fear someone might be listening in, "knows that the situation is hopeless. Bombing raids on industrial areas and population centers have already taken a mighty toll and destroyed the morale. There is no more hope. The people know that. Only the high command tries tenaciously to overlook this fact. Yet, we are powerless; and if we said anything to the contrary, we would certainly be shot as traitors."

My parents nodded in agreement all the while the Weidners spoke.

"Irma and Paul," they started up once more, "we both have the feeling that Jonah, our beloved Jonah, will not come back to us. That's why we are taking it so hard."

In retrospect, they were partially right. Jonah did return within a few months but heavily injured, a broken young man.

Father that night said, "We may very well go through the very same heart-rending experience with Janos."

But Herr Weidner replied, "Janos is four months younger than Jonah. That might save him. They are now going month by month of the year 1927 in which these young kids were born. Janos has a good chance of never being taken. They have four birth months to go before they are getting around to him, and who knows how many, many thousands of kids they can take every month. By the time it is his turn, the war will be over, let's hope. We are wishing you the very best of luck. We want to see Janos around for a long time."

Momentarily, my father's face lit up and I saw a fleeting glimmer of hope flush across the sad features of his face.

Meanwhile my mother had busied herself at the stove. Water was boiling for tea and a kind of coffee substitute we now drank. I smelled the frying of potatoes; and later I realized that she had scrambled the last six eggs we had left. She was a good, kind, and generous woman, always intent on lifting people's spirits when the moment demanded it without thinking of later needs. My parents even bedded the Weidners down in our house for the night.

They vehemently objected but stayed. I could sense that they dreaded going home to the empty house that night.

Father was home now every day since they had closed all schools and the university. His professorship had been placed on hold. He felt displaced and often seemed awkward as if he did not know what to do with himself. Even though his professional world had collapsed, he still busied himself at his desk a lot, sorting papers, making notes, leafing through books as if he were preparing for his lectures. Ordinary life had come to a standstill but not in our house. Ensconced, like in a cocoon, we tried to live as ordinarily as possible thanks to my parents. Through all the darkness, danger, misfortunes, and depravations, they tried very hard to carry on their daily domestic life as if nothing much had happened. With their heads held high and their backs straight and yet a steady faint glimmer of fear in their eyes, they seemed intent on conveying that nothing could ever destroy us or disrupt our family life.

Father had been in the war for a brief time (he really had been too old for service) but came home last year after he lost his leg below the knee and not through a heroic deed. It was a tragic, freak accident caused by a friendly grenade. He now hobbled around the house with an ill-fitting prosthesis. Sometimes, I thought, the sight of him would kill me. He was always a proud, straight man, and even now he still appeared that way in how he carried his upper body, even though his hair had turned almost white within a few months after his return and his face had become deeply furrowed. I watched him closely without being obtrusive. I felt even then that he was already a broken man in spirit. My mother hid her emotions better than he did. She tried to be cheerful in the face of adversity. She cared for my father tirelessly. They had sent him home before he was healed, and his wound still hadn't completely healed even now. There was no room for light cases like his in military hospitals. Mother tried nursing him with much dedication and tried to be creative in preparing meals with the few ingredients still available to us, mostly potatoes.

The only real joy they felt, it seems, was when they saw Effie and me together. I detected it in their faces, how their eyes briefly lit up when they looked at us standing together, as if they were seeing a vision of the future. Effie was my childhood friend and the daughter of my parents' good friends. We had always lived in close proximity and had played together since I know not when. She was just one year younger than me. Effie came over as much as her parents would allow her. She and I, being now devoid of schooling, studied together. Methodically and conscientiously we went through our books as if it still mattered in these chaotic times.

It was during those afternoons we sat hunched together over our books that I first took notice of Effie's quiet and unobtrusive beauty—her lovely, flawless, pale skin; her shiny dark hair; her large dark green eyes; and, above all, her long, slender, immaculate hands. It happened during one of our study sessions, as she turned her head and looked up at me, so trusting and dedicated, that I bent over quickly and planted a kiss on her pale lips. As soon as I had done so, I became consciously confused over my action. I had never wanted to do that before. I was just about to apologize to Effie when she pressed her forefinger against my lips without saying anything. Her face showed no sign of disapproval; and in her eyes, to my surprise, I detected a glimmer of approval. Effie, shy and withdrawn Effie, you are surprising me, I said to myself. What would I have given in that moment to know what she was thinking! That afternoon, I made no reference to what I had done. We just resumed our studies and pretended to be as serious as always, though I could not ignore a strange sensation coursing through my body, sweet and almost irresistible. It was the next day that Jonah was taken away.

When I met Effie again two days later, the same irresistible sensation flooded my body as soon as she lifted her face to mine entering the room. Ever since Jonah left, I felt with certainty that they would also come for me. My parents had begun to consider smuggling me out of the country. They pursued wild trains of thought of how they could save me. But then their integrity and conscientious natures prevailed. I suspected that, in the end, they entrusted my fate to God. They never attempted anything. And we waited. I never communicated my feelings to them so as not to worry them; and I never spoke of the eventuality that they might come for me.

One night, alone in my room, my fears of having to leave had become so acute and so repressed that I knew I had to talk to someone who would understand. If I talked to Ida, she might go and alert my parents as to my fears. To my parents I could not talk. We had already come to some kind of silent capitulation of maintaining the status quo. I thought of Effie. She might be able to understand and listen to me. The following afternoon when she came into my room, ready to crack open the books, I whispered into her ear.

"Effie, I really need to talk to you. Please hear me."

"Of course I will hear you, Janos. I know you must have premonitions. But I didn't want to bring it up; I have been waiting for you to tell me."

"Effie, I know they are going to come for me, soon, I feel it. I don't think I am afraid to go, but I am scared about my parents. Will you be a daughter to them? Will you be with them as much as you can?"

"I most definitely will," she answered very plainly and sincerely. "You can count on me being with your parents. Though I know I will not be able to replace you."

"Effie, there is another thing I need to talk to you about." I hesitated. How could I talk to her about this?

"Why have you stopped, Janos? I am waiting to hear what this thing is." She was always so kind, so patient.

I tried again, "Effie, two days ago, when I impulsively kissed you, I suddenly realized that you meant more to me than just a friend. I began to see the woman in you, and I suddenly desired you. I have never felt such a transformation before. It's difficult for me to speak that way, but in light of what is going to happen, I must say at least this much: perhaps, when I return, you would allow me to pursue my feelings for you."

I looked at her face and saw how she suddenly began to blush. The color started on her neck and moved upwards until her whole face was afire. I had never experienced such a reaction to anything I had said to another human being before. It felt painful for me, and all I could say was, "Effie, I am sorry, I don't want to make you feel uncomfortable."

As soon as I said this, the blush vanished from her face as a cloud vanishes from the sun. She had herself amazingly composed within a few moments.

"Janos," she suddenly said softly but very straight forward, "I have loved you for quite some time. I never hoped that you would reciprocate. I was just satisfied to be in your presence."

"Oh, Effie!" is all I could say. I swept her up in my arms and held her so tight I was afraid I would take her breath away. I felt her body respond to mine and felt her arms tighten around me. We clung to each other as two people just about to drown. That afternoon I kissed her long and wildly, at first her lips, then her neck, and then her delicate, budding breasts through her dress. I was happy and she seemed happy too.

To my surprise, it was Effie who first very shyly approached me about going further. She argued that if I did have to go away, as I felt I was bound to, we should seal our love.

"I am willing to wait an eternity for you, Janos."

I was so moved by her shy offer that I held her gently in my arms for quite a while.

"Effie, you know I do not want to do anything that might hurt you or that you might regret in times to come. You will not be able to count on me for anything. Think of that--I will be gone."

There was no dissuading her.

"In my heart I know, I don't want to give myself to anyone but you," she said with quiet dignity and strength.

I had not expected that much will and determination in Effie.

"Effie, I want the same as you but, please, let me think about it. I want it to be the right thing for both of us. Tomorrow, I'll let you know; and you will have time to think, too. Let's not rush into anything."

I was hesitating not because I thought I did not feel love for Effie but because I did not want to heave any responsibility onto my parents or Effie while I might be off on an odyssey of a most uncertain outcome. Effie agreed to think it over and wait.

The waiting period I had suggested passed quickly. I knew right from the start that Effie and I were bound to become lovers if only for the briefest time. When she came shyly into my room the next day her eyes searched mine for an answer immediately.

"Effie," I said right away, "I do want us to be together. For that, I promise you, I will never abandon my will to come back."

We hugged and kissed. I had no idea how we could spend a night together, not when two pairs of parents were watching us with Argus eyes.

"Janos," Effie whispered into my ear as I embraced her, "leave it to me to make the arrangements. Just come to me when I give the sign."

Again I was utterly surprised. I was just beginning to get to know Effie, her willpower and her tenacity.

"All right, Effie, take the lead and I will follow," I promised her, feeling the tenderest emotions for her.

Effie knew that she could best arrange our rendezvous. She had an aunt, her mother's sister, who was of a liberal leaning. She and Effie were very fond of each other. Aunt Edna had never married; but in her youth, plenty of stories had been circulating about her. Now she lived alone and apparently unattached. Effie had discussed our situation with Aunt Edna, and the two had hatched a plan. Effie was going to stay with Edna, and she would let me know when it was time to come. I only had to tell my parents that I was going to stay with my friend Peter for one night.

Edna had taste and was still glamorous, even now in her fifties. She received me with a hearty hug as she greeted me at the door. Effie was right behind her, her face looked lovely, fresh, and animated, and her eyes full of expectations. I again felt the same sweet sensation she had elicited in me for some time, only now it seemed more intense.

We ate with Edna and after that she left us alone, withdrawing politely with an excuse that she had to finish an important letter. We were thrilled; we had a lovely, unsupervised evening ahead, something we had never experienced before. We admitted to each other that we felt quite grown up and surprisingly relaxed. Maybe these awful, turbulent times are speeding our growing up, I thought to myself. In normal, peaceful times, Effie and I would never be here like this unengaged, unwed, and with no future whatsoever. A sense of sadness suddenly welled up in me, sadness because I could not offer more. I sat down quickly next to Effie on the couch and took her in my arms. We sat and kissed for a long time; and I felt ecstatic as her sweet delicate scent engulfed me. Suddenly, I knew what it felt like to be a man. It was my time to act. I swept Effie up and carried her into the room that Edna had set up for us, a lovely, private room in which love could flourish. Soon I lost all sense of time and space as I made love for the very first time.

I tried to focus on Effie. Effie below me; Effie above me. She was everywhere and nowhere and I was in the center of everything, experiencing the most effusive feeling of outpouring until I felt myself diffusing into nothingness and, at the same time, becoming diffused into all there is. When we came to rest, our bodies entangled, Effie seemed to be glowing with a new emotion. I was glad to see her happy because I was not sure how much I had kept her with me during those rapturous moments.

We fell asleep quickly in each other's arms, but were awakened rudely, seemingly after a short while though hours had passed, by the wailing sirens near Edna's house. This ominous wail shocked us into full wakefulness within seconds. We knew instinctively what to do--get dressed and rush to the shelter. Edna blew into our room like a guardian spirit urging us to make haste. My thoughts immediately turned to my parents.

Out in the street with the three of us running at top speed, I suddenly shouted to Edna and Effie, "I must run home. I can't do this to my parents, not being home. They would expect me to return since I was supposed to be at Peter's. Effie forgive me. I'll see you tomorrow."

Edna objected vehemently, trying to point out how foolish and dangerous my endeavor would be.

"Go, Janos, if you have to," Effie shouted encouragingly, "but be careful."

"Thank you, Aunt Edna, and I love you, Effie," I shouted back and broke away in the opposite direction.

I made it home in half an hour. Flashes of light like a wild thunderstorm flared up all around and deafening explosions roared in the distance. My parents had left the back door open, for they anticipated my coming. I found them and Ida huddled in the cellar.

The next day I waited for Effie in vain. I could not explain to myself her staying away no matter how hard I tried. It must be for a good reason, I finally convinced myself, for I had just gotten to know Effie's determination, will, and reliability. I knew I could count on her to come back. I would just have to wait until tomorrow.

That evening we heard the hard, ominous knock on our front door. Six uniform-clad men with shiny helmets and polished boots, their rifles with bayonets swung over their shoulders, came for me. Within twenty minutes I was gone, taken away by these stern men into the night while my heart ached for my parents, for Effie, and Ida.

8

The Training

On this still winterish evening, in breathtaking coldness, and silent snow falling, I was pushed rudely through the canvas opening up into the back of a truck, waiting outside our house. As I landed inside, practically on my face, I sensed that others were already inside although I could not see them in the total darkness. I groped forward deeper into the interior of the truck bed until I felt the first pair of feet and legs of someone in a sitting position. I pulled myself up into the same position and slid carefully towards the truck bed's railing, meanwhile murmuring an apology under my breath.

"Quit this shit! Just sit down and mind your own business," someone with a rather young-sounding voice hissed at me.

At that moment, the truck started, jolted forward with a leap and a start, but soon enough was roaring through the streets.

I did as I was told. I sat and kept quiet, shivering even in my heavy woolens in the chill of this winter night. Three more live bodies were practically flung onto the truck bed as if in the greatest of haste, I figured in about twenty to thirty minute intervals. After that the truck sped along smoothly for a time that seemed an eternity. No one spoke on the entire trip. I thought I heard a moan now and then or someone sobbing in a muffled sort of way. All new recruits, I thought to myself, collected like cones in the forest as fodder for the state's all-consuming war furnace. Then, I deliberately shut off my thoughts; I could not bear thinking of Mother, Father, Ida, and Effie, yet that is where my mind wanted to take me quite persistently. But there, in the darkness that felt almost soothing and kind to me, as the truck sped and bounced along now over, I gathered, incredibly rough terrain, I vowed to myself again, as I had to Effie a couple of days ago, that I would not waiver in my will to survive this ordeal, no matter how long and arduous the road.

We came to an abrupt halt. Voices shouted in a muffled sort of way. The canvasback was flung open, and I could see the dim outlines of several men.

"Get out and line up single file," shouted a harsh voice.

I counted fifteen of us—the catch of the day or the roundup of the night, however one might think of it, this thought shot through my head. We had no bags, just the clothes on our backs. "No need to bring anything," the stern soldier had said in our house, "the army will provide for everything."

We were led to a group of barracks, I presumed, for I could faintly distinguish a group of flat buildings in the darkness of the night. No lights anywhere. The fresh snow felt soft under our boots. Our captors unlocked a door of the first building we came to. We were herded in and commanded to take the empty beds nearest to where we were standing. One of the soldiers switched on a dim flashlight so that we could just make out the rows of beds stacked three high. The large room, taking in the length of the building, was bitterly cold. I could see the steam of our breath rising in the faint light.

"Get into bed and get to sleep right away. The latrine is at the far end of this building. We'll start with your training at five in the morning. There is no time to spare." With that, the soldiers, our abductors (as I liked to label them in my mind), left except one.

I had caught a glimpse of our group, all youngsters like me, in the dim shine of the flashlight. We did not speak to each other that night, perhaps out of fear or out of heartsickness. Each of us secured a bed quickly. I suppose on everyone's mind was just the warmth and the small comfort the bed would provide for us, and I don't think anyone doubted what the soldier had said about starting at 5 a.m.

In retrospect, I don't know how everyone survived those grueling five weeks in the wintry countryside and the merciless, sterile whiteness of everything: assembly for duty at five in the morning every day in the bitter cold; standing at attention for at least half an hour as all names were read (I figured there were about 500 young recruits in the camp, all stolen under the cover of darkness from their families); hours and hours of marching, sometimes through deep snow to the point of exhaustion (none of us was used to this kind of physical hardship); obstacle course training on ropes and steep concrete slopes, and low wire grating, barely one foot off the ground. The drills were rounded out by gun care instruction, shooting practice, and pep talks at night about the honor to serve the fatherland.

I realized soon that a definite attempt was made to keep us from getting to know each other, from forming friendships and attachments that desperately homesick young men would try to seek immediately. Camaraderie, normally an integral part of the military, had been cut out completely, so desperate an endeavor the war must have become. An unspoken code of silence prevailed, made manifest through constant reminders to keep silent unless spoken to. I felt tortured as I stood in isolation, looking into the closed faces of my fellow conscripts and realizing that I would want to get to know them. A desperate need to communicate, to share my feelings, to hear others' thoughts overcame me. I will go insane if I cannot tell anyone what I feel, my mind kept telling me. Yet I survived as most of the others did, a bit paler, a bit thinner than when we had arrived five weeks ago, in this isolated place. I had come to a point where I almost yearned to hear the hated sirens of the city.

By now it was the day before Christmas. On the morning of Christmas day, at assembly, we were told we would be released to our families on this day and collected again the next morning. After that we would be assigned for active duty to the companies that had already been chosen for us. A hushed murmur, like a sigh of relief, like a sigh of joy, like a hopeful moan when water is passed to thirst-stricken men, went through the five hundred lonely, beaten up souls. What joy this will bring to my family, who, no doubt, will have no idea of my coming, I thought. We had not been allowed to communicate with anyone during the length of our training. Finally, I thought, I'll be given the chance to say what I could not say when they suddenly took me away. It will be the last chance to convince my parents, perhaps, and Effie, of my inner fortitude, of my will to return.

The severe winter conditions had not abated for weeks. Under cover of darkness, the trucks bounced and lumbered across the rough terrain we had crossed weeks ago. Now they were fully loaded with young men squeezed in so tight that it was difficult to take a deep breath for fear that one would expand one's chest too much and rob a fellow trainee of space. But we had endured so many hardships already that this one was easy to take.

We were let off the trucks in groups in different parts of the city's suburbs. God, please don't let an air raid happen while I am on my way home, I prayed. We split up as soon as we were standing in the street, but not before we were reminded with the threat of execution not to forget to congregate tomorrow morning at five for pick-up in the same places where we were let off today.

"Remember, if you don't show up, we will find you. We will leave no stone unturned."

I ran through the streets until I reached our house, tore into the backyard, and knocked on the back door so as not to frighten my family. It was still very early for a Christmas morning, and it seemed an eternity until the door was opened.

What flash of joy in father's eyes and yet also what expression of disbelief, like successive images flashing across a movie screen, I saw in those first fleeting eternal moments as we stood face to face!

"Janos!"

"Father!"

He pulled me in and gripped me tight and ever tighter around the shoulders like someone who has just lost his footing might do. I folded my arms around Father then, and while we stood there seemingly a long time, I looked over his shoulder and saw Mother and Ida dart down the hall, their faces beaming. For me and, no doubt, for them those where moments of overwhelming joy, a gift that could never be matched. But especially for me this renewed contact with human beings was opening a floodgate of pent-up emotions of the past five solitary weeks. I wept as profusely as I never in my wildest thoughts imagined I could be capable of.

They had me talking for hours and wanted to know in detail the events and experiences of the past weeks. I was careful not to paint them too bleak and threatening for fear of arousing their deepest concerns. I did not want to heap more worries onto them than they were already carrying. I told them of my will to survive and reminded them what better day to start than on the day of the festival of hope--Christmas day. But there were no lights, no tree, no candles this Christmas, no culinary delights that Mother used to tantalize us with in past years, as far as I could think back. Yet there was lots of warmth that emanated from our souls as we huddled together in the evening over a cabbage and potato stew and later around the pot-bellied stove. No one thought of going to sleep that night. We stayed up until four in the morning, until it was time for me to head for the pick-up point. I broke away quickly in the cold, dark morning hours with short, firm hugs and kisses on their cheeks. In a way, I was glad that the darkness swallowed me up quickly. I could not bear seeing these sad, grief-stricken faces. My task before me, as I suddenly saw it, was to remain sane and alert in every present moment to stay on the winning side of life for the gain of some viable personal future. I could not strengthen and deepen my resolve more than I had already done.

As I hurried through the dark, cloudy winter morning with frozen snow crunching under my steps, I thought with uneasiness of one scene and one admonishment I had come across yesterday. During this Christmas day of our reunion, as all four of us had briefly withdrawn into our rooms, exhausted from hours of talking, I had gone down the hall to fetch another sweater from the living room. As I passed by my parents' room, I saw the door ajar. I slowed to almost a standstill and peered through the open door. Mother was kneeling in a corner that she had decorated long ago. Her face was tilted upward in devotion and her hands were pressed together as in prayer. Her gaze was fixed on a crucifix and a picture of the Virgin Mary right next to it. I had no doubt that she was praying for the life of her son. I will never ever be able to erase this picture from my mind's eye of Mother kneeling in pure devotion at her little private shrine. With this one picture of her, I realized where she must have always derived her strength and cheerful demeanor, her will to uplift the ones who were in need. I only watched her momentarily for fear that she would see me in this her most private moment. I never knew the depth of my Mother's belief before. Now I was convinced it ran deep, and I almost envied her.

The second incident occurred mid-morning after my arrival. Father, Mother, and Ida had expressed their sadness about Effie having to be absent. They told me how Effie's father had pulled strings and managed to take his family for the Christmas holiday to relatives in the country. He put his life on the line because no one was allowed to travel anymore. I wished Father, Mother, and Ida hadn't shown so much pity for me then, not so much with their words (they did not bother me too much), as with their facial expressions. It was not pity I needed, just human warmth and direct contact. I admitted to myself privately that my heart ached for being denied one last meeting with Effie, but I did not talk to them about it. I was convinced my parents, and I thought also Ida, realized what had happened between Effie and me, not in detail, but, I am sure, in a general sense. They told me how devoted to them Effie had become since I left and how her face would glow whenever the talk was about me. At one moment, when Ida had left the room, Father, with Mother right next to him, had said to me out of the blue in very soft yet serious words, "Janos, if you return, your mother and I would like to see you do right by Effie. She is such a wonderful girl and nothing would make us happier than to join our two families. Just remember that the holy sacrament starts with the first steps taken by the individuals involved."

I realized then that they knew simply through their own, keen observations. But I also felt certain that Effie had not betrayed our secret consciously and with words. I realized she would never have done so. My parents just knew from her altered behavior towards them. From that moment on, when my father spoke those admonishing words, I suddenly felt bound, a feeling I abhorred when it was imposed upon me from the outside. Yet, in my own heart, I never doubted the sincerity of my feelings for Effie then and my indomitable will to return. It was not until several years later that I was able to wrest myself through to the recognition that no person should ever be bound except through the dictates of his own heart and soul.

9

In The Field

I was the first to arrive at the prearranged pick-up place on that cold and dark morning. Standing alone, the future looked just as cold and dark to me in these moments as that forbidding pre-dawn while I waited to be taken away to a fate already decided. I was certain, I could sense it in my chilled, weary bones, that this fate of mine had already been nailed down at some impenetrable and distant but minutely efficient command center. The details of what the insignificant contributions of one barely seventeen year old Janos Jablonsky would be in this vast war effort had already been recorded and passed on to the executors of fate. They were coming for me shortly. I could hardly believe that the powers to decide and direct this vast effort would stoop so low. They must be desperate.

My thoughts were suddenly interrupted by a voice approaching me from behind. As I swung around, I looked into a young, pale but likable face dominated by large gray eyes that were directed at mine searchingly.

"Tell me quickly how you feel. I need to know. I am still overwhelmed with the love my family poured out yesterday. It seems so mockingly unreal in this cold darkness. I know it is only just beginning for us. That rotten training was nothing. Man, I am scared. My name is Gerhard van Dorp. I saw you all throughout training. I followed you with my eyes and thoughts to a point of complete frustration. If I could only have talked to you! This shit war! This shit military! These shit sergeants! These sweat and blood suckers! No offense, please. I don't know whether you share my sentiments."

The last words were hissed under his breath for fear that someone, some unknown and unsuspected someone, might hear them. We quickly and simultaneously looked around. The reality check assured us both that we were totally alone in the chilly darkness.

"Gerhard, man, I am glad you are talking to me. I thought I would go insane during those five grueling isolation weeks. How in the hell could they do that to us. Bastards! They have lost all sense of the humane! Who knows what's going to happen to us. Hey, thanks for your trust, brother," I whispered to Gerhard.

It felt good this outpouring. It thrilled me. I had suddenly made a connection to someone outside my family and old friends, and I was just about to embrace Gerhard to emphasize my gratitude to him when I heard the roar of a truck turning the corner into our street. It shattered our fleeting camaraderie and intimacy, and it stopped me dead in my friendly movement towards Gerhard.

Two more young men showed up silently out of the darkness, just as the truck came to a screeching halt next to us. A soldier jumped out in a great hurry and commanded us to get in the back. It was pitch dark under the thick canvas cover. I was surprised how many of my fellow comrades had already been picked up. Again, no one talked or even whispered. I lost track of Gerhard on that dark, bumpy ride to the Military Personnel Distribution Center, and I was not able to make contact with him again.

That same day I was shipped out by truck to my designated company. It was a supply convoy delivering everything from weapons, ammunitions, heavy equipment, clothing, food, and medical supplies to the front lines that were now positioned well within the borders of our country. The army's retreat had been slow but steady from deep within Russia; and their casualties were massive, counting into the millions. Now they were again almost at the point where the once proud, invincible forces had set out years ago to conquer all of Europe and Russia. I counted myself lucky to be commandeered behind the front lines. I still wore the full-length, white down suit we had been given at the start of our training together with a heavy pair of rubberized boots. It was a suit normally worn by alpine rangers. It served as a camouflage as well as for warmth. Supplies of military clothing had become scarce and I thought, they must have figured, this white alpine suit would serve us well for our snow training.

55

Now that I had joined Sergeant Gutmeister's supply convoy, my clothing was highly inappropriate, dangerous, and even ridiculous, especially with the change in weather from snow to rain, from white to muddy brown. But I was to be stuck with it for a while until Gutmeister, the master organizer, as I came to know him, procured one day, unasked for and unsolicited—I would not have dared to approach him—a regular enlisted soldier's uniform for me. Gutmeister, although staunchly loyal to his command and a regular, conservative kind of guy who followed written instructions to the 'T', also had this wonderfully compassionate side to him, especially when he liked someone. He would put himself out for a friend as I had never witnessed before or after I met him, as long as he felt they were on the same wavelength. With the change in weather setting in, Gutmeister could see how desperately in need I was for a change of uniform.

The fateful year of 1945 was rapidly approaching. It was now a couple of days before New Year's. Nature had thrown itself into reverse. What was a snow and ice storm just one week ago, that would have hampered our movements, had turned into near torrential rains and mud, throwing a different set of obstacles our way. It was as if nature, anxious to advance the winter season into spring (and to advance the progress of an ill-fated war towards resolution), had leaped ahead of itself, blowing strong, warm winds across the Alps from the south that drove dark rain clouds before them. Rivers almost overnight emerged from under their sheets of ice, rushing along with renewed vigor and purpose and picking up speed as the rains and the melting snow kept feeding them. As in a vision, I expected every day the first spring flowers to emerge in the just uncovered meadows that our convoy passed on the way north. I did not know how I could have conjured up thoughts of flowers, spring, and renewal at this dead-of-winter time when everything seemed so senseless and all our insane machinations seemed to crumble around us.

It took us sometimes hours to move the convoy along just a few miles over roads pockmarked with small and large craters and littered with vehicles burned out and shot to pieces--great, dark, ominous hulks like some grotesque prehistoric creatures, the victims of nature's cataclysm. By now the enemy had become very brash and daring, attacking our convoy in broad daylight with their agile little flying machines. Diving down at us with machine guns blazing, they sought to extract our blood, like swarms of gigantic bugs moving in for the attack.

Sergeant Gutmeister was a most amazing man. He must have been the most loyal soldier the military ever had. As far as I could see, he followed commands and written instructions religiously, even later when they became more and more out of touch with the realities of the fighting forces in the field. But he was also brave and loved and appreciated his men. They did whatever he commanded, even though later on they began to talk among themselves disparagingly about his carrying out instructions they thought were irrational and meaningless. Gutmeister had saved the lives of his men again and again in the face of an ever more overpowering enemy, but he had lost machinery, vehicles, and supplies more than he had wanted to.

Gutmeister had taken a liking to me and showed something like fatherly concern for me although he was just ten years older. He had been with the war effort since the beginning, and he had survived all these years as a shrewd organizer. His life really only became threatened in the past several months as the enemy sought to wipe out the supply lines and thus force the war to an early end. But they had not reckoned with men like Gutmeister. He was made of the stuff that proved indestructible and indefatigable.

Gutmeister had a toolbox he hung onto day and night. He hardly ever let it out of his sight. Even when he was attacked and had to flee his truck, he hung on to this box. I touched it one day to see how heavy it was. Gutmeister, talking to a group of his men some distance away, saw me lift it. He shot a stern glance towards me, and his hand raised up in a negative gesture. I immediately let the box go. Later he brought the incidence up by saying almost apologetically, "Jan, I am sorry, but you must never touch that box. Do you understand? It is what keeps us going mechanically. Only I must handle it."

I promised never to touch the box again. The little I had felt of the box, I realized it was very heavy. But Gutmeister was a strong man, well built, with muscular arms and broad shoulders, and an extraordinarily solid bone structure, though he was not a very tall man. He would be one of the few men who could wield such a heavy box around at all times.

"I will teach you to become a good mechanic, Jan," he had promised me and had added with conviction, "it will be the most useful and invaluable skill you will ever acquire."

I thought it very kind of him to want to teach me though I was not at all convinced that that skill would become my most valuable one. I also valued other skills highly, perhaps more highly, and there is where Gutmeister and

I departed in our aspirations. But I would only find out about that later. Right now I had only vague ideas that differed from his, ideas not yet fully formed.

Gutmeister had commanded me to sit in his truck, between him and his co-driver, when the convoy was on the move. It must have been my youth and inexperience that moved him to be especially protective of me. He also possessed something like a sixth sense when it came to the enemy. He seemed to know when they were coming even before there was any indication to the rest of us. He had gotten himself a set of whistles and had distributed them to all his drivers. Once he blew his whistle out his window with an ear-splitting sound that I thought inflicted irreparable damage to my ears, each successive driver followed suit. This whistle alert was done incredibly rapidly as if it had been practiced for a long time and had been honed to perfection. At the sound of the whistles, the entire company knew what to do.

The next time Gutmeister was to blow his whistle, I had dozed lightly as we moved along a relatively undamaged stretch of the road. I was shocked into painful consciousness by the high-pitched shrillness. At the same time I felt myself being rudely jerked out of the truck as Gutmeister and I plunged together into the deep, foliage-covered ditch next to the road. In those split seconds as we hit the bottom of the ditch together, the small enemy fighter plane swooped down on our convoy so low, so dare-devilish, that I thought its underbelly would strafe the cab of our truck. We could have made out the pilot's face, I am sure, had we been standing, but we stayed down in the protective weeds. But someone in the rear of our convoy had jumped the ditch and hid in the bushes beyond. He saw the pilot and sprayed the cockpit with his automatic rifle, just as the pilot tried to pull his plane to a higher altitude. We heard the shots and dared an incautious move. We lifted ourselves up. In a few seconds it was all over. As the small fighter plane pulled over off the road, away from our convoy, in a strange, wide, downward instead of upward turn, one wing touched the ground. It flipped over, almost in slow motion, and then it burst into flames with an awesome roar, followed by a thunderous explosion. The whole company had tossed away its caution by then as they peered over the rim of the ditch. After the explosion, a chorus of shouts erupted from the ditch as if our team had scored the final and decisive goal. They had defeated one, one of the very few I would witness over the coming, final months. We had sent caution to hell in those moments, but lucky for us—there were no other planes that day, just the one maverick that seemed to be bent on mocking us, wanting, perhaps, to tell us that we had lost it.

"Jan, you must never daydream in the face of the enemy," Gutmeister said severely when everything had calmed down. "He lurks everywhere these days. You must be responsible for yourself. I will not always be able to save you."

"Yes, Sergeant, I can see where I have failed, and I will never let that happen again." I was quite shaken after this incidence and did not let my attention flag after that.

One evening, as we were lying in the back of our truck (those trucks had become everything to us, including eating and sleeping quarters) on top of the supplies stacked high, and just before going to sleep—I think the other two guys had already gone to sleep—Walter Gutmeister said something that made me think for quite some time.

"Jan, how could your parents have ever given you, a true German kid, such an abominable Slavic sounding name? What was wrong with them? Were our fine German names not good enough? I fault them for doing this. We need to keep things pure, you know."

He was very serious. He said it with such conviction that it startled me. What's in a name? I thought. I had never seen anything wrong with my name though I was not especially fond of it either. But sometimes I even liked it because I thought it made me different. However, no one in our circle of friends or relatives had ever, to my knowledge, admonished my parents for my name as Gutmeister now had.

I was just about to defend them, when I heard myself say, "Sergeant, just keep on calling me Jan. I like it. Let's forget Janos. It means nothing to me." I could just make out his smile in the half darkness.

"You are clever, Jan, you will go a long way. At your age I would have defended my parents and my name hotly."

I let out a little laugh but did not say any more. And the subject was never brought up again. I was 'Jan' to him from then on.

Just yesterday, Gutmeister had given the command that we would now only travel at night. I doubted that anyone in the company would have thought this possible due to the condition of the road. But we also could not risk any more daylight attacks. Gutmeister also commanded that every man only sleep four hours in a twenty-four hour period. I knew that everyone in the company quietly grumbled about this command. No one wanted to sacrifice his sleep, especially since the rations had also been halved. They felt they needed the sleep to retain their strength. Gutmeister, however, set the example by only sleeping three hours each night. If he could do it, everyone felt they also could. Since he was fair to them in everything that truly counted, they felt they could not let him down.

When it came to repairing the trucks, Gutmeister was always out there in charge and with hands-on. Although he had his mechanics, his specialists, in the company, and he was the commander, he never stood back and let others handle the emergency. His feats in putting damaged equipment back together and to make it work was phenomenal. He was inventive and resourceful and thought of tricks and measures that no one else could have thought of. Still, in his estimation, he had lost too much valuable equipment to the enemy; and he blamed himself for that severely, I am sure. He now hatched a plan that carved our days into ten hours of night driving, four hours of sleep, and ten hours of building an emergency road through the woodlands adjacent to the road. The entire company worked on it, even he himself, with shovels, pickaxes, and saws. The woods would allow us more cover if the new road succeeded. The terrain was fairly flat and sometimes little had to be done to the ground. The hard parts were the trees that needed to be felled. We worked feverishly, as if that would save the war. It wasn't a smooth road because we paved much of it with small branches of the large trees. Though it was supposed to follow the old road, the new one swung around sometimes in wide curves to avoid open areas. Later, as the road neared completion, we hardly lost any more trucks. But by then our super human efforts were largely in vain. It just demonstrated to me the willpower of one man.

By the end of April, spring had come with a force and beauty that year as I had not experienced it before. It was profuse! Wildflowers blanketed the meadows in vivid colors as if a giant had left his artist's palette on the ground. As if by a miracle, the forests had burst almost overnight into a sea of intense green. Thick tangles of vines and grasses had already begun work on obliterating the burned and bombed-out hulks alongside the road. I clearly sensed this wonderful creative force that will renew all, not only nature but what man had destroyed; and, for a strange reason, I thought I felt more alive in those days before the end than at any other time in my life. It seemed a strange twist in my nature not to mourn the certain defeat but to affirm secretly the healing power of nature. Everyone around me had become quiet and withdrawn as if the whole company had gone into private mourning. The jokes that had kept us amused as long as we were on the move for a grand purpose had fallen silent. Even the stories of female conquests had lost their attraction in the face of the worsening news. The advancing enemy army from the East was only fifty miles away and closing in rapidly. The western allied forces were sweeping in from the north, west, and south. It would take only days until we were taken prisoners. I had gotten to know many of my fellow soldiers during our long convoys. All, I thought, were decent guys with private lives they feared in shambles or wiped out—sweethearts, wives, children, mothers, fathers, siblings, friends. I shared their fears and concerns; I commiserated with them. God knows how often I thought of Effie and my family. But then, I felt there was something more, something that I saw embodied in this beautiful spring that no one else seemed to notice. But I could not name it at that time and certainly not discuss it for fear that I was thought irreverent in the face of the immense human tragedy unfolding.

10

Capitulation

The day came when we stopped moving, when our convoy took its last gasp as a viable entity. We had just passed through a small town; and on reaching the meadows skirting it on the other side, we drove off the road. That meant Gutmeister and his leading truck drove right into the middle of the meadow and everyone followed until the entire convoy filled it. As in everything, a sense of organization and precision still prevailed. The vehicles formed perfect concentric circles with Gutmeister's truck being part of the inner circle. I then realized that Gutmeister with his guiding sixth sense had given up. He knew then that to carry on would be hopeless and wasteful. He called his men together and told us so. The enemy, he had learned, was now twenty miles to the East and the other one moving in from the west, north, and south was almost that close. We were already encircled. But no word of an official capitulation had reached us yet. Our radio operators were glued to their apparatuses. We would know as soon as it happened.

The first days of May were upon us. The sun shone hot and the sky was of an iridescent blue. Despite the beauty and clarity of the day, boredom and lethargy settled like a heavy fog over our company. By day the men walked into the fringes of the forest, lay down, and dozed. No one talked much. The mood was morose. When darkness fell, they came out of the forest and settled back into their trucks for the night. We still had a slim amount of rations that was carefully allotted amongst us. And so we waited long, tedious days. No one fled, although the possibilities for getting away existed. We all feared being caught by the enemy forces and being shot as deserters. We had heard that the enemy forces were large. They must have been intent to take in every last German soldier.

Finally, on a most beautiful, warm, and wind-still morning, a day in May that one would want to celebrate, the announcement came. The German high command and all German forces in the field had capitulated. Though our company had expected it for quite a few days, most of our men were overcome by emotions. Some openly wept like children who had lost their favorite game. But sometimes I wondered what tears they really were. Were they tears of joy that the ordeal was finally over and that perhaps they would be able to go home; were they tears of grief that the forces had fought so hard and yet lost in the end; or were they tears of pity for all that had been destroyed--the fervor, the passion, the enthusiasm, the dedication, the trust, the institutions, the families, the millions of lives, the country's material wealth, and their own youth? Feeling strange as if I were just a bystander, I simply observed but shed no tears. To be truthful, I was never really able to tune in, to be fully engaged. Maybe it was my youth that prevented me from becoming absorbed into the movement that had carried these men along for years. Yet I believed I knew what they thought and were yearning for because I was keenly aware of the loss of my family and Effie. I hated to think of their disappointments to come, for when I listened to my inner voice during those long nights in the open, I heard it whisper to me that there was no end in sight for me, not yet.

The next day the enemy forces came upon us. We heard the rattle of their tanks and felt the earth tremble way before they reached us. And there they were, a massive contingent of jeeps and trucks and tanks. They were American and Russian forces combined. Through a loudspeaker they asked us to come forward, out of our encampment, and lay down our weapons. This we did. I was moved to tears when Gutmeister also turned over his cherished box as he was commanded to do. The German translator asked us to fold our arms behind our heads. American and Russian soldiers circulated amongst us, padded us down to make sure no one was hiding a gun. They also got our names and the company we belonged to as well as each soldier's number. The ones that passed by me looked at me with startled expressions. I thought that maybe they had never seen a soldier that young and green as I was. I had lost at least ten pounds since joining the army and my face looked small and pale, no doubt.

The loudspeaker rambled on: "You must stay here for a while. We have got your arms and we will also take your vehicles, machinery, and supplies. You are to camp in this field until further notice. The victorious American and Russian forces will hold negotiations about who will take you over. Both armies are laying claim to you at this moment. It may be tomorrow or the day after and you will know. We are still waiting for the respective generals and their staff to arrive. We ask you to be quiet and patient. Your fate will be decided with due speed."

When the announcement was done, most of the contingent left. Some of their soldiers now started our vehicles and drove them away. Two trucks, one American and one Russian remained. The troop of soldiers that stayed behind herded us into the middle of the field and surrounded us with their guns drawn. Anything that had adorned our uniforms such as indications of our ranks had been torn off. With one fell swoop, we had all become equals. Even Sergeant Gutmeister's uniform was now as plain as mine. It was an odd feeling. I suddenly stopped seeing Gutmeister as my superior, and he began acting like a friend towards me, no longer like my father or my master. He asked me to stay close to him so that we may be taken or released together. Everyone's hope was that we would be taken by the Americans.

As we sat on the ground and waited, a whisper, quite unnoticeable, went from man to man, "American!" And a thumb would be flicked up low to the ground. That game went on for hours. That is how we collectively willed an American takeover that worked for half of us (for our company was ultimately split in half), but not for my friend Walter Gutmeister and me.

After two days in the merciless sun and two nights in the chill of an open field, the dice were cast. We stood on one side of the field while the other half of our company stood on the other side after we were split apart. It was like an emotional rift so deep that on our long march north, Walter and I and everyone else felt as if we had lost half of our souls. We never saw the men we had lost to the Americans again.

11

The Long March

Our Russian captors wasted no time. One more night in the field, and in the morning four horse-drawn carts arrived, each with a dozen armed Russian soldiers on top. We were grouped into rows of four and marched out of the field with two horses and their carts in front and the other two in back of our marching column. All the Russian soldiers except one on each cart positioned themselves at equal intervals along our column. At crossroads along the highway, more columns of prisoners and their guards joined us as the day wore on. Soon this column of beaten men resembled a great, slow-flowing river, lazing through its banks on the way north.

Before setting out, we were told through an interpreter that we were to march north through the mountains to a railway collection camp. The distance amounted to 250 miles. One formidable march, I thought to myself, one that some of us may not survive. "Don't try to escape. When caught, you will be hanged on the spot."

One soldier on a cart held up a noose as if to say, "We mean business."

"Bread will be issued three times a day. Water is scarce since we have little means of carrying it. The local population will hopefully comply with our request to assist with water. If you need rest, step out of the column and sit down on the shoulder. You must rejoin the column before you see the last pair of horses. If you have to relieve yourself, step out of the column but keep walking until a guard can attend to you. Don't try anything foolish; we will shoot on sight. If you get hurt, don't expect treatment. We have no medical supplies. They are scarce and needed for our brave fighters who sustained heavy injuries inflicted by you."

The instructions were simple and intimidating enough. My face must have expressed fear.

"Jan, don't worry about what they say. Stick religiously to the instructions when you need to do something. But, please, give your utmost concentration to your walking. Channel all your will and energy into this one activity. I want us to survive this ordeal and still have a little stamina left when we get to the camp. We won't talk much, just the most necessary communication. Talking will sap our energy."

"Thanks, Walter, I agree with everything you have said." I whispered to him.

"Oh, one more thing, Jan. When you have to relieve yourself, give me one tap on the arm and I will step out with you. We must not lose each other. When you need to rest, give me two taps so I will know. I will give you the same tapping signals."

He quickly grabbed my hand and pressed it firmly as a signal, so I interpreted it, that we would stick and hang together through all hardships. All the while he was saying these things to me and giving me the sign with his hand, he kept his face directed forward with an impenetrable expression. His lips barely moved. I counted myself lucky to have such a friend.

We had marched but a half a day when we first came across this horrific sight. Our guards had truly meant what they had said. We had worked our way up a steep stretch of road and came through the first forested area. I loved looking at the beautiful tall birch trees and their delicate leaves that dappled dabs of dancing light on the backs of the men before us. When my gaze moved ahead at one point and to the left of the column into the forest because of the screeching birds, I saw what would become the nightmare of my dreams for some time to come. Three bodies, stripped naked, were hanging from the lower branches of a tree. As we came nearer, I saw that the bodies had already started to decompose and the stench was so nauseating that some of the men ahead of us threw up the last pitiful ration of bread we had received some hours ago. Vultures were clinging to the bodies, tearing off bits of flesh in a feeding frenzy. The dark column of silently marching men did not faze the gruesome scavengers. They kept tearing away at the flesh. These bodies were no doubt left hanging there as a deterrent to us. I doubt that anyone after that contemplated an escape. How incredibly cruel to us and how incredibly sacrilegious to the dead men, I thought to myself. I averted my eyes and was never tempted to scan the forest again though I smelled that stench several more times on our march. I could cope with the stench but not with that gruesome sight.

The long march lasted eight days. During some of the night hours, we were allowed to sleep uncomfortably on the road. In the last couple of days, men who were initially straight and proud now just hobbled along. Many assisted each other in the end, and the Russian guards did not prevent it. As we came through villages and towns, people had put out buckets full of water along the street. If we wanted water, we had to do it on the run. There was hardly time to lift the ladle to our parched lips and to take a good drink. The streets were eerily empty like that of ghost towns I imagined. There were no gawkers, no onlookers—though sometimes I saw a slight movement of a curtain behind which, I suspected, people were watching us, perhaps with pity and sorrow, for no one knew what would happen to us.

Throughout the march, the weather held steady with clear skies. The sun was hot, almost punishing. I never thought I would ever wish the sun away. To avoid feeling the pain of the calluses on my feet, I kept staring at the head of the man in front of me so undividedly concentrated that it became in time a blazing ball right before my eyes. I became mesmerized with this transformation that in turn absorbed long lapses of time. It also suspended my pain while it lasted.

As we reached the collection camp and I had a chance to remove my boots, I could not believe my bloodied feet had carried me this far. Oh, Effie, Father, Mother, and Ida I am glad you cannot see me now, it shot through my mind. You would fear for me. But having survived this march, I knew that I had become incredibly tougher and could endure much more.

12

Journey East

When we finally stumbled through the gates of the collection camp, dazed from fatigue and hunger, Walter and I felt apprehensive immediately. There were no passenger trains, only boxcars, a multitude of them, on the tracks. The camp was basically a railroad yard, converted into a prisoners' holding pen. A vast area around it was fenced in, three meters high, we judged, with barbed wire coils at the top. Primitive guard towers had been thrown up at equal intervals along the fence. They were manned day and night with trigger-ready guards. Massive search lights, as they swept the camp at short intervals, turned nights eerily into day.

We estimated that two hundred thousand captives were camped in the fields around these railroad tracks. There was no shelter. They baked in the sun by day (most of them were sprawled on the ground in their undershirts) and shivered under the stars during those cool May nights. There were no blankets either. The worst of it was, there was nothing to do. By day, the men milled around aimlessly, as disorganized as a colony of bees might be that has lost its queen. There was nothing left to rally around. Worse yet, the prisoners became mired in boredom that deteriorated into lethargy and apathy the longer they were penned up. Even the heaviest work would have been welcomed with a sense of joy just to be able to escape this demoralizing inactive state. It was a scruffy mass of men with dirty, faded uniforms and unkempt hair and beards, a sad reminder of how quickly discipline can turn into dissolution. I do not know why at those times, when I kept looking at this beaten mass of humanity with my heart sinking, the soldiers' spit-polished boots on my parents' parlor floor kept intruding on my mind by day and followed me into my dreams at night--thousands of shiny black boots marching and marching, trampling everything underfoot that stood in their way. It appeared to me a mindless sort of marching with seemingly no destination in sight. But the shine never vanished. It was as if it mocked everyone that looked at it. Could those have been the same boots that now languished for days and nights on end, mud-caked and worn down badly at the soles?

When we arrived, we underwent again a tedious procedure as our names and ID numbers were recorded and checked against long lists fashioned previously when we were first taken prisoners. This red tape took at least one week. Stripped to the waist, our bodies were also checked once more. Any valuables we might still have been carrying were now removed once and for all. Walter's and my watches ended up in a little pile on the ground that kept growing by the minute. My thin gold chain with Effie in its locket also went. Walter seemed to have no other mementos, no valuables that could be taken away, except I knew he had been carrying a little toiletry bag pinned to the inside of his overcoat between the outer fabric and the lining. He had shown it to me once while we were still camped in the meadow before the march began. I had also seen him carrying a small roll of something that was now nowhere in sight as he was searched. I wondered were it had disappeared to. The toiletry bag was found since they searched all pockets and hand-tested the linings of jackets and coats. I saw the glee on the soldier's face when he found it. On opening its zipper and spreading its top open wide right before Walter and me, some gray and disgustingly slimy substance came to light that seemed to cover the entire contents. The soldier was just about to dive his fingers into the bag, but then, with a look of disgust, thought otherwise and dropped the bag at Walter's feet.

"You dirty German pig," he sneered at Walter with a frown and walked on to the next prisoner in line.

I could not help smiling. Clever Walter is still scheming and organizing things in his favor even under these worst of all circumstances, it went through my mind.

"Jan, we are saved," Walter whispered almost undetectably under his breath. "Do you know what valuables we have rescued? Soap, razor blades, and shaving cream and a pair of scissors and more. Just think of it, Jan. You'll come to see how fortunate we are. Trust me!"

I could already imagine the benefits, and it moved me to realize how sincere he was in sharing anything he had with me, the good and kind man. To this day I cannot understand how he could later turn on me the way he did, so utterly and completely wipe me out of his life.

"Walter," I whispered curiously, "Tell me, what else were you carrying on the march, that little roll of something?"

"Look here!" And he pointed with a sly and mischievous expression to his hips. Now at a closer look, he seemed, indeed, to have a larger girth than I recollected.

"It's a small air mattress," he whispered as he patted himself just below the belt. "I traded it for part of my rations way back in the meadow before we began marching. It will help us in the days to come, believe me Jan it will."

Little did he or I know that it would help save my life.

"Jan," he started again, "I don't have any hope that we'll be sent home, neither I think do you. You saw the boxcar trains. They are all pointed east and that's where we are headed. Are you up to it?"

"We have both to be up to it because we both want to survive. I have already summoned my will to do it long before I even came here. I have parents, a sister, and a girl to go home to. What about you Walter?"

"I have a sweet wife and two small daughters, and I know in my heart I will see them again. My will is bent on that."

He said it with so much tenacity and with so much conviction that I had to glance at him quickly to see what emotions might be revealed on his face. I had not known Walter to be an emotional man like some of the others who had openly wept in that field as the end had come. As I looked at his face, it appeared emotionless, a cold, determined sort of mien with shut eyes, except for the one tear that stole away from under his lashes and tumbled down his cheek. I was touched. I had not known Walter, the stalwart former Sergeant Gutmeister, to be a man of demonstrative emotions. Even when his men had openly wept, he had been stoic. I did not want to say or ask any more. I was afraid to open the floodgate that, I now surmised, may contain a sea of emotions. It was not the time nor the place, not now. We needed to keep our wits together.

All I said was, "I believe you, Walter," as I averted my eyes. I do not think he realized that I had looked at him, for we were supposed to stand at attention.

We thought we were lucky. Our stay in that most desolate and discouraging of camps was short--only eight days. In the morning of the ninth day, we were part of a large contingent of men to be herded towards a boxcar train, the end of which I could not see. Walter and I became alarmed when we first peered through the open sliding door of the nearest car. It had been modified. It is to further punish and humiliate us, I thought to myself. Walter had seen it too, and I wondered what went through his mind. Another floor had been added to the car so that it now had a bottom and a first floor. This modification made standing for the occupants impossible. They could only lie down, sit, or crawl around on all fours, but it had the advantage that each boxcar could now carry twice as many prisoners as before.

Luckily, Walter and I, sticking always close together, were directed onto the bottom floor. We could see right away that it would be easier to get in and out if the train stopped on its way east. They needed to let us out once in a while I reckoned for some exercise and to get rid of the buckets of slop.

Walter and I settled down into the corner of the car nearest to the door. He had scrambled in ahead of me and knew exactly what he wanted. Always getting the best out of even the worst situations it shot through my mind. The car filled up quickly. Each man had just enough space to lie down and stretch out. Four low steel buckets with wooden lids (thank goodness for the lids) were fastened to a post in the center of the car. There were no mattresses, no straw that the men could lie on. Everyone had to sleep on the bare wooden planks.

Within two hours, the train was set in motion. The large door was shut, and we were engulfed by darkness. We had not been told what the destination would be; all we knew, through our own sense of direction, was that we were heading east.

The siding of the boxcars was poor; its originally green planks had shrunk as they had dried during the hot summers so that now there were cracks between the planks. Some boards had holes where knots had been. They had fallen out as the wood had dried. These openings now let air in for our benefit—I do not think we would otherwise have survived the intense midday heat—and minute amounts of lights. As our eyes got used to the initial darkness, for we had come in out of the blinding sunshine, it turned out to be a semi-darkness that we could live with. The men on our floor set immediately to work on a plan that would allow us to know where we were heading. Since the train would come through a station now and then (we knew it would never stop there), it was decided that we would place two men uninterruptedly at convenient holes in the wood. These men had to report on what they saw of the countryside and the cities as well as tell us the name of the town or city as the train ran through its train station. The shifts were rotated during daylight every hour. It was not an easy task to sit still for that long a time with an eye steadily at the observation hole. But we were all glad to know how far we had traveled and what the countryside looked like. Also, the duty kept us somewhat alert and occupied. We were hungry for the information that was gathered.

As we crossed the Polish border into Russia, the names of places became meaningless to us since we could no longer read the writing. We gave up and stopped looking. The loss of interest in the outside world seemed to have started the decline of our bodies and minds.

The train crawled along at what seemed like a snail's pace. Twice every day the train stopped dead on its tracks for several hours in remote and isolated areas. It was then that we received our bread and water rations, could walk short distances back and forth alongside the tracks for a little exercise, stretch our crooked backs and aching limbs, and make our blinded eyes see again, all under the watchful eyes of the guns. There must have been several thousand men onboard this train.

Within the first week, prisoners were taken ill in one car or another with high fevers and dysentery. As time went on we heard their moans on our floor too and on the one above us. There was no medical help; no one looked after the sick except the fellow prisoners closest to them. Some prisoners, who were the weakest and in poor health from the outset, began to die. During the second week of our journey, each time the train came to a halt, the dead were removed before the living were allowed to disembark. The corpses were quickly taken away by some of the guards and most likely buried in shallow graves along the embankments, but always out of our sight. Emotional breakdowns now began to happen too with almost uncontrollable sobbing or intermittent yelling. The healthy tried to calm those poor souls to avoid everyone from going crazy.

And then came the terrifying incident on our floor. One of the men started to bang his head against the planks and let out horrific yells with every hit. He was a husky man who swung his arms around at anyone who tried to prevent him from beating himself up. For the longest time no one could come near him for he seemed to have more strength and fighting power than anyone could have imagined. Eventually he collapsed into a heap on the floor with blood streaming from his head. Walter tore his undershirt apart and wrapped it around the man's head as he bedded him down on our mattress. Never having formed a clear conception of hell before, I now knew this was it. It was not the sort of hell depicted by our priest in a netherworld-like place, neither was it Dante's literary hell, but the real hell created by human beings. I would have gone crazy too, had not Walter, almost incessantly, told me stories of his childhood, his adolescence, and his war years. He told them with excessive details as if he tried to stretch each story over as long a period of time as possible. He loved to talk, and I appreciated this diversion. He spoke always in low tones, and over time the stories repeated themselves. It was almost as if he tried desperately to keep himself from going crazy too.

At the outset of our trip, Walter's mattress gave the two of us comfort that others did not have. We traded off--three hours for him, three hours for me. But as time wore on, we let other needy prisoners use it, just so that they could get a few hours of rest. Most of these emaciated men, lying on the wooden boards day and night, had developed large blue and black areas on their buttocks, backs, and hips. With fear and concern in their eyes, they showed these marks to others on their walks along the train tracks, and took, I am certain, some consolation in seeing that others suffered in the same way as they did. Only Walter and I seemed to be free of these terrible marks.

It was during the third week that I developed an acute sore throat. At first I hid it from Walter. But when the fever set in, he knew I was very ill. I remember his bedding me down on the mattress he retrieved from one of the other prisoners. He must have tended me day and night. He had somehow gotten two rags. He had also organized some kind of metal container in which he saved some of his drinking water. The two rags he applied alternately on my burning forehead. It was not long before I lost all sense of where I was. I heard Walter's voice as if through a tunnel commanding me to wake up, to stay awake. Once in a while, his voice became so persistent that I opened my eyes against my will, and I would see Walter's face above me. I could not understand the worry I saw in his eyes in the semi-dark gloom. I tried to smile at him to wipe the worry off his face, but could not sustain it. I shut my eyes once more. Those were the lucid moments. The rest were lost in a recurring dream of standing on a rocky ledge under blue sky overlooking a magnificent blue ocean. The sea was calm and non-threatening. As I turned around, I saw behind me a steep rocky cliff rising up to a high road way up above. Some figure I did not recognize stood way up high trying to throw a rope down to me, but it did not reach me. I could have never climbed that smooth rocky surface by myself. The figure kept on shouting to me, but I did not answer. I liked where I stood, at the ocean's edge. It was so calming. I spent much time just contemplating the tranquil sea and was tempted to jump in. All the while, at my back, the activity for my rescue was still going on. I glanced up once more. There were other figures now besides the one that desperately tried to help me. They consisted of another man and three women. I thought immediately of my family and Effie. I waived to them with happiness in my heart, but they extended their arms, thin long emaciated arms, towards me in a gesture of desperation. I could not take their pain. So, I turned again to the soothing expanse of the sea. Still tempted to jump in but hesitating, I suddenly saw rising from the deep in the distance three white-clad women walking across the water towards me. They appeared so tranquil and so benevolent that I felt gladness in my heart. As I waited for them to come close enough and to take me with them perhaps, I heard again the clamor at my back. And then I saw Walter's face above mine. I revisited that dream many times and woke temporarily to Walter's face just as many times. But every time I was just about to enter into a communion with the women, I was pulled away again and again. So I never discovered their mysteries or their intentions for me.

After fighting hard for the dream to linger and as I tried to conjure it up again and again to keep it in my grasp, I became more and more exhausted until I willingly slipped into darkness.

13

Anna Petrovna

I lay there very still as if my movements had been restricted; and as I looked around me, I saw a world of dingy whiteness--walls of grayish-white that could have been part mold and part dirt from years without new paint, muddy-white curtains that hung around my bed, and yellowish-white sheets. I had expected the next world to be at least of a pure white. Suddenly, a great fatigue and disappointment settled over me again. So I closed my eyes once more (I was surprised that I still had them). I had no body, it seemed, for I could not feel it. Why then did I have eyes? I could not sustain this thinking process. It was too strenuous. So I departed once more into the fog from where I had emerged, and that seemed kind and soothing.

The next time I ventured out of the protective mist again and used the eyes I knew I still possessed, I saw a woman's face above mine. This is not how I thought an other-worldly spirit would look: a somewhat exotic face with high Tartar cheek bones, large blue-gray eyes, sallow, pale skin, and dark blond hair pulled back plainly and fastened in a twist at the nape of the neck. It was an older but still pleasing face with a hint of former beauty, full of strength and determination now, and even a certain coldness, although a touch of sophistication of old, I thought, still lingered. At least her smock was gleaming white and in stark contrast to all the other dirty whites surrounding me. As I kept my eyes open, her face began to smile and an amazing warmth suddenly spread over her, perhaps, artificially severe features. This smiling countenance was the face she only showed to me I later realized. It was her private face that she normally shared with no one, for much later I would watch her in action in her capacity as official camp physician and when she was called on to talk about health and food matters or to solve food controversies the prisoners had instigated.

"Janos I am so happy you have come back to us," she said with a softness I had not expected her to be capable of, not when I had seen those initial features in the first fleeting moments of my awakening. "You are in the infirmary of Prison Camp No. 805, also unofficially called Dom Sovieta, near the city of Rodonski in the South Western Soviet Union. It's close to the Black Sea. You are thousands of kilometers far from home. I am sorry for that, and if you still have a family, they would be shocked if they saw you now. You were nearly lost to this world. It is a miracle that you are still alive considering the condition you were in when they took you off that train. I don't think the prison administration would approve of what I have been doing for you, but that should not worry you. It was your youth that compelled me to be defiant. I could sense your innocence."

She had said all of that in fluent German. The words had gushed profusely from her mouth as a spring would that had been capped for a while.

"You are still very, very ill," she started up again and continued, "If my diagnosis is correct, you are suffering from rheumatic fever brought on by what, I believe, was a streptococcal infection in your throat, a very sore throat. Your fellow prisoners who handed you over to us said your ailment started with a sore throat followed by a high fever that rendered you delirious and then unconscious. The reason why I think it is rheumatic fever is that, while examining you, I noticed the hot and swollen joints of your arms and legs. That is an arthritic condition characteristic of rheumatic fever."

I now listened to her with full alertness and with growing concern. I appreciated her honesty. She sounded kind and yet with an air about her that tolerated no nonsense.

After taking in a deep breath, she started again.

"Listen to me carefully, Janos. We have tied your arms and legs, and you must lie perfectly still at all times, for the pain in your inflamed joints would otherwise surely drive you crazy. At the moment, I have no effective means to ease your pain because we have no aspirins in the infirmary, though I will now do my very best to somehow procure a supply."

Her tone had become increasingly more serious, and I dared not ask any questions for I sensed she had more to say.

"You must be very patient and follow all my instructions. In time, I hope, the inflammation will subside for you are very young. But you are undernourished and you are in a weakened state. It will take time, perhaps a long time."

She took another deep breath and continued.

"What is more dangerous than the arthritis is that rheumatic fever can affect your heart. The condition is called carditis. Your heart muscles and valves could become affected. If they do it could be mild and you would eventually fully recover; if the condition is severe it could lead to heart failure. I have already listened to your heart but I have only detected a very slight murmur, which is as yet a feeble indication of carditis. I hope the murmur will not become more pronounced."

I now looked at her with alarm and she noticed it right away.

"Janos, please don't worry and stay calm," she said pleadingly. "Please understand I just want to be very honest with you. I want you to know what we are up against. I think I know that you will follow my instructions if you are well informed." She hesitated a moment and then said, "I have something else to tell you. I cannot promise you that I will be able to keep you here, but I will try my best to retain you under my care. However, the camp administration is unpredictable. So far, they know little of your case. I have kept it hidden. That's why you only see one staff member besides me. The officials in the administration have little compassion for the German prisoners; and I have really no more than they have. But I want to try to save you." After a short pause she added, "Oh, I am sorry, I forgot to tell you; my name is Anna Petrovna. I am the prison doctor. Now that you are awake, progress, I am hopeful, can be speeded up. At least we will be able to give you solid foods and we will start tonight."

The words had rapidly tumbled out of her mouth as if someone was standing behind her ready at any moment to shut off the flow. But she kept on smiling throughout, a small, faint, almost sad smile. I was grateful to her for I thought I fully realized that she may be tarnishing her reputation or worse with the camp administrators if they found out about her determined efforts to save me. For what was I to her and them really: just another expendable number? Much, much later after the tragic events that were to occur I would find out what had been motivating her to go against the grain of the system.

"Thank you, doctor, very much," is all I could say, for even those few words made me tired as well as the thinking I had been doing. I felt I needed to rest and closed my eyes. For some reason I was glad to be still on this earth and sank into a dreamless sleep.

I think it was the smell of food, the grainy smell of porridge, I thought, that raised me out of my sleep. A male attendant, Boris, as I found out later, sat at my bed. He was holding the small bowl right below my nose. Yes, that warm grainy smell was what had roused me for I felt suddenly very hungry. Boris had a pale, broad face with pale gray, rather veiled eyes. He carried his face like a mask. He showed no emotions. Yet he was gentle with me as he spoke in Russian that I did not understand. Later on as Anna started to teach me, I understood that he always said, "Now you must eat, you young bird." These words, it seemed, were so utterly contrary to his reclusive demeanor. He patiently spooned the porridge into my mouth in tiny quantities. I could not eat much since swallowing was a feat. At last he drizzled some milk into my mouth, and then he was gone, quietly, as he must have come in.

Now that I was eating, they removed the IV. And, as the days wore on into high summer, I enjoyed looking at the summer sky through the little window above my bed. That's all the view I had for months. Eventually they removed the restraints on my arms and legs. I had no idea what the camp was like or the surrounding areas. They also started to prop me up in bed during the day. Anna Petrovna stopped by at least once every day, smiled and nodded at me encouragingly but said little. Boris kept on feeding me, still small portions because it was tiring for me. But, in a few weeks, the portions became bigger and I felt myself regaining strength. My joints still hurt fiercely when I moved them, but I liked that better than not feeling them at all. So I purposely started to exercise them a little and suffered the pain.

As soon as I could sit in bed propped up, Anna Petrovna came in one day and said that she wanted to talk privately with me. After closing the curtains, she sat down on my bed, something she had not done before. She leaned close to my ear and spoke softly.

"You are young and intelligent, I can see that. You need to exercise your mind. Would you like to learn Russian? I estimate that you will still be here for a few months. If you tried to walk now, you would soon realize that your legs wouldn't be able to carry you, not yet, and your heart would begin to race. I will let you know when you are ready to take your first steps. But for now, I would like to see you start exercising your mind. Your mind has a great influence over your body. I'll provide you with paper and pencil and, perhaps, a rudimentary book."

She was always so matter of fact. Even now, when she made this incredible proposal, she said it as if she proposed giving me some new medicine.

"Of course, there is nothing I would like better than to learn your language," I said with as much enthusiasm as I could muster, for I had just been given the gift that could save me from these dreary, dreadful days hidden behind this curtain. "And the sooner I start, the better," I heard myself say.

She could not have missed my eagerness and, indeed, she did not. That same afternoon, she handed me a few pages, tightly hand-written. They contained the Cyrillic alphabet opposite the German alphabet. They also contained simple words and phrases in Russian, the words written out with the lettering of both alphabets. I was ecstatic and tried to throw my arms up at her as if I wanted to hug her, but they fell down beside me due to the excruciating pain, which came almost as soon as I had raised them. I grimaced with pain.

"Janos, I know how appreciative you are. You don't need to show me," she said simply.

"I am so happy! I will work on these lessons from the time I wake up until it gets too dark for me to see. I promise you I will master it, for I want to so much."

I am sure she was happy about what she had heard, but she did not show it openly. After she left, I sank back as in bliss. Here was something I could sink my heart and soul into. I also suddenly realized that Anna had produced all this hand-written material in no time after she first mentioned the lessons. There was no way she could have written all of this down between the announcement and when she brought the pages to me. She must have written it the night before, or even long before so sure was she that I would take her up on it. Nothing would ever move me so much as this realization did. Oh, Anna! is all I could murmur to myself.

She had instructed me to keep the paper and pencil hidden as much as I could, especially when I knew that Boris would come to feed me. She had also said that someone else would replace Boris soon and that, perhaps, I would like the change. But she had remained cryptic about it.

Whenever Anna Petrovna came for her official visit, she would hear my recitation of the words and phrases she had given me, and she corrected my pronunciation until it sounded perfect to her. I did well and seemed to learn fast. For the first time I realized that I had a talent for languages, more than I had realized it in school when I learned French but was not very focused. It

79

must have been this life and death situation I had found myself in that made me more eager and concentrated to learn. Anna was pleased with the progress and soon we conversed in very simple words and sentences. She thought up little routines each day. Then one day she showed up with a simple primary school book.

"This is your reward for the good work you are doing. It cost me much finagling to get it. For these efforts I want you to learn it by heart and to recite it to me with the book closed."

She suddenly laughed a little as if she had become self-conscious and threw her head back slightly. In that pose, she looked younger and more pleasing than I had ever seen her since I first opened my eyes months ago. I figured Anna was just past middle age at the time I first met her. She must have been quite attractive and, perhaps, very idealistic when she was young, I thought to myself. Sometimes I wished I knew what she was thinking, what her private life was like, and why she was helping me.

As I began to feel better, I thought again about my loved ones at home. It pained me to think that they had no knowledge of my whereabouts. Ever since I left them almost a year ago, the day after Christmas, they had received no sign from me. I did not really know, but I believed that no one had been able to write since we entered this camp. But if the prisoners had written, I certainly had had no opportunity. I was totally cut off from the others. I always came to the conclusion that my family and Effie must think me dead. That was a heart-rending thought for me, one that almost threw my recovery into reverse.

It was Anna who kept me going, who lifted my spirit, who nudged me on to learn, to make the best of the present, to prevail, and to, perhaps, emerge as a victor. At the beginning of my ordeal, when they had taken me from my home, I was so certain that I would survive, that my will alone would see me through. Now I was not so certain anymore. Now I saw myself more like lying prostrate before the forces of life, and it was up to them to see me through or cut it short. I do not really know whether it was this protracted illness or the human hell I had witnessed that had curbed my drive to survive, had somehow curtailed that indefatigable will I thought I had. I also realized that, in any case, my will alone would not be able to see me through, but that I was dependent on the good will and compassion of other human beings.

I was also thinking more and more of Walter. Would he know at least where I was and what I had been through? One day, as Anna sat by my bed practicing groups of words and phrases with me, I told her in Russian (I thought she would more readily respond to me if I tried to express myself in Russian) that I had had a good friend on my way to this camp, a fine man who had saved my life twice. I expressed that I was afraid he had no knowledge of what happened to me and that he must be grieving this loss.

She asked me, "What is his name?"

"Walter Gutmeister," I replied.

From the expression on her face, it looked to me as if she was contemplating, perhaps some occurrence, some incident she had come across recently.

Then she said, "A prisoner came to the infirmary, not ill, but just requested to see me. He was denied access to me. He has come back several times. Seemed very persistent. He cannot see the doctor unless he is gravely ill. Even light illnesses do not go further than the orderlies. These requests from the prisoner have been reported to me, but I do not have to and did not respond to them. It could have been your friend who wanted to find out about you. I am thinking of his persistence. I will just send an anonymous note to him, alleviating his fears about you even if he was not the man who came looking for me. But I am almost certain it was him, for wouldn't a friend be looking for a friend even if he were directing undue attention towards himself? It is never wise, you know, to make unusual requests in these camps. The more you keep to yourself and avoid making waves, the more favorable you are looked upon. The system doesn't like individuals that stand out. By the way, I am glad we are talking about these matters concerning prison camps. Soon you will enter the camp for the first time and I want to caution you. Tame your youthful spirit, go along with the flow, and you may even be sent home some day."

"Anna," I replied (she had ask me to call her that when we were in private conversation) "there is no spirit to tame anymore. I feel I have been swallowed up by the great river of life. I no longer have the desire to go against the stream but to swim with it."

"In a way, I feel sadness welling up in my heart that someone of your youth has already lost his fighting spirit, and yet I think your new mode of being will see you through. It's a wisdom often learned much later. Some, perhaps, will never master it."

She suddenly, abruptly changed her discourse. "I will try to find your friend, Janos, and will get a message to him."

With that she rose and quickly left my alcove. It always seemed that she at first overextended herself in our short private conversations, especially now that we conducted them in her language because I repeatedly felt this sudden pulling back, this recoiling back behind her official mask. Great God, I would desperately question Him in those frustrating moments after she left me, why can't we human beings keep on communicating heart to heart, since I feel we are all of the same stuff?

14

Mei Chi

As I leaned my head back one morning against my pillows, eyes half closed, I saw her swooping in through the curtain towards my bed like a small exotic bird. She was very petite. Her hair was black as lacquer and her eyes black as a moonless night; her skin in contrast was pale and smooth, fresh and new-looking like a child's; black tresses fell over her forehead almost down to her almond-shaped eyes, shading them softly; the rest of the hair was shoulder length, cut off in a very straight fashion. I was glad I was positioned like I was for, I think, she thought at first I was sleeping. I felt she did not notice right away that I was watching her. I had never seen a young woman before so foreign, so exotic, so mysteriously different from others I had known. She must not have been much older than me. For a moment, she stood close to my bed, seemingly not knowing what she should do. She held the bowl in front of her. I really wanted her to think I was asleep. But within moments the smallest smile stole across her face as she opened her mouth and spoke in perfect Russian (I don't know why I had expected some foreign, far eastern language).

"I know you are not asleep, Master Janos, (it was strange to hear her call me Master, it sounded so incongruous in view of my situation) it's time to eat. I am Mei Chi your new attendant. I will not only bring your food but also do physical therapy with you. Doctor Petrovna has requested me to do that. She wants you to get well as quickly as possible. You must not linger much longer

83

in this infirmary. I know your case. I hope you don't mind my being female. Forget about any qualms you might have in that respect; I am only here to further your recovery. Please let's work together. Please cooperate."

She had said all of it in a soft tone and yet with great firmness. I marveled how she managed to employ these two opposites with great ease.

I opened my eyes, knowing that I could no longer pretend. She had seen through me. I felt myself blushing faintly and did not really know why. I thought of my beard that had grown long as well as my unkempt hair. I must have looked like an old man to her and yet I wanted her to see me as a young person like her. Inwardly, I felt ecstatic that someone close to my own age would work with me. God, forgive me, my inner voice said fervently, perhaps you will show me that communication is possible.

She came closer yet and handed me my bowl and spoon. "You must eat it, all of it. I'll be back in an hour. Then we will start the therapy. Doctor Petrovna said we must work hard to get you out of here. I don't quite understand the hurry, but she seems unsettled these days."

With that she was gone with her short white smock, her dark blue cotton pants, and her black hair bobbing as she turned abruptly on her heels. I was very happy that she would work with me and that I had understood what she had said to me in Russian.

She was back in an hour. She undressed me to the waist (after she had asked in a delicate manner for my permission) and started working with my arms, shoulders, and elbows. When she had finished manipulating them with her small, yet strong hands (it hurt, but I was almost enjoying the hurt, for what overpowered the feeling of hurt was the sweet feeling of being touched and manipulated; no one had touched me in a long time), I noticed that she always paused awhile with the palms of her hands on the joints. She closed her eyes while she did it and seemed to concentrate but without effort while her face remained calm. I could feel some soothing warmth emanating from her palms, at least I thought I did. Just this slightest of touches felt immensely soothing. She followed the same procedure when she manipulated my knees and ankles. Then she had me turn over and worked my back, always ending her manipulations with these exquisite moments of the barest touch. At last, she had me lie on my back, and she covered my heart with both hands. I thought it felt as if it derived new strength.

All the while Mei Chi worked my body, she described in a calm soothing voice beautiful natural scenes--forests, rivers, mountains, the seashore. And when I asked her afterwards whether she had ever been to that wonderful seashore she described (I had never been to the seashore myself since I had grown up far inland), she admitted with a blush that she had never been there.

"I grew up in Mongolia," she said simply, "far from the sea. I have seen pictures of the great ocean and the white sands that fringe it. I do not need to see or touch it. I carry it in my heart. We believe that we carry everything that exists in our innermost self. That's why I can make it come to life."

She said this so simply as if it were commonplace practice. The therapy was then finished and I knew she would depart quickly, for she never lingered. But she came three times a day (six times when you considered the few moments she spent handing me my bowl).

It was the second time she came that she had brought the scissors. She said quite matter of factly that she would cut my hair and trim my beard if I would like that. Naturally I would like it. She explained that the healing would not progress very well unless I felt good about myself in every part of my body. So, she trimmed my hair that used to be blond but was now of a dark, dirty color and matted down from lying in this bed for months without bathing. She said nothing and made no comments but worked with speed and a sure hand. I was certain it was a task she normally did not perform. She cut my hair very short and trimmed my beard as close as she could to the skin. Next time, she said she would bring a basin and wash the hair.

She did bring the basin with warm water, a little sliver of soap, and a cloth. She first cleansed my body with the cloth, then lathered up my hair with the tiniest amount of water. The rest of the water she used to rinse the hair.

"Oh, how wonderful this golden hair!" she cried out in delight, and then quickly held her hand over her mouth as if she regretted that these words had escaped her.

She worked such a miracle in my soul that at last it felt resurrected. She would not take my thanks and whisked away her cleansing tools as quickly as she could. She seemed modest and self-effacing, yet emanated a quiet strength, even power that she knew just how to direct.

Later on Anna confided in me that Mei Chi would have become a true healing physician in the ancient sense of this craft if the war had not intervened and if her family had not been driven apart. Mei Chi believed her parents, ethnic Chinese dwelling in Mongolia for decades and wealthy trades people at one time, to be dead. Mei Chi was brought to Russia in her teens and sent to a nurses' training school. Anna said she had known Mei Chi for two years in a previous prison camp and had sent for her under the pretext that some camp official was gravely ill. But she really needed her for me because

Anna thought my recovery was not progressing as it should be. She knew of Mei Chi's healing power. I thought I sensed that she was beginning to get nervous, for the longer I stayed in the infirmary, the greater the chance would be that someone might turn her in.

Mei Chi had been working with me like she did on the first day for two weeks. Then she willed me to get up. As I stood for the first time on my feet after months of confinement to the bed, I thought my legs would collapse from under me. But Mei Chi took my arm, placed it around her shoulders, and helped me to move forward. The walking practice was now added to the usual therapy, and in two weeks I was walking back and forth in the room outside my alcove. Though I was thin and emaciated still, I could feel some strength returning, and soon I walked around in my room for long periods of time. Mei Chi's touch even followed me into my dreams then, dreams in which I seemed to come alive under her touch and regain incredible strength that stayed with me even when she kept on disappearing into the distance. I tried to hang onto her, but she would somehow very cleverly slip away.

Two more weeks and Anna came in one afternoon as I was practicing my walking. She was impressed and her expression was happy.

"Janos, you are ready to leave here. I will arrange for some light work in the camp for you. You must leave this infirmary for my and your sake. Although you could benefit from a couple more weeks, I have to let you go. But I will give you an official note that will allow you to see me briefly every other evening after the evening meal for several more weeks. I must keep on checking up on you for you could have a relapse and that would be grave, indeed."

"Since I must go, I'll be very happy that I will still see you quite often. Thank you, Anna, for being my savior and teacher."

She then handed me a small package wrapped in brown paper. I knew what it contained when I took it from her.

"Oh, Anna! Books?" is all I could say. I pressed the package against my heart. Her nod and faint smile told me that she knew what I felt. Tiredness seemed to emanate from around her eyes. Placing the package on the chair next to me, I stepped towards her. I wanted to hug her and hold her, but she stood so rigid and so erect all of a sudden that I held back. I knew then that she did not want me to come any closer. Sometimes, her split-second mood changes baffled me. I never quite knew where I really stood. Anna left me quickly that afternoon.

That night, with feelings of trepidation but also of excitement, all at the same time, I awaited my entrance into the camp with eagerness. I would finally be among the men again I felt I belonged to. Being a prisoner of war once again instead of an invalid, I was now more than willing to take on the hardships.

15

Camp Dom Sovieta

He saw me immediately as I entered the enormous room filled with prisoners taking in their evening meal. Sitting at rough-hewn tables and benches, they were just finishing their meager meal of watery soup, black bread, and water. I heard him shout above the din of hundreds of voices talking,

"Jan! Is that really you, Jan?"

He jumped up and came sort of waddling over to me. I had never seen Walter walk that way. He had always had such a firm gait. He must be very tired I thought. They must work him hard. Suddenly, all three hundred eyes were on me, and I started feeling hot. After months of seclusion in the infirmary, I did not seem to be able to handle all this attention, I realized. But Walter was already right in front of me.

"Let me look at you, Jan. You look great! (I doubted the correctness of his assessment.) Thought you would never come back to us. But then I got this note a few weeks ago saying that you were OK. I tell you, Jan, nothing could have made me happier than receiving that message except seeing my wife and daughters again. Wonder who instigated sending it to me? Ah, never mind. So happy to see you, kid."

And with that he threw his arms around me and held me tight for a while. I folded my arms around him too. Everyone in that huge room must have heard my story for all the men started clapping and stomping their feet as

Walter and I stood there embracing each other. There is not much else happening, so every story gets circulated from man to man, I thought. In the next moment I felt like I had come home.

"I am so glad to see you, Walter. Seems you are doing OK. I have missed you and thought of you a lot. It's quite a miracle that I am here. I'll tell you about it later." He set me free and I saw the happiness in his beaming face.

"Pal, we can start working actively about getting out of here, now that we are together."

He said it with a lot of hope and conviction in his voice so that I was almost convinced that that was exactly what we were going to do. Meanwhile the men's attention had once more shifted to themselves.

"Let's go over there, Jan, and sit down." He pointed at an empty bench along the wall. As we sat down, he said under his breath with his face right in front of me, "It's really the shits here, Jan. They are feeding us abominable stuff, nothing but water and bread. You can discount the soup. You'll know when you see that broth. Dishwater they call it, that's what it is. After our meals, we feel so heavy with that brick of bread and all that water in our stomachs that we can hardly walk and barely manage to drag ourselves to our bunks and lie down. It's done on purpose! I tell you. They want to wipe us out, one by one. They have already gotten old Brandeis. Remember that finicky old guy in our boxcar. He couldn't stand the rags we had to wrap around our feet. Traded a bunch of his meals for a pair of socks. That did him in. He died a couple of months ago. By the way, I'm getting off track here. Watch! In a moment you will see everyone taking off to the sleeping rooms."

Then he became a little disjointed in his thinking. I guess he could not get everything out quickly enough.

"And no proper facilities, Jan. Well, you'll see tomorrow. I guess you don't even know what this prison is all about. They'll show you tomorrow. Nothing but exploitation! Hard work! Hard work! And more hard work! And then this lousy food! How can they expect us to keep going? I swear those physicals tell the story. We have to drop all of our clothes every couple of weeks in front of that cold bitch of a doctor (I ached for Anna) who does the evaluations. All she is interested in is seeing whether we still have butts left. They can tell by the butts, you know, whether we are still fit for work. Without a butt, they won't let you stay. They'll ship you out and you'll never be seen again. Don't know what happens to these poor bastards. Sorry, Jan, I am dropping this on you like a ton of bricks right from the start. But better to hear it from me than anyone else, don't you think? I figure the sooner you know the better. That's all for now. More later. But, tell me, where are you sleeping, kid?"

I was stunned about all I had heard. But I looked at the little scrap of paper I had been given in the infirmary.

"Second floor, room twelve, bed 25."

"Oh, I know where that is, not far from my room. Listen, Jan, I wish we could have our sleeping quarters together. But they won't allow that. We are being rotated every two weeks. Don't want us to get too friendly with the guys in the beds next to us or above us. So, it won't happen that we will ever be close during the night hours. It would be so great to be able to talk to you before going to sleep. I love talking to you, Jan. But, listen to this: I want us to stand next to each other at assembly in the morning so that we'll be sent on assignment together. I think that'll work. Just watch for me. I'll always wait at the door for you at 5:30 in the morning. Jan, you look distant! Did you get that?"

"Yeah, sure that'll be great. But for a few weeks I will have to do kitchen duty. I am not cleared for outside labor yet."

"Oh, I see," Walter said with disappointment in his voice, and it showed in his face too. "But remember what I have arranged for the future. As soon as they let you out, I'll be waiting at the door at 5:30 sharp."

Walter had been rattling off like a machine gun. He must not have found anyone who liked to listen to him as well as I did. Maybe he had gotten nervous. Maybe he is not as sure of himself as he had been, I thought to myself. After that exchange and a handshake, we went our separate ways. I climbed up the stairs to the sleeping quarters. Just those two flights of stairs made my heart race again though not as badly as I had felt it before. I guessed I was still not really well. But you must not think about it, just keep going I admonished myself. I was very tired now and immediately sank onto my bunk and fell right asleep. I was glad the guy above had not yet come in.

Someone tapped me on the shoulder lightly, and I woke with a start. I had slept fitfully, and I couldn't remember any dreams in the morning. It was still pitch dark. Someone whispered, "You are the new kitchen help. Please come with me." I got out of bed and followed. I had no idea how he had found me, and I had no idea what time it was. The kitchen was already lit up and some guys were already working. Now I saw the guy who had woken me, a little guy of slight build and with glasses.

"My name is Harold. I am the one responsible for getting the kitchen folks together in the morning. I appreciate that you didn't dally. I'll be off to get the others."

So it was that my days now began at 4 a.m. General wake up call was at 5 a.m. and assembly for the work crews at 5:30 a.m. as Walter had mentioned. Kitchen duty was easy and boring, but it allowed me to heal some more. It also allowed me to sneak a little more food than my normal allotment, a little extra mush at breakfast, a little more black bread. Anything extra I could swipe would help me I figured.

After breakfast that day, Harold showed me the camp. I could not believe what I saw. When I first stepped out into the yard and glanced up at the building that housed us, I was astounded. The building was a monstrosity--huge, almost fortress-like. It was twelve stories high and built in a fancy, ornate manner like a giant wedding cake. I wondered whether all official buildings in Russia looked like that, ornate and pretentious.

"This building you are looking at was once the administration center of this south-western region, a bureaucratic monster," Harold explained. "It was called Dom Sovieta. It got hit a few times during the war and then it burned out. See the black around the windows of the upper floors? It's not being used anymore, except for our camp. It houses twelve hundred prisoners of war, and they occupy the ground floor for daytime use and three stories above that for sleeping quarters. The infirmary and the camp administration use a portion of the fourth floor. That's it. Otherwise it's abandoned. There is no water on any of the floors, except the fourth. All other plumbing has been ripped out. The latrines in the yard we had to dig ourselves. I heard you have been sick a long time. So you were not part of the digging."

Pointing to a low, primitive, hut-like structure in the yard, he said disparagingly, "What you see over there is what you get as far as sanitary facilities. Open latrines, eight of them for 300 men. You can't waste any time once you get in because someone will be clamoring for it. Well, you wouldn't want to spend any time in them anyway. They stink to high heaven. Hold on to something when you are inside, otherwise you might faint and never get out of there. By the way, there are four prison yards like this, and they are all alike: eight latrines for three hundred men and one water faucet. See over there? And the men have to piss a lot, all night long. Those poor bastards that are on the third floor. All those stairs!"

Harold sounded disgusted. He had spoken rapidly, in very low tones. Everyone seemed to be doing that, I had noticed. I guessed they wanted to get their frustrations with the camp system off their chests, but were, at the same time, afraid to be overheard. Guards were always around inside and outside the building as I quickly learned, not only Russians guards but German prisoners trained as guards as well. The latter were not easy to identify. It was one of those ingenious tricks of the prison administration to use prisoners to watch over and spy on other prisoners.

I looked at the wall that enclosed the yard, a high formidable concrete wall with barbwire coils on top. They must have built this wall when the building was converted into a prison camp, I thought to myself. It cut out the view down to the mighty river that flowed past this building. I had seen the view when I had peeked out the window in the infirmary as I had learned to walk again. It was quite a ways down to the river since the building stood prominently on its high and tree-crowned northern bank overlooking a wide area all around. The river's southern bank in contrast was low with sandy shoals and merging into steppe beyond. The city itself was a short distance over to the West enshrouded in smog belching from its heavy industry smokestacks. I guessed that in its heyday the building we now occupied had been the epicenter of the city around which all life revolved: births, deaths, marriages, trials, taxation, policing, politics, and more. I wondered where that life center of the city had shifted to, perhaps to a new monster of a building that housed all these facets of life. Certainly this mighty building that used to serve those vital functions was now way past its declining stage, for providing shelter for these bruised and beaten up souls like ours was more like catering to death than to the life of a city.

Next Sunday, mid-morning, Walter came up to my bed. Most men went back to bed after breakfast on Sundays. That day they stayed in bed as much as they could to rest up for the next hard work week ahead.

"I've brought you a gift, Jan," he said grinning from ear to ear, and he dropped a tiny parcel, wrapped in a rag, on my bed.

"Walter, I appreciate this, but you shouldn't. You need to keep all you've got to yourself." Out of curiosity, I was already undoing the string that held the parcel together.

"Nonsense!" he replied.

Out of the parcel fell a tiny box of razor blades and a little piece of soap that had been cut off from a larger piece.

"I want you to be able to shave once in awhile and wash your face real good. It'll make you feel like a human being again. These blades are yours to keep. You just have to get the razor from me when you want to use it. I have only one. Remember that little bag I had way back when? These items are part of the goodies it contained."

I was moved and said, "This is my good old friend Walter all over again. I really, really appreciate this gift. No one else would give that away. You can't even get those things anywhere." With that I leaped out of bed, and grabbed him for a bear hug.

The cold winds had started blowing in from the plains to the southeast. The change had come suddenly, a change from dry moderate temperatures to dry cold. It was now the middle of November. Luckily our winter suits had recently arrived, (one would never know whether shipments would ever be on time), heavy one-piece quilted cotton suits, quilted gloves, quilted caps, and rubber boots that could be worn over our regular boots. These thick clumsy outfits were to get us through the winter, the first, long Russian winter I would experience. Little did I know then that there would be more winters like this one for me to go through.

16

Changes

The very short sessions with Anna every other evening let me somehow cope with the deadening duties I was assigned inside the camp. I was certain that I was more imprisoned than the men who performed hard labor on the outside. There were moments when I truly envied them. Every morning, when I watched their columns leaving the compound, I wanted to be with them. I could have endured the hard labor much more than these tedious chores in the prison's kitchen. Time was dragging. Only when I was in Anna's company did my spirit revive. These half-hour sessions of mainly practicing my Russian skills were like a precious libation that kept me alive and sane. But still I felt such a small amount of it was fed to me each time that it was barely enough to get me through the next two days.

Anna, though very gracious, always maintained her distance. Even until then I knew nothing of her life. Every time I was with her, Walter's words kept reverberating in my ears: 'That bitch of a doctor.' At first I thought it must be one of those incongruities of existence that an individual can be life-giving as well as life-denying at the same time. When I reflected on this duality, I came to the conclusion that nature as a whole was really like that. But I had always imagined human beings to be one way or the other, either supporters of life or destroyers. Anna changed my neat categorization. She made me uncertain as to the world I had constructed for myself. I would have never been able to ask her or to talk to her about the duality I saw in her, but maybe there was a good reason for it. I felt I could not and should not judge her; neither could I tell her what Walter had said. I could never ask her what made her do the one--preserve life--and also do the other--curtail it. To me it was as if she were two people that had been merged into one person by mistake. How was I to reconcile all of this since only good had come from her to me?

When I was with her, Anna kept on challenging me. We now conversed almost entirely in Russian. Rarely did she have to resort to German to make me understand a fine point. Every Sunday, as much as I could, I read the book she had given me (I kept everything she had given me hidden in my bed as she had instructed me to do), and I worked hand-in-hand with the little dictionary that had been part of the gift. It was Tolstoy's "War and Peace" I was reading, an officially forbidden book. Even when I was reading I kept pretending I was asleep, my head half covered with my blanket. Progress was tediously slow. I had to fight for and conquer every page to extract its meaning. But this immense challenge meant more to me than anything else at the time. I think I became obsessed with it. At first I kept my reading and studying hidden from Walter, but he always showed up quite unexpectedly. It was hard to keep things from him. Others left me alone and wanted me to leave them alone. But Walter found out soon enough with his inquisitiveness.

"Jan, what you are doing is downright dangerous," he said one afternoon.

At first I didn't know what he was talking about. But then I knew when he continued.

"That's not a book the current regime approves of. Besides, you are losing track of why we are here. Watch out that none of the Russian guards gets to see it." This was just the beginning of his admonishments. "Mastering that language will not keep you alive, or being versed in their literature, either. And besides, what will you do with it if you ever get out of here?"

I had no reasonable answer to what he had said, except I knew deep down that it was of utmost importance to me, that I loved languages—I yearned to know how other people expressed themselves and thus shape their unique way of existence—and that it kept me alive and sane. In those moments when Walter tried to dissuade me and I had almost shut him out by refusing to hear him, I, nevertheless, noticed painfully that he had changed his former 'when' to an 'if.' It seemed so minute a change, trading these two little words for one another, and yet it was significant. It was significant for I knew Walter so well. Was he beginning to lose his seemingly indomitable will? And when I reflected on it for some time, I came to the sad conclusion that he may be on the verge of losing it. I do not remember when exactly this change occurred. Maybe Walter had not even noticed it himself, and I had not recognized it until now. I could not bring myself to point it out to him either. I was just fervently hoping for him, for me, for all of us, that this subtle change would be rather meaningless, that it would not mean our belief in a future different from this abominable way of life had slipped irrevocably towards despair.

When going into or leaving the infirmary in the evening, I sometimes caught a glimpse of Mei Chi. She always seemed to see me, too, though her acknowledgments were of the subtlest kind—a faint smile or just a slight nod of the head. Every time I saw her, my heart and body went out to her. My heart yearned for the wonder of healing she had shared with me, and my body yearned for her touch. It yearned not so much for her manipulations of my limbs and joints but for her light touch that came always at the end. Perhaps I did not even yearn for that touch but just for her life force connecting with mine. I had dreamed many dreams of her. They continued to be inconclusive, frustrating. She was always challenging and awakening the spirit in me, but she seemed, at the same time, always out of my grasp.

I yearned for her company as I yearned for Anna's, but in an entirely different sense. Anna satisfied intellectual needs I had; Mei Chi fulfilled the needs of the heart, spirit, and body. But even the yearning I had for Mei Chi, and it became stronger the longer I was out of touch with her, was not the same as that I had experienced for Effie. Neither did I feel the same sweet stirrings in my loins for Mei Chi when I was with her that I had felt in the presence of Effie. My yearning for Mei Chi was of a subtler more complex kind, more difficult to interpret. It seemed to involve her and my essence but it also went beyond that. As I now think back, I understand the confusion that reigned within me then. At the time, I think I tried to explain the influence she had over me as that one kindred life force would have over another. Maybe I wasn't that far wrong even at that time when I had so little experience.

Over the next few weeks, my yearning for Mei Chi became so persistent that I felt I needed to take risks and to do everything in my power to be in contact with her. I was even willing to deceive Anna to achieve meeting with Mei Chi again. I knew I had to engage Anna's help for there was no other way to Mei Chi but through Anna. So it was that I told her that my joint pains had flared up again.

"Is there any possibility that I could receive more physical therapy that helped me so much in the past?" I asked her one evening immediately after I entered her room.

Her face became alarmed. (Oh, how I regretted doing this to her.) I was immediately afraid that she might have detected my deception. What relief then when I heard her say in reply, "Perhaps Mei Chi could help us once more. Now I think we cut off her treatments too soon. I will talk to her and let you know very soon."

There was no hesitation, as far as I could detect, on her part to elicit Mei Chi's help once more.

That night I performed better in my conversation with Anna than at any other time before. It was the first time I saw some signs of elation in her and the first time, I realized, that she thoroughly enjoyed being the teacher, a profession she probably should have chosen over medicine had she been given that choice.

To my surprise, next time I met with Anna, Mei Chi was with her. I blushed as I entered and saw her sitting next to Anna. I had not expected it to happen this fast. It was the realization that my little scheme had worked almost too well that caused my embarrassment. They both recognized the state I was in at the same time and began to smile.

Anna said matter-of-factly, "I see you are not used to too much female company. We will change that." And with that she broke the uncomfortable spell that had settled over me.

I hastened to reply as truthfully as I could, "You are mistaken, I love to be in both your company."

They both then laughed and nodded their heads in unison as if to say mockingly, "Yeah, we believe you!"

My evening calls at the infirmary had been changed. It was arranged by Anna that I would now see her three times a week and Mei Chi three times in half-hour sessions. I gave myself completely over to Mei Chi as she worked on me in the same way she had done before. She worked my joints, my back, and always ended with my heart. I let it happen with my eyes closed, and every time as her hands worked my body I sank for a short period of time into a bliss so transcendent that I afterwards thought my physical being had dissolved momentarily into nothingness.

One evening (I had shaved my beard off with Walter's blades, and he had trimmed my hair), as I lay on the small floor mat in Mei Chi's tiny, barren room she occupied next to Anna's, she touched my face with both hands when she had finished her therapy. She had never done that before. Her touch called me back from that wonderful place where I was dwelling at that moment. I opened my eyes and saw Mei Chi's face right above mine. Her eyes, always mysterious, were so black they appeared to me like pools in the night, the bottoms of which one cannot fathom. She kept on holding my face in both her hands.

"Master Janos you are a beautiful man, even now in your emaciated state. But that will change in time, for this is not the life you will lead forever." She sounded serious as if she had just had a revelation of the future. "Your limbs and heart do not need any more of my work. They are close to being healed. I know it and you will know it soon too. But it is your spirit that still needs a little healing. If you want me to, I will teach you some of the techniques I know through our ancient wisdom, techniques that you can use to preserve your life energy. You see, I am a Buddhist. No one in this country knows that except you since I am telling you now. I want to give you a gift that may get you through this time of confinement to prison life. Tell me whether you want to follow me into this world of mine. Be not afraid of turning me down. I do understand that you have a different belief. I will fully understand and nothing will change between us. My respect for you will always be there. Search your inner self and when it has told you what it wants you to do, then let me know. Our sessions will be coming to an end soon. It is never good to prolong something beyond its usefulness. I must report to Anna very soon that you are healed as much as you can be. It is my duty. But I would like to give you some tools as a gift, if you would like to accept them."

Mei Chi had never spoken this much to me and with such intensity. I mainly knew her speech through her imageries she conjured up while she performed her healing work.

Her hands were still holding my face. By now I was fully conscious. I had not let her face out of my sight while she spoke. Never had I thought that such a woman existed--so young, so innocently pure, so mysteriously beautiful, so full of ancient wisdom, and so certain of her power. I could no longer stay in my reclining position. With a sudden, powerful movement I pulled myself up into a sitting position opposite Mei Chi. Her hands had dropped off my face as I abruptly raised myself. Her features expressed surprise at my sudden action. And as I then sat face to face with her, I said with a passion and a thirst for knowledge that I did not realize was ever in me, not in that intensity.

"Mei Chi, do not send me away without my answer tonight. I do not need to commune with myself to find out whether I should accept your wisdom and your teaching. My whole self, even now, this minute, tells me that I should pay attention to all that you are willing to impart to me. Please accept my affirmative answer tonight."

Her face burst into a smile, and she just simply nodded her OK.

"Master Janos, I think we will have only four more sessions, so we must work fast. Please concentrate on bringing me all the attention you can muster." With that she bowed, and I knew it was time to leave. But before I did so, I said one last thing to her.

"Mei Chi, I will not return unless you promise not to call me master anymore."

She then laughed a bell-like, youthful, almost girlish laugh that I had not expected of her; and it was suddenly for me as if a wall between us had come down.

Then she replied very seriously as her laugh had quickly subsided, "I will consider your request, Janos."

I felt almost as if I had won a victory as I turned on my heels and left.

17

Hard Labor

It took only one meeting with Anna to convince her that I was now ready to do hard work. I sounded very determined. At first she tried to dissuade me, but as she saw my resolve, she wrote out a release after checking the sound of my heart once more.

"OK, I can't detect a murmur in your heart anymore." Because she said the words slowly and haltingly, I thought I detected a tinge of regret in her voice. Though I could have been wrong since she quickly added, "All parties that need to know will be notified; and on the third morning you will have to report for assembly."

Indeed, on that morning Harold did not come by at 4 a.m. as he usually did, instead I was awakened by the shrill electric bell that jolted almost everyone out of bed at once. I was surprised that I had slept through to this point. There was no dallying. Everyone was rushing to get down to the morning meal. I buttoned up my quilted suit hastily and was almost the first to enter the mess hall. We all carried our own spoon (a prized possession) that was always kept in one of our pockets. We never placed it anywhere else. We always carried it with us; and it never needed washing. After using it, we licked it clean before slipping it back into the pocket. If you had no spoon, you would be forced to eat with your fingers. We were advised at the very beginning that the camp would not issue a new spoon to anyone if the original were lost. So we guarded them like fine jewelry.

On entering the mess hall, I grabbed a bowl and got into line quickly. There were always some guys that tried to bully themselves into the front of the line. If Russian guards saw it, they would force the bully to the very back of the line and, if need be, with the threat of a drawn gun. The German guards would stand by and do nothing. They seemed to like some controversy flaring up now and then, for jumping the line would never be accepted by the other prisoners without hassling the bully back to his previous spot. That morning, I was one of the first to be served. It was the smart thing to do to be first in line. The servers were more generous in dishing out to the first guys than to the last for it was commonplace that at the end there was hardly enough mush left to go around.

I sat down at one of the still empty tables but did not even feel hungry. I felt strangely excited. I knew just how surprised Walter would be to see me report for work, finally. I wondered whether he had been waiting for me every morning at the main door, as he had said he would. I had not seen him for a while; but since I knew Walter so well, I was certain that he would be there. You could always count on him. If he said something, he meant it. There was never any wavering. I thought it strange even at that time that there was someone who would never change his mind, never reconsider. Neither would he have accepted or condoned someone else's point of view if it was different from his, nor even respected it. He was so sure he was right.

I had to force myself to eat, for without food, I knew I would not be able to keep going the ten hours we had to work. The hot mush did feel good as it slid into my stomach, and afterwards I was glad I had made myself eat.

I knew I was too early when I reached the door that led into the assembly yard. It was only 5:15 a.m. I had no idea how cold it would be on these mornings deep in winter. A blast of icy air hit me as I went out the door. It was still pitch dark. No one was in the yard yet. I guessed with this coldness no one would be so foolish as to arrive even a few seconds early. I turned down all the flaps of my fleece lined cap, the one for the forehead, the one for the back of the neck, and the two for the ears that could be tied under the chin. I took a rag out of my pocket, placed it over my mouth and stuffed the excess part of the rag into the cap around the cheeks and the chin. All that was left of my face was the eyes and nose. I kept standing there and began to feel very cold, but I did not want to miss Walter. Finally he came, probably right on the dot. His face beamed.

"This is the day I have been waiting for!" he cried out. "Just stick close to me, Jan. Do as I do, always. You first need to learn the ropes. I'll try to lighten your load as much as I can. You need to get used to this backbreaking grind. Okay, Jan?"

"Okay, Walter, lead the way. I am so happy you have come."

"Sure, I wouldn't do otherwise. You feel okay now?"

"Yeah, I am anxious to do some men's work."

The yard filled up rapidly now. The men never dallied, for they wanted to have the shortest assembly possible, especially in winter. Standing for long periods in this icy cold was nearly suicide. Even the Russian guards (on the outside there were no other but Russian guards with guns slung over their shoulders) seemed to be in a hurry on this bitter cold morning. They would lead us to the work places and were supposed to monitor our activities throughout the day. But the first order of business for them was to call out our numbers (as far as the prison administration was concerned, we had no names), and we were expected to respond. It went fast that morning. It was not always like that as I would experience later. When there was no response to a number, confusion would reign; and we could not leave until it was cleared up why a number was absent. Depending on how many numbers were missing, assembly could take an hour or more. But this morning we were quickly led out the gate as we formed the customary rows of four with sixty men per work group. A couple of guards headed the column, others marched alongside us. We never knew where we had to go on a particular day. They sent us off to where a labor force was critically needed, mostly for work that Russian workers did not want to do or were in short supply for.

"I think we'll hit the same construction site as yesterday in the center of town. That building is making progress. The first two floors are finished in the rough. Sometimes during the day, we can sneak down to the lower floors and get a little rest and warmth. If we can find some scraps of wood, we might even be able to light a fire, on the sly, you know. That's how it goes in the coldest part of winter. Our guards, you will find, keep mostly out of sight. They'll hide a good part of the day in the parts of the building that are enclosed. Oh, by the way, lunch will be brought in at midday. Just soup and bread."

Walter had said this quickly and under his breath. I could hardly catch everything because of the snugly tied flaps covering my ears.

"Did you get that, Jan?" I nodded so as not to unsettle him.

"Just stick close to me. That's the best advice I can give you, kiddo. Just copy me, at least for the first few days, until you've learned the ropes. Always try to do everything as slowly as you can. That way you reserve energy. Find short cuts; take lighter loads, anything that will benefit you. Winter is a good and a bad time--good because the guards don't watch us that closely, bad because it's so damned cold. You must be careful not to get chilblains. Could turn into gangrene if they get too bad. Once that sets in, you'll have had it. Don't forget to stomp your feet as much as you can and keep those toes moving."

All I could say was, "Walter I am so happy to be with you."

"Hey, relax! We'll make a great team."

We had entered the city in no time because our camp was just on the outskirts. It was still dark and there was little street lighting. People, on their way to work, I guessed, kept hurrying past, dark figures bundled up in layers of clothing. You would have never been able to recognize any of them even if you had known them. They never paid any attention to us. I guess they were used to our columns that marched through the city day in and day out. Now and then we passed a horse-drawn cart and once in a while a truck lumbered down the street. We had to make room for it and moved over to the side temporarily. The pavement was uneven and had potholes. Usually we marched along with eyes glued to the ground to avoid stepping into a hole, not that we could have seen these holes. There were no stars that night, but the icy wind kept blowing unabated. It never stopped, not even during the night. There was a dusting of snow on the ground. As I later learned, it never snowed very much in this region except on occasion. But the winds kept blowing from the steppe to the east, winds so strong and icy, they did not allow much vegetation to flourish. Further north there were forests, but this city was just to the south of them and in the path of those unceasing winds. It was strange that this city dwelt on the fringes of a climatic divide. If it had been built a hundred miles north from where it was, its climate would have been more benign. Perhaps the city would have had a different character altogether then, a more friendly and lively one. As I got to see more of this city, I realized how drab it really was; not a single building displayed any architectural beauty. There were obvious signs that the war had been raging around it. A lot of the buildings were bombed out or burned out. Most of the exteriors were pockmarked from the heavy shelling that had gone on around there. Nothing seemed to have inspirational value, not even their churches that were now, of course, in disuse and boarded up. People seemed taciturn and morose as they went about their business. Maybe all of their imagination had come to fruition in that monstrosity we now occupied. If so, it was a sad monument to their spirit. As the day dawned, a blood red sun rose in the east, its rays traveling through layers of smog generated by the heavy industry on the northeastern fringe of town. During the day, it was a pale, washed-out sun in a grayish white, undefined sky.

At the construction site, we had marched at least forty minutes and it was still dark, a half dozen overseers were handing out tools--trowels for the guys who were laying the concrete blocks, buckets for carrying the mortar, and wooden boxes for carrying concrete blocks. All building materials had to go up to the third floor. There were no lifts for them. I knew that Walter would probably be a good brick or concrete block layer. He responded when the overseer called for those prisoners to come forward who could do masonry work.

I tugged at his sleeve in desperation, "Walter I can't do that kind of work. I don't have the foggiest." I whispered to him.

"Sure you can, Jan. Just respond to the guy." I was fearful, but I responded as I was told.

So it happened that Walter and I laid concrete blocks all day long. He was a damned good teacher, and I was quite satisfied with my work at the end of the day. Though not light, it was still the easiest kind of work on the construction site. You would never want to carry mortar or concrete blocks. That would surely do you in over time.

"I'll promise you, you'll learn fast, Jan. It's not hard. I'll show you, kid. You must learn to bluff, otherwise you won't make it," he whispered to me before we started the job.

We both had our trowels and headed up the rough, unfinished concrete stairs. As I looked around, I realized that most of the masons were Russians. We prisoners were all dressed in the same baggy suits but they were not. You could easily tell us apart.

Walter, as soon as we emerged onto the vast third floor with its partially completed walls, hurried over to an area he thought would be good for us to work on. I knew he had something in mind by picking that particular spot. I later realized it was close to the back stairs that led down to the completed second floor. Later we would spend some time in one of the rooms below us, trying to get warm. We even had a little fire going for a short time until we were chased out by Russian guards. They bellowed at us, "You dirty prison bastards. Get back to work." They threatened to hit us with the butts of their guns. But I realized that it was all rather staged, that they sounded fiercer than they meant to be. Walter confirmed my observation later when I got a chance to ask him while we were back at the mortaring job.

"Yeah, Jan, you are a keen observer. They feel they need to do their duty once in awhile and, besides, they wanted our fire. In general, the little guys have some compassion for us. It's the higher ups that try to do us in like that damned doctor."

Again, I felt awful for Anna, but good too that I had, for the first time, made a keen and correct observation, and it had been confirmed by Walter. I really felt good about that and even thought at the time that I might survive prison after all.

On the march home, it was already dark. Walter suddenly said, "Listen, Jan, we need to get a little extra food. I keep losing weight and that worries me. We must take advantage of that construction site as long as we can. There are a lot of materials people would be happy to get. I'll tell you what I'm thinking. What I have in mind is not without risk, but it would earn us some money that would buy us extra food. Now I am thinking your learning Russian was not such a bad idea after all. There are always guys hanging out around the construction site, trying to look for opportunities to get a sack of cement or a few concrete blocks. What we could do is this: I could organize a few materials in a corner of the building downstairs. Then I'll point out certain guys to you that I know are the scavengers as I call them. Your job will be to approach one of them in Russian and to ask him whether he needed something. He'll nod. Tell him what he can get and tell him the price. Of course none of this is without danger, but believe me it's done all the time. Where else can people get materials? You can't buy anything. So, people resort to stealing, and sometimes they go right to the source by buying from the workers. I don't want to force you into it, Jan. Think about it and tell me whether you will come in on it. We'll share the proceeds, of course."

I thought about his plan for a while and then said, "I'll give it a try, Walter."

"Let's do a trial run tomorrow then, just on a small scale. I'll organize a bag of cement in a hidden corner of the building at street level. You'll approach the guy I'll point out to you. Offer it to him for ten rubles. Anyone would go for that. You feel all right with that, Jan?"

"Yeah, I think so. I'll do my best."

Sometime during the afternoon the next day, when we knew the guards were warming themselves again at our fire, Walter said the bag was sitting inside the doorway by the sidewalk below us. I was surprised that Walter was able to hide anything that quickly. I had not even noticed that he had been absent. We were standing by the wall we had begun to mortar up that day. It was chest high.

He said, "Look at that guy down there with the large overcoat. He has been waiting there for quite awhile. I know he wants to buy something and, besides, his coat gives me an indication that he is serious. Saw him yesterday as well as the day before. He can hide a lot in that coat. Go down and say some friendly words to him. If he is receptive, try to make a little conversation with him. Feel him out as to why he is waiting. Talk about the expensive building materials. You'll know right away that he wants something if he is very friendly and willing to talk to you. There is a whole market culture out there. Friendliness and eagerness on the part of the guy you approach will be a sign that he is genuine. Then tell him what you have and what it costs. If he wants it, he will step closer to you and hand you the money unobtrusively. Never try to run with the money, always tell him where the goods are. If you try to cheat him, he'll make a hell of a fuss and you'll be in trouble. You don't want to try that, Jan. Always deliver. If he is a good contact, he'll be back tomorrow."

"Yeah, I think I want to do it, Walter. I want to see how persuasive I can be. I like to test the Russian I know."

"OK, we'll watch the guy a while longer."

After half an hour, Walter said it would be fine to go now. He had previously shown me where the cement bag was. I was a bit nervous. But as I got down into the street and walked up to the guy still standing on the sidewalk, he turned to face me right away. No ordinary person in the street would have done that. They would not have given a hoot even if I had yelled at them. I realized right away that it was a sign and I could talk to him. I said but a few words to him and he nodded. Then I mentioned cement. He immediately asked, "How much?" His OK came much faster than I had expected. Either Walter had set a good price or the guy was desperate. I had no idea how much a bag of cement cost in Germany, let alone in Russia. Before I knew it, the guy had made some unexpected move towards me and past me. Just as he walked past me very closely I felt something being stuffed into the large hip pocket of my suit. I was stunned. He continued walking beyond me a short distance, then turned around as if he had changed his mind and came back towards me slowly. "Where is it?" he said even before he reached me with his head pointed straight ahead. He never looked at me. His mouth hardly moved. "Keep going. Third open doorway. Just inside." I had barely said that and he was past me. I figured the rest was his business. I went a short distance along the sidewalk then turned around. I saw the guy coming out of the doorway with one arm across his chest as if trying to keep the coat shut against the wind. Before I could reach him, he went across the street and disappeared down a narrow alley. I was stunned how well it had gone, but my knees shook more than I had ever experienced. The whole encounter had not taken but a couple of minutes. I ran up the stairs to Walter, and he started laughing, maybe out of joy for the money or because he had been watching the game being played out in the street. In the end I thought he was overjoyed that things had gone so well. Then I handed him the money.

"You are a natural, Jan," he said, and patted me on the back.

Next day, Walter went across the street and joined a bread line. Even though ordinary Russians standing in line got quite angry with him (a prisoner was not supposed to take away their bread), he did not budge. They told him fiercely, "Leave! You don't belong here. We'll have you arrested." But Walter paid no attention, kept hanging on to his place, finally got to the bakery window, and got his goods. Tenacity was another one of his traits.

Walter and I were to repeat this sort of business quite a few more times. We became a good team, and I became very good at talking to and dealing with ordinary Russians.

That evening when I was still elated about the transaction I had so successfully completed for the first time, I met with Anna. But I did not tell her what had transpired during the day. She loved my good spirits; and we had the most animated conversation ever and, sadly, one of the last. I also felt daring that night. I asked her point blank whether she could improve the camp situation as far as hygiene was concerned like running water next to the sleeping quarters and improved latrines.

"And what about some raw vegetables and a little meat at times. The prisoners can't make it very long on that diet they are getting."

She was taken aback by my requests. I could see it in her eyes that had narrowed a little. And for once I thought I detected some ambivalence in her towards me. Apparently, she did not know what to make of my requests. I guess no one in the prison had ever dared to approach her that way. But I felt I was coming into my own, was possibly becoming a man. The fact that I had turned eighteen a few weeks ago and today's success made me dare her.

I could see successive emotions cross over Anna's face. How was she to deal with me in the face of those direct requests? I again remembered vividly what Walter had said about her, and I expected suddenly, it came like a flash to me, to see her other side. But momentarily she had composed herself and answered coolly but not unfriendly or as if offended.

"Janos, you are asking too much of me. My powers are limited. I have to strictly conform to the duties, responsibilities, and defined liberties of my position. I cannot possibly accomplish all that you have asked for without compromising my position."

She paused a moment and there was complete silence between us. I still expected her to reprimand me.

But then she said, "Janos, the answer really lies with you. You will be able to accomplish all these changes better than I ever could. Join the Antifascist Association. They call the organization also ANTIFA. You are someone they would be happy to train. You speak Russian now fluently and you are very young and not set in your ways. I can put you in contact with the administration. If you go through the training and show yourself to be a good prospect, you will be able to push through improvements that will benefit your comrades greatly. I know you are a brilliant learner. They would be ecstatic to have you. You are also persuasive. They would have you lead the indoctrination sessions in the camp. In turn, the benefits would be many. Think about it, Janos. I know you want to help your comrades survive."

I thanked Anna for her suggestion and said that I would consider it and soon left her after that. I was intent to give this possibility a lot of thought.

At the time, I thought there is nothing in the world I would like to do more than to help my fellow prisoners with any method at my disposal. And, I do not want to conceal the fact that there was not a little curiosity in me to experience their methods of affecting or even changing my beliefs. However, as it turned out, I would not act on Anna's suggestions until after the dreadful events of the next two months.

18

Of Work, Death, and Life

The night before our next work assignment, I lay in my bed thinking intensely of my family and Effie. What a difficult day my eighteenth birthday a few weeks ago must have been for them, I thought. They would not know that I was alive, and I still had no idea whether they were alive or dead. We had not been allowed to write to our families, and no mail had come into the camp from the outside. I felt such pain in my heart and anxiety pangs that night that I thought I would surely expire before morning came. I cannot remember how and when I finally fell asleep.

The next morning our work changed drastically. We were loaded onto trucks and driven north for hours until we hit the forest. We were to log selected trees that had been pre-marked. We were issued huge handsaws that had to be worked by two men, axes for removal of the smaller branches, and a tool like a pickax for dragging the logs onto the logging road. A period was now to begin during which our work crew performed some of the hardest work during our imprisonment. We were all very exhausted at the end of the day so that we could not remain seated in the back of the truck as it carried us for hours back to the camp. We were all lying asleep, partially on top of each other. We did not wake up until the guard back at the camp shouted us awake. I had never in my life seen a more bedraggled bunch than our work team as it headed for the deserted mess hall. Everyone had already eaten. We were hours late. They served us specially and extra food as long as we were on the forest job.

Walter had saved me during the day by taking on some of my work. I was not able to sustain the strain of that kind of labor. Every time the guards stood around the fire they had built for themselves, we sat down but not for long since the cold of the snow quickly penetrated our clothes at our seats. Walter saw to it that I was doing the easiest work, removing small branches from the logs. He was sawing. The hardest work was not even sawing the trees but dragging the logs out of the forest onto the logging road. Depending on the size of the tree, as many as twenty men had to drag those logs little by little with their pick irons, sweat forming on their brows despite the cold. I knew they would not last long, not with the abominably unbalanced meals we received.

We worked at the logging camp for weeks. One day, pretty much at the beginning of our work assignment, some of our men were dragging an especially large log down a steep embankment. I do not quite know how it happened, but the log suddenly started rolling. The men below it were able to jump or run out of its path, except one. That monster log rolled right over him and crushed him to death. I could not go to look at his corpse. Walter told me his rib cage had been crushed as well as his skull. He probably died instantly. The guards rolled him into a piece of canvas and had him ride with us on the truck bed for the last time. When I contemplated the accident, I was overcome by dark thoughts. The realization of the tenuousness of life hit me once more with full force; and, of course, I had no idea that it was just the beginning of my encounters with death. I could not get the image of the silken thread out of my head, that thin, delicate silken thread through which we were attached to life. How quickly it could snap!

On the Sunday night after the accident, I was to meet with Mei Chi for one of the last two officially sanctioned sessions we were allowed to have. Our last meetings had been rescheduled for Sunday nights since I now came home too late for meetings on weekday evenings. She had been teaching me during the last two get togethers simple precepts and practices of Buddhism. I had already learned breathing techniques from her. That night we were to start what she had called a meditation practice. I was so exhausted physically and emotionally from the previous week's work that I felt I needed to take to bed instead of working with Mei Chi. But the evening meal revived me a little, and I made my way to Mei Chi's room after all. As I entered I found myself in a world so different from the horribly strenuous and tragic realities of the past days that I thought I had stepped into a dream world.

Her barren room was transformed by the soft, muted shine of three candles. At first, Mei Chi was not visible to me. I thought she had not yet entered and possibly wanted me to get used to the new atmosphere. But as my eyes adjusted to the soft semi-darkness, I was able to make out the pale skin of her face floating like a lily very still in a pool of blackness. I soon saw that this blackness surrounding her were her hair and the black suit she wore. She sat on the floor with her legs drawn up and tucked under her body behind the tiny table that held the candles. I stood without moving for a while as she sat silently with her eyes closed. I dared not speak; I dared not disturb her. I felt as if I had entered a holy space that my voice would desecrate if I spoke. So I stood still until she opened her dark shimmering eyes in the light of the candles, moved her body effortlessly into a standing position, and almost floated towards me. The creation of this almost otherworldly atmosphere was so perfect, so all-embracing that my senses, my emotions, and my body came to rest in it effortlessly. It made the pain of my day activities vanish.

"Janos," she whispered almost inaudibly, "remove your shoes and your heavy clothing and sit down as I sat when you entered." She knelt down in front of me and undid my shoes. I lifted each foot automatically so that she could pull off my boots. I do not know why I let her do this. She undid the fasteners of my quilted suit and I helped her automatically as she tried to remove it. I did not dare speak for fear of breaking this wonderful spell of peace that had settled upon me. I was in an atmosphere at once holy and utterly soothing, yet sensual at the same time. I became aware of the sweet incense wafting towards me that must have added an air of sensuality to this purely peaceful ambiance.

Mei Chi took my hands in hers, something she had never done before. I had felt her hands so intensely on my body before, but she had never until now given me the chance of holding them. They felt incredibly small yet strong in my hands that must have been twice as large as hers. I was very aware of the hard calluses I had acquired in the past weeks of hard labor. Mei Chi held my hands quite steadily and in that manner guided me to the little table, where she freed her hands and indicated for me to be seated. Nothing was said and I was most willing to follow her into her ritual.

Mei Chi seated herself opposite me with the candles between us. She began to speak softly, "Keep your eyes on the candle light. Choose one to be your flame. Concentrate on it until all thoughts have left your mind. The flame will become fixed in your mind's eye after some time. Close your eyes when you feel that it is happening; observe the flame becoming alive within you and try to bring it to your forehead, just between and above your eyes so it will become your third eye. You may not be successful at first, but try again. Eventually you will succeed, and you will feel yourself engulfed in a peace that defies description. Let's do this together now."

I followed Mei Chi into her world of peace and thought-suspending freedom; and even that first evening I thought I had entered a world of bliss. Besides becoming keenly aware of that glistening flame in my mind's eye, I also suddenly held the image of two shiny strands of silk that breached a dark chasm. Those thin strands crossed over in the middle above the abyss, and one lay on top of the other lightly touching. I could not see what the silk strands were connected to on either side.

After some time, I do not know how much time had elapsed for it seemed an eternity, Mei Chi pulled me out of my meditative state by gently speaking to me. I opened my eyes on hearing her soft words; and I felt strangely, yet wonderfully refreshed. She came over to me and held my hands once more. This time I was more conscious of her warmth than before and thought I felt her pulsating life within them.

"This is all for tonight, Janos", she said very softly. "Next time, we will practice mantra meditation. All of these practices will enable you to replenish your strength just when you think it has ebbed out of your being. But it will take lots of practice to perfect these arts of emptying your mind so that it can be filled with the infinite life force."

All the while Mei Chi spoke, her face held just a touch of a smile. It was then for the first time that my heart went fully out to her, for the interest she had taken in me, for the services she continued to perform, for the teaching that had gone on for months now, teaching in a direct and an unspoken way. Though my body felt still and as if it had been newly formed, my heart erupted in joy. I could not help placing my hands on her shoulders as she stood before me, this small dark figure with her translucent face. My hands touched the silk covering her shoulders—I remember thinking to myself: Silk in this abominable prison camp? Nothing could be more strange and absurd—and I pulled her ever so gently towards me until my lips touched the tiny bridge between and just above her eyes. It was a gesture so gentle and so benign in my mind that I suddenly realized I had never known myself to be that way. At that moment I felt her arms enclosing my body and we remained like this for the longest moment in my life. I could feel her heart beating and knew that those silken strands I had seen in my mind's eye before had crossed for real.

It was Mei Chi who pulled back gently from her embrace of me. "Janos," she whispered barely audibly, "you must go now. The time is up. We must not go longer. I will see you next week." And she added as an afterthought, "I have never been happier in my life than tonight."

She had placed the mundane announcement and the most personal reflection so closely together, so inextricably tied up with one another, that I at first did not grasp the meaning of the latter part. But when I did, all I could say, "Oh, Mei Chi! How wonderful!"

As I looked at her for a sign that would confirm what I had heard, she had already assumed a formal position with her hands pressed together in front of her chest and her head slightly bowed towards me. I felt I could do nothing but leave and contemplate the happening later. I felt I needed to be respectful of her pulling back and observe her wishes. And then to my surprise, as if she had read my thoughts and my confusion, she said quite serenely, "Yes, Janos, our lives have touched tonight."

"Oh, yes! That's what I have felt, too." I said it very simply but with emotion in my voice.

Then I turned and left her room. It was not until I closed the door behind me that a multitude of images barraged my mind, making my head spin. I had to lean against the wall for a few seconds before heading down the corridor and to the stairs that led back to the prisoners' sleeping quarters.

Work in the forest continued unabated and there was no change in sight. Anna had reduced my sessions with her from three times a week to once a week. She had told me so the last time I saw her before I was sent to the forest. She explained that we could only see each other on Sunday afternoons since I would come back late from work during the week. Besides, she had indicated that my condition had improved to a point were frequent visitations were no longer necessary. She also said that it was good for her and for me that way. There were never any full explanations from Anna. I had to guess what might have transpired. Did she truly mean what she said or was something entirely different behind it? Perhaps someone in the administration had made a remark to her and made her more cautious. Perhaps she suspected being watched. If I could have only found out. But as it was I had to try to live with these gnawing thoughts. Everything in this system was always so concealed: the plans for our future, the secrecy connected with the work places, the fact that we were not allowed to write, Anna's never opening up to me although we had become quite close on some level. My thoughts would have driven me crazy if I had not been able to practice what Mei Chi had taught me. Her practices worked wonders for me--the meditation and the breathing exercises as I sat up in bed late at night as everyone else lay sound asleep. I could even conjure up the candle's flame in my mind and make it move. Mei Chi's practices always eased me into a deep, refreshing sleep despite the hardships of the day. Although some of the dreams that centered on Mei Chi kept reoccurring, strange dreams of her always eluded me. I could not explain to myself why they persisted, even then when we had both realized that our threads had crossed.

One late Sunday afternoon at dusk as I sat downstairs in the great hall daydreaming, I suddenly jumped up and ran upstairs to my bed not even knowing what I was looking for. But I found it right away, a note that had been tucked just under one side of my pillow. It was barely visible. It was from Mei Chi and said, "Do not come tonight. All prisoners must attend the special assembly this evening. Go there. Your friend, Mei Chi." I was supposed to see Mei Chi that evening but not Anna anymore. My sessions with her had come to an end the week before. I ran back down the stairs to the mess hall and was confused why I had gone to my bed. There was no way I could have known that the message was there, neither could I remember why I had gone up. I thought there was something else I wanted to get but simply could not now remember.

Shortly after the beginning of our meal, when all prisoners were present and the serving was done, it was announced that there would be an assembly one hour after the meal that everyone must attend except the sick. I heard a hushed grumble run through the assembled crowd of exhausted men. They must have been cursing the request just as I had not been able to refrain from cursing when I found the note. To them it still was news. I had not shared my knowledge with anyone. Full assemblies like that were very, very rare. Something important must have happened, I thought. I guessed there was a lot of conjecturing going on as the men finished up eating. No one wanted to return in one hour, for all the men could think of was dragging themselves to their beds. But there was no choice.

As we returned to the hall, the entire prison administration was assembled and seated at one end. The officials (six of them and all men) who pulled the strings behind the scenes, but were normally invisible, had suddenly emerged in the flesh and in full uniform. I do not think many of the current prisoners had ever had contact with them or even seen them. The entire infirmary staff was lined up, including Anna and Mei Chi. Off to the side, the prison guards were seated. I noticed Anna sitting with a severe face and very stiffly upright on her chair with Mei Chi in a more relaxed position next to her. There was a hushed silence in the room. Everyone seemed to expect a momentous occasion with all the brass lined up before us. Then one of the men got up and spoke in Russian that was immediately translated.

"A grievous complaint has been lodged with our administration concerning the food supply. Although we are doing the best we can for you, we want to air and discuss this complaint here openly tonight. We think it to be ungrateful of you for bringing it up, especially in view of the fact that our own people are not faring better than you. But we want to show you our willingness and patience to hear your concerns, and I will have Dr. Petrovna take over from here."

Anna stood up and stepped forward. She stood very erect in her white doctor's coat. She appeared taller than she had seemed to me and more formidable. Her face was severe and seemingly permanently set that way. No one could have guessed that it could look very different, even loving.

"I want to discuss the complaint about the food with you, specifically the fish we started serving last night. I want Bernhard Seidler to stand up and formally lodge his complaint once more so that you can all hear it. I will then make an evaluation of the complaint for you. I will try to be fair, but whatever I decide will be implemented." She said this with much firmness and authority in her voice. She is formidable I thought to myself. Then she continued, "Bernhard Seidler, please stand up and repeat the complaint."

I saw Seidler rise from his seat. I realized who he was, a prisoner who had recently joined us. He was from Berlin. You could hear it right away from the dialect he spoke. He had the most booming voice I had ever heard. Since his arrival it always seemed to float just above the din of the eating crowd. It was very annoying. If it had been possible, his voice could have been heard throughout this bottom floor of the building if the other parts had not been walled off.

Seidler began, "I want to put forward a complaint about the fish we have been served the past couple of nights. Though I appreciate the change in food and the addition of protein, I must say that we cannot eat them the way they are cooked. We would never eat them that way at home with all the bones and guts in them. We can't stomach it. And besides, we are here, I believe, to help you rebuild your country that we have destroyed. I will gladly do that, but I can't eat those fish, not the way they are. If I could eat them, they would give me more strength, and I would be able to help you more with the rebuilding of your country and…"

Here he was rudely interrupted by a voice that shouted out of the crowd with overtones of rage. I realized right away that it was Walter's.

"You idiot! Shut up! Are you crazy talking about guilt. Who is guilty here? No one. We did our job as we were called on to do. You traitor of the fatherland! You damned, crazy Berlin dog, you!"

I looked at Walter who was not seated very far from me. I could see thick blue veins on his pale forehead. He was madly angry and ready to jump at Bernhard's throat if he had been able to get to him. I looked from him to Anna and saw her make a sign with her hand towards the guards. Three jumped up simultaneously and dashed over towards Walter. In no time, they had grabbed him, and as they hustled him out of the hall he kept on shouting, "Traitor of the fatherland. Damned you Berlin bastard." On and on he went until his voice was just a faint reverberation as he was half pushed, half dragged out into the yard. I felt very bad for Walter. I had never seen him so violently angry. All right, I thought to myself, he was a bit preachy and inflexible at times, but he had the best heart and a lot of compassion. But this incident should have given me a warning.

Meanwhile Anna had collected herself.

"Bernhard, I have taken your complaint to heart," she said rather coldly so that I realized her hard stance immediately. "I have tested the fish myself. They are nutritionally sound and of high food value. I will demonstrate to you that anyone can eat them just as we have been serving them to you. It's just that you prisoners want to be obstinate. You should be glad that we provide variety in your diet."

With that she motioned to one of her nurses who held a plate in her lap. The girl came forward and held the plate toward Anna. Anna picked up the small fish by its tail and started eating it until it was gone.

"I have been the guinea pig right from the start, and I have approved the fish to be released for consumption. I suggest that you eat them if you want to survive, Bernhard. If you don't we must assume you have different motives." With that she had obviously finished her presentation.

The six higher ups started clapping approvingly towards Anna for her handling of the situation. The one who had spoken before stoop up and said, "Assembly dismissed. You have heard the doctor. I can only but second her advice." With that he turned to his comrades and they began to talk among themselves oblivious to us. The guards got up and made us leave. I thought of Anna's performance. How tough she could be, almost to a point of ridiculing our men. Who knows, her fish might have been prepared differently. Who would know the difference? You could not tell from the distance. As I left the hall, I thought, Oh, Anna, you beloved savior and you abominably cold-hearted authoritarian. They had thrown Walter into a solitary holding cell for obstinate prisoners on reduced rations of bread and water. He remained there for two days.

19

Tragedies

It was now February. More than a year had passed since I became separated from my family. For some reason, the events of that last reunion at Christmas came back to me in full clarity and with the full force of its emotional content. I suddenly had dreams again of my parents and Ida. They also occupied my daydreams when work and prison life allowed me to have them, as on those hours-long morning and evening rides to and from the forest. My family and also Effie had for months receded into the background of my conscious life and my dreams. Their energy had become overshadowed by people and recent events that had entered my life with overpowering reality. Now, just a short time after the first anniversary of our parting, my memories began to overwhelm me. Later on I thought it might have been something else, some premonition, that pulled me back to certain scenes of that last family Christmas day: our huddling together around the stove, our closeness and love, Mother's desperate praying, and Father's reminding me of my manly and moral duties.

It was only a few days after I had started thinking again intensely about my family when I was called to the infirmary as I returned from a day's labor in the forest. The orderly who opened the door did not say a word but ushered me in and gestured to follow him. He led me to Anna's room. As I entered, she sat at her small desk. She smiled at me, sort of a sad and tired smile, and nodded. Picking up a small piece of paper off her desk, she came towards me.

When she stopped right in front of me, she looked steadily into my eyes as she spoke.

"Janos, you have received news from home through the Red Cross."

With that she passed the piece of paper to me. It was not just a piece of paper; it was an open card. It must be a very grave situation that allowed this card to penetrate deep into Russia and land in the hands of one of the most insignificant prisoners of war. What could have happened, I thought? As soon as this question formed in my mind, I tried to look at its sender, at the handwriting, but everything was just a blur to me. I averted my eyes, looked over to the side, and then forced myself to look again. It was almost as if something inside me refused to consciously see what was written. I cannot keep going like this; I must face whatever it is, it shot through my mind.

The first thing I clearly saw then was the name Ida Jablonsky. It's from Sis! Then it must concern Father, Mother or even Effie. These thoughts seemed to confirm some deeply felt anxiety that began to surface as soon as Anna had mentioned the Red Cross. All I needed to do now was turn the card over, and I would know what had happened. But there was such reluctance in me that I just stood there staring at Ida's name.

It was Anna's voice that pulled me out of this seeming paralysis.

"Janos, you must read the card and face the news," she said with a softness in her voice that I had not thought was possible, not after the public performance I had witnessed.

Looking at her then, I recognized my old compassionate benefactor with an expression full of concern and empathy on her face. I did turn the card over but only saw certain words spring out at me from that small tightly hand-written white space:

Father ... re-injured his leg ... recurring gangrene ... three more operations ... unable to walk ... heart gave out ... December 22 ... Mother despondent ... treated for depression ... retreats from reality ... hope you are alive ... need you desperately ... Effie great help ... very close ...

It seemed like the only way I could read this card was in telegraphic style. I tried to be easy on myself by acknowledging that that was all I needed to know. I think I must have stood there as if I had been struck by lightning. I was transfixed and without emotions. It was then, seeing my pitiable state, that Anna embraced me for the first and only time. We stood there together, I do not know how long. It seemed an eternity. At first I did not even realize what had happened. But then I woke up to the arms that enfolded me. It was Anna holding me like one who needed to be comforted desperately. Then I suddenly felt my sorrow. It swept over me like a deluge and I started sobbing violently in her arms. She kept on holding me tight and I felt this comforting pressure even through this thick wall of my grief. Anna never spoke a word, and it was good like that. Words would have been like swords cutting me to pieces.

Her patience seemed great. She kept on holding me, and it was I who stirred and gave the sign to be released. She respectfully complied and stepped back. I had sobbed and had wept profusely in her arms. I don't think she quite grasped what she had done for me in those moments. It was not so much that my father was no more, that he had been taken away from me before I could commune with him one last time, it was the suffering he had had to undergo before he left that gave me the sharpest pain right through my heart. If I could only have been given the news that he passed away peacefully. I could, I think, have embraced his death with some sort of calm resignation. But he had suffered already so much when I had left him over a year ago. Oh, God, my heart cried out, You are trying me hard.

I knew I had to leave Anna. She had done all she could for me. And now I even wanted to be alone with my grief. She realized I was breaking away, but before I could turn, she grabbed my shoulders, pulled me close to her, and kissed me on both cheeks. As she pulled her head back, she squeezed my shoulders so tight that it hurt. I knew what she meant.

"Anna, thank you for your concern and your friendship, for all the good you have done me. I love you very much." And before I could shed any more tears for my dead father, for her, or for me, I hurried to the door and left. Had I had any knowledge then that this was the last time I would ever see Anna, I don't know what I would have done. A day or two later she arranged for a blank card to be placed on my bed and a note that said she would try to work with the Red Cross to get this card delivered to my family. She instructed me that I must confine myself to thirty words and to leave the card at the infirmary.

Day and night I mourned for my father. During the day I threw myself into the labor in the forest with such vengeance that I sometimes feared I would do myself harm. Walter, as always, was a supportive friend. He was very respectful of my grieving, asked few questions, but helped me with my work as much as he could, always taking on something I should have done. At night I was visited by the most vivid dreams surrounding my father and me, beautiful dreams actually of wandering with him through lovely valleys and climbing tall mountains. Their heights allowed us to overlook vast expanses of the most verdant countryside. But the most wonderful aspect in those dreams was that my father was whole again. He seemed older and yet the same age as mine and handsome as I had known him as a child. There was a timeless quality about him that I had never recognized when he was alive. All throughout the dreams I had the feeling as if he and I were really one, one and the same being. Although on awakening I pondered this strange unreal quality of being one with him; yet in the dream it seemed the most natural experience I could have. These dreams I had of father were, in a way, so realistic, so powerful, and so uplifting that their influence carried over into my life after a while, so that I even began to feel strangely elated over time. It was incredible to me how he in death reached out to me beyond time and space to heal my wounds of grief.

It was shortly after the news of my father's death that I had one more formal session with Mei Chi. As I went to her I thought that I would not be able to concentrate on her teaching and that I would have to tell her so no matter how much it would disappoint her. She, who had been so close to me since our last encounter, now suddenly appeared distant. But all that changed as soon as I saw her. As I entered her room, she stood right inside the door with the delicate sheen of candlelight behind her forming a pale aura around her body. I looked into her ivory face and saw tears streaming down her cheeks.

"Janos, I fear so much for your well-being after this heart rending news. I cannot begin to tell you how much I feel your grief. It is my grief all over again," she said with a faint, trembling voice that seemed on the verge of being extinguished with every word it brought forth. She then stepped forward very close to me and laid her arms around my neck. (I knew she must have stood on her toes to reach up that far.) It was such a wonderful warm gesture coming from one so reserved and formal that I could do no other than fold my arms around her body, her small, fragile body. We stood there for a long, long time it seemed, in a tight embrace, face leaning against face and heart against heart. It was then that I felt my heart going out to her again, felt it swell so large until it engulfed the whole of her and me in one all-embracing bubble. In that moment I could not think of my suffering, only of hers that seemed in magnitude so much larger than mine.

She was the first to loosen her arms, but I did not want to let her go, not yet.

I kept holding her tight as for dear life. I felt her head bending back and as I looked into her lovely face, I kissed her again in that spot between and just above her eyes. I kissed her tears as if trying to obliterate them, and at last I kissed her mouth, her small delicate lips. She did not advance towards me neither did she withdraw. She held very still and her hands rested on my shoulders.

"Mei Chi," I finally whispered in her ear after relinquishing her lips, "I know how much you have suffered. My fate is nothing against yours. But I love you very much, Mei Chi. Now that I have found you, I never want to lose you. I want to love you, always. We must never lose track of one another. Promise me that. I know under these circumstances it will be difficult. But if we are both dedicated to each other, it should be possible."

"Janos, you are so young, so loving, and so idealistic. And though I love you, too, and have for a long time, almost since I first saw you, I can never promise you anything, for I don't know whether I will be able to follow you. Our fates are on such different courses."

"What do you mean, Mei Chi, by 'they are on such different courses?' How do you know? If we want them to be on the same course, we should make it possible."

Then she said suddenly with much clarity but also with some reticence in her voice, "Yes, I wish that, too," but no more. In that fleeting moment's hesitation, it seemed to me that it was a strange, reluctant answer, perhaps even evasive, but then it became swept up and overthrown in that wonderful feeling of my heart. From then on my actions seemed to take on their own direction. I lifted Mei Chi up into my arms and carried her to the small mat on the floor that she slept on. She never resisted, not for one moment. As I crossed the room with her, she flung her arms around my neck and pressed her delicate face against mine.

As I laid her down and myself next to her, I suddenly said to her (to this day I don't know where this sudden knowledge and recognition of my state came from), "I need to be very close to you, but I don't think that I will be able to fulfill all your dreams or mine. Please accept me the way I am."

We were now lying very close, body against body. I guess I had intuitively known that something was different with me, for I did not have the same sweet sensations in my loins I had when I was with Effie, even though my feelings were more complete, more all-embracing for Mei Chi than they had been for Effie.

Pressing a finger across my lips as if to seal them, she whispered, "Janos, please, don't speak. Let everything just happen as it will. Anything and everything that happens between us will be wonderful. I will embrace and accept all as it reveals itself."

With that she unbuttoned my shirt and loosened the tie string of my trousers. Her right hand reached up getting a tiny bottle from a shelf above us. She poured a few drops on my chest. As the fine scent of pure jasmine essence engulfed my senses, her hands, her beloved hands, stroked my chest gently and moved ever so slowly lower and lower down below my belly. I, lying on my back, let it happen, this most delicious of touching; and while she continued, she kissed my face and lips gently. What blissful state I experienced then as I had not known before. It felt as if in those moments all weights that life had pressed upon me were lifted. How much I loved her then, and yet the stirring, the passion did not happen. I think she knew, knew right from the beginning, sooner than I had even suspected, that what I needed and wanted would not come to pass. Yet she was tireless in her sensual stroking and fondling, as she had been when she worked on my body during my illness. It was so fine a feeling for me that I wanted it to last into eternity. But then, quite suddenly, the need of touching her arose in me. Taking her hands off me gently, I half rose up and pressed her down tenderly. Opening her smock, I began returning the stroking she had done for me. I pushed one arm under her shoulders and so held her slightly towards me. That beautiful, delicately pale skin of her body, like that of her face, shone up at me like water lilies in moonshine. I had never explored a woman's body before. She allowed me quietly to move from her sweet, pure breasts into her most private recesses. It felt as if I was entering some rare, hidden but exquisite temple for the first time. And as I dwelt there for a while, her eyelids began to flutter lightly and her lips parted at the same time as a fine ripple like that of a spring ran through her body. Momentarily, she opened her eyes and smiled at me, such a lovely, deep smile, as I had never seen on any woman's face. She freed her arms suddenly and threw them around my neck as she snuggled her half naked body against mine, whispering, "Oh, Janos, you most wonderful, wonderful man. You give so much happiness and well-being." Then a shadow floated across her face, and in the next moment she was up, buttoning her smock and running her hands over her hair as if to smooth it.

"I am so sorry," she said softly, "but we must part. Reality came back to me suddenly, and I realized you must go." And, after a slight hesitation, she added simply, "I love you, Janos, very much."

I knew she was right; we should not have extended our time beyond what was allotted.

"This was our last official meeting," she said very quickly. "But let me see what I can arrange. I do want to see you again and if I don't, I think I will die." I had never heard the kind of passion in her voice as I now detected. "I will give you a sign, give you directions, once I have figured something out. Check under your pillow. Everything that has been happening until now was sanctioned by Anna. From now on we will be on our own, and it will not be without danger if we are discovered," she said in haste.

"I will do whatever you can arrange, Mei Chi. I, too, need to be with you again. I will wait no matter how long it takes." I kissed her quickly on her lips and left immediately, hurrying down the corridor towards the exit into the prisoners' quarters.

It was within a week that I found a small slip of paper that had been wrapped around a little key. The paper contained a note instructing me to come through the infirmary back door that was hardly ever used. Mei Chi's room was right next to it. I was further instructed to come only every other Sunday right after the evening meal. The meeting could only be a half hour in length for fear that someone may discover my absence. I understood that in the past my absences could always be officially certified if there were any questions because they were on Anna's orders. I was more than anxious to be with Mei Chi even if it could be only at these lengthy intervals and for a very short period as she suggested. I knew she was very cautious, and I felt I needed to follow her suggestions. When I received her note and key it was still three days until I was to see her.

Meanwhile Walter approached me one day with great concern. I could hear the fear in his voice.

"Jan, I have lost the ability to see at night. I don't know what is happening with my eyes. If I go blind, I'll be doomed. How is your eyesight?"

He was very upset and worried. I told him that I had no symptoms. He begged me to guide him in the early morning darkness and in the evenings when we returned from the forest. It was already dark by then. I promised that I would never leave him alone in the dark. He hugged me, cried, and thanked me. It was the first time I ever saw Walter shed tears. Though I had no clear idea what had happened to him, I thought his seeing problem might be nutrition-related, for there had been no improvement in the monotonous fare we were being fed. I asked him to see the doctor. He was almost violently opposed to the idea and said that he didn't want to see that cold bitch. She would probably make things worse for him. I tried to convince him, told him of her fine, considerate treatment of me during my illness. It took a lot of talking until he agreed that he would go. When I saw him again the next morning, he said he had seen her, that she told him his problem was most likely due to a vitamin deficiency that only fresh vegetables could cure. Since those were not available, she was sorry not to be able to help him. Walter was devastated. He had always prided himself on his good eyesight.

"What will become of me?" he asked with so much discouragement in his voice that I could not help embracing him.

I held him for quite a while until I sensed he had drawn enough comfort from my closeness. I did not know what to say or how to give him hope that his eyes would improve. At that moment I could not see where help could come from. Everything had just about stayed the same as long as we had been in this camp. It was hardly enough to sustain life for a long time. We had observed the disappearance of a number of fellow prisoners over the months. Walter had kept track of them more than I had. He knew every prisoner who had died and those who had just vanished, for with his social disposition he was acquainted, I could swear, with all three-hundred men in our section.

I began to think why it was that I did not suffer the same symptoms as Walter. I then thought of the small food items Anna had given me every time I saw her. She always made me eat immediately whatever she offered. Not once had she let me take anything, not even the tiniest morsel, back to the prisoners' quarters. I realized then that these small gifts of food—a dry piece of cheese, an apple, a carrot, or an onion—had really been life-saving gifts. I also realized that Anna had gone way beyond her role of prison camp doctor in giving me extra food, which was probably part of her own ration. Had the administration known what she was doing, she would have been severely reprimanded or perhaps even convicted for the crime of aiding a prisoner of war. I don't know why I was seeing these things clearly all of a sudden but had not done so before. I was also thinking more and more of the suggestion Anna had made to me about how I could help my fellow prisoners. At times, I was very close to acting on her recommendation, but then, somehow, I let it slip.

As good fortune would have it, Walter and I were transferred to another work site within the next few days. We were elated to leave the forest behind in which we had toiled with our work group for weeks and weeks, day in and day out in virtual isolation. Although in a few moments of rest, as we sat down on a felled tree, I had looked up into those mighty evergreens. They then appeared to me as the silent witnesses of our toiling and suffering. But they were suffering, too, I realized, in that we had invaded their clan and taken out their best, their brightest, and healthiest. Like a living community they had stood together for many decades through summer heat and winter storms, through driving rain, through swirling snow, and howling winds. None of nature's undulating passions and violence could mar them; they kept on standing, erect and proud facing all of nature's assaults. Seldom did one of them grow too old or too weak, and succumbed. It was man they could not stand up to who was decimating them. I don't know why those thoughts crossed my mind as I contemplated the forest in those precious few moments of rest. I have always had an affinity for nature, but I think it was my association with Mei Chi that had deepened it.

An icy cold had settled once more over the land close to the official beginning of spring. Even that mighty river below us was frozen over. We marched to work in every scrap of clothing, worn in layers upon layers, that we possessed. The new work site was welcome. It was a new construction site. I assumed the previous one we had left several months ago had been finished by now. Now we were building the walls on the second floor, a huge open expanse, whose interior walls would be added later. Our Russian guards made bonfires on the rough concrete floor, just to stave off the freezing air. They tried desperately to keep the mortar from freezing. They even allowed us masons to run around the perimeter of the building every half hour to keep us from getting frozen to death. Even while placing the mortar and laying the concrete blocks, we were in constant motion as if we were performing some strange ritual as we worked. Walter and I again collaborated in selling off some stolen materials as before. We had become very adept and sneaky in completing the deals. And it was always Walter who would procure some food items with the earned money, anything he could get, even if they were just a few frost-bitten onions.

We had been at the construction site for several weeks and I had seen Mei Chi secretly several times. I never thought that anyone had seen me enter or leave the infirmary. I always took the greatest precaution. Our encounters were very brief but full of the sweetest experiences. We were so close to each other that it sometimes felt as if our souls had merged. Even under these worst of circumstances, there was a wonderful peace and tranquility between us, no doubt due to Mei Chi's orchestrating our meetings. I don't know how she managed, but she always added this special sensual quality. We were never able to consummate our love in a purely physical sense even though Mei Chi never tired of trying to achieve a change in me with her delicate manipulations. But after a while she began to fan my hope verbally by trying to convince me that my condition, especially because of my youth, was just temporary. I did all I could to make Mei Chi happy. For some reason, I felt always more concerned about her than about me. I loved her with all my heart. I thought my feelings for her derived from such depth within me that I could not ever see them waning. Sometimes we would just lie together talking about freedom and a future together. We could foresee great hardships still ahead that, in the end, we thought we could overcome. Mei Chi was most reticent at first to engage in any such discussions, but my passionate drive towards creating a vision of the future in the end caught on with her and ignited also her imagination. And there was always that wonderful experience for me how she entrusted herself to me and let me create some sweet sensations for her. Looking back now, those were some of the most precious moments in my life when I dwelt in Mei Chi's world.

Outside, the deep freeze continued unabated. With no end in sight for this harshest and longest of winters, everyone seemed to be affected alike. We were all now engaged in pure survival, free men and prisoners alike. Our guards had become more lenient, probably because of a drive to protect themselves, but I always liked to think that they also thought of us. They had shifted the early morning assembly to inside the mess hall, for in the yard their suffering would have become nearly equal to ours. While we were readied for the morning departure to the work site, trucks already warming up were lined up outside. We had never before been driven to a work site in town.

It was on one of those freezing days, when the air above and around us seemed to consist of thick and frozen vapors, that even the sun could not penetrate the atmosphere except like a pale, fuzzy, diffused source of light placed behind a frosted glass. But in the mornings it rose in a spectacle like a phantom out of its primordial blood and in the evening it descended back into it. This day with all its natural and human events is forever etched into my mind and soul, indelibly, until they, too, will cease to exist.

We had been driven home after a day of accomplishing little on the construction site since we had had to keep ourselves on the move almost constantly to avoid freezing to death. As had never happened before and was never to happen again, we were sent back to camp in the late afternoon. As we climbed off the trucks, I immediately noticed the change. A contingent of soldiers, bundled up against the icy cold and with faces almost obscured by shawls wound around their heads, surrounded the building. I let my eyes sweep over that great, dead facade of the building before I stepped inside with the others. Its usual whiteness this late afternoon, as the sun was setting in its pool of blood, was tinged crimson. For some strange reason, it appeared to me at that fleeting moment, as my eyes were dwelling on its mighty facade for a few seconds, like a monstrous mausoleum ready to entomb us all.

And then this incredible tragedy unfolded before me. From the first moment that I realized what had happened I became as someone, a double of mine perhaps, who witnessed everything with no emotions. We had gone up to our sleeping quarters to rest since we were back too early for the evening meal. In the great hall we had encountered some flurry of activities, Russian guards and soldiers hurrying back and forth, their faces solemn, almost grim. Before we parted to go up to our separate sleeping quarters, Walter said to me in low tones, "Something unusual must have happened today. I sense there was something going on, but we may never know about it." I looked at him and shrugged my shoulders as if to say, who knows, Walter, what it is, but I don't want to think about it. I think he understood. Because we were both tired and cold, we headed off in different directions. As I came to my bed, I was surprised and alarmed to see an orderly standing next to it. He said nothing but passed a little folded paper that had been taped shut with surgical tape. He was gone before I could take my eyes off the little scrap he had dropped into my hand. Something is not right in the infirmary, it shot through my head. I thought of Anna and Mei Chi right away, but I could never have imaged the horrible events that had transpired.

The little message was from Natasha, Anna's assistant. I didn't really know her but had seen her once in a while. She asked me to come to the infirmary immediately. The only other thing it said was to admit me, and it was signed by her. If I could have flown I would have done so. But I tried to avoid anybody noticing me and, therefore, walked very slowly and in a roundabout way to the infirmary. Although my mind started racing immediately trying to explain to itself why Natasha I had never had any dealings with would ask me to come. I suddenly expected the worst.

It was she who apparently waited for me behind the door, for it was she who opened it. She wasted no time and suspended all formality. It seemed she was intent on only reporting the bare facts.

"I had you come here because I am supposed to give you this letter from Anna. She was taken away at noon. We don't know where to. It all happened very quickly after they found Mei Chi murdered in her room. Boris had led Anna to Mei Chi and admitted to the deed there and then but refused to give any motive or to answer any questions. He never said much to any of us. We always thought he was strange and somewhat mysterious. Anna had asked some of her orderlies to detain Boris. He never objected. She asked others to attend to Mei Chi, but she was already dead with a knife through her heart that was still there. They removed the knife and washed Mei Chi and cleaned her room and placed her on her pad. By then we all knew. Anna immediately notified the administrators and they must in turn have notified the central prison administration in Moscow. Directions must have come quickly. Before we knew it, the army came in and removed Boris and Anna. We are uncertain of their fates. It all happened under Anna's watch and that does not look good for her. I think though that Boris is doomed. As for Mei Chi, we are all in shock."

She had spoken so hastily that I could hardly follow her. As she prattled on, something seemed to be dying within me until all feeling was gone. Consciously, in my mind, I suppose, I was following her report, but my emotional body had died little by little as my mind absorbed the gruesome news. Both Anna and Mei Chi, the most precious people in my life, were gone, wiped out with one stroke. I cannot bear this loss, I thought.

"Where is Mei Chi now?" were the only words I could manage to expel almost soundlessly.

"She is still in her room but will be removed shortly. The living had to be taken care of first, I suppose."

"I must see her once more, Natasha." I pleaded with her.

"No! That is impossible."

"Natasha, my life depends on it," I suddenly blurted out with so much desperation in my voice that she looked at me startled. I don't think she realized my total involvement with Mei Chi.

"Natasha, please," I began again. "Mei Chi helped save my life. I need to honor her by taking leave of her. You must understand that. She has done so much for me and given so much of herself."

"Yes, we all realized her goodness," Natasha now conceded. I saw that she looked at me differently now than before. And before I could even gain some inkling of hope, she said suddenly, "Follow me, then."

She took me down the hall that led to Mei Chi's room. I retraced the steps I had taken so many times before, and every step seemed to ingrain itself in my mind now. My heart began to ache suddenly, but I felt desperately that I had to contain this ache, to store it up until later when I could let it consume my heart if it was going to.

At that moment Natasha opened the door that I had opened so many times myself and behind which had always awaited me some blissful experience. Now I stepped over the threshold and immediately sensed a coldness and emptiness. Natasha, realizing perhaps that I had fallen into some state of mental paralysis, grabbed my sleeve and pulled me forward towards Mei Chi's body. I looked down and here she lay, stretched out and covered to her chin. The only part exposed was her beautiful alabaster face fringed by her shiny, black-lacquer hair. She seemed asleep and serene with a peaceful expression on her face, a strange incongruity for one who had died so violently. I knew it was irrational, but at that moment it felt to me as if she had preserved her face just for me so that I could carry it with me through the rest of my days.

I didn't know that I was still capable of words, but I was surprised to hear myself whisper almost inaudibly (or was it someone else who stood there instead of me), "Mei Chi, I love you. You will always be with me wherever I go, just as I promised."

At that moment I felt a tug in the back. Through all this physical numbness I knew what it meant, and I hastened to bend down and kissed Mei Chi's lips one more time.

"We must leave now," Natasha said, slightly impatient.

"Yes, I know," I heard myself answer politely. I got up and followed for I knew she had done much more for me than was wise or safe for her. As we left the room, I never looked back, for I knew what I wanted and needed I was carrying away in my heart.

20

Grieving

Clutching the letter Natasha had pressed into my hand, I entered the prisoners' quarters. Like a ghost I appeared to be wandering in timeless space. What seemed an eternity I had spent in the infirmary was probably not more than ten minutes. I found myself in the mess hall on the ground floor. I had no recollection of the actual steps I had taken to get there. The hall was empty. All activity I thought I had noticed there earlier had ceased. Where were they all? I stood there for a while not knowing what to do. Inside me it felt as if a dark, gaping space had opened up ready for me to fall into, and yet I also felt, at the same time, as if I were filled up to the point of bursting. I couldn't explain the contradictory feelings to myself. But even if I had wanted to, I don't think my mind would have been able to sort my feelings and emotions out or to determine what was really going on inside me. A certain numbness and haziness pervaded all parts of my being. Suddenly, I took notice of the paper in my hand. And, as if someone had been guiding me, I went up the stairs to the sleeping quarters. As I entered the room, I saw every bed was occupied. How strange, I thought, all the men are sleeping and yet there is still a faint light outside. Then some memories from earlier in the day came back. I thought of the sub zero temperature, the freezing air, the little work we were able to accomplish, the fires burning on the open floor of the building, the guards who did not seem as threatening as usual, the sudden announcement that we would be sent back, and the sun beginning to wallow in its blood bath in the late afternoon as we were off-loaded at the camp. These happenings now seemed like strange precursors. Beyond that there was this inexplicable hiatus in my thinking, nothing but blank space. I lay down on my bed and closed my eyes until I again became aware of the paper I had in my right hand. I brought it up to my eyes and turned it over several times. It was a folded piece of paper sealed at the edges with small bits of tape. It was not addressed to anyone and yet it had been handed to me. So, there had been instructions! Suddenly I had the urge to see what was written inside. I removed the tape and unfolded the paper. It read:

My dearest Janos,

Before I am taken away, I want you to know what you have meant to me. You see, something inside myself compelled me to help you and to take you into my heart. When you were first brought to me sick and close to death, so young, so innocent and pure, I suddenly had the vision of having known you for a long time. And there was this unusual resemblance. I could not help myself but to take you in and to fight for your life. You see, not too long ago, I lost my only son, Sergei, in the war. He was not much older than you. So, I cared for you as I would have cared for him. My heart will always be full of joy when I think that you survived and that I took part in your recovery. As for the future, I hope that you will be released some day and that you will be granted a full, long life after that. Even when I am gone I will still be able to pray for you. Though almost everything has been removed from me--my child, my husband (he too fell victim to the war), my possessions, my beliefs (they have tried very hard to take away my beliefs and, I must say, they partially succeeded), but I still know how to pray in the deepest part of the night. So, I will always engage my energies for you as long as I live. You have a brilliant mind and you are very talented. And if you should get out, you will do well. Teaching you has given me one of the greatest joys in my life, and it came at a time when much within me had already died.

I love you,
Anna

P.S. Janos, my heart aches in mortal fear for you. I hope you will stay intact when you learn of this dreadful, horrific happening. I will never be able to get over the loss of Mei Chi. If I could only be with you. But since it happened under my watch, I know, they will come for me before the day is up. In cases like these there will be no dalliance, no formal investigation. It's viewed like a cancer that must be cut out immediately. To be truthful, I don't know what will happen to me. Please keep on thinking of me as I will be thinking of you.

Blessings and love.

Oh, Anna! Anna! a defeated voice inside me cried out, why didn't you tell me earlier? Our relationship could have been so much more than it was. I could have been so much more to you had I known. But you will always be at my side till the end of my days. That much I will promise you. I love you, too.

From this moment on, a feeling emerged in me as if I had been blessed with two mothers. Both had contributed so much to me in the way they knew best. It appeared to me now as if the second had been meant to take over from the first when she lost her power to guide and sustain my young life.

I read the letter once more before I folded it and hid it in my pocket. As I contemplated her words and revelations in those moments, I suddenly realized that she had written the top part carefully, in a precise and slightly stilted script probably quite some time ago. In fact, the paper seemed yellowed and a bit frayed as if it had been folded and unfolded numerous times. The bottom, in contrast, had been hastily scribbled, possibly just before they arrived to take her away. What was to become of her, I could not imagine. So, I understood then that she had prepared this letter possibly months ago, and I believed now that she must have suspected for quite some time that they would get her some day. Even I had periodically had at least a vague notion that she was overextending herself, but I had not given it too much thought. Though she suspected, she could not possibly have known how her removal would come about, that I was sure of. How deathly sick in her heart she must have felt as they drove her away. I could no longer sustain this train of thought. I turned over in my bed, hid my head in the pillow, and bit into the pillow so hard that I thought I would fracture my jaw or crush my teeth. It was plain fear, fear of screaming out loud in pain that kept me lying like that (I don't know for how long), every muscle tense in my body, until the shrill bell jolted me out of that state.

As I lifted my head and saw everyone around me scramble out of their beds, I knew that we were called down for our miserable evening meal. All I knew then was that I needed to appear composed, for no one had knowledge of the loss I had experienced that day, not even Walter. Walter knew only little of my relationship with Anna, hardly anything beyond her efforts to save me and her efforts to teach me Russian. He knew nothing of Mei Chi. He would not have approved if he had known the full extent of either relationship. So, it ended up that I was all alone, that I had to work through the pain of these losses in virtual isolation.

Like everyone else I retired to my bed right after the meal. Walter had inquired hesitantly and indirectly as to the meaning of my brooding mood, for he and I usually had some lively discussions concerning the events of the day, about our little exploits that we had successfully handled. He seemed happy about the few rubles he had hidden in the lining of his suit. He liked to pat that part of his chest where the money was sort of in an unobtrusive way, a gesture only he and I understood. I liked to see him like that, for I knew it gave him pleasure to think that he had beaten the system in his own way.

He had also begun to fashion little trinkets out of pieces of Plexiglas or metal he had found at the construction sites and in a workshop in the rear of our camp building. He went to that workshop on Sundays after he had been able to become acquainted with some of the Russian workers. They let him use the machines, the drills and sanders and anything else he needed. In turn he gave them some of the wares he produced that they could sell for themselves. One day, Walter showed me with pride a great big knife he had forged, sanded, and polished to a high sheen in that shop from a piece of raw metal he had found. He kept it hidden inside his mattress until he could sell it.

To me his skills and inventiveness bordered on the artistic. Though somewhat fastidious and very tenacious, he was also very creative. But tonight he let me be, except for his initial reticent inquiries. He was always respectful when he realized that something was going on inside me. In that way, he was quite sensitive. He never prodded to know what it was that bothered me like others would have done. He waited patiently until I would tell him, if I had something to tell him. Sometimes, I would never tell him.

We parted when we went to our separate sleeping quarters. I wanted to take to bed immediately, for I needed space to myself to begin mourning for Mei Chi. I had repressed the memory of her for several hours, and sometimes I think I unconsciously expelled her from my mind until I had parted from Anna. I never thought that a double tragedy, as had struck me that day, could be assimilated without losing one's mind or descending into the night of irrationality. It would have been so easy to allow myself to be anesthetized as it had happened in those first moments as I staggered out of the infirmary, numb and half unconscious. None of these states I realized in these moments in the dark of night I wanted to allow myself to succumb to, for I thought both women wanted me to live. They both had worked hard to keep me alive and sane. They had demonstrated it to me through the care and compassion they had given me. They had also taken it upon themselves to teach me in the areas of their expertise. These thoughts were racing through my mind and it was with a painful heart that I ascended the stairs. I hoped that I could commune with Mei Chi, perhaps tonight, for to me she was not really gone and would never be really gone. She had become too much a part of me. I even felt that, perhaps, her spirit would imbue mine and would always be there, so closely entwined our souls had been. That's why I had been so desperate to see her one last time and to read the message she had left for me as she faced her horrible demise. It was certainly not the reason I had given Natasha when I begged her to lead me to Mei Chi. The more I began to contemplate her final expression that night and in times to come, the more I became convinced that it had been meant for me. It came to embody the beauty she and I had looked upon but also the beauty she believed extended beyond this earthly journey.

That night as my fellow prisoners around me had settled into various states of sleep from the most restless to the depth of unconsciousness, from the most peaceful to the most disturbed, I sat up in my bed trying to commune with Mei Chi. It was then when I sat very still in total darkness, when I gave myself up to the pain and loss I felt, that the living flame she had taught me to capture and retain would not appear in my mind's eye. But instead an image emerged out of the dark depth that I had earlier seen within myself. Instead of feeling myself dragged into this abyss, the image slowly floated up towards me and assumed Mei Chi's features. It was just like I had last seen her face, and I realized that I had truly carried her away with me as I thought I had when I left her room for the last time. And so I sat there as if transfixed, looking into her beautiful, delicate face. And then came the tears that would not come before. I wept them silently, tears that had filled my interior to the bursting point. But strangely enough, as the floodgates opened, I was not at all sure whether they were tears of grief or tears of joy or a mixture of them, for I was now certain Mei Chi would always be with me and influence me. And just after her peaceful features had faded from my mind's eye and I laid myself down, the very first bird-like image of her rushed into my mind as she swooped through the curtain into my alcove, the private, solitary space I had occupied alone for weeks already. "Mei Chi, you rare, exquisite creature, you healer, teacher, lover, and mystic, I will love you forever," I breathed into the all-embracing darkness, and with those words on my lips I fell exhausted into a dreamless sleep.

21

ANTIFA and the End
of a Friendship

It is difficult to understand now how the mundane and the most basic elements could have ruled our lives almost totally. They assumed center stage, as happened when two days later a trainload of beets arrived at our camp. Walter and I knew as soon as we jumped off the truck that something unusual had occurred. Harold was standing there. He had apparently been waiting for Walter, for he walked right up to him. By now everyone knew the kinds of skills Walter possessed. He received requests from different people, guards and prisoners alike, to do this or that for them or create this gadget or that tool. Here was Harold gushing excitedly about the trainload of beets that had been shipped on the doctor's orders and how they needed a machine that could peel them. He asked Walter point blank whether he could build one.

"That might not be impossible," Walter said thoughtfully.

"Then come and see the administrator for food and supplies, Lieutenant Nikolei Bolkov, right away," Harold answered excitedly. "We want to start serving them as soon as possible. But we need someone who speaks Russian, an interpreter, so that you can talk with the Lieutenant. I don't know who to ask."

"No problem!" Walter said with a smile and Harold looked at him with incredulity and with his mouth half open.

"I didn't know you could speak it, hardly any of the prisoners can speak anything of substance!"

"Oh, it's not me really, but it's Jan over here. He'll do it for us." Walter said as he pointed at me.

Harold glanced at me admiringly and said eagerly, "Follow me, guys."

Well, Walter and I worked out a good deal for both of us with the Lieutenant. He gave us two weeks in which to build the machine. Walter had insisted that he needed my help. It was granted. And the Lieutenant promised to find the materials and parts that would go into the machine. He ordered the workshop in the back of our building that Walter was already familiar with to free up a space for our project. We were elated. We could work for at least a short period of time indoors and at our own speed. It seemed like Walter and I were a good team and our skills worked hand in hand so to speak.

Every day, as we walked to the workshop, we passed the enormous piles of beets stored behind our camp. Walter always snatched a few and dropped them into one of the pockets of his quilted suit. He had slit holes in his pockets so that the beets actually fell through down to where the pants were stuffed into his boots. It looked funny as he walked because he carried the weight of the beets, or whatever else he might have dropped in there, around his calves. One day he was so loaded up, he could hardly move. His leg weights required a very slow, gingerly kind of stepping out. He tried to avoid the beets from swinging back and forth around his legs. That could have unbalanced him in his forward progress. The sight of him was so funny that I started laughing out loud, something I had not done since I had entered the camp. "Walter, you are a sight!" I cried out. I could hardly stop laughing. Walter became quite angry with me. Realizing the extent of his anger, I settled down and kept quiet. For him, stealing food and transporting it back to his bed where he hid it was the most important endeavor of his current life. For him there was nothing more serious than the procurement of food.

I was happy for him that within one week his night vision returned. He came running over to me one morning as I entered the mess hall. I could see the excitement on his face.

"Jan, I can see again. I have my vision back," he cried out, even before he had gotten to me.

"Walter, I am so happy for you. You know the beets did it, don't you. It's the only change in our diet. What do you think now of the doctor? I know you hated her."

"You mean the new doctor, Jan? I haven't even been to see her.

"We have a new doctor? I didn't know that."

"Most of us know that. Where have you been, Jan? The old doctor is no longer here."

"But Walter, it was the old doctor, Anna Petrovna, you saw weeks ago. She ordered these beets, and it must have been on account of your visit with her, I am sure of that. Did you not hear Harold say the other evening that the load of beets had been ordered by the doctor?" I reminded him.

I wanted so badly for him to stop talking disparagingly of Anna, that he would recognize at least some goodness in her.

"Puh, I did not listen to all of Harold's prattle the other day. Just heard what I needed to hear."

"I just wanted you to understand that Anna was responsive to your needs, Walter. She helped you the only way she knew how. I just wanted you to see that. She could not have made any promises on the spot," I said to Walter hoping that he would at least recognize and appreciate her concern for him and what she had done.

"I guess, so she did. She helped me. But I still hate her. Well, it doesn't matter any more, for we got a replacement."

In some ways, Walter was incorrigible. It was that stubborn, inflexible, irreconcilable side of him coming through that I had trouble with. If he pegged someone for something he disapproved of, he would not budge and change his mind, probably never. I had never tested this side of him myself to see how far he would go. In Anna's case it was hopeless. I wanted to throw up my arms in defeat. But at least I realized now that Walter knew nothing of the tragic events in the infirmary and why Anna was gone. I realized for the first time, how secretively the prison administration worked. It was as if a wall existed between them and us, except it was permeable one way. They knew everything about us. Perhaps they had even known everything about me, Anna, and Mei Chi. Perhaps even Boris had been their henchman, and he is not even suffering the kind of punishment that Natasha thought he would get for certain. Maybe he was planted. He was a strange character, I thought, right from the start when he was helping me while I was deathly ill. I was surprised at myself that I could have these thoughts, to be that cynical. But the fact remained--they knew everything, and we didn't know anything about them and never would.

There had been a number of disturbing incidences in our camp lately. The steady weight loss experienced by all our men, carefully monitored by Walter, was a great worry to all of us. Nothing could be done to halt the weight loss unless there was more and better food or less heavy work. The prospect of either of these happening was dismal. Walter and I were fortunate that he and I—mainly he, to be truthful—were able to organize a little extra food for ourselves. The night blindness incident, affecting many prisoners, was another. A third had started a couple of weeks ago. Suddenly, all men in our unit, all three hundred of them, had become infested with body lice in such a severe manner that their bodies literally crawled with them. You could reach into a man's shirt and pick up a handful of lice out of his chest hair. The administration, being concerned for themselves and to prevent an outbreak of disease, ordered an emergency delousing process immediately.

Being sent for delousing was a painful and dehumanizing experience, albeit a very necessary procedure. Instead of being rousted out of our beds at 5 a.m., we now were made to get up at 4 a.m. twice a week. We were marched through the early morning coldness for almost an hour to the delousing shed. In an unheated room we were ordered to strip naked, to bundle our clothes, to secure them with our belts, and to hand them in to be steam treated. Meanwhile we were herded into a shower room where cold water was sprayed from the ceiling for a few seconds. That was supposed to get us wet enough to soap ourselves down with the little soap powder that had been spooned into one of our hands. We were instructed to work fast at every stage, for the time allotted was always short. They did not want us to lose too much time from work, we guessed.

No sooner had we smeared the powder over our wet bodies, then water started spraying from the ceiling again, but hardly enough to wash off the soap. Immediately after washing off, we were herded into the next room where our bodies were supposed to dry while we waited for our clothes to come back from the steam chamber. But that room was also very cold and there were no towels. Upon entering this room, our bodies being wet, we got chilled to the bone so quickly that a mad running around in circles and a wild jumping up and down ensued. To an outsider looking in it would have appeared as if we were all wildly intoxicated. These gyrations went on for at least half an hour until our clothes were carried in so steaming hot that we could not touch them at first. Yet all we had in mind was to get dressed immediately. It took painful minutes until the untied clothes had cooled enough to put them on. But they were still damp from the steaming process and cooled down so quickly while we were putting them on that we hardly felt warmer than when we were naked. As soon as a group of men was dressed, they were immediately marched back through the cold darkness to the camp for breakfast and assembly. A day's work still lay ahead of us.

All these incidences affecting the prisoners' health and well-being affected me emotionally to a point that I physically hurt when I thought of all the filth, inadequacies, and malnourishment. Even the simplest hygiene was substandard. The latrines in the yard had not been improved since we first occupied the building. They were at best makeshift. We had no running water still, except the one faucet in the yard. The men could hardly ever wash and had to trudge down the stairs, two and three flights of them, three or four times a night out to the latrines in the yard to urinate. They had been wearing the same clothes including the same underwear for all the months (six of them) since we received the quilted winter suits. Nothing was ever washed. Some men had developed sores on their legs because of their filthy underclothes. Our condition was slowly, but steadily, deteriorating. I could sense a disaster happening, an outbreak of an epidemic of some kind, perhaps, or more deaths due to infections and malnutrition. But most of the men, I noticed, carried their plight stoically. I guess they had given up to expect more or to expect improvements. Their spirit became steadily diminished to a point where their senses became dulled, their demeanor listless, and their eyes expressionless. Now that I had lost Anna and Mei Chi, my awareness and attention turned more and more towards the men.

Directions in life become changed so rapidly at times that one hardly notices when they are in the process of changing. So it happened with me for I suddenly realized what I needed to do from one day to the next. Only days had elapsed since we started the delousing program. As I returned from work one evening, I went straight to the administrative offices on the fourth floor. I would have never known how to get there had Walter not been asked to build the machine that would peel the beets. Since I had gone with him, I knew where to find Lieutenant Bolkov and that's where I was heading as if on automatic pilot. I knew he wasn't the right man to see, but he would connect me with the right man if he thought I was good material. I don't know why I was so certain of that, but I was dead right. My certainty probably derived from the conversation I once had with Anna. When I talked to her, months ago, about the camp conditions that bothered me, she had hinted that I could have an influence if only I were willing to undergo some ideological training. Well, after these very recent and utterly disturbing experiences, I was ready for anything except actually laying my life on the line.

Lieutenant Bolkov greeted me quite cordially. I realized he remembered me. We chatted in Russian for a while. I was pleased how well it went. I still had not told him why I had come, and he, for some unexplainable reason, had not asked. But I knew I had to do it even though I felt a slight tug inside me and a slight hesitation that nudged me to hold back and to reconsider. But a seemingly independent voice from the depth of my being was much stronger than I realized, and it spoke suddenly loud and clear.

"Lieutenant," I heard myself saying, "I would like to gain an understanding of the Russian experience. Not too long ago someone recommended a course to me that I might be able to participate in. Is there such a course of study?"

"Jan," he replied, obviously quite interested in what I had said (he had even remembered my first name), "I am not the right man to talk to. But I advise you to see Commissar Bukarin. He will tell you exactly what chances you will have to be accepted. I think they are very good considering your fine language skills and your youth. You could be quite valuable to us." After a pause, and a few seconds of reflection, he continued, "Wait here, Jan, for a few moments. I will see whether the Commissar is still in his office."

Bolkov was back in a couple of minutes and an obviously high-ranking Russian officer was following on his heels who looked at me sternly and critically. I could feel his penetrating gaze on me immediately.

"This is Jan…," Bolkov started to introduce me to his superior, but realized that he didn't know my last name. I stepped a little closer and introduced myself to Bukarin.

"My name is Janos Jablonsky. I am eighteen years old, and I have the desire to take a course to learn more about Russia, its system, and its ideology." I added with firm resolve in my voice, "Is there such a course and would I have a chance to be accepted? How would it profit me, you, and, perhaps, my fellow prisoners. All I know right now is that I love your language."

He now looked at me with interest. "Janos, you are the type of young man we would be interested in. You already possess a skill that is valuable to us. It will speed up your learning process drastically. But we need to know from you whether you are sincere and quite serious."

"I can assure you I am," I heard this independent voice reply.

"You will have to attest to your seriousness in writing if you are accepted. The courses are disseminated by the Committee for Antifascist Activity, in short called ANTIFA. So, now, let me tell you who will profit and why since you asked this question frankly. You will profit because you will achieve extensive knowledge of our system, gain an elevated status with all its benefits of better food, better clothing, and an office on our floor. We will profit because you will help us run the camp we will assign you to; you will be responsible for prisoner welfare, indoctrination, and training of German prisoners as auxiliary guards. Your fellow prisoners may profit because you can request certain changes that may be approved after we have carefully studied your requests. The prisoner of war population is valuable to us because they are helping us with the rebuilding of mother Russia. But we have no intent of coddling the prisoners. You must understand that." He had spoken very firmly and I felt he meant everything he said.

"I do understand everything you have told me and I think it's fair. I could abide by it. The only thing I would like to be quite frank about is that I would like to be assigned to this camp if I was to be trained."

"Ah, I don't know whether we can promise that although I am not unwilling to put your wishes in writing and send it forward with your request. I would even be willing to emphasize your wishes. I would go that far. But even after that you would still take a chance."

"I understand," I answered quickly, "and I am willing to take that risk."

He seemed obviously pleased with me now, and I was quite certain that he would do everything he could to have me return to this camp and be part of his administration. I was now quite certain that he liked me as much as Bolkov did.

It was only two weeks later that I was called back to Bukarin on the fourth floor. He gave me the good news that I was accepted and would be sent away within one week for a four-week course in a city up north. I hadn't told Walter anything about my plans and my resolve. I was quite excited about the prospect of achieving perhaps some changes in the camp. I was willing to work very diligently and as diplomatically as I knew how to convince the administration. Walter was another matter. I didn't know how he would react to my plans. I had some inkling that he would not look upon them favorably, but I had not in the slightest expected what was about to unfold.

The same evening I received the news from Bukarin, I let Walter know during the evening meal that I needed to talk to him privately. He asked me to come up to his bed later on. He thought we could talk out in the hall. "What's going on, Jan?" he was very curious. "Why the secrecy and privacy? What could be so unusual?"

"Walter, you will know very soon and you will understand."

We met within half an hour outside his sleeping room. He seemed aghast when I first told him. We spoke as quietly as possible for fear that someone could hear us.

"Jan, I am sure you can't be serious! If you do this, you will become a traitor to the fatherland! Do you realize that! Maybe you are too young to understand. I know that's it! That's it!"

If I had not asked him to be as quiet as possible, I know he would have yelled out loud.

"No, Walter, you got it wrong. I am very serious. Something good will come out of this." I answered with conviction.

He would have none of it. He just carried on and wouldn't consider anything I said.

"I tell you, you are absolutely crazy, Jan, or you have already been brainwashed into it by someone, perhaps that nasty doctor. I am warning you, Jan, you will become a traitor, and I hope you know what that means, if you go through with it," he suddenly hissed at me.

I saw a redness working its way up from his neck quite rapidly until it had engulfed his face within seconds. And the blood vessels began to swell at his temples. I became alarmed.

"Walter, you are making too much of this. I thought you would be with me. Think of yourself and all your fellow prisoners. Think that you want to get home to your wife and daughters some day. If you and the others can all benefit, then it will be worth my effort."

But he scoffed at what I had said and continued almost sneeringly (where was this wonderful compassionate and kind side Walter possessed and that I knew so well?).

"Your effort, you call it Jan, your effort? It is nothing but a traitorous undertaking and I will have no part in it. I would rather perish right here in this miserable camp than to have any part in it. You are on the verge of betraying everything that is part of you and me—your family, your homeland, your friends, the German culture, everything."

He had worked himself almost into a frenzy. Having become almost breathless, he stopped for a moment to catch some air. Then he started again.

"Jan, I am telling you one more thing which may bring you back to your senses. I can no longer be your friend if you go ahead as you have planned. There is no way I can consider you my friend. Even though our friendship has been wonderful and dear to me. But you are betraying me also with your unbelievable intent and everything I stand for."

I was speechless. Here stood a man in front of me who was willing to totally reject me, reject me out of hand because I wanted to do something he would not and could not approve of. A deep sadness and hopelessness suddenly overcame me. I felt very fatigued and old within the few minutes of our exchange. What traitorousness, what betrayal was he talking about? In my mind, in the face of our slow and steady demise, there existed no such thing. And I knew then I would forge ahead. It was very clear in my mind that I had to do it. What was the loss of one wrong-headed very dear friend in the face of what could be gained? Little did I know what this one dear friend turned enemy could accomplish.

"I am sorry, Walter, that we don't seem to see eye to eye in this, but I must go ahead. I am very sorry," I said wearily. "But my friendship towards you will never cease, Walter, no matter what you say to me. You cannot tear that from me."

With that said I felt tears coming on. I turned on my heels as fast as I could. This would be the last exchange Walter and I would ever have. But I did not waiver in my resolve, and I was sent away within a few days.

22

The Course

The further the bus carried me north and the longer I sat without collecting my thoughts in some ordered fashion, the more my current situation became unreal to me. My thoughts and emotions had been a problem since the bitter clash with Walter a little over a week ago. Thoughts had kept racing through my mind wildly in an ever more unruly fashion until I felt unable to cope with them. Attempts at sorting them out, of pursuing even a single one long enough to make sense out of it had failed. Even Mei Chi's practice at night in the dark did not always work for me. And yet, there were nights when I experienced some small triumphs. It came when I finally succeeded in stilling my mind and her peace-giving image came floating up from the depth.

As the bus lumbered north and virtually retraced the daily ride to the forest (we were now following the same road the work truck had taken seemingly a long time ago), it appeared to me as if I were now embarked on a forbidden journey. And yet, at the same time, my current endeavor seemed so simple and straightforward. Was not my single-minded goal to achieve improvements in the life of my fellow prisoners? And yet Walter's rejection had tossed me into a boiling cauldron of wildly swinging thoughts and emotions that I had not been able to get out of for days.

The Russians had been fair, almost kind, to me. They had given me a simple uniform (jacket, trousers, as well as new boots and underwear), plain and unadorned. It had felt good getting out of the quilted work suit I had worn for months. The winter was conquered with its freezing temperatures. A few weeks of rain had washed away the dirty remnants of crusty snow and ice. And on this day during my ride north the sun was out in a delicate, spring-blue sky.

Bukarin had arranged for me to be taken into the center of Rodonski in his private vehicle. I had boarded the bus alone. The Russian who had driven me stayed behind and waited until the bus left the plaza. He even waved to me. We had chatted amicably on the way into the city. He must have known where I was headed and what I was about to undergo. Here and there I had noticed weeds of fresh green growing in the cracks of the sidewalks. They were like harbingers of life returning to the city. I noticed that even the people walked differently, faster and with more vigor than during the winter, maybe just because they had been able to shed some of the layers of clothing they had worn in the icy cold. For me it felt strange to have gained a state akin to freedom after more than one year of imprisonment and under the steady watch of the guards. I was amazed the trust Bukarin had invested in me by letting me travel unguarded. But as I reflected on that thought, something nudged me way in the back of my mind, and it suddenly occurred to me that I might not be traveling alone after all. Who knows, some guard in plain clothes may have been sitting in front or in back of me. I surely couldn't tell. As I looked around me at the faces in my vicinity, I found them closed and self-absorbed. I felt as if we had all been enclosed in our own bubbles, destined never to touch each other's lives. The more I thought the more I believed that someone among these people must be watching me, but as long as I stayed the course, I would never find out.

Ever since the disappearance of Anna and the murder of Mei Chi, I had detected traces of paranoia and distrustfulness in me that I never thought would lodge themselves in my naturally trusting disposition. Also, Walter's sudden disavowal of our friendship had hit me hard. How could such a close bond as he and I had experienced and such selfless caring on his part be severed and discarded at once and with such finality? I guessed there was something in life that I had not been exposed to until then. With incredulity I looked at it now: it was Walter, the most loyal friend I had had in adversity, sickness, and in the face of death, who had now demonstrated to me that in the final analysis the bond and loyalty to the collective will take priority over the personal by leaps and bounds. It was this allegiance to the people, the race, the fatherland, the traditions, the ideology, the belief system, the common religion, and the political system that took precedence over any love for and devotion to an individual. As in him, it really was the connection to the collective that seemed to stir a far greater passion and fervor than any personal relationship. Was it not Walter who, some time ago, had professed to love his wife and daughters above all else but who had also said he would rather perish than violate his allegiance to his country? That is why he saw me as betrayer and traitor! And what about my bonds and allegiances? How did they stand up to his? I searched and felt myself solely connected and bonded to the members of my family, to Effie my first love, to Anna my savior, to Mei Chi my healer and soul mate, and to Walter my friend. I realized then that even in my personal relationships I had already crossed over into traitorous territory by Walter's standards. Even worse, for beyond the personal I only had a vague notion of a collective bond. This bond, I guessed, had never formed in the chaos of the war years. There was then this irreconcilable difference between me and Walter as he perceived it. And it was the reason why our friendship could no longer exist in his mind. I felt different though. I could have accepted and respected his devotion to the collective and also remained his friend. I could have even accepted his personal rejection of me as his friend because of my transgression. But what I could not accept was what occurred after that due to his machinations.

For four weeks now I had suspended any judgment as to what we were led into, even at times when I felt the claws of indoctrination tightening around me. I had thought of myself more like an observer than a full participant. And yet I believe I understood everything taught to us (there were fifty students in the course) better than anyone, as reflected in the high scores I had earned: in Russian history, in revolutionary history, the tenets of communism, the differences between communism and fascism, the causes of the war and its aftermath for Russia with twenty million dead and a devastated country. The teaching was intense and concentrated. Ten hours a day, six days a week. I absorbed it all with much interest since I had never had any knowledge of the Russian experience. In the end, I knew I had gained some understanding of a new worldview, one that I was not necessarily willing to adopt as my own. At the completion of the course, I felt I was ready to go out into the field and to accomplish my goals and to live up to the duties that would be imposed on me.

Sometimes even four weeks can make a vast difference. As I had parted from my teachers and fellow students, I realized how abundant nature had suddenly become. Early summer was in full force. It was then the middle of

June 1946, and traveling south on possibly the same bus that had carried me north just a few weeks earlier, I marveled at the transformation of the land and spring's profuse outpouring. We had been kept inside the building the entire four weeks and had been fully occupied with heavy class and study loads. We were fed well in comparison to the inadequate prison fare I had been used to for so long, but we were only allowed to breathe fresh air in the interior, stone-paved courtyard of the building that housed us. The only nature I saw then was a small blue square of summer sky.

I realized that Bukarin must have pulled some heavy strings, for I was about to be returned to the same prison camp I had left four weeks ago. Now, as the bus rolled through the countryside, I gave myself over to observing nature. I had six hours of reprieve, the time it took to return to Rodonski. On this road south, as we traveled through collective farming country north of the great forest region, adjoining apple orchards had burst into millions of blossoms so delicate and precious that they brought tears to my eyes. And underneath the trees sometimes small patches of yellow daffodils. In those hours on the bus, like a starving man, I consumed every scrap of natural beauty my eyes could lay hands on. Even the plain green meadows became a feast as no other.

As the hours ticked away, we left the open fields and orchards. We now entered miles and miles of forest, the same I had toiled in to exhaustion for months in the dead of winter. For one who had felt half dead for such a long time, it was a glorious sight. These mighty evergreens seemed more alive than I could remember, as they now stood in diffused sunlight that fell in fine shafts upon the forest floor. I felt a strangely elevated mood settling over me, one that lasted for the rest of the journey. And when at last I saw the low skyline of Rodonski and the mighty building that was our camp in the distance to the east, I realized with an amazing gladness in my heart that I had been allowed to come home, where all my current memories, attachments, and sufferings were still housed.

23

Improvements and Ostracism

As the bus lumbered into town, the thought crossed my mind that none of the prisoners knew that I would be returning, not even Walter; and most likely the great majority didn't even realize that I had left. I still felt awful about Walter's outburst before I left, but I hoped against hope that he would come around once conditions were starting to improve in the camp. Before I could pursue my thought further, the bus stopped at the city square. To my surprise, Bukarin's car was waiting for me already. I recognized it right away. Their internal communications, I thought, work like a well-greased machine. I was almost willing to bet that they knew every step I had taken in the last few weeks. Andrei, Bukarin's driver, who had driven me into town when I was about to begin my journey north, was leaning against the car waving at me as I stepped off the bus. I waved back in remembrance of our cordial chat on the way into town. As I walked over to him and as I came closer I saw his face beaming at me. He was obviously happy to see me. Andrei was not much older than I, and there had been a feeling of familiarity and camaraderie between us right from the beginning.

"Comrade Janos, welcome home," he said smiling and with a twinkle in his eyes.

"Oh, please, don't do this to me, Andrei. I can't handle it," I said light heartedly but inwardly not a slight bit alarmed. They are trying to make me totally one of their own, it crossed my mind in a split second.

"I hope you don't mind me calling you Janos. We'll be seeing each other a lot from now on, you know."

"No, no! I would like that very much."

"I have been asking the boss about you as often as I could when you were gone. He didn't mind telling me in detail how well you were doing. He is very proud of you, you know. I am sure he will take you firmly under his wings. He even told me you came out on top in the course. It speaks well for you." The words had practically been bursting out of his mouth.

"Andrei, please give me a break!" I tried to tone things down.

He seemed to understand, and our conversation immediately turned from me and my achievements to a more casual topic. I appreciated his sensitivity, and I liked the way I could make conversation with Andrei as if we had been friends for a long time. And besides, he had a refreshing sense of humor. He was one of the friendliest and sincerest Russians I ever met. I realized that fully later when things began to fall apart for me.

It was now close to six in the evening as we stopped in the back of the monstrous building that was our camp. Avoiding the prisoner's quarters, Andrei led me straight up the backstairs to the fourth floor.

Bukarin and Bolkov had obviously been awaiting me since they were both being seated in Bukarin's office. They both stood up at the same time as we entered. Their faces were beaming. They simultaneously stepped forward in my direction. I turned to Bukarin first and shook his hand formally. He then grabbed me spontaneously, pulled me towards him into a bear hug. He held me firmly for a while and I felt his formidable strength. What luck, I thought, I have the highest boss on my side. I should be able to accomplish much for my fellow prisoners. In a sudden surge of gratitude I hugged Bukarin firmly back.

As he released me, he held me at arm's length, looked at me, and said, "You are looking well, Janos. It seems like they treated you well for your face looks more rounded than before. And, above all, congratulations on your fine work. You have brought recognition and honor to me and our administration here for selecting you. More than well done, Janos!"

I was very happy I could please him that well. I then turned to Bolkov, and I hugged him with all the strength and good will I had in me. I think he was taken aback by my forcefulness for I felt him stiffen under my embrace. But I felt much gratitude towards him, too. I suddenly knew that I would be able to work well with these men; for I had not let them down, in fact, I had gone beyond their expectations. They respected that.

They led me proudly to a small office on the same floor as theirs. What luxury! It contained a simple desk and chair on the plain concrete floor, a small potbellied stove, two easy chairs and a small, low table in between. One wall had a simple bookcase and there was a cot in one corner that I assumed was my bed. But the best of all was the window. It afforded me a view over the river below and the vast grazing lands, the steppe, to the south. I felt overwhelmed and the thought immediately entered my mind that I did not deserve this much privacy and comfort. It did not seem fair to me in comparison to my fellow prisoners. What had I done to be entitled to this? I had simply studied their history starting with the Revolution and their political system with sincerity and listened to them with an open mind when they lectured us about what we had done wrong. I had not given up my independent thinking, my inner freedom. I never would.

I turned to Bukarin and Bolkov and thanked them profusely. I also acknowledged Andrei who had been part of this fine reception. I let them know that I wanted to be at their full disposal and was looking forward to taking their instructions. I made them feel as well as I could that I was ready to work in any way they wanted me to. Those were my sincerest intentions then.

For months I carried out the tasks assigned to me with much dedication. I trained prisoners to be auxiliary guards and impressed upon them in the subtlest ways to be fair when they dealt with their fellow prisoners. I held indoctrination sessions, as they were called, and presented the Russian side fairly without being preachy. Most important for me, in my meetings with Bukarin, I had suggested to him certain hygienic improvements that could avoid disease, would improve the prisoners' spirit, and improve output. I also began to press as soon as I felt the time was right for improvements in the prisoners' diet. I was happy I made progress. Prisoners were selected to work on bringing water to the sleeping quarters on the second and third floors. One room on each floor was set aside to serve as a washroom and urinal. In the shop behind the prison building prisoners fashioned sinks and urinals from scrap metal and Bukarin procured the necessary pipes for the water lines. Soon the prisoners no longer needed to drag themselves several times during the night down long flights of stairs, stand in line in the yard in the cold night air, and wait for their turn to urinate. They now gained more sleep and felt a little more refreshed the next morning. They could also now wash themselves in the morning or at night, and that helped in keeping the lice at bay.

Another contingent of prisoners worked on improving the latrines in the prison yard. Instead of open trenches, they now dug big holes and built outhouses over them that had wooden floors and wooden seats. From the German prison guards I had trained, reports filtered back that the morale in the camp had improved and that the prisoners' self-esteem seemed to have been raised.

Soon after these improvements, large shipments of cabbage, carrots, and more palatable fish than the kind Anna had been forced to promote arrived. Though the improvement in the diet was slight, it helped in lifting the prisoners' spirits.

During all these months I kept largely out of sight of the prisoners. The few times I was among them, they hardly paid any attention to me. I did run into Walter on a few occasions. Our meetings never went well, to say the least. Most of the time he kept his eyes averted, trying not to acknowledge me at all. But sometimes I forced the issue between us and approached him in a way that he could not avoid me. When our eyes met, his hateful glance pierced me every time like a sword right through the heart. How excruciatingly painful it was! At every intense encounter like this one, Walter would hiss something under his breath like, "You God damned traitor, don't cross my path again. I don't want to see you any more. We are done. Stay out of my way." But I kept on forcing the issue again and again at lengthy intervals. It felt as if I were driven back to him seeking the same abuse I knew for sure I would endure as long as the confrontations continued.

Walter's hatred and contempt did get to me over time. Eventually, they were with me every minute of my waking life and invaded my nightly dreams like a pair of poisonous snakes. In helplessness and despair, I sometimes wrung my hands in the middle of the night and cried out, "Why, oh God, why?" But an answer would not come. On the one hand, I was happy that because of me the prisoners' lives had improved; on the other hand, I didn't know how long I could live under the scourge of Walter's hatred. It affected me badly. Yet during the day and in my contacts with Bukarin, Bolkov, Andrei, and the rest of the Russian staff, or anyone, Russian or German, I came in contact with, no one would have ever suspected what was going on in my mind and soul. The only influence that could abate my desperation for a while in the depth of night was Mei Chi's image that still intruded itself steadfastly with its calming loveliness. It was as if she wanted me to know that she was still with me and that I was not alone. I think her appearance alone gave me the strength to carry on as long as I did.

But then, as the improvements kept on advancing, my situation took a turn for the worse. The next time I found myself in the prisoners' quarters and walked across the dining hall where everyone was assembled and seated, I suddenly heard a voice shouting.

"Traitor!"

That shout hit me like a lightening bolt. I momentarily stood transfixed, unable to move or think. And then another shout from three hundred throats rang out.

"Traitor!"

It was such a ferocious, deafening roar, so brutally direct and so instinctually primordial that I felt myself transported into a primitive world where the transgressors and the unwanted were judged, shamed, and ostracized communally. These transgressors were mercilessly cut off from the lifeline of the clan. And then in a flash I was brought back to the situation at hand. My thoughts returned clearly and in an organized fashion: they too are doing their work communally and in cold blood. Theirs is a world of black and white with no exception. I knew then that Walter had done his work well. He was their leader—an efficient leader and a persuasive manipulator. He knew very well that the crowd would follow him once he had stirred it up and that in this way he could get at me most effectively. Oh, Walter, how wrongheaded and yet how powerful you are! You always manage to influence my life whether for better or worse. Then I turned towards the crowd and fully looked at everyone. I faced them openly, almost defiantly. They took my stance as a cue. Their fists began to pound the tables as the rhythmic shouts, "Traitor, traitor, traitor ..." intensified.

At that moment I felt such an electrifying force being hurled at me that it hurt physically. I knew then for certain if they had had stones, they would have stoned me to death. As I stood and this realization swept over me, the Russian guards suddenly rushed in with their guns drawn and pointed into the crowd. The roar abated swiftly, and the hall fell quickly into an eerie silence. I suddenly felt so emotionally drained that fleeing from this hall of judgment and condemnation was my only impulse. Turning on my heels, I rushed out and up the stairs to the sanctuary of my office. I sat there in silence and without emotions, I don't know how long—until darkness engulfed me, until a new day began to dawn in the east.

Soon everyone in the administration knew what had transpired. Security became tightened. The armed Russian guards became very visible in the prisoners' quarters. They were everywhere—in the sleeping quarters, the washrooms, the dining halls, the yards. Their presence was menacing. Gone were the days of relaxed supervision when the armed guards were mostly out of sight. I felt sorry for this coercive atmosphere and held myself inwardly responsible for it.

Very soon following this incidence, Bukarin called me to his office. He expressed his regret for what had happened. I detected great concern in his voice.

"We must never let this happen again," he said sternly. I thought he would show concern for me, but as I soon realized, it was only concern for himself and the reputation of his administration when he said, "I am certain of it that informal reports have already been received by Moscow. News travels fast and in clandestine ways. I am working on my report now. It needs to be sent off speedily otherwise it will be a strike against me. I called you here to forbid you to ever enter the prisoners' quarters again. I do not want you to be seen any more so that there will be no repeat of this upheaval. Also, do not ask me for any more improvements at this point. The prisoners must be punished and be more strictly guarded than before. The showing of arms will keep them in check. I am sorry for the recent events. You have been a good man for us to this point. We need to wait and see what will happen. In time, we may see an abatement of the problem, but then it may never go away."

He said all of this with bureaucratic weightiness and with little emotion in his voice. It became clear to me that the only skins that really mattered to him were his and those of his fellow administrators.

While I pursued my train of thought, I heard Bukarin say with little more feeling than was in his previous speech, "I am sorry for the situation, Janos, and for you. You have been a great asset to us so far. But now we must see. I am truly sorry, young man. Please avoid contact with the prisoners for now."

With those rather kind but non-committal words I knew I was dismissed. Bukarin suddenly became engrossed in the report lying on the desk in front of him.

I formally said, "Thank you for your trust, Commissar Bukarin."

He glanced up at me briefly, smiled, and nodded his head, while I turned slowly away from him and left his office.

Outside in the hall, Andrei was waiting for me. His open face expressed such concern and compassion as I had not seen in anyone in a long time. He grabbed my hand and whispered, "I am so sorry, buddy. You were doing so well. Let me know whether I can do anything for you. We should find some way to talk privately."

He let my hand go and walked past me. I knew he also had to protect himself. Everyone had to protect himself. But at least, he seemed to be a real friend. It showed in his face. The only friend I had left.

24

Return to Hard Labor

In the morning of a cold and crisp early winter day and after a long sleepless night, my mind was made up. The past months had ticked away uneventfully. I had no more contact with my fellow prisoners. Nothing could have occurred in that respect. I stuck to Bukarin's request faithfully. I didn't even go near the prisoners' quarters. My life had also become uneventful. No more guard training, no more indoctrination sessions. All had been suspended indefinitely. I still retained my outward status, my uniform and my office, but it now felt just like another form of imprisonment. I was still well fed, and, ironically, my full physical strength and vitality had returned. Bukarin and Bolkov were always friendly, but it was an even, impenetrable friendliness worn like a mask behind which remained hidden the real emotions and the real motives and intentions.

Once I heard the faintest knock on my door in the middle of the night. Sleeping fitfully night after night since the dreadful event in the mess hall, I got up and opened the door. It was Andrei who begged me to let him in. I waved him in.

"I am sorry, Andrei, but this is a very foolish thing you are doing visiting someone who has been ostracized twice."

I knew I spoke the truth, for I had nowhere to go. The prison administration had ostracized me just as much as my fellow prisoners had.

The difference was just a matter of degree. I could not continue to hold on to what I was able to build for myself in this camp; and, slowly, the conviction had grown in me that I must leave this camp.

"Janos, I know I am foolish, but I must let you know things will improve, just wait and see."

"No they won't, Andrei. They will only deteriorate more over time. I already know what I must do, " I said very calmly.

I realized how good it was that Andrei had come. I could finally verbalize what had been brewing in me for weeks now—a decision that was at first like an unspeakable secret. Talking about it now and bringing it to light, I suddenly knew, was the final step before making it reality.

"You should do nothing. The situation will improve over time, believe me. It is firmly in the hand of the camp administration. I could bet you would now be able to move around among the prisoners unassaulted."

"I know I could, Andrei, but at what price? Only at the price of fierce repression. Neither I nor the administration are willing to have that happen. But I thank you, dear friend, for trying to give me hope."

"I am not trying to instill hope. This is how it's going to be: the negative sentiments towards you will blow over. The prison population will change. The administration is only waiting for that and is biding its time. You will be fully reinstated, believe me. Don't you think I know at least just a little bit what is happening? Janos be patient."

"I am sorry, Andrei, I can't anymore. I have resolved to request a transfer to full prisoner status in another camp. Please, understand me, Andrei. I need to do this for myself to find peace no matter what will become of me." I had spoken the last sentences in a pleading manner, hoping that Andrei would understand how resolved I was. He did not let me down.

"Janos, pardon me, but I think you are now foolish. However, I also know you well enough that I realize your resolve is strong and has, no doubt, slowly matured within you over the past few months. To be very honest with you, I know in my heart that you will be taking this step. The only thing I want you to know is that I am your friend. I will try in my little ways to help you. Though I am just at the beginning of my career and have not much status, I will find ways to keep in touch with you. Since yesterday, I am not Bukarin's driver any more, but have been promoted to his personal assistant."

Suddenly I realized how wonderful this relationship was and how fortunate I had been of meeting Andrei. Even if he could never so much as influence in the slightest way my impending fate for the better, I was immensely grateful for his friendship. He had spoken those soothing words rapidly and with much feeling, and as I looked into his face in the semi-darkness, I thought I could detect the mingled emotions of concern and understanding. I impulsively embraced Andrei. He slung his arms around me keeping a tight grip on me. We stood there for a long time holding each other in the candle lit semi-darkness like two shipwrecked sailors knowing they are about to drown.

Andrei left shortly thereafter, and I knew that in the morning I had to ask for a meeting with Bukarin as soon as possible. The meeting was granted the same day. As I stepped into Bukarin's office with a hint of reticence, he looked up from his desk at that moment. He must have noticed my momentary hesitation for he immediately started in.

"Janos, how are you? I know this is a difficult period for you, but we hope the atmosphere will change, and in time you will be as productive as before."

So I was right and Andrei was wrong! The word 'hope' in Bukarin's statement had lunged out at me. It sounded very vague in comparison to Andrei's affirmation last night that things 'will' change.

Then, suddenly, and even before I had finished my thoughts, I heard myself say quite formally, "Commissar Bukarin, I am here to request a change to full prisoner status in another camp. I am very sorry to say that I am no longer able to fulfill the position you have so kindly assigned to me. I will always be grateful for the trust you invested in me. But I am firmly resolved that I must leave."

I had no idea what reaction I would get. It could have ranged anywhere from understanding, regret, disbelief, relief, to hostility. During the moments I had spoken, Bukarin had averted his eyes and fixed them on his desk. His hands were firmly planted on the edge of the desk in front of him with his thumbs curled under and his elbows spread out to the sides. It looked to me as if he were steadying himself. I kept my eyes on him. When I stopped speaking, an awkward silence arose between us. Bukarin made no move, and I dared not start up again. But I still kept on looking at him. It seemed like he was wrestling with something inside of him. I could not imagine what thoughts and emotions turned over in his mind during those moments. Then he looked up, his face unreadable, his eyes narrowed down to slits. He studied my face for some time while I kept my gaze directed steadily at him. We were like two animals locked in a standoff that could erupt sooner or later into a clash of physical force against physical force, especially if one showed the slightest weakness. But since I held his gaze under his critical inspection, he finally let go.

"Janos, I think you are resolved but I am certain you have not begun to fathom what this request will mean. You will experience a change that may break your spirit. Your request will have to go to Moscow. They will not look at it lightly or kindly. They will make the decision, not I, where you will be placed. I have no more to say in this matter. All strikes are against you in this society once you abandon your course. I know you don't know what you are doing, but you will do it anyway, is that right?"

"Yes, that is right, Sir."

"Janos, Janos, I wish it hadn't come to this," he said with traces of sadness and regret in his voice. But he wasn't a man who would cave in to emotions. He would not have gained the position he had if he had let emotions reign. Momentarily, he composed himself, and said with full show of his authority and bureaucratic efficiency, "I will present your case to Moscow immediately. A decision for your transfer could come within one week. Of all cases, one such as yours will be processed speedily." And after a slight pause, he added, "Is there anything else you want to say?"

His last words sounded a little as if he were begging for a change of my mind. It appeared to me that I could have changed my mind at that point, and he would have accepted that change. I know I wanted to cave in at that moment, but I couldn't let it happen.

"No, Sir, there is nothing else I have to say except thank you from my heart for your trust, your fairness, and the experience you have given me."

He just sat there and nodded. "That's it then, Janos. I'll be contacting you."

With that I knew I was dismissed. It broke my heart that we could have gone from the initial, profusely cordial reception when I returned from the course to this sad, officious parting.

25

Lost   Connections

The bus lumbered north at first for quite a distance, but then it changed
course, veered straight east and followed the edge of a scrubby forest for a
while until it entered a vast plain, the steppe country. It was two hundred
miles to my destination. An armed guard had boarded the bus with me and sat
directly behind me. He had not spoken to me. He just kept a watchful
distance. The outlook for my future was dim, at least from the vantage point
of that bus journey.

In the two weeks it had taken to obtain the directions from Moscow and to
send me on my way, winter had come on with icy winds blasting in from the
east. There was plenty of ice but no snow yet. At least at Dom Sovieta they
had provided me with the prisoner's quilted winter suit, the fleece-lined cap,
heavy rubber boots, and gloves. These garments alone could not assure my
survival, but they would at least give me a chance. I must admit they had
outfitted me well. I did not see Bukarin again, not since the last, fateful
meeting with him. Also Bolkov had kept his distance. It was as if they both
had disappeared from the camp. It was a sad state of affairs. They had
completely distanced themselves from me. Bukarin apparently had given the
assignment to Andrei to get me ready for my transfer. Andrei had provided
me with clothing above and beyond what he was supposed to give me.
Somehow he had procured a second set of winter underwear, hand-knitted
woolen glove liners, and woolen socks. I was so moved when I found these

treasures in my bundle of clothing that I spontaneously burst into tears for I knew exactly what should have been issued to me. These small fortunes that came to me among the large misfortunes that life had been dealing me helped in keeping my hope alive. There had not been another chance to meet privately with Andrei like we did that night in my office. But he had hidden a note in my bundle that simply read:

Dear Janos,

When all of these dreadful abominations of war, these prison camps, have been shut down, and I can be reasonably certain that you are a free man again, I will search for you until I find you. Always remember my friend, life itself is change and that is the certainty and hope we have. My thoughts will be with you until then, always.
Your friend,
Andrei.

If Andrei harbors this kind of hope then I will too. This thought later became a steady companion of mine that never left me until the end of my travails. But as we traversed this bleak and barren landscape, I couldn't avoid thinking of my destination. I was on the way to a coalmining prison camp, one of the worst places of incarceration. Besides Siberia, we prisoners had always dreaded to be sent to a coalmining camp. We thought of it as one of the worst kinds of punishment. We had always counted ourselves lucky to be at Dom Sovieta. It was an easy life in comparison to what awaited me in the coalmine. Dom Sovieta I just left afforded us to be in town on construction sites or out in the fields and forests. It afforded us sunshine and rain and the sky above. From now on I was going to be toiling in dark tunnels like a mole under a sunny field of corn.

As I sat on that bare and drafty bus rattling east, thoughts entered and exited my mind in ever more rapid succession for I was leaving what had been the semblance of a home for more than a year and a half. I was leaving behind friends and enemies and the spirits of the departed who had been so good to me. Would anyone be brave enough to follow me to that Godforsaken hole in the earth I was about to be heading into? Would Mei Chi still make her life-promoting appearances? And would the spirit of Anna still surround me as it had in every part of that monstrous building? And what about Walter, Bukarin, Bolkov, and Andrei? I had already forgiven Walter despite the pain and anguish he had caused. It had suddenly come to me like a revelation that he was just a cog in the vast machinery of life fulfilling its part as we all do, that he was just a pawn on the great chessboard of life fulfilling the moves that the game held in store for him. Though I never laid eyes on him again, I had made peace with him in my heart and soul even before I left Dom Sovieta. It felt good for at one time he had given me life when I was on the brink of death. And he had instilled confidence in me. I could never forget that. And who knows how his contradictory spirit would continue to have an influence on my life. Through Andrei I had found out that the administration had extracted the truth from other prisoners about Walter's leadership in the standoff against me. They had not punished him beyond a few days in solitary confinement. But they were keeping a close watch on him. Any more agitation on his part and he would be removed. I sat on that bus hoping that he could restrain his temper and loosen his inflexible beliefs. It was much to hope for, but I wanted him to survive.

26

Camp Cherminsk

Long before we reached the new camp at the outskirts of Cherminsk, I saw an enormous structure looming at a great distance. It mesmerized me for it looked like a black monster rearing up on its hind legs on the plain's horizon and growing larger by the minute. We were heading straight towards it. Two massive columns pointed heavenward like two giant horns belching angry, black clouds into the gray winter sky. The pervasive easterly winds, driving the soot-laden clouds westward, had flattened them into dark bands that stretched in a broad swath across the sky as far as the eye could see. Nothing else besides this spewing giant could be distinguished. Whatever it was, factory or power plant, in my state of mind this dark monster of the desolate plain rose before me like an ominous symbol of what might be awaiting me— darkness, exploitation, decline, and, perhaps, death. My thoughts were full of doom in those moments and reached the lowest point in my prison experience. For the first time since I had stood before Bukarin with my unexpected request, I suddenly understood what he had said about not knowing what I was doing. His words now reverberated clearly in my mind in the solitude of this journey into the unknown. They kept me tightly in their grip. Now I also understood why at the very end of our exchange he had given me one more chance to reconsider for 'Is there anything more you want to say?' he had asked me. I now remembered clearly that his words seemed to beg for a change of mind, and I found myself inwardly crying out: what have

I done to myself? In this light, the certainty of my resolve as I had stood before Bukarin seemed, indeed, foolish and rash.

I sank to such depths of despair that I hardly noticed the small town moving into view with its low and nondescript skyline. And beyond it, on its eastern side and towering over it, stood the giant, but viewed from this short distance, quite ordinary power plant that had menaced me for over an hour with its ominous darkness. Judging from its size I knew it must have been supplying a vast region with electricity, and I realized that my impending destiny was to become its slave to help fuel an insatiable appetite.

The bus came to a halt abruptly at a drab city square devoid of trees and ringed by bleak and plain one-story buildings.

"Get up and move," a voice sounded gruffly at my back.

This voice jolted me immediately out of my thoughts. I felt a slight prod at the back of my head like a gun's nozzle poking me. I jumped up, moved off the bus, and waited at the foot of the stairs for the guard.

"Let's go, and stay at my side," he said in the same gruff voice without looking at me, "and don't make any weird moves, I am ordered to shoot."

I stayed at his side and tried to maintain the same hurried pace he was setting. We walked through town, past more drab, low buildings towards its eastern fringe, I guessed, for we were heading in the direction of the power plant. A low mountain range, half shrouded in winter haze, was now barely visible in the distance beyond the city and the power plant. The wind was icy. It attacked our faces mercilessly with thousands of tiny needles. At last we walked down a long wide street at the end of which I could see, I thought, the largest building in town. It had four stories and was surrounded by a high fence with barbed wire coils on top.

All the city streets we passed had been virtually empty. We had arrived in the early afternoon, probably around two o'clock. The people must have been at work or huddled in their houses or flats out of the cold. We passed very few shops, and the ones we saw had empty windows hidden behind iron bars. I thought it was the most unappealing town I had ever seen, dismal in comparison to Rodonski, and I could not imagine what kind of life could thrive in this town. The walls of buildings and houses were tinged in a dirty gray, no matter what their original color was. Everything seemed makeshift and without design, and it appeared as if the power plant had spawned this town of dirty houses when it was built maybe twenty years ago.

The large roughly finished concrete building we had approached as we hurried down the long street, I now recognized as the prison camp. We ran right into its heavily fortified fence, and walked alongside it for a while until we came to a gate on its southern side. Two armed men were guarding it. We were still ten meters away from the gate when my guard commanded me to stop and wait there. I immediately stopped while he continued on to speak with the two guards while still keeping an eye on me. The three put their heads together and talked for a while, my guard glancing over in my direction periodically. It appeared as if they knew each other. There was an air of camaraderie about them as they huddled close together. I thought I could hear them joke and snicker for the time they stood together. I envied them their intimacy, and I realized how alone I now was. Eventually my guard turned around and waved me over. While they were talking I had started jumping up and down to keep my feet warm in the icy, penetrating cold. Frostbite was what we always feared most in winter, for it could mean in its severe stage the loss of a limb and at its worst the loss of one's life.

We traversed the yard and stepping up to the building, the guard pushed me without a word through a door into some sort of office. After that he left quickly. The young clerk behind a desk in an otherwise bare room hardly looked up at me. What followed was no reception, just an impersonal camp registration during which I had nothing to do but to stand there. Not a single question was asked. While I stood and waited, the clerk worked off some sort of document the guard had flicked on his desk before he disappeared. In a short while he asked me to step into the next room where another clerk took over. His main task was to sew a number patch on my suit which he did there and then after I had relinquished my suit to him. From here on out I became again just another number.

As the clerk later walked me up the stairs to the second floor, he assigned a bunk to me and commanded me in broken German to wait until dinner assembly time at six in the evening. I dared not tell him I could speak Russian for fear that I would stand out among the prisoners before I even settled into this camp and before I had the chance to test its atmosphere. My resolve was to fit in as inconspicuously as possible and to make no waves. Of course, I did not know what the document had said. Would it alert the camp administration to my former position? Would I be marked from the moment I got there? Afterwards I was never able to find out what was going on behind the scenes and what they knew. They left me basically alone even after the change came. All I hoped for during these initial moments at this camp was that I would be allowed to be a prisoner without a past and with no future, someone who would just be allowed to do his duty. With this resolution I sank onto my bunk right after the clerk left. The bus ride and my intense thinking had exhausted me. It was a long time yet until six o'clock.

I must have drifted off to sleep for I suddenly felt someone pushing me.

"Get up and follow me down to the mess hall." I was startled, and for a moment I did not know where I was. I blinked at the man bending over me. By his clothing, I recognized him as a prisoner.

"I guess you just arrived," he continued, "My name is Gustav, and I have been here for a little over a year. It's a hard life and it's an impersonal atmosphere. Don't expect to make any friends here. Everyone is looking out for himself, trying to save his own skin. But, mostly, the men are exhausted when they come off their long shifts. They just can't be bothered to pay attention to their fellow inmates. Just wanted to let you know so you won't get your expectations up. Face reality right away, man, and you'll be better off."

With those words, spoken hastily and with low energy, he hurried down the stairs, and I followed him with reticence into the mess hall.

There must have been already three hundred men assembled on long tables that spread clear across that cavernous hall. And I guessed this hall took in at least half the bottom floor of the building. At the bottom of the steps I hesitated. I stood there lost and in a state of bewilderment while other prisoners in droves came down the stairs rushing around and past me towards their tables. After the initial encounter, Gustav had gone ahead of me and never looked back to see whether I was following. I didn't even have time to tell him my name. I suppose he wasn't interested.

As I later learned about the meal procedures, everyone had to be seated and everyone had to be in his seat before prisoners were allowed to form long lines at the food counter. If a chair was empty, the prisoner seated next to it had to raise his hand and report the empty chair to the closest guard. Feeding could not start until it was determined who the missing prisoner was, where he was, or what had happened to him. If we were unlucky an empty seat could mean a long delay in getting our food. If we were very unlucky, as it sometimes happened, it could mean lukewarm or cold food. Prisoners always pressured each other to be on time for meals. Every day the men of a different table had to form the first food line. To be in the first line was coveted. It meant a little more food, for the servers were more generous at the beginning as there was still plenty of food in the containers. It was a bad day when one's table was last. The sequence in which the tables lined up never changed. It assured us that we had the chance of being first and inevitably that we were periodically last.

As I was standing there in a daze at the bottom of the stairs and not knowing where to go and where to sit, someone tugged at my sleeve. I spun around and faced another Russian clerk. He too spoke in broken German.

"Come with me. You new. I get you seat. Remember always same seat every day. Wait until your table goes for food. Here is your spoon. Do not lose," he impressed on me.

I followed him to a table in the middle of the hall. I guessed there must have been thirty tables in that long, rectangular hall with twenty men at each table. When I got my seat, I was reminded once more.

"Always same seat."

"Yes, I will remember."

"Someone will see you after meal with work assignment."

He was gone before I could ask a question. Everything appeared to happen spontaneously in this camp as if unintended. Yet later I realized that everything was minutely organized. Someone apparently always knew where you were or what you did. The higher camp administration remained virtually invisible. But a cadre of clerks and guards watched our every move. This camp must have been quite easy to run for most of the prisoners were worked to the bone. In their exhausted state, they had no energy left for demanding changes or starting an agitation of any kind. I doubted that Walter could have ever succeeded in exerting the kind of influence over his fellow prisoners in this coal mining camp that he was able to carry out at Dom Sovieta.

Once a week we had to see the camp doctor. The procedure was simple. We had to strip in one room and then enter the doctor's room stark naked. He just briefly looked at us as we stood before him. I was sent on into the next room every time he saw me. He said nothing, just looked me over front and back, and waved me on. And yet, I knew, I steadily lost weight while I was working in the mine. Other prisoners must have met a different fate during those examinations for later I noticed, when I became familiar with the men around me, that some periodically disappeared and newcomers took their place.

That first night I was there, it must have been one of the best meal times. No number was missing that evening and we got our rations quickly—a thick vegetable soup with an occasional lump of fatty meat, water, and two kilos of bread. I was amazed about the substantial fare. They must be extracting much more labor out of these assembled men than they ever did at Dom Sovieta I thought to myself. This was a more solid meal than I had ever received since I entered the prison system. We ate in silence. At the end of the meal, the hall emptied as rapidly as it had filled. I sat there without making a move and without knowing what to do next. Then suddenly I felt a tap on my shoulder and heard a voice behind me saying, "You are prisoner 864271." I looked up into this young guard's closed and officious face, and nodded.

"Come with me. I will tell you about your work assignment." He spoke German well. He barely had an accent. We traversed the hall and entered a small room at its end near the steps I had descended earlier.

"You will start work tomorrow morning. Show up in this hall at three for the morning meal. Get up as soon as you hear the bell and come down as soon as you can. It's best to follow our orders promptly. If you make no waves, things will go smoothly for you. You will have fifteen minutes for your meal. It's best to be among the first at the food counter. At three thirty sharp step out into the yard where the work groups will be assembled. Be there on time and no one will have to wait. You will work a sixteen-hour shift in the mine, and you will get thirty-two hours off after every shift. Part of the mine has had a shutdown because of flooding, and part of the main entry shaft near this camp has collapsed. You will be marched to a secondary entry shaft. It will take an hour. A shovel or a pick axe and a rubberized coverall that you will wear over your winter suit will be issued to you when you get down into the mine. Be on time, mind your own business, and you will be all right."

After this last sentence, I knew the guard was done with giving me instructions. I bowed my head slightly and thanked him and let him know that I understood. I turned on my heels, left the room, and walked upstairs.

My bunk felt like a sanctuary. No one said anything to me after I entered the sleeping quarters; no acknowledgements of the new person in the room took place. It seemed like everyone had already gone to sleep or was pretending to be asleep. I welcomed the silence and anonymity on that first evening. As I lay down my thoughts roved far and wide. They touched on everyone that evening who had ever been dear to me; and as a I dozed off and fell into a half sleep, a parade of loved ones ensued—childhood friends, my family, Effie, Mei Chi, Anna, Bukarin, Solkow, and Andrei. Even Walter was part of the line-up. I remember thinking how happy I was that he had decided to come too. They formed such a wonderful line-up, all of them together like that. They all looked their very best, their faces smiling. Holding their arms stretched out towards me, they tried to touch me but their arms were too short. No matter how much they stretched them, they could not reach me as they strode past. I wanted them desperately to touch me, but they couldn't. And I wanted to get closer to them, but I couldn't either. I remember thinking how happy I was to see them all, how much they meant to me, and how sad I was at the same time that I could not reach them. Nevertheless, I couldn't get enough. The parade started over and over again but I could not make contact even though I strained towards them. It all stopped abruptly when a shrill sound intruded and made all these wonderful people disappear. Then I realized I had woken up to the morning bell.

I was the first prisoner in the black yard at 3:30 a.m. None of the guards were there yet. I almost felt like a fool being so anxious to be on time. But within a few moments the yard started filling up with both guards and prisoners and the spotlights were turned on. I could sense everyone was anxious to start moving on that stabbing cold morning. A wind was already blowing and that made it even colder. The guards, no doubt thinking of themselves, did not tarry. They divided us into work groups—sixty men in each group in formation of fifteen rows with four men abreast. Two armed guards lead and two guards followed each group. The marching pace set by the leading guards as soon as we got past the gate was so fast that we soon broke out in a sweat despite the icy cold. We marched, what seemed to me like an eternity. But the guard who briefed me had said last night it was only one hour. Several times during our march, I tried to glance at the men on either side of me hoping that they would at least acknowledge me. After all, we were comrades in suffering and oppression. But I never succeeded in having either my right or left marching partner look at me. They stared sternly straight ahead until we reached the mine entrance.

The guards who had marched us for an hour left us once we reached the low huts clustered around the mine entrance. They crowded into one of the huts where a fire was probably blazing. Mine guards quickly took over and directed us towards the entrance hut. Twenty men at a time were quickly shoved onto a steel platform dangling from steel cables. As that platform descended into the vertical shaft that seemed like an abyss to me, another one ascended at the same speed to the top to pick up more men. The two platforms worked in tandem. The platforms were not enclosed except with a rough framework of steel bars. We were tightly crowded together. The men who formed the perimeter of the group hung on to the steel bars. The men at the core were held in place and were so tightly squeezed together by the outer ring of men that they did not have to hold on to anything. Being part of the group's perimeter, I braced myself against the steel bars and hung on for dear life. On my side, there were just inches to spare between the descending platform and the sheer rock walls. Even though it was pitch black in that shaft, I could sense and smell the moist odorous rock wall as we sped past. If the inner core of men had pushed outward, it could have been dangerous for the men who formed the outer ring. Their heads or arms could have been pushed partially through the bars and been dragged along the rough rock wall. I saw the danger in that immediately. I braced myself against the steel even more firmly than before and with my back pushed inward towards the core of men. I knew I would never allow myself again to be at the perimeter after that first descent.

Before we stepped onto the platform, I recognized Gustav as one of the men in our group. I did not think he noticed me being bundled up the way I was. I stationed myself next to him hoping that I could extract some information from him. He was my only hope to gain some pre-knowledge.

As we descended down into the blackness, I ventured in a whisper, "Gustav, it's Janos, the new guy. Remember? I need to talk to you. I have no idea what we are going into."

"What do you mean? We are going into a coalmine, that's all."

"I mean I have never been near a coalmine, let alone entered one. How far are we going down? What work will we do?"

"The platform will take us to 200 meters. From there we will have to traverse a steep cross shaft that will get us down to the main shaft at 500 meters. It will be treacherous going. Water is flowing down the cross shaft like a babbling mountain brook. It's low and narrow down there until we get to the large horizontal shaft of the main mine. That's where they will assign the work. There are only four kinds of work you can be assigned to: knock the coal loose with a pickaxe, shovel the coal onto the trolleys, push the trolleys up to the vertical exit shaft and onto the platforms, or you can be assigned to work in the new section of the shaft. The latter is the easiest but also the most dangerous work. It's where they blast out the new extensions of the existing shafts. You could be assigned to clearing the rock or you might be assigned to the bracing of the new section with heavy timbers. The danger in working in that newly blasted area is a cave-in. We have lost men there several times this past year; horribly crushed to death, almost beyond recognition. But then you could be lucky and not be one of them. The good part is that the area is well lit and you don't have to suck in that coal dust that you get with pick and shovel which destroys your lungs. And the work in the new section is rather slow, for the blasting has to be done carefully and in small increments. They can't afford to blast the hell out of this mine. Once these old tunnels start rocking, the whole vast honeycombed underground might collapse, and then God help us."

I could hardly believe Gustav had given off all that information in no time and in a breathless manner. I finally had a clearer picture of what I was getting into. I hadn't expected it to be good, for I had my premonitions already on my way to this camp.

"Thanks, Gustav, for the info. I appreciate your clueing me in. I had no idea what's ahead of me."

"You won't be green very long, I'll guarantee you that."

With that rather caustic prognosis, Gustav settled back into his silence. I still wanted to ask how he managed to survive for over a year, but I could sense that he didn't want to talk anymore. He seemed out of breath for I heard him suck in the cold, damp air in short, anxious gulps like one who fears he might suffocate. Yet I was grateful to him that he had given me that much. I thought I would draw him out later for some more information, perhaps after we got back to our bunks.

The platform jerked to an abrupt halt, and the men scrambled off immediately. Seconds later the platform lifted up and was gone. I kept close to Gustav because I had no idea what we would do next, yet I did not dare talk to him again. No one spoke. The area where we had gotten off the platform was dimly lit. Some of the men in front of me started disappearing into a shaft single file. I thought it must be the low and narrow cross shaft that would take us to the main shaft. Before I knew it, I was shoved into that shaft by the men in back of me. I could barely see. The light was dim. I had to feel my way along the rock wall. Beneath my feet, the rocky ground sloped steeply downward. Water gurgled under me. I had to tread carefully and keep my wits about me so that I wouldn't slip and fall. And then an intense fear suddenly arose in me. If I fell now no one would stop. The men would just keep going and trampling right over me. I saw my end right there and then in that miserable narrow and dark passage. There would be no help, no compassion, no looking out for one another. Then suddenly thoughts like electrifying currents jolted life back into me: I must not let these conditions get the better of me; I have survived until now and I will get through this; if Gustav could why couldn't I? From then on I felt my way down the narrow passage with great care, and after twenty minutes, or was it half an hour? our group of twenty spilled into a brightly lit cavernous underground hall. Looking around I could see high and wide passages leading off in different directions. Over to one side guards stood handing out the work equipment. Again I had no idea what to do. I watched the men going up to the guards and asking for this or that tool. Some got what they wanted, others didn't and had to take what was given to them. I couldn't figure out how it worked so I stood back. A guard who had surveyed our group came over to me.

"You new?" he asked.

I nodded.

"Take pickaxe. You will knock coal out of rock wall. Two weeks. After that you can request change. Go over to group of men in back of you. They will take you to work site."

I did as I was asked. I took the coverall and the tool and joined the group of men in back of me.

I toiled all day in a hole in the rock wall in one of the newly timber-braced shafts. I don't know how long I had toiled knocking black, glistening lumps of coal out of the rock. Sometimes I was on my knees and sometimes up on a ladder as I kept picking away with my mind dead all the time. And then I came to a point when I could do no more. Feeling utterly exhausted, I sat down on the ground. I held my head in my hands and tears started streaming out of my eyes like springs activated by a vast well of grief inside me. Oh, mother and father, how can I get through this? Then someone tapped me on the shoulder.

"Don't do this! You must be strong. And you will get used to this. This is just your first day, isn't it? It hits us all like that at first. Come now. Get up. It's almost time for our meal break."

I looked up into a blackened face. Only the glistening white of the eyes stood out. That coal black face was so surreal a sight that I thought for a moment I had descended into Dante's Inferno.

"Snap out of it, man. I tell you. Don't let it get the better of you."

These words did snap me out of my state. I nodded and got up. As I stood face to face with this blackened man, I realized that I must have looked even stranger with my black face furrowed with light streaks that the tears must have left on my cheeks.

"Thanks for talking to me. It helps. By the way, my name is Janos."

"I'm Helmut. Don't thank me. I just remembered how I felt at the beginning."

At that moment a bell shrilled through the underground passages.

"Let's go have something to eat. Follow me." Helmut led the way back to the cavernous room.

Somehow I made it back to the camp and my bunk that evening after fourteen hours underground and two hours of marching. I was weary to the bone. I had difficulty getting my clothes off, my hands trembled so badly. But then I stepped into the shower room on the same level as our sleeping quarters. I hadn't seen a shower in years. The cleansing action of the water, it was just luke warm, was a wonderful experience. It felt as if I was being washed clean of that first day's harrowing experience. Even though it couldn't wash away the physical exhaustion, I felt the running water lifting my spirit to a point where I could look forward to the meal, my bunk, and the thirty-two hours I could spend recuperating before I had to descend into that hellhole again.

Eight months I toiled in that mine. Winter turned into spring, spring into summer, summer into fall, but I hardly ever saw daylight. It was dark when we left in the wee hours of the morning under mostly starless skies and dark again when we returned at night. The rest of the time I just ate and slept. The work days came and went like dreaded experiences one has to go through, but then I recuperated every time during those hours and hours of dreamless sleep, almost miraculously. But I was beginning to think of myself more as a robot than a human being. I moved from hacking the coal out of the rock to shoveling the coal onto the trolleys, to pushing the trolleys to the platform that would carry them above ground. Then, one day, the dreadful accident happened as I was working with the trolleys.

It took eight men to pull and push a trolley up a rather steep, narrow shaft to the level of the loading platforms. It was at the end of our work shift. We were to tackle the last trolley for that day. The men were tired and sort of stumbled around with exhaustion. We were eager to get that last trolley up the incline. Everyone strained and did their utmost, I thought. When we were half way up, one of the two men who pushed in back apparently stumbled and fell to the ground. The other man let go of the trolley to help the fallen man. With two men off the trolley, the six of us pulling with ropes in front could not hold it for long. It started slipping down hill. Soon, the six of us couldn't hang on to the trolley any longer, and, suddenly, it got away. The men in its path, poor guys, must have realized they were in deep trouble. The one who had helped the fallen man was able to get him to his feet. They started running down the narrow passage. There was nowhere to go but down. But they couldn't outrun the trolley. With its heavy load it picked up speed fast. And then the horrifying thing happened. The six of us stood there powerless. Even before the trolley reached them, the two men racing down the tracks stumbled and fell, and the iron trolley went right over them. As the trolley raced out of the narrow shaft into the main cross shaft, it missed the curve, jumped off the track, and slammed head on into a rock wall. It crushed a third worker who was down below in the wrong place at the wrong time and virtually flattened him against that wall.

Guards who had seen the trolley shoot out of the shaft sounded the alarm immediately. And suddenly swarms of men congregated around the accident site down below us. It was a dreadful sight—three men crushed into pulp and killed instantly. In those heart-rending moments, a wave of icy coldness swept over me, and I slowly felt my whole being turn into a column of ice. I felt neither pain, nor guilt, nor dread, nor horror. It was as if I, too, had ceased to exist. I could not move from the spot like the others, but I could see everything before my mind's eye. The men, at our trolley, who had run down to the accident scene, came back later and dragged me virtually all the way back to the platform that lifted us out of this terrifying place. I realized then fully how incredibly fragile the silken thread is that tethers us to life.

In the aftermath of that accident, no inquiry took place and the remains of the men were handled by the administration. We, their work mates, were left with the sadness, the guilt, the recriminations, and the feeling that we could have done better. I came to suspect that the three men were being rapidly replaced, for this camp, associated with the power plant, must have had the highest priority in keeping its prison population constant. I had noticed that there was hardly ever an empty seat in our mess hall and new faces appeared in our sleeping quarters regularly. Everything worked in perfect harmony: in came the men and out came the coal to keep the wires humming and the smoke stacks belching their black clouds that blanketed everything for miles around with a gray soot. Even the pure snow in winter as it fell from the sky and threw a soft white blanket over the landscape was turned into a dirty gray cover in no time.

After three months I asked for work in the new tunnels that were pushed ever deeper into the ground in a desperate endeavor to produce more coal in a mine that seemed close to being exhausted. I remembered Gustav saying the work was dangerous but that it had its definite benefits. I kept on losing weight because of the hard, physical work it took to produce the coal. The weight loss was a constant source of worry for me. In the blasting area the work would be slow, precise, and relatively clean. I would be able to preserve my energy at least somewhat. I also dreaded the coal dust that had already invaded Gustav's lungs like an insidious, slowly but steadily advancing menace. I hated the black dust that invaded every pore of my face, scalp, and neck. No matter how much I scrubbed these parts, I could not rid them of a grayish tinge. In those days as I contemplated the switch, I felt I was entering into a desperate gamble with Death, the outcome of which might have very well been in his favor.

The gamble in the end paid off not for him but for me. Five months I worked in the blasting area without a major tragic incidence. There were small injuries because of falling rocks but no cave-ins. Over that time period, I was certain I saved my lungs. I definitely stabilized my weight, and cleared my skin. I thought I was actively saving my life because of the new work I did, but in the end it was really saved because of forces and people working for me I could have never dreamed of.

I was lying in my bunk in one of those deep, dreamless states when I was persistently shaken awake. It must have taken quite some time to rouse me from sleep. And even after I had awoken I still seemed like someone who had lost his hearing and his power of comprehension.

"Get dressed," the young man who had shaken me said calmly. "I'll be back in ten minutes. I expect you to be ready."

I suddenly recognized that voice and the fluent German it spoke. As I looked up into the young man's face I recognized the guard who had informed me about my work assignment eight months ago. Even before I finished contemplating the event of that first day in the camp, the guard was gone. Now I was wide-awake. Something special must have happened! No one would wake me during my thirty-two hours of rest unless it was very important. We were never woken up except for meals. We were too valuable a tool for producing the coal. They knew we were useless and couldn't function unless we got our rest.

I was ready in a few minutes. I ran into the washroom and looked at myself in the mirror. I washed my face, wetted my hair, and trimmed my beard a little with the scissors—a gift from Walter—that I kept hidden inside my suit. Since Walter and I had used up his precious razor blades—I don't know how long ago—I always kept my beard trimmed as close to the skin as possible with those coveted scissors he had given me. Even in the darkest hours, to be groomed as much as possible was important to me. This personal ritual dated way back now it seemed, since the time Mei Chi first started caring for me and performed these basic grooming tasks for me with love and affection. I never forgot how high she had lifted my spirits then. After that I did not let myself deteriorate to a point where no one, not even I myself, wanted to look at me. I didn't know why I had those thoughts and memories at that moment.

Possibly I realized deep within myself that I stood before a significant turning point. Then I suddenly realized that I might have lingered too long. I knew time had stood still but for how long I couldn't tell. I began to worry that the guard may have come for me and left because I was not ready for him. I rushed back to my bunk. No one was there. I quickly gathered together my few belongings in a piece of cloth, including Anna's books and writing materials, sacred things to me by now. I had not finished my task but for a few seconds when the guard came back for me.

"Make sure to take everything you have and follow me," he said in a distinctly friendlier manner than I remembered from our first encounter.

I grabbed my bundle and indicated to him that I was ready. It was then, as we descended the stairs, traversed the downstairs mess hall, and headed for a back door that a faint apprehension and tightness arose from the pit of my stomach up into my throat. What if this wake up call would plunge me into something worse than what I had already gone through? Could they have found out about my background and the events that took place at Dom Sovieta? I could hardly imagine what else it could be, but then I remembered the guard's friendly face and I became confused. My reason was telling me something else than my stomach. He unlocked the door we had been heading towards, and we stepped into an entirely different world than the prisoners' quarters. Behind it, and what I had never suspected, were the administrative offices. We walked down a long corridor in which guards and clerks were lingering and chatting. And there were closed doors behind which I suspected sat the powers that directed every minute movement in this dreadful camp. The guard stopped at one of those doors and asked me to enter. He stayed behind. As I stepped into that room, which looked like the offices I had known at Dom Sovieta, I saw in front of me a young, immaculately uniformed prison official.

"Good afternoon, Janos," he said, "I am sorry we had to disturb you, but we have received recommendations for you that we want to implement. My name is Sergei Leskov. I am the deputy director of this camp. Please be seated."

Confusion ran rampant in my mind. I could not believe what was happening and doubted its reality. I had held my hands clasped behind my back during this first and only encounter with Leskov, and I now started bending one of my small fingers until I thought it would snap in two, and I was overcome with pain. I grimaced slightly. Only then did I realize that it was not a dream but that I was wide awake and I sat down as I was asked to do.

177

The deputy director looked at me, it seemed like, with wonder for a short time, and I immediately tried to have my eyes meet his gaze openly and unguarded. His face changed too. It revealed nothing anymore, no emotions, no friendliness, but no unfriendliness either. After what seemed like long moments of silence during which I tried not to show any discomfort, he started to speak and came right to the point.

"Your name is Janos Jablonsky?"

"Yes," I affirmed.

"Upon recommendations of the deputy director of your previous camp, we are going to move you from mine duty to one of our auxiliary workshops that keep our mine and power plant operations supplied with any tool, any piece of machinery, or any repair work that they are in need of. You will work in the metal fabrication and welding workshop on a trial basis for three months. If your skills are such as the recommendation has outlined, you will be able to continue in that line of work," he said in a very formal manner. "We expect you to follow all work rules strictly, and we will watch you closely during your trial period. Your supervisor will report directly to me. The deputy director at Dom Sovieta must know what your skills are, for he says that you have demonstrated exceptional skills. We are very willing to try you out. We are always in need of skilled craftsmen." He spoke in German, and he spoke it fluently.

As soon as Leskov started talking about my skills, my mind started racing back at a desperate speed to my time at Dom Sovieta. In those moments I felt hot and chilled throughout my body in rapid succession for I wanted the change so badly but felt it might be a case of mistaken identity. I was no skilled craftsman and I never quite finished my high school education. The war had thwarted that. I could not imagine who could have recommended me for these improved conditions and, at the same time, put me to the severest test of skills I truly believed I did not possess. My mind ranged over work assignments I had had but none fit the description of work I was asked to perform now. Then, suddenly, when my mind's search had netted barely a skill that would have been sufficient for this new assignment, I remembered Walter's and my officially sanctioned collaboration in the beet peeling machine project. I had learned so much from Walter at that time for the machine involved welding, fashioning precise metal parts out of scrap metal, and fitting pieces together that were barely suited for each other. These tasks required skilled and deft manipulations and sometimes redesign to make the pieces fit. Supplies and parts had been scarce and without possessing an abundant dose of inventiveness, that hardly I but certainly Walter possessed, that machine would have never been built. Walter had all the skills needed; I was trying to acquire some of them at that time. Why had it taken my mind so long to think of this work experience? But that was surely it! I remember thinking at the time when Walter and I had been assigned to the project that the Procurement Director Bolkov must have assumed I was a skilled worker of Walter's caliber and had consequently allowed me to work with Walter. So, it must be his recommendation. But why would he take such an interest in me and since when had he become Deputy Director? In the end, just before my requested transfer to the mining camp, he had completely shunned me. I never saw him after I had lodged my transfer request. He had purposely avoided me. My thoughts now became utterly confused, and I became suddenly aware of my face expressing that confusion. And just then, at that moment, I realized that Director Leskov had stopped talking a while ago. As I looked at him I saw that he was sitting quite still behind his desk watching me.

"What is wrong, Janos? I hope you allow me to call you Janos. Are you not feeling well?" he inquired.

"Oh, no, thank you, I am feeling quite well, ... uh, ... I am just feeling so honored to be called on for this new duty," I said quickly and I added, "I will perform the work to the best of my ability, of that you can be assured, Director Leskov. Thank you very much for giving me a try."

Apparently these were the right words I had spoken.

"Fine, we will see," he said and stood up. "Mikhail, our work assignment assistant, who led you to me, will take over from here on."

I rose also. "Thank you again, Director Leskov." I knew that our conversation had come to an end and that I must leave his office immediately without further statements or questions. I bowed slightly to show deference, turned, and exited his office. Mikhail was, indeed, waiting for me outside.

"Believe me, this has never happened before. Not in my three years of duty here has any prisoner been moved from the mine to the workshops. That simply does not happen. The coal miners stay miners until their strength is spent or until they are moved to another camp. You must have someone very special working for you," he gushed.

Then, as if catching and restraining himself (both he and I knew that he was not supposed to prattle like this in front of a prisoner), he went on in a more formal tone but not cold and unfriendly, "I am going to show you to your sleeping quarters now. You may rest for the remainder of the day. Listen to the dinner bell at six and follow your fellow prisoners down the stairs to the shop workers' mess hall. Ask one of the hall guards where you should sit. In the morning, at 6 a.m. you will again be woken up. Again go down to the mess hall. After your morning meal, at 6:30 a.m. sharp, I will be waiting for you at the door that leads out into the yard. Meet me there and I will take you over to your work assignment. Normally, there will be a workers' count in the yard, but tomorrow, since I will be accompanying you, you will not have to attend the count. In the future you will have to. Any questions?"

"No, not at all, but thank you very much, Mikhail," I replied and I quickly added, "I hope you are not offended that I called you by your name. My name is Janos."

"Oh, no, that's all right," he said hastily and turned to lead me upstairs to my bunk. There was no more talk between us except that he pointed to the bunk that was assigned to me. And then he left.

I sank down on the mattress, my head spinning. I was at once thoroughly elated, apprehensive, and utterly exhausted all at the same time. I closed my eyes and I began repeating over and over again "What luck, what luck, what luck …" until it became a mantra of sorts that lulled me ultimately into a deep dreamless sleep until the dinner bell woke me.

As I opened my eyes, a young man, a fellow prisoner, of slight build, blond, and bright eyed, was looking down at me.

"Hey, I am surprised! How did you get here? Come on let's go down for the grub. By the way, my name is Fritz. What's yours?"

He was not much older than me. His tone was so startlingly different from what I had been used to during my eight months of toiling in the mine that I thought I was still dreaming. But then I looked at Fritz and recognized that he was real and that his face expressed patience and that he was smiling at me.

"Honestly, I don't know, Fritz, how I got here. I have been transferred from the mine to this section. I am still in the process of sorting things out. I can't believe yet that I am here. I am happy to meet you. My name is Janos."

I got up while I spoke to him. I tried to smooth out my clothes (prisoners mostly wore the same clothes day and night) and patted down my hair.

"Go and freshen your face and straighten out your hair in the washroom next door. I'll wait for you here."

"OK, I won't be long."

27

The Hungarians

That evening when Fritz woke me up to take me down to the shop workers' mess hall, a much smaller hall than that of the miners, I carried in me diametrically opposite feelings of elation and fear. I remember thinking: I am done with that Godforsaken mine, that hell hole, forever. Someone has rescued me, some mysterious benefactor. I think I am worthy of this rescue. I will be. But then immediately fear asserted itself: But what if I couldn't do the work? What if my skills proved quite inadequate for the new work assignment? What if there had truly been a mistake? What if I couldn't produce and they would think of me as an impostor and traitor? A worse fate than the one I had just escaped from would await me, no doubt. And so it went incessantly, a stream of opposing feelings. It was devastating to experience such lack of confidence and be so gripped by fear. I couldn't even concentrate on what Fritz was saying right next to me when we were still in the bunkroom and shortly after while we were descending the stairs.

Fritz was very lively and babbled away like a spring brook as if he had known me for a long time. I felt comfortable with him too. What a change from morose Gustav! Yet during those moments between getting up from my bunk and going down for the meal, Fritz's voice only reached my ears faintly, almost unrecognizable as if heard through a long, narrow tunnel. But as we entered the mess hall, I was shortly to snap out of those contentious emotions when Fritz led me over to one of the Russian guards. Fritz simply asked him if this newcomer at his side could sit with him. Without ado, the guard just nodded his okay while hardly looking at us. As unbelievable as it might seem, that exchange was able to jolt me out of my unnerving inner turmoil. I suddenly realized things were different here, possibly more humane, more forgiving, easier going than what my previous experience had conditioned into me for eight solid months. That small difference of a guard not caring where I sat was incredibly good news for me since I had just escaped from the most rigid and oppressive camp rules and camp atmosphere I had ever thought possible. My worries and apprehensions were instantly taken off my shoulders like a heavy winter coat lifted off and left in the hall when entering a warm, inviting home. Right away I felt change taking place inside me. I felt freer than I had for a long time and followed Fritz with eagerness to one of the long tables that seated twenty prisoners each.

"This is where I usually sit. But that doesn't mean that you or I have to sit here. I know all of the guys around us, and we all know each other well. That's why I always stay in this area. Nobody makes me. I will introduce you later. I could go to any table except to the three at the far end of the hall. They are reserved for the Hungarians. As you can see we are almost all assembled, but they, I mean the Hungarians, have not arrived yet. They have an incredible amount of freedom. No rules seem to apply to them. They don't even work much. You will soon be able to observe them. They are definitely being treated different from us. I guess the Russians have more of an affinity for them than for us. You will see. But let's not think about that now. Let's go and get the chow." Fritz had expelled all of this information in one rapid, breathless stream.

"Don't we have to wait our turn?"

"No, as soon as we come in, we can go and get it. Why do you ask?"

"Oh, never mind. It's just that I came from a minutely organized and very repressive section of this camp. I still have to get used to the change. It will take me quite a while."

"Don't worry, you will almost immediately get used to it. According to my experience, people are incredibly adaptable. I have seen much harder times too. I had no problems adjusting almost right away. In comparison to what I have seen, the treatment here is mild if not downright good."

Fritz and I got our food—it was the same thick vegetable stew with fatty lumps of meat as in the mining camp, but here in the shop workers' camp, we only got half the bread ration. Yet, it still seemed a generous ration, for I could not imagine that the shop work would require more than a third of the energy that the coal mining work required. I felt an incredible gratitude welling up in me. If this continued, I could now see myself surviving this desperate prison life.

As Fritz and I sat at the table, in contrast to his chatty self, he ate his food in silence, almost reverently, while I took some time out to look around. This mess hall had a friendlier and lighter appearance than the one next door. Some brightly colored paper scrolls hung on the high walls—scenes that depicted forests and towns, rivers and rolling hills, castles and ranch houses, meadows and fields. They were beautiful to behold—luminous scenes of a most desirable country. I was astounded that art was allowed to flourish here and, at the same time, very happy that I would be able to look at these scrolls every day and draw sustenance from them. I knew instantly that they would help me in holding up my spirit. I needed and desired no more.

Then I counted the long tables and their seats. There were ten tables in this hall and seats for 200 prisoners. But then I remembered that Fritz had said three of these tables were reserved for the Hungarians. Those tables were still empty. As I thought to myself that they might be on a different timetable, I suddenly heard faintly stomping footsteps on the stairs as those of a hundred pairs of boots. At first, these footsteps seemed to come from way up high, possibly the third floor. But in a short while, the men belonging to those stomping boots came spilling down the broad stairs into the hall. They came in pairs, as a tightly knit group close together, not one hundred but sixty of them, mostly young men in civilian clothes. Contrary to us with our uniformly drab and dirty prison clothes, they were so well and freshly dressed and groomed that their sight took my breath away. To me they appeared like a beautiful, long extinguished apparition that for some reason had been resurrected at that moment and literally swept past me.

"Wow, what is this? Am I seeing right?" I turned to Fritz in an outburst of surprise.

He had not lifted his head during the Hungarians' procession. I guessed he was thoroughly used to it, a show he had witnessed morning and night as long as he had been in this camp.

"You'll get used to this, too. They are the privileged ones in this camp. They really don't mean a thing to us because you won't get to know them. They won't let you. They keep to themselves. From all I have experienced, they are a closed, impenetrable group. They are proud and talented, offsprings of the Hungarian upper middle class—sons of professionals like doctors and lawyers. Off limits to us. I don't think they even see us."

I was surprised. Easy-going Fritz was expressing very strong feelings. They seemed feelings of antipathy mixed with envy. I couldn't really tell since I didn't know him well enough.

"This is interesting! Never in my life would I have thought to experience this in a prisoner of war camp for German soldiers."

"Well, they are only prisoners of sorts, mostly collaborators with the German forces in the early stages, at least some of their family members were—their parents, their uncles, who knows. Now that I have heard that Hungary has turned into a communist state, they may not be traitors in the Russians' eyes any longer. They may soon be shipped home. Anyway, that's the gossip around here."

Fritz again became engrossed in his food and stopped talking while my eyes searched out the Hungarians as they sat and chatted spiritedly at their tables. Some had gone over to the food line. I was very curious, for anything different always excited a deep curiosity in me. Most of these young men were tall and slim, dark haired, some with curly hair, some straight. Their hair was well cut and groomed, their faces shaved except for moderately heavy mustaches. They wore knee-high leather boots, like German officers had worn in better days. They wore black, slim-cut pants that were tucked into their boots. Their shirts were mainly white, some light blue or pale yellow, well and full cut, especially in the sleeves. Over their shirts they wore brown leather vests, loosely tailored and open at the front. I loved their liveliness and even felt a twinge of envy when I observed their camaraderie. How I longed to be in a circle of friends. This feeling of group closeness had been denied me for years now.

When the meal was done, I realized how tired I was. The events and emotions of the day had taken their toll. All I longed for was to be left alone, to be able to reflect on all that had happened and all that I had seen.

"Fritz, I am sorry I have to go. I am totally bushed. I need to get some sleep," I excused myself.

"Sure, man, go right ahead. I understand. We'll talk later. Maybe we'll even be in the same shop. And don't worry about anything. You'll be all right."

"By the way, in the morning I'll be picked up by a guard to get situated in the shop. Don't worry about me and don't wait for me."

"OK! Take it easy."

With my excuse and Fritz's understanding words, I quickly licked my spoon clean, stashed it away in my suit, returned my bowl to the counter, and stumbled up the stairs. I really was tired and worn out. Even though I had the urge to use the washroom and thoroughly cleanse myself, I thought it would be better to forgo that ritual until morning. If I dallied in the washroom, the others might come upstairs and prevent me from retiring to my bunk. I could talk to them tomorrow.

As I lay in my bunk moments later, I closed my eyes and released a deep sigh. It came from a place so deep within me that I felt it stripping away all my anxieties about life and death as it slowly worked its way to the surface. Immediately after, I conjured up the images of my loved ones, one by one. I needed to share with them my newly found certainty of life and how there was hope of it to continue on. All of them looked at me lovingly. Andrei came last. He also seemed happy and touched my chest with his right hand where the heart is. With his doing that I fell into a deep sleep.

The next morning, when I reflected on the peaceful moments I experienced just before I went to sleep the previous night, I could not reconcile them with the disturbing dream I had, it seemed, just before waking up—a dream of taunts, rejection, and, I thought, even ridicule. We prisoners were all loaded onto trucks to be taken to an indefinite destination. When it was my turn, there was not a space left in any of the trucks except the one that transported the Hungarians. I was commanded to sit in the back of that truck with them. I felt very reluctant and hesitant to comply. Suddenly a big and gruff-looking guard came over, grabbed a hold of me, lifted me up, and literally shoved me onto that truck. As I landed on their truck, a wild protest ensued from the Hungarians. They jeered and sneered and laughed wildly. Some pushed and pushed until I almost fell off the truck. But I had taken hold of the railing on one side and hung on for dear life. When they couldn't push me off, they all recoiled from me and moved as a tight group into one corner of the truck. They seemed like one solid, impenetrable mass of bodies to me. I felt thoroughly ostracized and yet I yearned to be among them.

At that instant and with those feelings, I woke up with a start, confused and shocked over the treatment I had just received. But when I realized it was just a dream I tried to push the images away but couldn't shake them. I could hardly imagine that the Hungarians, if I ever got to know them, would act that way towards me. I ascribed the images to my continuing state of rejection ever since the incidence instigated by Walter at Dom Sovieta. I told myself to be careful and not let Walter's rejection or Fritz's negative impressions of the Hungarians affect me too much. I knew I needed to keep an open mind and to see for myself what their attitude would be should I ever meet them.

I was now fully awake and realized that the morning bell had not rung yet. A faint glimmer of morning light fell through the uncovered windows. I got up silently and refreshed and groomed myself in the washroom, the ritual I had postponed the night before. Suddenly a surge of energy as I had not known in a long, long time, years maybe, coursed through my body. I was ready for the new experiences the day would bring. I could not believe how I enjoyed myself in the empty washroom. When I finished my tasks, I sneaked silently back to my bunk and rested during those precious moments before the bell rang. I watched the dawn rising for the first time in eight months, and I was looking forward to seeing the sky, the sun, and the trees again without which, I knew, I would have died a slow death, first mentally and spiritually and in the end physically as well.

At 6:30 a.m. sharp, when I rushed through the door leading into the yard, Mikhail was already waiting for me.

"Hi, how are you," he said.

"Fine, excellent I think. I am happy to start this day."

"So let's go."

We crossed the yard in silence and stepped out through a heavy iron gate past the armed guards. We were not checked. It was a cool but clear morning that promised to be a beautiful, sunny day. As we stepped out the gate, I looked to my right and my eyes swept along the tall, chain-link fence with the coils of barbed wire at the top. That fence ran into the distance as far as my eyes could see. It enclosed an enormous prison camp complex.

"This way, Janos!" Mikhail said. He must have sensed my sudden hesitation as I contemplated that prison fence.

"OK, I'm with you. I am just stunned to be outside the prison compound and that it's going to be a beautiful day," I answered rather calmly, but with stirred up emotions just beneath the surface.

We crossed a road that ran along the fence and beyond it, and, hidden among trees, I saw a long row of low metal buildings on the opposite side of the road.

"All those buildings over there house our workshops," Mikhail pointed out as if he had read my mind. "You are assigned to building No. 12. I'll take you to your supervisor, introduce you, and then you'll know where to go every day. Hope you will like your new work," Mikhail sounded friendly, but this was no buddy talk. I realized he kept his distance. I knew officially he had to.

"Thanks, Mikhail. I appreciate everything you do for me. I thank you very much," I responded.

I always felt a twinge of hurt when I detected that coolness, that wall between the other person and me. In fact, I hated the many different walls that separated us from one another, walls thrown up by conditioning, indoctrination, obedience, expedience, or sheer fear. Mikhail and I were about the same age. Why couldn't we dismantle that wall and establish some sort of personal communication. But Mikhail apparently did not want to and I needed to respect his decision.

My train of thought ended suddenly when we arrived at door No. 12. Mikhail went ahead and opened it, stepped in, and I followed. At that point he turned around and said to me, "Listen, things are done differently here than what you have been used to before. We invest a lot of trust in you. You will have freedoms you have not had before. Deal wisely and cautiously with them. I have to warn you. These freedoms are just as easily withdrawn as they were given. Now, I'm about to introduce you to your supervisor. He is a Russian civilian. Both regular Russian workers and prisoners from this camp are working side by side in these shops. Hope you can get used to that. Try to get along with your supervisor and you'll be fine. He is a nice and patient man, a little gruff at times, but he has a good and kind heart. But communication will be difficult for he only speaks broken German. Please be patient and you'll be all right."

"I'm glad to know all this, Mikhail. You can't believe how much I appreciate this information."

"It's good to hear that. I have found, no matter how downtrodden German prisoners are, they still, almost always, adopt an attitude of superiority. I don't like them for that. It won't help them."

"I hear you, Mikhail. Don't worry, my new supervisor and I will get along well because I will work hard at it and I will let him lead."

With the distance Mikhail had been trying to maintain between us, he was, to my surprise, going to slip again briefly through the wall like he had done yesterday. I respected him very much for that. The switch happened in the way he responded to my last remark.

"I am very happy that you have such a good attitude. I was right when I sized you up eight months ago when I first saw you. I sensed you were different than the rest, and I was sorry to see you go into that mine, I really was. I couldn't believe I could have that feeling at the time. Good luck now, Janos! I'll be seeing you around."

Before I could reply, he had turned his back to me, walked on, and I followed him. We walked towards a burly, middle-aged Russian in blue overalls.

Mikhail spoke to him first in Russian, telling him that I was his new worker and that he needed to work closely with me at first. He also said that he thought I was a good man. Of course, without his realizing it, I understood every word he said. Mikhail added that weekly reports had to be sent to Deputy Director Leskov on the work quality I was demonstrating and the general progress I was making. The Russian only nodded. Then Mikhail turned around and introduced us. His name was Ivan Borisenko. He nodded slightly and said, "Welcome," and a few other German phrases of the worst pronunciation and grammar I had heard in a long time. Speaking that language was obviously a struggle for him.

I smiled at him and said in German, though I was very tempted to speak Russian, "I am happy to work with you."

He smiled a little and just nodded again. I thought he felt uncomfortable as well as a little embarrassed. At this point Mikhail excused himself and left us alone.

I knew that Ivan and I would be able to get along better if we spoke Russian than if we struggled along with his poor German. If we spoke his language, he could thoroughly instruct me and we could, perhaps, become a team. With that broken German of his our working relationship would not be as successful as it could be, I knew. Ivan would probably feel inferior when he struggled with his German. So I broached the subject right away.

"I speak a little Russian. May I try to speak in Russian to you? I love to speak your language." The last sentence I had actually spoken in Russian.

I thought I would let Ivan decide how he wanted to communicate. For just an instant, I thought he looked very perplexed as if seeing something he had never seen before. I could imagine, he probably had never heard anything like that before—a German prisoner speaking in fluent Russian to him. But then his pockmarked face froze into a mask with his eyes staring coldly and steadily at me. God knows what went on in his mind! I looked him straight in the eyes with as much of an open expression in my face as possible. In those moments, we were like a dog and a cat crossing paths for the first time, frozen opposite each other, sniffing each other's scent, furs along the spine ruffled and standing on end, and neither one knew what the next move was going to be—attack, retreat, or acceptance of each other. The longer Ivan maintained his impenetrable stance, the more unsure I became of my proposal and myself. I was just thinking that I should have left everything the way it was when, suddenly, his eyes started twinkling and he burst into a broad smile. It felt to me as if a sheet of ice covering both of us had melted instantly under the sun's rays after a long deep winter's freeze. When I saw Ivan's genuine smile and his hand reaching across the divide to me, I grabbed it instantly and shook it long and firmly.

"I like your suggestion, Janos, we will work better that way," he said with a steady nod of his head.

What relief I felt! I wanted to hug him but thought it might not be appreciated. That might have ruined the precious trust and friendly reserve he was able to muster towards me. When we let go of each other's hand, Ivan was the first to recover completely.

"Let's go and get to work. I'll first show you the shop and the parts I am working on right now. Later I'll introduce you to the guys. I think we will work well together if you work hard and show a good attitude. Please follow me."

I was happy it had gone so well.

Ivan led me straight into the machining section of the shop. I was quite overwhelmed. Most of what I saw I encountered for the first time in my life. The scene was bewildering. Later on when I had become thoroughly familiar with the shop, I knew I had made acquaintance that first morning with drill presses, lathes, milling machines, and metal bending presses. All this machinery made my head spin. I nodded a lot as Ivan moved from machine to machine, explaining what each could accomplish for the metal fabrication workers. I wanted to show him that I was attentive and interested, but I didn't quite grasp all of the functions each machine was used for.

Ivan moved along quickly then as if he felt he was wasting his own work time.

We stepped into the welding section where sparks were flying everywhere and I followed him curiously. The scene appeared to me like a veritable fireworks display in progress. And in the midst of all these sparks there stood the arc welders, broad-legged, with their big welding helmets and heavy asbestos gloves, appearing like some strange, ungainly creatures from outer space. Much later I learned that our eyes should have been protected from the intense light of the arc, but they were not and we sometimes looked right into the light. We moved on to a separate, more isolated section where the gas welders stood among the flying sparks. As Ivan explained, they were working with a highly flammable, explosive oxygen-acetylene gas used for the welding and cutting of steel. He mentioned to me that I wouldn't do this kind of welding for quite some time. Little did he know that I barely knew anything about welding.

When we returned to his and my future workstation, I was still somewhat bewildered but elated at the same time. I thought we were off to quite a good start, and it indeed remained a good relationship as long as I was assigned to Ivan. Ironically, he became not so much my supervisor but my teacher and mentor. He and I realized quickly that I possessed few skills for the work I was supposed to do. The little welding and machining I had done for Walter was not enough to prepare me for this job. But this discovery did not faze Ivan in the slightest. He handled his responsibility towards the camp administration and me in his own way. Sergei Leskov received good weekly reports about me and never became aware of the true state of affairs. My gratitude towards Ivan knew no bounds, and I never let him down.

In many ways, Ivan reminded me of Walter. He was his Russian counterpart in skills, craftsmanship, and inventiveness. Both were able to create material miracles from scraps they scrounged from the surrounding countryside that was littered with heaps of rusting metal parts. But Ivan was much older than Walter, perhaps in his middle forties, my father's age. His hair was already gray and always appeared unkempt. His broad face, crisscrossed by hard, deep lines and covered with a rough skin, truly had a gruff look to it that belied his patience, good nature, and occasional sense of humor.

As a cool early spring turned into a warm late spring and a hot summer, Ivan allowed me to open the large doors of the shop every morning and so, to my delight, we invited the outside in. I watched the chestnut trees first unfurl their tender, furry shoots that they turned in a couple of months into thick, dark green canopies adorned with tall, white stacks of blossoms like giant candles. True miracle workers, all of them. I reveled in seeing the green grass that grew in patches in the yard and the weeds and wildflowers that twisted in, around, and through the discarded parts, machinery, and general junk. Nature seemed strangely profuse to me during this spring and summer. But then I was as one severely deprived whose hungry eyes see suddenly more than before. Nature literally waved and beckoned to me, and I spent all my breaks lying or sitting in the grass under the trees amid the jokes and needling of my fellow workers. I was the only one preferring the out-of-doors and sitting in the grass to lighthearted gossip and quick card games. But I was happy and filled with hope.

At least a couple of times a week, Ivan brought me a hard-boiled egg and once in a while a cold piece of chicken. "With compliments from the Missus," he would say and smile his broad, twinkly smile. His wife raised chickens on their apartment's balcony, he had confided in me. Otherwise he kept his private life secret, and it would remain so for the duration of our working relationship. But looking at his deeply inscribed countenance, I knew he had suffered a lot. I was immensely grateful to Ivan. All I knew how to reciprocate for his kindnesses was through total dedication to my work. I worked long hours every day, six days a week, and socialized little with the other workers in the shop. Ivan was happy. We consistently exceeded our weekly quotas, and he benefited steadily through a little extra merit pay. We prisoners were not paid. Officially, we were supposed to receive wages for our work outside the camp, but those phantom wages went straight into the coffers of the camp administration. They were payment for our room and board.

At night I chatted with Fritz a little before I happily sank into my cot. Life had become relatively easy and uncomplicated. I liked it that way and desired nothing else. I thought, if it only remained that way until they send me home, I will be a very happy, lucky man. Little did I know what was still to come— an array of events, experiences, and emotional upheavals I would not have wished upon myself at the time. But life, the unceasing river washing over us, will not stop at our deepest desires or our desperate cries for time out. Life will engulf us no matter how exhausted we are and will keep leading us into its rapids, and so forcing us into struggles until the very end.

It all began when Ivan became ill for a few days. I was alone in our section of the shop, and as usual I had neither eyes nor ears for anything but my work. Bent over the workbench, I doubled my pace to try to work for both of us. Once as I straightened up my back to relax a little and glanced sideways, I noticed a tall young man at a bench close by working on a large, thin metal frame. He seemed intensely involved. His darkly handsome profile and well-groomed head caught my eyes immediately. As he was engrossed in his work and did not seem to notice me, my eyes lingered longer than they would have had I drawn his attention towards me. I recognized him as one of the Hungarians, though he wore a long, colorfully stained smock over his regular clothes. Otherwise, only his fine leather boots were showing. He must have sensed my looking at him, for he suddenly glanced over and our eyes met. I immediately averted mine and fully concentrated again on my work. Though I sensed his periodic glances, I never let them distract me. And then suddenly I knew he was standing right behind me looking over my shoulder. I could feel his energy but I did nothing and kept working.

"Hey, young, diligent worker, why won't you look at me? Why be so impolite? I would like to talk to you."

He had taken this step despite the possibility that I would totally ignore him. And then came this one word that hung in the air between us for a while, a desperately inquisitive "Why?"

I truly did not want to be bothered since it would take time and concentration away from my work. At the same time, I have never been one to be grossly impolite. So I turned around, slowly and tentatively and faced this young insistent intruder. I faced his inquisitive gaze squarely. He was taller than I and he looked slightly down at me. His eyes were very dark, handsome, and seemingly bottomless. He said no more, but just stood still, waiting for my next move. It was a standoff of some sort, like two alpha males sizing each other up before the fight begins. But then the situation took a different turn, for he suddenly threw his head back and started laughing out loud. This laugh lasted no more than a few seconds. I thought he tried to catch himself quickly for fear that his laugh would be interpreted wrongly, and he began to speak softly.

"Hi, my name is Stephen Teleki. I know we are in the same boat; and all I want is to talk to you. How difficult can that be? Why the reluctance? Why the standoff? You can refuse me later if you don't like me. What will you risk? Tell me, what's your name?"

"Janos."

"No, that's not possible. Not a countryman?" He seemed thoroughly perplexed.

"No, not a countryman just a great, great grandfather by that name. I don't know where he got it from. By the way, my last name is Jablonsky." And so the ice was broken between us as it had been between Ivan and me. I felt relieved.

"You are the artist!" It suddenly came to me.

"How would you know?" We had been speaking Russian and it came naturally to both of us.

"Your stained smock led me to your luminous scrolls." Again, he tilted his head backwards and laughed out loud, heartily and freely this time.

"You are a fine observer. I like you even better now than before when I listened to your fine Russian over a period of time and was very impressed. I knew then that I had to get to know you some time."

Almost involuntarily, my hand went out towards him and he grabbed it firmly with both hands and shook it. We became instant friends.

"If you can make time in the evening sometimes, I would like to invite you up to our quarters. My friend who is an astronomer of sorts has built himself a telescope. Now we are building a ladder that will allow us to climb from our floor to the roof. I want you to be there when we are ready. Let's get out of our confinement and contemplate and lose ourselves in the vast reaches of the universe. Please, promise me you will come," he said almost pleadingly.

I thought I was not hearing right. This invitation was too good to be true. How could these young men contemplate such luxuries for the mind and spirit when the rest of the prisoners in this camp and in all camps across this vast Russia could only think of food and rest to keep their emaciated, tortured bodies and spirits alive.

"Thank you, Stephen, for your invitation, but I don't know whether I can free myself. Frankly, I am scared. I have recently slaved in the mine and hardly made it. I cannot jeopardize my current position. I need to get out of here alive." I was full of hesitation but Stephen was unperturbed.

"Janos, I know how this section of the camp is run. As long as you work hard and long during the day, you have your evenings off. You are not being observed at all when you are in your sleeping quarters. You are still paranoid from the conditions next door. You can free yourself on an evening now and then and ascend the few flights of stairs to our quarters. I will invite you again and again until you will finally give me your assurance that you will come. Mark my words! I am not one who is easily discouraged. But I also only make a move when I am absolutely certain that I want to make it. I want you as a friend, Janos; I am absolutely certain of that. I have studied you long enough."

I had no idea that Stephen had studied me; and now it was my turn to laugh out loud as I had not laughed since I was a child. Stephen just stood there and grinned at me. He liked my outburst.

"Please, Stephen, let me think about it. I cannot commit this minute. Please, understand."

"Sure, I do. But remember I will be back. We will contemplate the universe together. But now get back to work."

"Thanks, Stephen. If you only knew how much you have already given to me without your invitation. Your wonderful, luminous scrolls have lifted my spirit to a point where I know I can go the rest of the way."

"I am very happy to hear that." He smiled at me gently this time, took a slight bow and went back to his station at the bench. I went back to work too, and we did not speak again that day or for quite a few days to come. Stephen certainly gave me enough space and time to think and to digest his incredible offer. Fritz could not have been more wrong.

28

Marika

Two weeks went by. No trace of Stephen. As the days passed, I became excited just contemplating his invitation. In recent months my physical body had been so starved and neglected that, as a consequence, my mind and spirit had all but died. No real food for their life support had been given to them since Mei Chi and Anna had ceased instructing me. Now that, as the days went by, I saw no trace of Stephen, I began to yearn for his appearance, for the possibility, the excitement of communion and contemplation with kindred spirits.

At noon time one day, I was sitting under my beloved chestnut trees devouring a piece of chicken Ivan had brought for me that day. I felt happy about the way my body had responded to the relatively generous camp food, the little extra nutritional help I received from Ivan, and the less strenuous work assigned to me. No longer did I have to undergo the weekly scrutiny by some cold, unfeeling camp doctor whose task it was to sort out the fit from the unfit. In fact, I had not been checked over by a doctor for several months. No one seemed to care anymore what the status of my physical condition was. But I knew myself that I had improved, that I had even gained a little weight. Those incessant worries of starvation had vanished. I was just thinking how very lucky and graced I was when Stephen's unmistakable boots appeared before my eyes in the grass. Even before I could look up at him, he had thrown himself into the grass next to me.

"Hey, Janos. How are you? We are ready, and you are invited to come up tomorrow night at eight to look at the stars and planets if the heavens will bestow us the gift of a clear sky."

Nothing could have been more startling at that moment when I contemplated the state of my health and well-being than Stephen's throwing those unexpected words at me. Even though I had softened my thinking over the past fourteen days as to what I dared or dared not do, this light-heartedly thrown out invitation tightened something in me again against throwing caution into the wind. But then, as I looked into Stephen's face and saw his sincerity and his pleading expectation, I just burst out, "All right! I'll come. I'll be upstairs at eight."

In those moments just before I started speaking I truly did not know that I would say those same words. But here they were and stood happily between us. I guess something within me, be it curiosity, yearning for mental and spiritual food, yearning for friendship, yearning for breaking the mold had driven me to committing myself. Apparently, deep down, I wanted no less. Stephen had grabbed my hands immediately even before I finished speaking. Even though I couldn't completely understand his seemingly genuine enthusiasm, I accepted it at face value and let it affect me. Here we sat holding hands tightly and pressing them harder and harder until our knuckles hurt like in some competition of endurance.

"This is great, Janos. I'll be glad to introduce you to my friends. They'll like you and you'll like them. Glad you mustered the courage. I know at least somewhat how you must have felt these past two weeks but I thought it would be best to give you ample time to think things over. At this point, you don't want to jeopardize anything, I know. I think, though, that it will be all right. It hasn't been this easy for us as it is now since we were taken prisoners. We went through quite severe hardships for some time, but now things have changed, and we can ask for and do almost anything. But what we really want is still not being given to us. We want to go home, pure and simple, just like you. We don't know why it is not happening. It's hard to be patient. So my friend, I'll see you tomorrow."

"Yes, you will."

With that he got up and started walking away.

"Thanks, Stephen. I'll be there for sure," I called after him.

He turned around briefly and smiled and waved as he kept on walking with those long springy strides of his that made him almost bounce across the yard.

That afternoon I performed miracles in the shop in Ivan's eyes. I worked at such an efficient and fast pace that our daily quota was reached at three in the afternoon. When three o'clock rolled around, Ivan stepped up to me and patted me on the back.

"Janos, you are a wizard. You are getting better every day. I am amazed," he cried out, utterly pleased.

"Sooo! Let's keep on working until 5:30 at this pace, and you will soon be the number one producer in this shop complex. Honors and extra bonuses will be coming your way," I replied enthusiastically. At my wild prediction, we both burst out laughing.

"You are the best boss I ever had," I said with all the sincerity in my voice I could muster.

Then it happened as I had wanted it to happen right from the beginning: Ivan grabbed hold of me and pulled me into one of those Russian bear hugs that took my breath away. He held me a long while, clasping me exceedingly tight in his arms.

That late afternoon, at closing time, as the big shop doors swung shut, I walked across the road back to the camp a very happy man. My spirit soared so high, I could hardly contain myself. I wanted to be good and kind and friendly and generous to everyone, even the most unassuming person. And if that wasn't possible now, I thought, I wanted it to be that way after I became a free man. That I swore solemnly to myself at that moment.

From then on, back at the camp, I made it a point to socialize with the guys in our sleeping quarters as much as I could. I would talk with them, draw them out, encourage them to talk about their families, their loved ones, their apprehensions and fears. I joined in their card games, their bedtime stories. Fritz had introduced me to as many guys in our sleeping quarters as he knew himself, characters all: Peter, Rudolf, Hans, Ingo, Werner, Günther, Siegfried, Bernhard, and more. Gone were the days of my envy of others' camaraderie at a time when I literally hungered for companionship.

The morning after Stephen's reappearance I awoke very early to a cloudless sky. The prognosis for the coming evening therefore was excellent. It was still dark; the stars still sparkled in the sky. I had no idea what time it was. I got up with my toiletry bag in hand and stood by the window. In the East the slightest glimmer of dawn was spreading across the horizon in faintly pink hues and as I stood transfixed, I don't know how long, the pink slowly turned to bright crimson just before the first rays of the sun burst over the horizon. This dawning day felt as no other day in my whole young life had felt. What had changed, I wondered. I was still a prisoner with no idea when the prison doors would open up to release me, to send me out into freedom. What had significantly changed was prison life: better treatment, less fear of getting hurt or killed, and suddenly the treasure of companionship. Just as day dawned for the world, so a better life seemed to be dawning for me. I tore myself away from the breaking dawn and stepped into the washroom where I had never showered and groomed myself with such care and enthusiasm as on this glorious morning. I was ready to face the day long before the bell rang. Then I remembered that it was also the day we would be issued the blue cotton summer suits at last. They would be clean and fresh for quite a few weeks to come and light and pleasant to wear. Off would come the quilted winter suits that we had worn for more than six months, day and night. They were more than ready to be discarded, dirty and torn as they were.

A workday at the shop had never seemed as long as on that particular day. Even as I left at 5:30 in the afternoon, a long two and a half hours still lay ahead of me. The evening meal for me went by in a daze. Fritz had attached himself to me but gave up on me the longer he had to put up with my unresponsiveness. I finally apologized to him as I noticed his silence.

"Sorry, Fritz, I need some space tonight."

"Hey, man, I understand. Don't worry. We all need some time to ourselves once in a while." Fritz was great that way; he always seemed to understand.

I had finished my meal way before everyone else and flew up the stairs as soon as I could. I hurried to my bunk for I needed at least a short time to calm myself. I closed my eyes, and to any onlooker I would have seemed asleep. Far from that. I had closed my eyes to still my mind for I did not want to contemplate the events of the evening before they even happened, I did not want to speculate what was to transpire tonight. And as I sank into a deep, thought-suspended, and timeless state, Mei Chi's luminous image came floating up, quite unexpectedly, out of pure space like a flame that suddenly illuminates darkness.

"Mei Chi," I whispered, "be with me tonight. Let me approach this coming event in the right spirit with gratitude and an open heart."

I thought she smiled an approving smile just as she was crowded out by the noise and commotion my friends made bursting into the sleeping quarters after their evening meal. But no one came up to my bunk; no one tried to roust me out of my solitude. What they thought I do not know, but I appreciated their respectfulness. I lay there for I don't know how long when I suddenly sat up with a start thinking I had missed the time I had promised to show up. I had no watch and it was already dark outside. I could not gauge what time it was.

197

The only one in our sleeping quarters who had a watch was Günther the watchmaker in civilian life. How he was able to get a fancy watch for himself in this prison camp, I don't know. But he was forever repairing watches seemingly for all the Russians who inhabited this camp.

Günther occupied the bunk next to me, so I said, "Hey, Günther, tell me what time it is, please." At the same time I tapped him on the shoulder, for he had his back turned to me while he was talking to a couple of his friends.

"Five to eight, Janos. Too early to be asleep, man."

"Thanks, Günther."

"You're welcome."

I jumped up and raced into the washroom for a glance at my face and hair. Minutes later I flew up the stairs into a world and an experience that has never had an equal in my life.

To my surprise, Stephen was waiting for me at the top of the stairs.

"Janos, I'm happy you are here," he greeted me.

"Likewise, Stephen."

He gave me a brief hug. Then, grabbing my upper sleeve, he pulled me eagerly into a dimly lit room filled with many of his friends and fellow prisoners. I stood in the doorway, unable to move for a while. Stephen had stopped also and let go of my sleeve for he must have realized how strange this sight had to be for me. I couldn't believe my eyes. Easy chairs and couches were grouped in different areas of this large room. They were filled with young men conversing animatedly with each other in soft, subdued voices. Others stood in groups chatting quietly. As these animated human sounds drifted towards me like gently rolling waves, I was transported back into childhood, standing, for the first time, at the ocean shore next to my father with my eyes closed, listening to the eternally repeating swelling and crashing of the sea waves.

I returned to the scene at hand when I heard Stephen say softly into my ear, "Janos, let's move on. I would like to introduce you, for the show will soon begin."

We had entered the room so unobtrusively that no one had taken notice of us. But now, as Stephen nudged me gently towards the first group, they stopped talking and turned their heads towards us.

"Hey, guys, I want you to meet a friend of mine I have invited to gaze at the stars with us. Please meet Janos."

Suddenly I found a whole bunch of friendly hands stretch out towards me. Could these hands and friendly faces belong to the same group of envied strangers that had swept past me just a few months ago? They were indeed, and I had to nudge myself to start shaking those hands one by one. I could not possibly have remembered all those names and faces—several Stephens, Mihálys, Józsefs, Páls, and Bélas. I did not see one astonished face in that crowd, just friendly smiles. No scrutiny, no questions, just simple acceptance. And as Stephen and I weaved between the groups, I, in turn, became more open and self-assured than at the moment I entered this room. There must have been about forty young men in this mainly candle-lit room, about two thirds of the members of the group I had first observed months ago in the dining hall. When Stephen had finished taking me to all the groups, someone spoke out loudly above the ebb and flow of the ongoing conversations.

"Guys, listen." Everyone fell silent. "It's time to go up to do our viewing and marveling. I got it all set up. It could not be a better evening as far as clarity and stillness."

Everyone was up in a flash and headed towards a wide-open window. The young man who had spoken led the way and was the first one balancing himself on the windowsill. He grabbed the rung of a steel ladder on the right side of the window, swung himself out, and disappeared. Everyone else followed one by one. Stephen and I were last. He urged me to go ahead of him. As I climbed up along the wall towards the roof's ledge, I wished the ladder would extend up into the sky and my climbing would go on forever. I imagined the freedom and bliss I would feel in climbing towards the stars. But then I landed on the roof and Stephen right after me. Everyone already crowded around the telescope in silent curiosity.

"My friend's name is Zoltán. He is the one who built the telescope. It's a miracle that he was able to get all the parts. He had to promise and sign a statement that he will leave the telescope behind once he leaves this prison camp. I guess the camp administration knows already where it is going to go after he leaves. Zoltán's father was an astronomy professor at the university in Budapest. When Zoltán was a teenager, his father built a telescope with him to instill a love for astronomy in the boy. Apparently, it worked. He is very good at what he does. He is also very knowledgeable. He reads astronomy books and journals all the time." I was happy that Stephen filled me in on the background that led up to this very unusual prison camp event.

"Guys, listen to me," Zoltán began at that moment. "I appreciate your silence, but you must also step back. We cannot all view the sky through the scope at the same time. Please seat yourselves in a semi-circle around the scope. Before we start viewing, I would like to tell you a little bit what we will be seeing and what we cannot begin to hope seeing. Tonight, in a rare display we will see both Mars and Jupiter fairly close together in the sky. This scope is strong enough to see features on the planets: red Mars and its plains, mountains, valleys, and long canal-like surface features. You can fantasize what it all means and what creatures could have created those hitherto unexplained features. You will view giant Jupiter and its twelve moons of which we will only see five or six. Some of them are very small, others are hidden behind the far side of the planet. Europa is its largest moon and some scientists think it has an ocean of water like our planet but covered by a sheet of ice. Jupiter itself, being more than one thousand times the earth's size, is believed to be enveloped in a gaseous layer of formaldehyde and ammonia, not an inviting place for us. So, without any more ado, I would like you to start viewing. I will train the scope first on Mars and then shift it for each one of you to Jupiter. Oh, by the way, what we won't be seeing with this limited scope are the further reaches of the universe. Even the nearest stars will still appear like tiny points of light to you and the galaxies will just be faintly cloudy patches. This is a prodigious and infinitely vast universe, and this small telescope will reveal, unfortunately, just a fraction of our own solar system. But even the little bit you will see is enough to fire up your imagination. So, let it roam as far as it wants to go. I have been up here quite a few nights now, and I have been awed to say the least."

Zoltán had spoken with much enthusiasm and reverence; and from what I could sense sitting among those young men, they experienced the same feelings that Zoltán expressed. In the dark, I grabbed Stephen's hand and squeezed it very tight and he responded. I think he knew how happy I was to be there. Stephen and I were the last to get up to view the planets. Everyone around us spoke in whispers, for no one wanted to disturb the still, dark, mysterious, and almost sacred atmosphere. Even sitting on the roof, out in the open, and looking up at the night sky illuminated by millions of cosmic lights, suns all and many vastly larger and brighter than our own sun, elicited an awe that cannot be felt, I was certain, in the grandest and finest cathedrals of our creation.

And then it was my turn. What I saw inspired me greatly. Suddenly our small menacing prison world dissolved into insignificance as these marvels of nature came into view for me. Then, at that moment, I felt a liberation of my mind and spirit taking place that lifted me way beyond these confining walls and encircling fence.

After Stephen finished his viewing, I spontaneously embraced him full of enthusiasm and gratitude. "You could not have given me a greater gift, Stephen," I whispered into his ear. "My mind and spirit are soaring like a falcon's ecstatic ascent towards the morning sun."

"I knew I would get that kind of response from you. You have struck me that way from the very moment I started watching you. I think I have a knack to be able to detect that in people. And you know, my perception has never failed me."

"Thank you, Stephen. Sometimes I think you may not be able to fathom what all of this means to me, but maybe you can."

"I think I can, Janos. When you come up to visit next time, I would like to show you my paintings. I am a liberated man since I have been allowed to paint again. For a long time I have been denied the pursuit of my art. It was a painful period for me, one that sent my physical and spiritual health into a downward spiral. Had it not been for my friends' steady caring and encouragement, I would have perished. If I can't paint, my whole being starves. It's become like an obsession when I can't do it, and when I am allowed to do it it's like a sweet libation that nourishes the whole of me. I can't express it in any other way. My whole family was at first taken aback by my artistic craving as they called it. This almost manic tendency showed itself early. All I wanted to do in my childhood was to draw and paint mostly out in nature. My parents thought it was excessive because I was not very interested in my schoolwork or normal children's play. They worried about me, I know. My father was a well-known lawyer. My mother was the daughter of a banker's family. Before me, no members of the two families were artists. Well, yes, my family had a penchant for music and art, and I was immersed in them from early childhood. But in the truly creative arena I was all alone and certainly not well understood by my family. They did let me study art at the university. They had that much good sense. But the war intervened, and I was not able to finish my studies."

I was moved that Stephen told me about his drive towards and obsession with artistic expression and about his family and childhood. My bleak experiences during my adolescent years seemed less aggravating and depressing to me now that I had heard Stephen's story. At least I never had the drive towards and obsession with one endeavor so early in my life. I probably was considered normal. I loved school, I loved to study, I loved to learn, I loved poetry, and I loved playing with my friends.

"How you must have suffered, Stephen!" I felt like bursting into tears. "At first you were not well understood. You felt very alone. And then you were thrown into a prison camp where art was out of the question. No wonder your whole self declined. But now you are able to express yourself. Think of it what a large dose of grace it took to move you back into this present creative state. And think of it that you will be set free much sooner than I will be. Of that we can be sure. You guys wouldn't be as privileged as you are if freedom were not close at hand."

"I hope you are right, Janos. I cannot and should not complain, not now. I am quite happy, and I think I can be patient."

"I am very sorry, Stephen. What time is it?"

" It's 9:30 already. I know you must go."

"Please forgive me, but I have to hurry back."

"I understand, Janos. We will see each other soon."

I had turned away from Stephen and was heading towards the edge of the roof. It was very hard to tear myself away. Stephen followed me and stood at the edge as I climbed down towards the window.

"I am glad you came, Janos," he called from above, and with that he disappeared.

Soon I found myself back in the Hungarian's social room that seemed worlds apart from our sleeping quarters, which was the only place where we could engage in a little socializing before going to sleep. I hurried out of the room, down the stairs, and towards my bunk. The lights had already been turned off. Except for some whispered conversations, it was quiet in the room. I lay down immediately and closed my eyes although I knew I would be awake for quite some time. I needed to think about the exciting events of the evening and to enjoy going over the experiences in my mind. Suddenly I felt a tug at my sleeve that electrified me with fear. Who could it be but a Russian guard having come to take me downstairs for an interrogation? I reluctantly opened my eyes and turned my head. The fear disappeared immediately when I saw Fritz's silhouette in the dark, faintly outlined against the window.

"Where were you, man. We missed you. Bernhard had somehow organized a chessboard. He had carved the pieces himself. We didn't know he had it in him. It's his gift to us. We watched the first game tonight between him and Günther. It was great; it was exciting. They were about evenly matched. You really missed something." I could sense Fritz's annoyance with me. I knew he liked to have me around.

"I am sorry, Fritz. I am very tired now. I'll talk to you and tell you everything tomorrow."

"Sure, Janos. Have a good night. I'll see you in the morning."

Dear, understanding Fritz! But I was happy he left me alone that night. Relieved, I closed my eyes again and thought that I could now go over the experiences of the evening when I was suddenly overcome by a vast tiredness and I sank immediately into a deep, dreamless sleep.

The next morning, when I was ready to go down for the morning meal, Fritz rushed over to me.

"Morning, Janos! How are you this morning?"

"I am just fine. I slept well."

"Tell me now, where did you go last night. I thought it was strange the way you disappeared."

"Well, I had an invitation to participate in one of the Hungarians' events."

"You what? You accepted an invitation from the Hungarians? You are shitting me, Janos. That is not possible. You know how aloof they are."

Fritz's voice revealed annoyance and incredulity at the same time, and I wondered about the wisdom of my telling him the truth. Nevertheless, I continued.

"I am not kidding you, Fritz. I would never do that. You are too valued a friend of mine."

"Well, I thought you were a dear friend of mine. But now that you have taken up with the Hungarians, I don't know. All my friends say that they belittle us, worse yet that they despise us. It doesn't seem worth it for them to be even civil to us."

"Fritz, you are wrong on that score. They are all very fine and sensitive young men. You would realize that if you got to know them."

"I don't believe it, Janos, and I don't really care. They are strangers to me and should be to you too. Culturally and socially, we have little in common with them."

"Oh, Fritz, loosen up. You are such a friendly and generous guy. I know that you are. Please, don't pronounce judgment over someone you don't even know."

"I know without knowing them. You can't tell me otherwise."

I couldn't believe this was the same Fritz who had shown me such intense friendship and understanding. As we entered the dining hall, he suddenly started waving. "Ingo," he called out, "I need to talk to you." At the same time, he took off and started hurrying towards Ingo without saying a further word to me. I knew it was just a ploy to get away.

I felt that I had been left stranded. Feelings of rejection as I had felt them a long time ago welled up in me. But this time I swore to myself right away that I would not give in to them. I needed to do what I felt was good for me. I wanted to be friends with Fritz and with Stephen. If either of them rejected me, it would be their problem and their loss. In the days to come I approached Fritz again and again in the friendliest manner I could muster. More then ever, I wanted to give him genuine friendship, but he remained cool and distant. And over time the other friends I had made in our sleeping quarter, one by one, acted cool and distant towards me. It was sad to think that this was Fritz's work. This time I grieved over the loss of their friendship, but I was not devastated to the core as I had been before. I did care for their friendship, and I thought I could have had both worlds. Now that this didn't seem possible, I chose without hesitation Stephen's friendship. But deep in my heart this choice also struck a chord of fear. What if my former friends alerted the guards to my periodic absences? I couldn't bear thinking of what repercussions that might have.

It was not until two weeks after the stargazing event that Stephen showed up again during my lunch hour. I had seen him working in our shop off and on during those two weeks, but we didn't socialize. We just exchanged friendly nods when our eyes happened to meet. That was all. I knew Stephen realized how much my work with Ivan meant to me. No doubt he respected my loyalty and dedication totally. But now, during this sunny lunch hour, he had thrown himself, like last time, into the grass next to me.

"Hey, Janos, would you like to come up tonight and look at my paintings. I would love to show them to you. Will you come? I want to know what you think of them."

"Yes, I would love to come. I noticed that you have been busy making frames."

"I need to protect my paintings, especially the ones in the dining hall. I also need to get some backing for them soon as well as some glass, otherwise they will deteriorate. I have been promised all the materials as long as I signed an agreement that the paintings will stay in Russia when I go home. I gladly did that. All my other paintings I keep rolled up, hoping that if I never hang them, I will be allowed to take them, though I don't know whether they'll let me in the end."

"Nothing would give me greater pleasure than to look at your work, Stephen. When do you want me to come?"

"Can you manage to be there at seven? Then we would have a little more time than during your last visit."

I nodded affirmatively. "I think I will be able to manage. I can't wait till tonight. I am already very excited."

"Thanks, Janos. I'll be happy to see you."

With those remarks he jumped up, waved at me, and was off in the direction of the prison building, while I would soon resume my work in the shop with Ivan.

At seven that night, Stephen was again waiting for me at the top of the stairs.

"It's wonderful that you could make it. Let me take you to the room where I am allowed to work. It's not a studio or anything close to that, just a room that I have access to whenever I want to paint. Otherwise it's a room that is used for storing files. Well, why am I talking about this now? Come along, you'll soon see."

He led me down the corridor past the social room I was in the last time I came up, past some sleeping quarters, and the washroom. At the end of the hall we entered through a door to which Stephen had the key. The door closed shut behind us. It didn't need to be locked from that side.

"We are now in the infirmary that takes care of our floor. It's different from yours. We have our own doctor. His name is Sándor. He is one of us, a young intern from Budapest. Believe it or not, he is a prisoner just as we are. We asked that he be allowed to take care of us and that request was granted. They also gave him an assistant, a young Hungarian woman. Her name is Marika. I did not know that the Russians kept women prisoners. She is definitely one of ours. She served as a nurse during the war. I think she is part gypsy, though I don't really know anything about her background. She keeps very much to herself. She seems a lonely young woman, but she is very caring. She arrived one day totally unannounced after Sándor had been installed as our doctor. We hadn't even requested that a Hungarian nurse replace the Russian nurse who was on duty when we got here."

"Thanks, Stephen, for telling me all of this. I find your life and privileges fascinating."

"You are not envious?"

"No, I'm not. I am just glad to see that someone is allowed to have a little better life than we have. But don't get me wrong. I am not complaining about my lot. It is very good in comparison to what I had before, as you know. It is all relative."

I was very happy that Stephen filled me in every time he introduced me to something new. He was very thoughtful that way. So far, he hadn't even asked anything about my background. He took me as a friend just the way I was. Meanwhile we had walked down a corridor and entered a room that was a strange combination of administrative archive and artist's studio. All four walls were covered with shelves right up to the ceiling. They were stacked full with files. A large table stood in the middle of the room that held all of Stephen's paints, brushes, paper, as well as his rolled up paintings, I gathered, for a shelf under the table held rolls and rolls of paper. Off in one corner stood a very simple easel and attached to it one of Stephen's new creations in progress. I was speechless for a while. Stephen stood just patiently next to me and allowed me to take it all in.

"Stephen, this is incredible! I can't believe this! This room is basically yours. Who would ever come in here to look at these old files?"

"Yes, I am very lucky. This is my sanctuary. But come on and look at my paintings."

He stepped to the table and lifted one of the rolls from under the tabletop. He untied the string that held the roll together and let the paintings, as many as a dozen I figured, fall on the table. At that moment I heard a faint knock at the door. But I could have been mistaken. Apparently I was, for Stephen did not seem to have heard anything. He busied himself with his paintings, flattening them out, pulling them apart, and arranging them on the table. Then I heard the knock again. This time Stephen did too.

"Excuse me, Janos, " he said and turned towards the door.

I had turned around too, and when he opened it, a young woman in a white smock stood outside. Her pale face expressed distress and pain. She seemed as tall as I was. Though she was slim, her frame appeared strong and her shoulders very straight. To me she was like an apparition. And for the few seconds before Stephen started talking to her I conducted a reality check by pinching my arm. When I felt the pain, I knew she was real.

The next moment, I heard Stephen say with concern in his voice, "Come in, please. What is the matter, Marika? Is he worse?" He closed the door behind her.

"Yes, I am afraid he is," she began in Russian. "His condition is getting worse. We cannot control his fever. He is now hallucinating. The doctor is fearing the worst. We have no penicillin left. Several times Endre called out your name. That is why the doctor sent me to find and fetch you."

I could see that Stephen was about to bolt for the door, but then he remembered me and turned around.

"Janos, I got to go. My friend is very ill. Please wait and look at my paintings. I'll be back. But if I'm not back within an hour, you may want to leave. I am so sorry, Janos."

He had spoken with great haste and with a tone of despair in his voice. They both left hurriedly. Stephen had not even taken the time to introduce me to the young woman. Of course, I knew who she was. Only once had she glanced at me and our eyes had met. Hers were large, green, and intense as those of some of the great cats. In the light of the ceiling lamp, her hair was of a deep red, pulled back severely and fashioned into a large knot at the nape of her neck. What struck me more than anything else was the translucent quality of her facial skin, like the pure sheen of rare alabaster. She had taken no real interest in me. I sensed that. But she had taken note of me. I recognized that in the momentary steadiness of her gaze directed toward me before she turned and averted her eyes. But hers was not a curious gaze. It reminded me of a person's detached gaze who had seen too much suffering in life.

When the door shut behind them, I turned towards the table with a heavy heart. I was hoping that Stephen's friend would somehow, perhaps miraculously, pull through. Somewhat absent mindedly, I started sifting through and viewing the paintings that Stephen had strewn onto the table. Their beauty and vividness, their exquisite shapes and colors drew out my full attention in no time and soon I was lost in them as if I had stepped into a different world. I felt that same uplift of spirit that I had felt the first time I gazed up at Stephen's luminous scrolls in the dining hall. No doubt he had the gift to convert a viewer's emotional state into an extreme sense of well-being. They were rural landscapes mainly, nature at its most beautiful, but city landscapes as well. All were created from memory, no doubt, revealing years and years of gazing at the beauty of all things. I knew this search for beauty started way back in his childhood. He had told me so. He had stored in his memory pictures his mind and soul had taken like a camera would, but unlike a camera's these pictures carried the stamp of his personal artistic genius. They were rendered not realistically but in brilliant colors and stylized forms and shapes, in a vividness that transcended their real counterparts. To me, at least, they spoke of a passion for shape and form and color that was unequaled in what I had ever seen. Before the war, my father had taken me to several art museums featuring traditional and modern art. Though I loved most of the pictures I saw and reveled in the peaceful, hallowed atmosphere of the museums, my psyche was never affected by any of them as it was affected by Stephen's paintings.

That evening, Stephen did not return within an hour as he had said he might. So I left somewhat disappointed but elated at the same time after I had rolled up the pictures carefully in the same manner as he had done. It seemed strange to me and somewhat unnatural to hide their exquisite beauty under the dark tabletop. I hoped that they would all be born some day into the world for the benefit of men and women like me who needed their spirits lifted to a higher plateau.

29

The Concert

I did not see Stephen for a week after he was called away from his studio. He did not come to the shop to work on his projects, either. I did not dare go up to the Hungarians' quarter unless I was invited. Though I had been introduced, I did not really know anyone except Stephen. So I waited. One day, at noon, he did come back in the same manner he had always done. Suddenly he sat next to me in the grass. When I looked into his beautifully carved face and dark eyes, I knew right away what had happened. His face was pale, his features drawn, and his eyes swam like dark, bottomless pools in the pallor of his face.

"I am sorry, Stephen. You must have suffered tremendously during the past week. I have never stopped thinking of you and your friend since that evening I was in your studio. My heart ached for both of you."

"Endre did not make it in the end. And he didn't go easily. He clung to life tenaciously. He fought and fought to overcome the fever and to stay conscious. But he was delirious most of the time I was with him. Several times we thought he would pull out of it. But his constitution was not strong enough. He was of delicate health to begin with, but he loved life and poetry. I knew he wrote secretly, but he never shared it with anyone. Almost everyone was unaware of his secret passion. I found his journal when I went through his few possessions. During our ceremony, when we put him to rest in our hearts, I read one of his poems. Though he perished, his poem was like

209

an ode to life. In it, he had harvested and distilled life's beauty as in a wonderful sunrise, in winter's fresh snow, in a tiny flower, in a mighty tree, and in a lasting friendship. I think it was one of his last poems. We were all very moved, for Endre was in life a quiet, gentle soul, one who never wanted to shine, be first, or be noticed. What broke our hearts was that his body had been whisked away by the prison authorities almost immediately after his death. Naturally, we wanted him to be sent home. At the very least, we wanted to give him a proper burial. No matter what arguments we put up with the administration, no matter how we pleaded and begged, all our efforts were to no avail. The policy, we were told, was that the bodies of the deceased had to be removed as quickly as possible. And so it was with Endre. When Sándor returned to the infirmary a few hours after our friend had died, Endre's body was gone. We don't know where they took him and what they did with him. He had simply vanished in the night. I feel his spirit will roam forever across this desolate land. When and if I get home, I will try to have him live on in his poems. I will devote myself to that. I will get them published."

Stephen's experiences of the last two weeks had burst forth with such force and speed as if a floodgate had suddenly been opened. I grabbed his hand that lay in the grass next to mine, but what I really wanted to do was to embrace him and hold him for a while to let the energy of my friendship soften the pain he felt over his dead friend. Yet I didn't dare do more than just hold his hand firmly for I was always watched by the workers in the shop, who sat together inside, eating and drinking, but also often glanced over my way. It seemed that they could not understand my need to be in nature during my time off. I would have loved them to come out and join me for a quiet lunch under the chestnuts. But no one ever did.

Finally I found words for Stephen, words that were, in my mind, pitifully inadequate to help my friend in his pain.

"My heart is sick with pain over the death of your friend, Stephen. I know that you will do everything in your power to keep his memory alive. I love and respect you for that immensely."

"Thank you, Janos. I am glad I came, and I am glad I was able to share this sad story with you. It feels good to be able to unload my pain. Thank you for hearing me. But life also goes on. Listen to me, Janos. Let's forget the pain for a few moments, for this is why I came today: some time ago, we had planned to celebrate the birthday of Ágoston, the leader and spokesman for our group of prisoners. He has worked very hard to bring music to us, and we are not short of musicians. Every instrument he obtained was like a major feat. We

Hungarians can hardly live without our folk music. It had been withheld from us for a long time, but Ágoston gave it back to us. His feat we must celebrate no matter what, despite death and despair. The plan has been all along that the celebration would be kept secret. It was meant to be a surprise for Ágoston. The band members and a group of us got together last night, and we decided that we must honor the living despite the death of our friend. Between the music and some dancing, someone will hold a speech in honor of Ágoston, and I will read Endre's poetry. In that way, we will be celebrating his life and work as well. What do you think, Janos? Will you come to the celebration? I herewith invite you. It will give you a chance to get to know my friends better and to feel more part of our group."

I was struck speechless by the turn Stephen's talk had taken from death's pain to the affirmation of life. How could he have, seemingly without effort, moved from one dissimilar realm to another with such speed? And yet it made sense. What is death but an integral part of life, for the latter does not cease when the former intrudes to claim its share. Life must always be celebrated as well as the memory of the dead. Endre would be honored if he knew he could be there in spirit.

"You seem struck speechless, Janos. What is it? Don't you want to come? I would so much like you to be there. Being at that celebration will do wonders for your life." In retrospect, I think, he had never spoken more prophetic words unless he had already an inkling of what would come about.

"Yes, I want to be there, Stephen. More than anything else, I want to be there."

"Now you are talking." The old, spirited Stephen had emerged like spring often suddenly emerges out of winter.

"I am sorry, Stephen. I just can't move as fast as you can between pain and joy. It'll take me a while longer to abandon the one and embrace the other."

"Oh, to me they are both equally important parts of the realities of life. Listen, if you conceive of life as a broad river then pain and joy are its banks. What we should try is to float down that river, somewhere in the middle, between the two banks. But sometimes we get hung up for a while on the bank of pain and sometimes on the bank of joy. Heaven forbid that we get stuck on one bank or the other. We must always return to midstream for life to proceed. Anyway, that is how I perceive life. Now you may understand my rather rapid movements from one state to another."

"I see what you are saying, and I think I understand. I will be contemplating your river journey in the days to come, and maybe I will decide to come on board."

I saw him smile then, and his strained features relaxed for the first time since he had sat down next to me.

"So, you will promise to come then on Sunday night at seven? We have permission from the administration because there will be noise involved in our celebration. We will negotiate permission for you to come. You need to be there for quite a few hours. Normally, I know, you can't be absent for very long. I don't think there will be any problem. Since Endre's disappearance, they owe us one."

"That's wonderful, Stephen. I didn't know you could make such a request. It will take a load off my mind if my attendance were officially sanctioned."

"Don't worry. It will work out that way." And after a short pause, he said, "Janos, I need to run along. See you Sunday night. I won't be waiting by the stairs because I will be busy. Just come up and go straight into the social room. I'll keep an eye out for you."

"I will, thanks." We both got up and shook hands, and then Stephen strode away a happier man than when he first came.

It was right at seven on Sunday night that I mounted the stairs. The mood on the third floor was electrifying. Festive sounds greeted my ears: talking and laughter, clinking china and instruments being tuned. Young men, dressed in white shirts and black pants rushed past me as I stepped onto the third floor landing. Everyone seemed elated and expectant. I felt strangely out of place in my blue cotton work suit. Though I had groomed myself carefully, I still felt and looked like a worker and totally out of place. Some of the young men in the corridor looked at me with astonishment, others recognized me from the stargazing event. They nodded or smiled at me. Others called out, "Good to see you again, Janos." Through the milling crowd, I worked my way into the social room. There I saw Stephen talking animatedly with some of the musicians. At one point, he turned around and glanced towards the door as if he was expecting someone. I knew he was looking for me. Then he saw me, and his face lit up. He waved me over, and he left the group immediately and came towards me, carrying a bundle under his arm.

"Janos, you are right on time. How wonderful to see you. You will enjoy this evening no end; I promise you that. If you do not feel comfortable in your clothes, you may want to change into these for tonight. Go and change in the washroom. You will feel more part of us." He handed me the bundle he had been carrying.

212

"How did you know how I felt when I stepped onto the landing?"

"I just know. I can put myself in your shoes. It's not that hard. Please, go and change, Janos. This celebration will mean so much more to you when you don't feel like an outsider."

"Stephen, I don't know how to thank you."

He laughed and said facetiously, "If you don't know how then just don't. I am just happy that you are here, my friend."

With those words he left me and rejoined the group he had been talking to, while I, after a few seconds of recovery time, turned in the opposite direction to look for the washroom.

I looked into the mirror when I was all dressed and was utterly astonished at my own transformation. For years I had worn those prison work suits during all waking and sleeping hours. I couldn't think back far enough, it seemed like, when I was still wearing civilian clothing. As I stood there and looked at myself, I felt lighter and more unrestricted than I had for many years, and my heart leaped with joy and expectation.

I weaved my way back to the social room. Although many young men were still in the hallway talking to each other, many more were already assembled in the room. The band had taken up its place on a large, elevated platform next to their instruments. Young men carrying trays were circulating among the crowd. As one of them approached me, I became overwhelmed at what I saw: sliced pound cake richly laced with raisins and dried fruits, chocolate cookies, pieces of dark chocolate, coffee, tea, sugar, and milk. I hadn't seen delicacies like these in ages. We didn't even have those any more during the last year I spent at my parents' house. I wasn't even sure they still existed anywhere in this world. At first I couldn't bring myself to take any of it that was offered to me, but the young server didn't want to move on until I had taken a cup and a piece of anything I desired. I wasn't even certain whether my stomach would take kindly to such fine food having gotten used to the rough fair given to us throughout the prison years. I finally took a piece of the cake. It looked so alluring that I couldn't resist. And I had him pour me a cup of coffee, real coffee—the aroma alone created a feeling of elation in me. I asked for milk and sugar as well.

How could they have ever been able to extract such fine food and drink from the Russians and how did it get here to this prison camp? It was, of course, a question I couldn't get an answer to. Even from Stephen I couldn't get the answer when I questioned him later on. In those moments, as those heavenly libations were offered to me, I took them as a gift from heaven, one for which I immediately gave thanks in my heart. Little did I know what other gifts would be bestowed on me even on that same evening.In the meantime, the band was fully assembled and most of the young men in the room had sat down on chairs and sofas along the walls. Ágoston was sitting close to the podium in a comfortable chair. I had observed how Stephen had offered this chair to him. Others were sitting on the floor in a wide semi-circle in front of the band. Others yet were standing along the side walls of the room. Then the band struck their first chords starting with the accordions. In came the basses, the flutes, the guitars, the cimbalom, and last the violins. They began slow and melodic at first at a tempo that started the bodies in the room swaying gently from side to side. Young men next to me closed their eyes and let the music filter into their beings where it in turn created a blissful expression on their faces that I had not seen before. It was like they were partaking of the finest foods and wine. Slowly, the music picked up speed and the violins became dominant while all the other instruments receded into the background. Faster and faster the violins sang their wailing song with such intensity and passion that it cut right through to the core of your soul. It produced in the listeners a feeling of excitement, even of frenzy, and, at the same time, a feeling of melancholy and yearning. The speed of the rhythm and the intensity of sounds kept on climbing; and when it could go no further, it was sustained at that top intensity for seemingly a long time, for time itself became suspended. And just at a point when I couldn't imagine that the music could sustain this climactic fever pitch, it suddenly settled back, without warning, into the original slow, melodic rhythm as the other instruments again became dominant. I felt like I had been on a roller coaster ride of sound, carrying me through amazing heights and setting me down at last into a soft lulling depth. And just when I thought this waxing and waning of sound would go on forever, it suddenly stopped. Immediately a cheering and clapping storm erupted so intense as if it came from hundreds of enthusiastic listeners when, in fact, there were about sixty present.

And so this exquisite evening with folk rhythms and folk songs, so special and unique to the Hungarian temperament, unfolded in unabated intensity and with a passionate force. I knew everyone around me was partaking of the sound feast as if they had been near starvation. And I, always having been fond of folk rhythms as long as I can think back, partook with them until my soul sang with joy and yearning, too.

During the intermission, Stephen came over to me. I had no idea where he had been during the first part of the concert. But here was his beaming face.

I had never seen him in such an excited state.

"How do you like it so far, Janos? Aren't you swept away by the rhythm and tempo? It's exactly like it was in the olden times. I can almost forget where we are."

"I feel that way, too, Stephen, and I hope they won't stop now. I am just feeling life, real life and real feeling returning to me."

When the musicians returned and had taken their place on the platform, someone gave a speech in Hungarian that was obviously addressed to Ágoston,. Next Stephen read some of Endre's poems. During his reading, a devotional stillness settled over the room, that I wouldn't have thought possible after the tumultuous musical renditions. But everyone around me listened as far as I could determine with reverence. The poems were read in Hungarian. Though I didn't understand the words, I knew they were moving everyone's feelings around me. Stephen had a deep melodic voice. It alone moved me with its beautiful intonation.

Immediately after the poetry, the music began again. They played a number of very melodic folk tunes at first, Hungarian ballads they must have been, celebrating every aspect of life: love, friendship, yearning, betrayal, jealousy, heroism, and death. One of the violinists was singing the songs in a strong, clear baritone voice. Then, without transition, the melodic tunes were transformed into the passionate, frenzied rhythm once more. It again revved up everyone's feelings to a fever pitch. Again it ended in a rather abrupt cessation that left everyone in a highly charged state of emotion, which sought to discharge itself in a wild cheering, shouting, foot-stomping, and clapping storm of applause.

For a long time, the bandleader tried to get everyone's attention over the microphone. He shouted, "Please, please listen." But it took forever, it seemed like, for the crowd to settle down. Finally he succeeded in getting his message across. Since everything was spoken in Hungarian, I had difficulty in knowing what would come next, but I was able to distinguish the name of Marika and knew that to follow was some kind of performance by her. At that moment, Stephen showed up at my side.

"I am sorry, Janos, that I am spending so little time with you tonight, but I am one of the main organizers of this event, and until now I was needed behind the scenes," he whispered.

"I understand, Stephen. Don't worry about it. I am enjoying myself as I have hardly ever done in my life."

"It makes me very happy to hear that. Let's go to the front row and sit down together. What comes now you will not want to miss."

So, we pushed our way to the front of the semi circle and had barely sat down, when Marika appeared on the podium in a wonderfully colorful folk costume and golden headdress. She looked stunning in the full, calf-length skirt, her black, tight fitting bodice, and the white puff-sleeved, low cut blouse. Ribbons, in the colors of the rainbow flowed down from her narrow waist to the hem of her dark blue satin skirt. These same ribbons cascaded down from her golden tiara over her long red hair. The skin of her face was even more striking in its delicately shimmering pearl hue than I remembered it from that night in Stephen's studio when I briefly saw her. Her eyes sparkled darkly green and with more intensity than I had in my memory. She wore heavy, dark lines around her eyes that accentuated them greatly and made them look much darker than in that glance I received from her in Stephen's studio. She was exotically beautiful, like a vision seen in a far away dream.

She sang in a deeply timbred voice, soft yet strong at the same time and immensely soothing. She was so feminine in her appearance and movements, so sumptuously beautiful in her striking costume, yet not delicately so, that I initially doubted her reality. And suddenly I saw myself as a man, starved and thirsty, struggling across a vast desert landscape towards a beautiful and enticing mirage. For a moment I thought how devastating it was to be in that deprived state and to encounter such a lovely, yearned for vision.

This visual feast, created by Marika, had me totally in its thrall. It released me only when the music abated, the singing stopped, and the room erupted in another wild round of applause. Marika smiled and bowed deeply. She took the microphone and announced something that I didn't understand. Again another round of applause erupted. She replaced the microphone onto its stand and stepped off the platform onto the floor in front of us in an amazingly shy and unassuming manner. She stood there with her head slightly bowed and her gaze directed to the floor in front of her as if she tried to avoid facing this all pervasive, all consuming male attention. Yet, I might have been mistaken. She might have been oblivious to what I sensed. She might have just been gathering her thoughts and concentration before the next performance. But while she stood there like that motionless, enveloped totally in her own self, like a gorgeous chiseled statue, an expectant silence suddenly fell over the room, palpable in its breathless, soundless density.

And then the band struck up a dance tune, light and playful at first and very melodic. Marika lifted her shining face and began to dance with delicate steps and slow, soft swaying motions of her arms and torso while her colorful ribbons rustled softly against her skirt. In time the music picked up. The rhythm accelerated as if being intent on reaching a stirring emotional peak. It began to pulse feverishly while the violins entered and created a strikingly separate cross rhythm. Marika was keeping pace with the music, accelerating her steps and body motions faster and faster until her feet stomped and her body twirled in a large circle with the passionate rhythm of the music until the dancer and the music became as one intricately woven fabric. Her skirt flew, her ribbons on both skirt and headdress fluttered in the air around her like festive, colorful streamers set in motion by the wind. I had never seen anything so stunningly beautiful—woman, music, and dance fused into a harmonious whole. Like me, everyone around me stood or sat in breathless admiration as her dance went on seemingly forever. But eventually the time came when the music fell back into its originally melodic rhythm and Marika resumed her soft steps and motions again. And slowly, ever so slowly, music and dance trailed off like an echo into the softest sound and motion until they died away altogether. For a moment there was utter silence in the room until everyone in the audience had collected themselves. Then the applause burst forth in stomping and clapping like the torrent of a rain-swollen waterfall. To rid myself of my pent up emotions, I participated as I had not done before. Everyone by then had jumped up honoring the musicians and the dancer in a standing ovation that didn't know its end. All musicians were standing on the podium, their heads bent, while Marika stood motionless before us, looking straight ahead, her animated face smiling brightly, and her arms extending out and upward.

It was the only dance she danced that night. I, for one, was so completely filled with her astonishing presence that I could not have watched any more. When I came to this performance I had no sense of the extent of my utter starvation for music, dance, and beauty. One small dose was enough, I realized, to overfill my senses and emotional capacity. I was glad when the band resumed playing soft, melodic folk tunes. At the end of this evening they never accelerated their rhythm, never exposed us again to the emotional frenzy that their performance had thrown us into earlier. They remained soft and gentle with us because we had already reached our climax. When the music stopped and the room was lit up, the band members stepped off the podium and lined up before us on the floor where Marika had danced her ravishing dance. As the musicians stood there, Marika in her shining colors came back into the room and joined the musicians at the tail end of the line.

Then Ágoston was asked to step out of the audience to shake hands with Kálmán, the band leader, who stood at the head of the line. As Ágoston moved on to the next musician, Stephen, who stood next to me, pulled me over to the musicians' line-up. I felt honored to be able to shake their hands and express my gratitude for the beautiful sound and pleasure they had given me. I spoke to them in Russian, and I hoped that they would understand. They nodded and smiled at me. When Stephen and I came to the end of the line, he waited for me until I was done shaking hands with the last musician. We both then stood in front of a still smiling Marika. Stephen did then what he was not able to do that night we were in his studio and Marika had entered with the distressing news. He now introduced me formally to her. This time I felt that her full attention was directed towards me. Her inquisitive eyes searched my face as if they wanted to fathom what was behind it. She held my hand so firmly and her gaze so steadily that I suddenly felt an intense heat rising out from the white collar of my shirt. In split seconds this heat had engulfed my entire face until I was certain that it glowed like a red lantern. I could not keep on returning her gaze, so overwhelmed was I by her presence. As I lowered my eyes, her head bent forward close to mine and she whispered in Russian, "I am glad to meet you, Janos."

She then turned to Stephen and shook his hand and chatted with him in Hungarian very briefly while I managed to recover myself. Then she said to Stephen very lightheartedly in Russian and for my benefit to hear, "I am happy you finally introduced me to your new friend, Stephen."

Stephen and I had already taken up too much time, for the next young man in line pushed his way towards us. We had to leave Marika. I was happy for that because in my heart I thought that I had never made a greater fool of myself than in those moments as I stood face to face with her as she kept probing my countenance and I crumbled before her. Though I was happy to have formally met her and to have looked at her beauty close up, I was glad to get away from her with that exposed weakness of mine. And I hoped fervently then that I would not have to meet her that closely again. I was even certain that there would not be another opportunity since Marika did not participate in the usual Hungarian prisoners' activities.

That night as I returned to my bunk, sleep would not come to me. I lay there until the wee hours contemplating what I had seen and experienced that evening. I fled for a while back to my childhood. I communed with my parents; I stood face to face with Effie and asked her forgiveness. I conjured up Anna and Mei Chi and prayed for their souls. I finally thanked the master

218

of the universe for this evening's wonderful, yet overwhelming experience. As I dwelled with all these loved ones of my past, my mind became more and more animated until I felt as if I had been intoxicated. Then panic set in. I saw ahead of me more years of prison life, more physical labor, more confinement, more inadequate nourishment and a slow deterioration of mind, body, spirit, and soul. What I had seen and experienced this evening was dangerously unsettling and possibly dangerously destabilizing the favored status I had gained and the harmony I was able to create between myself and my supervisor.

The one aspect of my life that bothered me no end and came to the fore and overshadowed everything I was contemplating during that dark night in my bunk among all those soundly sleeping bodies was the relationship with the fellow prisoners in our sleeping quarters. Over the weeks they had distanced themselves more and more from me so that by now a wall of silence had been erected that seemed impenetrable no matter how hard I tried to scale it. I realized I would soon have to ask for a move to other sleeping quarters. I was hoping that I could either keep to myself or try to establish some meaningful relationships after the move to new quarters. But I also perceived of the possibility that Fritz's influence could or would eventually extend into my new quarters. I felt utterly alone and even Stephen could not stave off this feeling no matter how I enjoyed and appreciated his friendship. Sometimes I felt I had made the wrong choice. But then how could I have made the wrong choice when I had followed the dictates of my heart? My swirling mind with its incessant thoughts became so dominant that night that all peace and rest seemed to be totally outside my grasp. And suddenly I realized the futility of it all. Thoughts were just thoughts and had no real substance beyond their power to menace and punish me. I closed my eyes then and tried to suspend all thoughts. I was only partially successful because thoughts kept on creeping back insidiously trying to take over once more. But I kept on suspending them again and again until I was just able to take note of them and let them pass. Then I knew I was on the way to have control over my thoughts just before I sank into an all pervasive stillness and quietude.

In the morning I was surprised how well I felt and how alert I was as I started the day. To my astonishment, a sense of trust in my life and destiny exerted itself, and I was happy to be able to place all my energies that day into my work with Ivan.

30

The Dancer

Work with Ivan was the most stable aspect of my life at that time, and I gave just about all of my energy to it. I was happy to see how Ivan benefited from my efforts. His gratitude showed itself in the little gifts of food he brought almost on a daily basis now, not just pieces of chicken and an egg once in awhile, but a few slices of bread at one time, a piece of cake, or a piece of fruit. I always received the gifts from him with the greatest gratitude. Sometimes I thought of Ivan as one of my saviors, right in line with Anna, Mei Chi, and the anonymous benefactor.

Stephen stayed away for two weeks after the concert. He was capricious in that respect. I never knew when he would show up. But when he did, it was always during the lunch break. We had now entered late summertime. The temperatures grew hotter by the day, but it was a dry heat and not that difficult to cope with. I unbuttoned my work suit half way down my chest and rolled up my sleeves as far as I could to achieve as much coolness as possible. In the afternoon, a steady wind rose up from the east that blew until sunset. It was this reliable easterly that made the hot summer days bearable.

I continued to sit under my beloved chestnuts in the middle of the day. Their beautiful candle flowers were gone now. They were replaced with ripening chestnuts still enclosed in their green protective shells. It would be autumn when these shells would open up to release their beautiful brown shiny nuts that would densely cover the ground beneath those trees. My eyes often dwelt in those trees as I lay in the grass in the precious few minutes after I had eaten my meager lunch and when the bell went off that signaled the return to work.

It was during those moments one day when I lay there in total peace that Stephen appeared suddenly out of nowhere. I hadn't even heard his footsteps. Suddenly he was looking down at me as from a great height for he was tall and slim. I sat up with a sudden start then.

"Hi Janos, I am back," he announced himself simply.

"Well, I am glad you are back. It's about time, isn't it?" I shot back.

He dropped himself next to me and laughed out loud.

"Are you still thinking about the concert? Be honest, Janos, you are, day and night." He laughed again.

"To tell you the truth, Stephen, my thoughts haven't touched the concert since that Sunday night when I lay in my bed and sleep would not come to me for hours. It was a fine concert, but to be very honest with you, this musical feast was almost too much for me to handle. Until your celebration I was not fully aware of my apparently fragile emotional state. I ought to be a little careful, I think. I do not want to lose my grasp on reality while I am still in prison."

"I am sorry, Janos, I didn't think our music made that deep an impression on you though I know it is powerful and it tends to stir up emotions. Please forgive me for having been insensitive with you just now."

"Oh, no, you weren't insensitive. Everything you said was fine. It's just me who is unable to handle certain aspects of life these days."

"In order to handle life you need to be more involved with it. If you allow me to make an observation it would be that I sense you withdraw too much into yourself. Seek new friendships and experiences, open yourself up to them, no matter what has gone before. We all get rejected at times like you think your German friends are rejecting you. If you can't overcome the rejection and rekindle the friendship then move on. You will miss too much of life if you don't." He sounded very persuasive and intense.

"I think I really needed you to come back to tell me that, Stephen. I mean it. You are absolutely right. I do tend to dwell too much on friendships and experiences gone astray," I responded so spontaneously that I surprised myself.

"Therefore, listen to me, Janos. I need to discuss an important issue with you. You are not aware of it, but since that time when Marika was sent to replace the Russian nurse, the handful of leaders in our group perceived a great danger to our band of Hungarian prisoners. You know, Marika is compassionate, healing, and beautiful, and she is one of our people. I am now telling you something that no outsider knows. The leaders met shortly after she came to us, and they, by the way I am one of them, decided that our entire group of men must swear an oath to the effect that they will never, as long as we are together in this camp, pursue Marika. As a group, we are close knit and very loyal to each other. The only person who could destroy what we have in male loyalty and friendship is Marika. Not that she would want to do that, but that our men would surely bring it about. So, in a solemn ceremony we collectively swore that we would abstain from Marika. This oath was very serious for all of us, like a swearing to lifelong celibacy. So far the men have stayed with the oath faithfully. We have had long discussions as an entire group about the need for abstaining from any and all pursuits of Marika, and we were in complete agreement pretty much from the start. Also, because we still recognize our weaknesses, we had to make it a policy to exclude Marika from our usual social get-togethers. Why tempt ourselves? She, by the way, fully understands our actions and has expressed her gratefulness to me personally."

"I had no idea that you as a group would go to such lengths to avoid conflict. I admire your willpower and foresight. I can very well imagine what could happen because Marika is a very attractive woman."

"I want to be very straightforward with you, Janos. The real reason I am telling you of our oath is a selfish one. Listen very carefully and with an open mind to what I am now proposing to you. We have in mind another great celebration, and we hope the last one in this prison because we believe they must let us go soon. So, five weeks from now, when seven of our men have their birthdays right around that time, we want to celebrate. All seven of us go by the first name of Stephen. Saint Stephen is Hungary's patron saint, and the birthdays of all males by that name are always celebrated in a special way. We want to have Marika dance again, but she said she would only be willing to perform if she had a male partner. She is right, the role of the male dancer during Hungarian folk celebrations is very important. But here is this dilemma: we cannot assign anyone from our group to her as a partner. It would go against our oath. We have had discussions back and forth between our men, and then the leaders communicated with Marika. She finally suggested, I thought ingeniously, that we should ask you to take on the role of the male dancer. We would do it legitimately and would seek the approval of the administration. And she is very willing to teach you. I know this revelation is blowing you away, Janos. I can see it in the expression of your face, but please do not say no immediately. You don't even have to say anything now. Take this request away with you, digest it, and think about it. I will come back in two days."

I was stunned when I realized the full extent of what Stephen was asking me to do. He had spoken very rapidly, and I had not interrupted him, for I thought he wished to first lay out his full proposal before me before I would comment.

"I am so sorry, Stephen, I really cannot give you an answer right now. My first inclination, to be honest, is to say that I cannot do it, no way. I don't even know that I am talented enough. But I am promising you that I will give it a lot of thought, and I should be ready with an answer two days from now." At the moment I made my promise, I wasn't even sure whether I could manage a reply in that short a time span.

" I fully understand, Janos, and I don't want to rush you. But please bear in mind that you would do us a great favor. And it is obvious that Marika sees potential in you. She is very discerning, you know. Believe me, she would not have suggested you if she was not quite certain that she could transform you into a dancer."

At that moment the bell, signaling the end of the lunch period, shrilled through the yard, as loud and annoying, as I had never heard it before.

"I must go, Janos. Thanks for listening to me. Don't get emotionally too upset over this. Whatever you'll decide, we will abide by it."

And so he left without realizing what great turmoil he had tossed me into. Afterwards it was difficult to get through the afternoon in the workshop. It took all my energy to just keep focused on my work. Even Ivan noticed that something was wrong for I worked absent-mindedly and in complete silence. Normally, we would chat at little during our work, or Ivan would tell me a story about life in his apartment house with neighbors so close and walls so thin that he and his wife couldn't help overhearing the most private talks, arguments, and other goings on.

"You are not feeling well this afternoon, Janos?" was Ivan's concerned and probing question.

"It's nothing, Ivan. I am just a little tired today. All will be fine tomorrow."

He seemed satisfied with my answer, but his question had jolted me back to reality. My full allegiance had to go to my work and everything else I did had to be secondary. I swore to myself to be careful from now on, and not to let other concerns and activities interfere with my work. When I was in the shop I could not let anything else intrude. That I swore to myself during these moments after Ivan had directed his question to me.

When I arrived back in the camp that late afternoon, Mikhail was waiting for me at the entrance. I was happy but also concerned to see him, but I smiled at him right away. I was apprehensive about what he would have to say to me. Could it be that Fritz and his friends had finally complained about me to the prison authorities? They would feel compelled to investigate my behavior. But it could also be that my request for a sleeping quarter change was approved and that Mikhail was charged with informing me of the administration's decision. I watched him carefully as I approached and tried to read his face even before he said a word. To my relief, he returned my smile and his face had a friendly expression.

"Good afternoon, Janos. I have good news for you. Your request to be moved has been approved, and I want to assist you with the move right now before the evening meal," he announced in a very casual but friendly tone.

What utter and complete relief I felt! Obviously, it concerned nothing else but the move.

"Mikhail, that is very good news. I am ready to do it right now," I replied, with as much enthusiasm as if I had just received the news of my release from prison.

The move was a very simple matter. We both ascended the stairs to the sleeping quarters, went to my bunk where I grabbed my small bundle from under the mattress, which was always ready and tied up. Off we went to the new quarters with Mikhail leading the way.

"I am glad, Janos, that you made the request to be moved," he said as we entered the new quarters, and he continued, " Some men are afraid to do that, and they stay in a situation that greatly bothers them. It sometimes affects their work output or the quality of their work, and we have to resort to a more severe measure than a move to another sleeping room because we do not know what is causing the work slippage, which is serious to us."

"I am glad you are explaining this to me, Mikhail," I said to him and added, "The men in the sleeping quarter are not as friendly anymore as they used to be, and that bothers me to a point where I think about it too much. I really felt I needed to move on and reserve my energy for my daily work."

"It's good that way, Janos. Sometimes people shift their allegiance irrationally and sometimes for petty reasons."

"I am very glad you understand, Mikhail. Thank you very much." I said to him with true gratefulness in my voice.

"I am happy to help you," he answered simply but with some finality in his tone.

I knew I had to be careful and not push my conversation with him too far.

"Well here is your new bunk. I hope things will work out for you. Glad to see you again." After a short hesitation, he added as an afterthought, "We are hearing only good things about you." Then he left me suddenly.

As I was standing there in front of my new bunk, I thought how unusual Mikhail was, always friendly but formal, except that he would sometimes throw in some small bit of information that caught me totally by surprise. I was never sure whether that simply reflected his basic nature or whether he genuinely cared for me personally. In any case, he had made me happy and I was grateful to him once more. I allowed myself a deep sigh of relief. The danger had passed once again.

The men in the new sleeping quarter received me that first night without much ado. They introduced themselves to me but then went about their usual activities. It was nothing special to them that a new person would suddenly appear, for the prisoners were an ever changing population though the changes were much less frequent in this section of the camp than in truly hard labor camps.

I was grateful to be left alone that evening. I retired to my bunk early. I needed desperately to sort out everything that Stephen had told me, and I had to make a decision about his proposal. But I had a difficult time getting started thinking about Stephen, Marika, the dancing, and the oath these men had sworn. In my mind they had almost gone to bizarre lengths to protect themselves from a disturbance that could unsettle or perhaps wreck the solidarity of their group. But since I basically admired the Hungarians and Stephen in particular, I did not spend too much time thinking about or analyzing their actions. Whatever they needed to do, I thought, they needed to do. But I, personally, did need to achieve some sort of clarity in my mind about their request to draw me into their inner circle and to have me work closely with the young woman whom everyone tried to avoid. If I hadn't felt the heat and weakness coming on as I stood in front of her that Sunday evening, I would have leaned towards allowing myself to accept their proposal. My role would be officially sanctioned. Stephen had said so. But it was this strange unsettling feeling I had experienced in standing close to her that unnerved and swayed me towards excusing myself. I had sensed strength and an almost magnetic power in her that had put my own strength to shame. Did I really want to challenge that strength and power and see myself crumble once again? That was my real fear. Though I didn't know what potential talents I possessed that could make me a reasonably good dancer, this unknown element was clearly of secondary concern to me. So what if I did not meet her expectations or standards, she could reject me, and I could accept that. But it was the deeper issue of her energy cutting across mine and subjugating or even obliterating it that I worried about. If she had affected me that greatly within those few moments, what would happen to me if I worked with her intensively for hours at a time. And yet there slowly emerged from underneath that fear of mine the realization that an enticing possibility of working with her and allowing me to develop the confidence of standing up to her was presenting itself. I had experienced so many horrendous hardships, heartaches, and a near death experience over the past few years that I was suddenly convincing myself that I would have the fortitude to face this challenge. I was surprised at myself how my inner reasoning took on its own force and drove me rapidly towards an acceptance of the proposal when I was so sure at first that there would be nothing but a decisive 'No.' Now I suddenly wanted to take on the challenge, and the part of myself that reasoned against acceptance became weaker and weaker until it receded into the background. Only that part that reasoned for the proposal stayed strong. It triumphed in the end. And I became certain that I would be prepared for Stephen when he returned. Had he not said that I needed to open myself up to new experiences. With this affirmative decision, I was doing just that. I suddenly felt happy that I could still make this kind of decision and that I could accept a challenge when it presented itself. That night, after I had found the resolution, I had no problems going to sleep.

I awoke refreshed and remembered the resolution I had come to the night before. I wished that I could have told Stephen that same day. Two days of waiting now seemed a long time to me. When he revealed his proposal to me the day before, I had thought he was allowing me too little time to think about it. Now I wished he were coming back today.

But he did as he had said. He came back the following day. He looked at me with so much expectation in his darkly handsome face that I couldn't hold back and blurted out right away, "I am going to do it." He wasn't even close to me yet. But now on hearing me, he started running towards me and threw himself so hard onto the ground that I thought I felt the earth tremble.

"You are not kidding, Janos? Don't be cruel with me," he said with disbelief in his voice.

"No, I am dead serious, Stephen. I am looking forward to the experience."

He looked at me in utter disbelief. It was very obvious that he had expected a flat refusal. But then he caught himself quickly as he looked straight into my face. He saw my sincerity, no doubt. He started smiling at first and then broke out in a peal of laughter that shook his whole frame. He slapped his thighs forcefully. And as he calmed down he said, "Janos, this is absolutely fantastic. I love you more than ever before."

"Oh, you don't have to love me for this, Stephen. I really want to do it, and I am anxious to start. But I have one requirement. I would like you to attend the practice sessions, whenever and wherever they are held."

"It's a deal, Janos," he said right away, and he grabbed my right hand with both of his. He shook my hand so firmly that it actually hurt.

"When can we start?"

"As soon as we get the permission from the Russians. I will see about it today as soon as I am leaving you. Oh, Janos, everyone will be thrilled, especially Marika." He was still holding my hand and squeezed it firmly once more.

I could hardly believe my own decisiveness. Just one day ago I was easily swayed and prone to choose refusal; now I was charging ahead into an experience of which I had no idea how it would end. But I suddenly felt an excitement and an aliveness as I hadn't felt in a long time. It was as if an exterior force had taken over my thinking and was making decisions for me. It didn't feel quite like I was in control. It was more like I was being swept away as in Stephen's broad river of life. Once in it, I had to submit to the mainstream of its rushing waters.

I suddenly heard Stephen saying, "Janos, where are you? You haven't said another word in quite a while. Are you having second thoughts?"

Now it was my turn to laugh. It felt good coming from my heart as it did.

"No, Stephen, you can count on me. This is a solemn promise. Go and convince the administration," I finally said as I recovered from my laughter.

"Okay, I will, right now." He jumped up and strode away. He turned around a short distance away and said, "Maybe we'll start tomorrow. Let's see how persuasive I can be." He waved once more and bounced across the yard with his long strides. I truly admired this man.

He did get permission that day, and he told me as I was leaving the shop late that afternoon. He had been waiting for me by the prison fence. "We'll start tomorrow night at seven. We can't lose any time. Are you ready for that, Janos?"

"Sure I am." I replied. I was happy and excited that we would start that soon.

"I am going to meet you tomorrow at the top of the stairs on our floor."

"All right."

We had crossed the prison yard and had entered the empty dining hall. His pictures were now framed and covered with glass. In this finished form, they were more beautiful in their vivid colors than ever. We were now walking side by side in silence, both pursuing our own thoughts. After I noticed the pictures again, I glanced at Stephen sideways and caught his chiseled, manly profile in my sight. He was beautiful, sensitive, a bit capricious, and one very dear friend of mine. I could hardly believe my good fortune.

"You finished framing your pictures, Stephen. They are more striking than ever."

I know I had interrupted some heavy thinking of his, for as he looked over into my face, he had that far away gaze in his eyes that wasn't particularly focused on anything. But his focus came back presently and he responded, "So you are holding my pictures still in high esteem. I am happy for that. I am enamored with them myself," and he again laughed this catching laugh of his that always seemed to throw doubt on the truthfulness of his last statement that had elicited the laughter.

By now we had reached the second floor, and we parted ways after a quick good-bye. I was happy to have a little precious time for myself before I had to go down for the evening meal.

My work the next day went well. I was feeling excited and alive and chatted with Ivan incessantly but still stayed focused on my work at the same time. He became very congenial, for he liked the good work pace and the socializing at the same time. For some reason the day flew by when I had expected it to drag until quitting time. At five thirty I literally flew across the road, through the dining hall, and up the stairs. I washed up more slowly and thoroughly than usual. I checked my appearance again and again in the small mirror that hung on one side of the room. Stephen had given me a razor and blades not too long ago, precious possessions that I had not known since Walter's days. I had not used them since he gave them to me. But that night something drove me to use them. The transformation was remarkable. Though I had kept my beard as short as I could by clipping it frequently, it made me look a lot older than I was. Now this smooth, slim face looked back at me from the piece of glass on the wall that didn't seem at all like me, fresh and incredibly young.

Stephen noticed the change, too, right away. I saw how his eyes widened when he looked at me coming up the stairs.

"You look great, Janos, almost handsome," he said with an impish smile on his face. "I was wondering when you would use them. I almost thought I had wasted a gift on you."

He laughed out loud as usual. That took the edge off his teasing words. I knew he was joking and having a little fun with me as usual. When he stopped laughing, he said very sincerely, "No, you look splendid," and he extended a bundle of clothing to me. "Here, don these for your first dance lesson."

I didn't hesitate this time. "Thanks," I said, and added, "I'll be back in a moment." I headed straight for the washroom.

When I came out, Stephen was still waiting for me patiently in the same spot. He had an approving look in his eyes. He didn't need to comment; I knew myself that I looked good.

"Let me take you to the makeshift dance studio. Come with me," and he gently tugged the sleeve of my white shirt and motioned towards the door at the end of the corridor. It was the same door we had used to go to his studio quite some time ago. How could I have ever, in my wildest dreams, conceived of this second entrance of mine! Arriving at the door, Stephen used his key and said, "You will be given one of these so that you can let yourself in. Then I don't have to wait for you every time you come for your lessons."

On hearing this, I was stunned how much trust the Hungarians invested in me, but I recovered presently.

"That is a very good idea, Stephen. Then your involvement in the practice sessions will take as little of your time as possible."

He just nodded, and we entered the corridor and walked the length of it, side by side, past many doors. Stephen halted at the last door. It opened into a fairly large, virtually empty room. Marika was standing in the far right corner next to one of three chairs. She was already waiting for us although we were a few minutes early. She came towards us as soon as the door opened with barely a smile on her face. This was not how I remembered her, gorgeously dressed and sumptuously beautiful. Her face was pale and devoid of makeup; her glowing red hair was pulled back plainly and knotted at the nape of her neck. She wore a tight, black, long-sleeved bodice and a colorful, calf-length skirt that was slim cut to below her hips but then flared out richly. She was no longer this beautiful goddess of the dance, but a simple young woman. The only thing that was truly alive about her at the moment she was coming towards us were her wide green eyes. They, again, seemed to have gathered up all the life of her pale face. How simple she looked and how much less self-assured than when I saw her last! How could I have ever felt so weak in her presence as I did that night of the concert?

As the three of us met in the middle of the room, she extended her hand to me, and I locked mine into hers in a solid handshake. She withdrew hers rather quickly, but before she did, she said simply and with a veiled look in her eyes, "I am very happy you decided to dance with me, Janos. You'll have a lot to learn within a short time. I want to start immediately."

"That is fine with me, Marika. You are the leader. I will do whatever you want me to do. I hope I won't disappoint you."

Our exchange had gone much better than I had thought it would. She carried herself in a cool and professional manner. I felt none of the intensity I had felt that Sunday evening. I felt no heat rising in me, sensed no intensity from her. I now thought what a fool I had been and began to question the correctness of my recollection. I knew instantaneously that I would be able to work with her. None of my fears seemed to hold true.

Stephen and Marika spoke only briefly. Then he turned and walked to the corner of the room and seated himself on one of the chairs. Meanwhile Marika began explaining to me that we would be going over steps and step progressions and sequences first without music to get the basics down. Later, she said, after a couple of sessions, she would bring a gramophone. And so she began immediately to position me in a certain way and herself opposite me.

"Watch the steps I am showing you. I will perform them in front of you many times. Then I will turn around so that you can begin copying them. I will start very slowly. By the way, we will perform only two dances during the concert, one slow dance and one fast dance, and we will concentrate on getting the basics for these dances down first. After that, we will go over them again, and again, and again until we could do the step combinations and movements in our sleep."

She had spoken softly but fast as she moved away from me. Suddenly her whole body became animated and graceful as if her being had stepped from one body into another, a more lithe and pliable one. Her torso and shoulders straightened up beautifully and her arms began to move slowly but rhythmically as if to a music that only she could hear. Then her feet in black leather pumps started a simple step pattern that repeated itself over and over again. I kept watching her feet and became almost mesmerized by her repetitive movements. The steps seemed simple enough, and I felt confident that I would be able to copy them. After a while she turned around with her back facing me. "Please, start copying my steps. Don't worry if you make mistakes. We will do the steps over and over again until you tell me that you got them."

I began copying her, haltingly at first. But Marika went slow and accentuated each step precisely. They formed a sequence. It took me a while before I mastered the entire step sequence. Then we started from the beginning, over and over again.

"I think I got it," I finally said with excitement.

Apparently she had been waiting for my words for she immediately turned around. When she was facing me, she said softly, "Please, Janos, show me the steps and don't worry about the rest of your body. You will learn later what to do with your torso, your arms, your shoulders and your head. "

I immediately started showing her the sequence I had just learned. I kept on doing it over and over again and laid my whole body and soul into it. I didn't know whether I was doing it right, but I suddenly felt this drummer inside me beating the rhythm, I could plainly hear him, and I followed him with my movements. I became so engrossed with this beating drum and my own rhythm that, for a few moments, I forgot Marika standing there in front of me, Stephen sitting in the corner, this room, this camp, this foreign land. The only thing that seemed to matter to me at that moment was that I was moving. Soon I heard Marika clapping rhythmically with the drumbeat inside me. She speeded up her clapping, so did the drummer inside me, and my feet and movements followed suit. Then Marika started mimicking my steps in front of me. She felt herself into my rhythm. She added arm and body motions that I began to copy. I felt myself more and more in the flow of these simple, repetitive dance movements. It was fun. I felt excitement in every atom of my body. The rhythm and the motion could have gone on forever. But suddenly my drummer stopped and I stopped abruptly. I felt hot and a little exhausted. I had never moved like that before in my life, not like that where I was guided by an internal rhythm maker. After I had stopped, Marika stopped, too. Her hands now clapped in applause as I stood before her.

"This was a wonderful first performance," she said delightedly, and she added, "We will make our dances a success. I am now sure of that."

Stephen had risen from his chair and came over. "That was great, Janos. I knew Marika would choose the right man." He laughed again as he always did.

That same evening we practiced more step sequences, and in the end welded them together into a short harmonious dance. My drummer didn't leave the entire evening. He started up as soon as I started moving and drummed tirelessly as long as I needed him.

By the time Marika said that we were done for the evening, two hours had passed. Time had been suspended for me, and the two hours seemed to have passed in a flash. Stephen came over and almost overwhelmed me with a hug so long and tight as he had never done before. When he released me he said enthusiastically, "Janos, you are great. You and Marika will be a sensation at the concert. I already know it."

"Now, you are going overboard, Stephen. This may have just been a freak beginning. You have no idea how successful the final product will be."

"Oh, don't worry, I know."

With that we prepared to leave. Marika said that she would bring the gramophone next time because she thought I would be progressing faster than anticipated. She felt we should be practicing with music right away. Both thanked me for being willing to participate in their celebration. Stephen suggested that I stay behind to change my clothes. He said Marika would take care of them until the next practice session. He stuck his hand in his pocket and pulled out a key that he handed to me.

"Let yourself in at the next practice session two days from tonight. Arrive a little early so that you can change before we come in. And, thanks again Janos. You are making us quite happy," he said with a clearly appreciative tone in his voice.

"Please, don't mention it, Stephen. It is my enjoyment."

Marika didn't say anything more. It was as if Stephen was the director of the show. She smiled at me before they left, and for a fraction of a second, as Stephen was already turning to leave, her eyes dropped their veil and seemed to sparkle momentarily just for me to behold.

I now began a double life that I thought I would never be able to manage—as an obedient, dedicated worker by day and an ardent and dedicated dance student by night. How I was able to reconcile these two roles I still cannot explain to myself to this day. I distinctly felt however at that time that I was somehow driven to participate in both for the one, I knew for sure, would keep me alive, and the other, the more enticing one, would eventually toss me into the middle of real life as I only afterwards understood.

The change started occurring the night Stephen failed to attend our dance practice. We had been dancing for nearly four weeks now to the folk tunes of Marika's old records and antiquated gramophone. The routines of our two dances had been worked out and we were just about to start refining them and fleshing them out. At first I was a little upset about Stephen's no show. His being there was part of our verbal contract. It was him who was breaking that contract and weakening our artistic endeavor, I thought to myself. Marika noticed my uneasiness immediately.

"Don't worry, Janos, Stephen will just show up a little late tonight. I am sure he was held up. He is very busy, you know, with the upcoming festivity. He is very much involved in the planning of it. Don't worry. The two of us can manage by ourselves, if we have to. I am not worried in the slightest."

She said these words with so much cool firmness and conviction that I thought my own concerns were rather silly. She seemed much more mature than I. I changed my mind immediately and replied as lightheartedly and nonchalantly as I could, "Let the show go on then with or without our friend. Who cares? We can handle it."

"That's what I say. So, let's begin."

She walked over and activated her gramophone. Having become very attuned to each other over last three weeks, we immediately went into the routine of our fast dance. By now I had also learned all the movements of the arms and the upper body. As we twirled and swayed and interacted in the dance, I suddenly felt freer and more passionate about my movements. Whereas in the previous sessions, I was always conscious of Stephen's critical gaze, I now felt a sense of freedom rise in me that was unknown to me before. With the freedom of being able to fully express myself also emerged a sense of passion about the dance and my own movements. My internal drummer worked harder and more intensely than I had experienced him before.

Marika must have sensed my greater intensity and involvement because I felt her following me. And a few times, as we danced opposite each other I detected again that, until now hidden, internal dancer emerge in her, the same dancer I had witnessed during the concert. She became extremely animated and free in her movements and expressions, her pale face suddenly animated with the delicate hues of an early morning sunrise and her eyes flashing as the sun's rays first pierce a clear horizon. Before my eyes, she became transformed, as intensely and wildly beautiful as I had seen her on that concert night. The difference was that she only shone for me this time. That knowledge aroused a strange excitement in me that seemed more concentrated in my loins than anywhere else. Though a part of me started raising a flag that read 'Be on guard! Maintain your reserve!' the other part virtually shouted, 'Give it your all! Keep freeing yourself from all restraints!' It seemed in those moments I could not help myself but let the reins go. I realized as I was sure Marika did, too, that our dance was wild, exuberant, and passionate and would be very successful if we performed it that way for the audience. But in these close quarters of this makeshift dance studio, I felt it was beyond my ability to sustain that intensity. In the end, there came a point when I was relieved that the dance ended and Marika immediately assumed the role of the teacher again. She clapped for me in applause and commented profusely on my talent to perform this dance at a much higher level than ordinarily seen. She appeared suddenly very cool and professional, but, at the same time, ecstatic since she expressed herself in these lavish comments.

We paused a while to catch our breath and remained silent in pursuit of our own thoughts. Mine were wildly disorganized and resisted any attempt to bring order to them. Then, after quite some time had elapsed, Marika rose and walked to the gramophone. From across the room she said, "We must still practice the other dance tonight even though you seem exhausted. But if you do as well as in the last dance, we will be able to quit for tonight. And from now on until the festivity, we will simply go through the dances in the same fashion as tonight. We must solidify them to a point that we could perform them in our sleep. But there is really nothing I can improve on anymore. We just need to stay in practice from now on, but our practices will be shorter."

"I see," I said, "That makes sense. I am willing to follow you whatever you think we must do."

"Thanks, Janos, for your trust."

She appeared quite serious and distant while she had spoken. I was relieved. I thought then it was very possible that we could go through this experience in a truly professional and artistic manner. Momentarily I watched her activate the record, and just as she turned towards me, the slow and lilting folk melody began. She raised her hand as she advanced toward me and I rose to her invitation as in a trance.

This time, our movements flowed slowly, yet we invested no less concentration and passionate dedication to this dance than to the last one. This one required of us to flow together more harmoniously in steady proximity. Our hands and arms became intertwined many times as our bodies moved in close alignment. Her face came so close to mine at times that I felt the urge to touch hers even if ever so slightly. Yet I never did. I reminded myself that I had sworn I would dedicate myself truly to the dancing and nothing else.

Again I was relieved when the dance ended. Though we both had performed very well, and Marika expressed her feelings about our performance profusely, I couldn't think of anything but to get away. My feelings had become so mixed up during the dancing that I desperately needed to gain distance to sort them out and to look at them if possible.

"Thank you for your praise, Marika. It makes me very happy, but I need to get away immediately. I feel very exhausted and tomorrow will be a taxing day."

The way she looked at me, she seemed a little disappointed. I knew she felt she should have gotten an enthusiastic response from me. I felt sorry I could not give it to her in those moments. I yearned for solitude.

All I could say was, "I am so sorry, Marika. Please tell me when you want me to come back."

"Tomorrow night," she virtually spurted out. "Can you come tomorrow night at seven? We need to practice the dances every day for the next ten days. After the festivity you will be relieved of all pressures."

"Sure I can. I will not let you down. We are very close indeed to the culmination of our efforts and you have performed wonders with me, I know."

With those words I left her standing in the middle of the room as I rushed out as if fleeing from her.

31

The Rapture

I raced down the stairs but started slowing down as I approached my sleeping quarters. Once I entered the room I walked as calmly as possible to my bunk. This calm reserve required quite an effort. Some of my fellow prisoners were already asleep, others were still quietly talking to each other. No one seemed to take notice of me. I had not really made any friends in these quarters since I was transferred several weeks ago. I was particularly grateful for the inattention that night because I desperately needed to think. I threw myself down on my bunk. In no time my mind was racing, going over and over what had transpired tonight—what we had said, how we had danced, how we had moved together in harmony and with passion, what strange feelings and sensations I had had, how Marika had responded to me. On and on the thoughts flew by in an incessant whirlwind, like autumn leaves swept up in sudden gusts. I knew I had to still my mind and let the underlying emotions emerge into an uncluttered mind. I tried to lie there in calm suspension for quite some time with my eyes closed. Then I suddenly saw through my confusion: I had fallen in love with Marika. I knew then, too, that the feelings had been confined under the surface as long as Stephen was watching over me, but tonight, as I was left to my own devices, they had broken through to the surface. No wonder I was confused, anxious, apprehensive, and perplexed. I realized that I was in love with her with mind, body, and soul, and probably had been since the night of the concert. It was not only tonight's dance that had stirred up the true passion. Once I saw everything clearly while I was lying there in utter stillness, I understood how difficult the next nine days would be—the practices, the performance, the close contact. I shuddered to think that I could allow myself to be in love with Marika in this hostile place. But I knew I could not bail out of my commitment, not at this stage. Yet any kind of involvement with Marika beyond the dancing could mean the end of her and the end of me. I could not do that to her. I could not let that happen to me. And yet I wanted to be with her above anything else.

"Wait a minute, Janos," I said to myself. "You have entered a contract with Stephen and even though there was a breach of this contract by him tonight, you still must uphold your part of it. You must, you must, you must! Your integrity requires that of you."

I became quite convinced in those silent moments in my bunk that I could do it, that I could uphold my end even to the climax of the performance. The success would be assured as long as Stephen was present. I would seek him out tomorrow and virtually beg him to do it. I had to. He would come to my aid. With those reassuring thoughts I fell asleep and awoke to my astonishment quite refreshed.

At lunchtime the next day, I asked Ivan to give me permission to go back to my bunk to fetch something I needed.

"Oh, sure, there is no problem. If anyone stops you tell him you have my permission, and if he doesn't believe you ask him to check with me. Just be back on time."

"Oh, I will, Ivan. You can be sure of that."

Off I rushed across the road, past the guard at the fence entrance. I waved at him, and he motioned for me to pass through since he knew me quite well. I walked calmly through the dining room, but flew up the stairs all the way to the third floor. I was now doing something I had never done before in all those months since Stephen had befriended me. He had always come to me when he felt he wanted contact with me. Now I was searching him out.

"Do you know where Stephen Teleki is?" I asked the first Hungarian I came across rather breathlessly. He threw me a curious glance.

"No, I don't, but go into our social room over there. You'll find some guys in there. They might know."

With those words he went on his way. I went over to the large room I had been in several times. At the far end four young men were standing in a group arguing intensely. I walked up to them calmly without being noticed.

"Excuse me, please. I need to find Stephen Teleki. Do you know where he is?" I asked pleadingly.

They swung around and faced me. A couple of the men recognized me and I remembered them. They mumbled a 'Hello' and 'Nice to see you.' But one of them said, "I am sorry, Stephen is in an important meeting. You won't be able to reach him for hours." I thanked him and excused myself.

I felt devastated and abandoned as I hurried down the stairs and back over to the shop. Ivan took notice of me as I came running back. He waved and smiled and nodded his head in approval from the interior of the shop while I went straight to my chestnut tree. I had taken my camp lunch and Ivan's offering of the day with me. I still had a little lunchtime left and would be able to munch the food in a hurry before the bell went off.

What was I supposed to do? I knew in my heart that Stephen would be absent again tonight. I just felt it. He had not contacted me; he had not explained himself; he had not apologized. I suddenly saw what he was doing. He would say something when I next saw him, but he would shrug his commitment off in the lighthearted and somewhat flippant way he was so good at. He would say, "I could tell you two were doing just fine. You didn't need me as a chaperone anymore," and he would treat it as not a big deal. He would laugh his usual laugh and I would just forgive him, no matter what he put me through. Such was his personality. No one would ever hold anything against him.

But my problem at hand was really not the absence of Stephen or Stephen himself. It resided with me. I was an adult and I needed to carry on by myself. And suddenly it seemed so strange to me that I could not handle my situation myself. I felt embarrassed, and I swore to myself that I was going to go it alone tonight and that I was going to make it a success.

On my way up to the studio, I was still firmly convinced that I could complete the practices without him. I arrived before Marika did and was able to change quickly. She came shortly after that in her usual modest practice attire. She was very calm when she acknowledged me with a slight smile and a "Hi, Janos."

I hoped we were on the same wavelength. She had, no doubt, thought about it, perhaps as much as I did. I was sure she wanted to remain professional for the rest of our involvement. I could sense that. She expressed it almost in a 'by the way' sort of attitude when she said, "I don't think Stephen will be here tonight. I haven't been able to talk to him all day. But my intuition tells me that he won't come. Hope you are okay with that."

"Yes, I am, Marika. Besides, I don't think we need him anymore," I said, as firmly and convincingly as I could muster.

I don't know why she sighed at that moment as she strode over to the gramophone. It seemed a strange response to what I had said. It seemed oddly out of place in view of the tone she had struck right after she entered the studio. My thoughts were interrupted as the music began and she came towards me, smiling a distant smile as if directed towards an invisible audience. She approached in a stance that seemed to solely indicate that she was ready to dance.

She had chosen the slow dance first this time, and I responded to her invitation rather mechanically. The dance went well but in an almost perfunctory sort of fashion without fervor, without passion, without enthusiastic abandonment. There were no technical flaws, but I never once experienced the same heightened sensations as the night before. Yet I felt relieved and proud that I could pull it off that way.

There were no profusely positive comments from Marika at the end as she usually lavished on me. She could not have commented negatively because I had performed technically perfect. She, herself, had not come to full life as she had the night before, either. At that moment I was wondering what was going through her head. She must have asked herself why I had changed so much.

"That was technically perfect," I suddenly heard her say. "Can you do the next dance right away, or do you want to rest for awhile?" she asked politely.

"I am ready to do the next one. Go right ahead and put on the music."

That dance went practically as the one before. There were no flaws and no missteps. Though we were thoroughly in tune with each other, the performance again lacked the passion and exuberance it had the night before. I never caught the slightest glimpse of Marika the sun goddess as I had seen her the night before.

She said again, "That was impeccably executed, Janos. You have really mastered the dance. I suppose now we are done for the night. I will see you again tomorrow night at the same time?"

"Yes, Marika, I'll be here. And thanks for your comments."

She dismissed my thanks with a slight movement of her hand as if she wanted to say, "Don't mention it."

A feeling of sadness suddenly flooded over me. I thought then that I had lost almost everything that was dear to me and that it was going to be this way for the rest of the time of our collaboration. We would perform perfectly executed dances on the evening of the festivity and that would be it. I suddenly felt abandoned again: first it was by Stephen through his failure to communicate with me and now by Marika through her reluctance to be open and a true friend.

So, I hurried off with a short, "Good-bye," and "See you tomorrow at the same time."

As I sped back to my sleeping quarters, I stopped first in the third floor washroom to change back into my prison clothes. I almost forgot to do that, yet it was important, for no one in my sleeping quarters knew what I was involved in, and it was better that no one knew. I felt sort of numbed as I hit my bunk. What had happened tonight? It seemed in my mind that I had lost two friends on the same day. But, ah, had I really lost them? Or was it my own attitude that caused these feelings? Wasn't I holding back because I wanted it that way, and wasn't it going exactly as I had planned? As I examined my actions carefully, I should have been content with the results they had created, but I realized I was not happy. What did I really want? That question I refused to answer for myself. Instead I suddenly experienced an incredibly weighed down mind, so heavy that I presently dropped off to sleep.

The next evening was practically a repeat of the night before. From a technical standpoint we danced very well but did not let our emotions and feelings enter in. As we finished the second dance and were about to part for the night, Marika positioned herself right in front of me. Her face was pale and emotionless, but her eyes were actively searching my face. I had not come under such close and penetrating scrutiny for quite awhile. She said nothing. Instead her eyes did the talking. It was as if she wanted to cull my features, my expression, for an answer. I was not prepared for such intense searching. Soon I felt my facade crumble when I experienced the same heat rising as I stood before her on the night of the concert. It began to engulf my neck and was about to creep slowly into my face. I turned away from her then, just to prevent her from witnessing my slow disintegration. At that moment, I heard her say to my back rather softly, "Janos, I need to talk to you come what may," and more firmly, " We really need to talk."

"What good would it do?"

"We need to reach an understanding, or we cannot go on like this any longer. Something has occurred that is blocking our performance. I need to know whether it is anything I have done."

"You have done nothing wrong."

My back was still turned toward her. I simply could not turn to face her.

It would have pained and embarrassed me too much.

"Janos, my dear friend, would you follow me to the infirmary? I beg you. We cannot talk here. This is an open room. Anyone could come in here at any moment. Please give me a few moments of your time. Maybe we could come to some sort of understanding. I still think I caused something that you don't want to talk to me about."

"It has nothing to do with you, I swear." I tried to speak calmly.

"Janos, will you accept my request? Will you come with me?" She pleaded again.

"If it means that much to you, I will. Though I can't see that it will change anything," I responded in a non-committal voice.

"Come with me then. It will be good for us to sit down in a more comfortable environment and discuss our common endeavor. Please follow me."

She turned even before I could, and I followed her rather mechanically as if some invisible puppeteer was pulling the strings to set my limbs and body in motion. We headed down the hallway, past the door through which I usually entered, until we came to a door at the end. Marika had steadfastly walked ahead of me. She never turned around to check whether I was following her. I guess she knew I was. She unlocked the door, and we passed through and entered a hallway leading to the infirmary. We encountered no one. Marika now turned to the left down another hallway and stopped at a door she again unlocked. She turned around and asked me to enter, and I slipped past her into the room. I recognized immediately where I was. This room was too personalized to be anything else but hers.

It was a plain, rather small room. The only true adornments were large pictures on the walls of Marika in various costumes and dance poses, mere large unframed, pinned-up photographs. In the far left-hand corner of the room sat a small wooden desk with lamp and chair and an adjacent bookcase. Next to it stood a wooden cot with a mattress. Its dark blankets were tucked in tightly and with precision as in military fashion. On the wall to the left stood a small, two-seater sofa, and on the wall opposite was a clothes rack. It carried in orderly fashion her nursing smocks, her personal clothes, her dance practice skirts and tops, and two colorful costumes. One of the costumes I recognized right away as the one she had worn the night of the concert. Two old suitcases stood in the corner. The lamp on her desk was left turned on. It was the only light in the room, and it lit the room only dimly.

Marika motioned for me to sit down on the couch but I kept standing. I felt relieved that the room was only dimly lit. It would make it easier for me to face her. When I ignored her invitation to sit down, she strode past me to the bookcase, took two glasses and a bottle off the shelf, placed them on the desk, and poured drinks for us.

"Don't worry," she said with a an open, disarming smile as she turned around to offer me the drink, "It's just a harmless cordial to quench your thirst. I hardly ever drink anything wicked."

It seemed these simple words and how they were spoken removed the barrier between us. She appeared now just like a lovely young woman, more appealing and more fragile in the dim light than I had seen her before with only her alabaster face and her large, smiling eyes prominent.

"Won't you sit down, Janos? It would make it easier for us to talk."

"I don't think it will take more than a few minutes. I really need to go, Marika," I maintained my stance stubbornly although I secretly enjoyed being trapped with her in this small, personalized, feminine room. I had not experienced such intimacy since being in Mei Chi's candle-lit room years ago.

"You do not need to go immediately, Janos. Relax at least for a few moments. You have been very uptight last night and tonight. I am thinking incessantly that I might be intimidating you with my sometimes very stern demeanor. I don't mean to do that, especially not to you. Your consent to dance with me means so much to me, I can't begin to convey to you how much. You see, I am virtually ostracized from the rest of us. The men around me act like they are part of a secret society that cannot and will not tolerate females in their midst. I do not quite understand their attitude towards me. I do not hold anything against them, please understand that, because they are treating me with utter courtesy and respect. But they refrain from socializing with me. Sometimes I experience bitterness because it somehow feels as if they are condemning me to solitary confinement. I feel that intensely sometimes, but they obviously don't see it that way. I would love to be part of their discussions, would love to be part of their stargazing. I know you were there once and I am happy for you."

It was like a dam had burst inside her and her feelings came rushing forth like a torrent. In that moment she appeared more vulnerable to me than anyone else I had ever seen. Suddenly a Marika emerged I had not known before, a girl almost, crying out for recognition and companionship. Stephen certainly had not portrayed her as someone desperately lonely. He had said that she fully understood and respected the male prisoners' behavior towards her.

As I abandoned those thoughts, I do not know exactly what happened then and how I could have suddenly acted the way I did. As in a trance I walked over to the desk and set my drink down. When I returned to her, I impulsively threw my arms around her and held her very tight. Part of me wanted it that way; the other part was scared. I did not say a word at first, and Marika did not try to free herself from my embrace. I felt her rigid body pressed against mine. Her arms hung down at her sides and her head was erect. But suddenly she laid her head on my shoulder, ever so gently and I felt her body relax at the same time as if she had capitulated. The most wonderful feeling then arose in me mixed with a warmth and tenderness I had scarcely known before. It felt like she had given herself over to me with such a disarming gesture that immediately unlocked something inside me.

And as from a great distance, I heard myself whisper into her ear, "I love and cherish you with all my heart, Marika. I don't want you to be lonely anymore. You mean the world to me. If we are ever allowed to leave this place, this terrible confinement, I want to go with you; and if we become separated, I will not rest until I find you again, even if it takes the rest of my life."

I had emptied out my love filled heart to her, and I had spoken words and made promises I had not been aware I was capable of making. For a split second I was stunned, I had totally committed myself to her there and then. Then I knew how strong and how sincere my love was for her.

While I whispered to her, I felt her lift her arms and fold them around me just as tightly as my arms held her. It did not take her long after my words were finished that she replied very simply in a whispering tone.

"I love you in the same way. But I would have never had the courage to confess if you hadn't spoken first. We will keep this as our wonderful, very own secret and no one will be able to take this love away from us."

She was the first to free herself from our tight embrace and lifted her face to mine with such expression of abandonment and such a soft glow in her eyes that my lips were magnetically drawn to hers in a kiss that seemed to last an eternity. It seemed our lips were drinking from each other so greedily as if to quench a thirst that was unquenchable. And suddenly I felt a sensation stirring in me that I thought was lost forever. Here was happening what Mei Chi, the wise one, had predicted would happen some day.

I think Marika had felt it, too, for she suddenly tried to release herself. I let her go, but the knowledge was between us. She was the first to regain her composure.

"I think we should part for tonight," she said very softly. " I would like for us to think about what has happened here this evening. Especially you must think. I do not want you to rush into anything you may later regret. I will cherish your words more than anything else that is dear to me. Just think of the consequences that may be the outcome of our union."

I was suddenly jolted out of my rapture. My head spun momentarily but soon began to clear.

"Yes, I should leave, Marika. You are making the right decision. But before I leave, I want you to know that I will never take my words back. They will stand as solid as a mountain."

Suddenly I felt very strong; gone was the weakness that had come upon me in her presence several times before. It never was to return. I left her very quickly after the last few words I had spoken.

For reasons I could not explain to myself at the time, I did not think much as I lay in my bunk a short time later. I just lay there, I don't know how long, and let myself be flooded again and again with those sweet sensations I had felt during our long embrace until I faded away into sleep.

And then I was suddenly dressing myself formally in a black suit for I was to go to a wedding feast. I did not know whose wedding it was. I thought it would be revealed to me when I got to the wedding place. I set out to find the place, but the countryside was rugged and it was rough going. A few times I almost tripped and fell over some rocks. I could have hurt myself but I didn't. The landscape was strangely dark, and I could not see very well. I became confused because it was supposed to be daylight. But I didn't give up. I tried to make progress and eventually did. By then my clothes were not as immaculate as they had been before but rather rumpled. I had originally dressed myself very carefully as if I was about to go to my own wedding. But I knew it wasn't my own. Suddenly the terrain ceased to be rough, it turned lighter, and I found myself skipping down a meadow. Below me I heard music, festive folk tunes, as those played at country weddings. I was happy that I had finally found the place. At the bottom of the meadow, I encountered a large crowd of people. Some I knew. They were old school friends of mine, but also prisoners I had met over the years. Suddenly Mei Chi came towards me beautifully dressed in a slim Chinese dress made of red satin and gold embroidery. She was very striking with her smooth black tresses. She took my hand and I willingly followed her. As by a miracle the crowd of people I had encountered parted freely. They left a narrow passage that Mei Chi and

I strode through. Suddenly we came upon an open space, a large lawn area, next to a country house. A lone young woman strode back and forth in great agitation. She was dressed in a most sumptuous, shimmering wedding gown, and her flower-adorned hair cascaded down her back. No groom was in sight. All her guests stood in a great circle around her while the music played wildly. No one made any effort to console the lonely bride in their midst.

"Look at her," Mei Chi said to me in her soft voice. "Do you recognize her? Go, she needs your help."

I saw her beautiful red hair then, which I hadn't noticed at first, her pale face, her slim waist in the tight-fitting bodice.

"I know who she is, but I can't help her anymore. She has become the sun goddess. Anyone who comes too close to her will burn up."

I clasped Mei Chi's hand tighter and pulled her out away from the crowd. She smiled rather sadly at me and kept on glancing backward as if she couldn't stop being concerned about the anguished bride. But I kept on pulling Mei Chi up the meadow and into the mountains. There was no way she could escape my grasp.

I woke up with a start then. It was still dark in the room, and I still clung to the dream. Its vividness held me in its grasp. Again and again I now saw the bride before my conscious eye and beautiful raven-haired Mei Chi at my side. I felt like I was reaffirming my allegiance to her as I had grasped her firmly and pulled her away into the solitude of the mountains. Is this really where I wanted to go? I thought to myself. And then suddenly her intent became clear to me. Mei Chi wanted me to care for the bride and the bride was Marika. That is the way she wanted me to go. But I was still holding on to a spirit instead of being the groom to the lonely bride. It all made sense all of a sudden. I had lived so long with Mei Chi, had been happy with her, and had obtained strength and nourishment from her. But now she had come to me to give me over to the bride.

A great calmness then suddenly overcame me. I knew how my path was prepared for me. I just had to follow it and just keep pursuing it. With those thoughts I fell asleep. In the morning I felt refreshed, and my first thought was that I needed to let things happen the way they were meant to unfold. I would not erect artificial barriers again.

One thing I knew for certain, I needed to stay the course with Ivan. I had not been negligent about my work with him and much good had come to me as a consequence. In a way, as Ivan would never even begin to realize, he was instrumental in my involvement with Marika. Had he not retained me as his worker and even given nourishment to me, I would not have come to the point where I was. In gratitude, I would stay devoted to him no matter what would happen.

Marika and I had only five more practice sessions left and after that would follow the performance. In the evening of that day I raced up the stairs early. I changed clothes quickly and waited calmly for her. I didn't mind the waiting. Just the anticipation of her coming seemed to satisfy me. I wondered how she would enter. And then she came through the door. Her face lit up instantaneously as soon as she saw me and a faint blush, like that of an impending summer sunrise, spread over her cheeks. She appeared happy and excited, the way I had not seen her before, and I spontaneously rushed towards her. My arms folded around her and held her as tight as the night before. While I felt her pushing softly against me, I heard her whisper, "Janos, my darling, we need to practice first." I let her go then and we both laughed simultaneously, a disarmingly happy laugh.

That evening we gave to ourselves the best performance yet. Our movements were flawless; they were precisely synchronized but flowed with an ease and abandonment as if we were moving with one heart, one soul, and one passion. We felt exhilarated when the dances were done for we knew that they would be immensely successful. They would fill the hall with such exuberance that they would set the audience on fire. We had both wanted it that way, and now we had achieved it, for nothing would change before the performance. I knew we both were sure of that. This practice ended like none had ever before.

"Please leave your practice clothes on and follow me in about two minutes. It's better that we are not seen together. You know the way, and I will leave the doors open for you. Just close the door that leads to the infirmary behind you after entering. It should be closed at all times. Let's hurry."

"I'll come," is all I could say and she was gone.

She had asked no questions. She had intuitively known the outcome of my thinking process. She had felt my abandonment and passion. And she was right; we did not need to talk anymore.

I entered her room without being seen by anyone, I was sure, and she locked the door behind me. Instead of her lamp, Marika had lit two candles. They threw a soft, intimate light over her room. Suddenly it did not appear sparse anymore, but sumptuously warm and inviting. It was she who embraced me first that evening. She stood on her toes with her arms folded around my neck to bring her face up to the level of mine, and she kissed me tenderly. I let it happen and gave myself over to the wonderful feeling of being desired. Freeing herself a little, she whispered in my ear almost coyly and with an almost quivering reticence.

"We must be very quiet, darling."

"Yes, I know."

I swept her up into my arms then, carried her to her cot, and laid her down gently. She moved over and onto her side. Lying next to her, face to face, I think an unreality overcame us both that made us doubt we were really experiencing this moment. We began to stroke and caress each other at the same time just to reassure ourselves that we were real. And then it happened so quickly and so passionately that time and space became suspended. I found myself floating in weightless space and knew she was with me. We traveled along in unison until we came to a place so marvelous and unearthly beautiful that we experienced a sensation as if being washed over with waves upon waves of bliss.

I was the first to return to reality and opened my eyes. I saw her lovely face below me. Her eyes were closed. She was silently weeping now. I shifted over without letting her face out of my sight.

"Marika, my love, what is happening?" I asked with concern in a barely audible voice.

"Forgive me, darling. I am just immensely moved and happy."

I was relieved then and took her into my arms. We lay like that, silently and tightly entwined, it seemed for an unfathomable time. There was only oneness.

It was Marika who called us back to reality, "We must leave each other now," I heard her say with incredible gentleness in her voice, and yet I was jolted out of my position immediately. I stood on my feet presently and reached down to pull her up to me.

"No," she begged, "Leave me here like this. I want to keep on experiencing us until I fall asleep. I kneeled down and placed the softest, gentlest kiss I could imagine on her lips and she responded in kind.

I got up and turned quickly away from her. Standing in front of the door, I patted down my hair and rearranged my clothes. Just before I left, I threw a quick glance at her to take her picture with me into the night. I hurried down the hallways, and when I came back into the Hungarians' quarters, a few young men were lingering by the washroom. I had no idea how late it was. Some of the men knew me and were obviously aware what I was involved in.

"How are the dances coming? We can't wait. Four more days!" one of them shouted.

"Oh, it's going well. It will be a good performance, I think."

"Good for you," said another one.

I disappeared immediately into the washroom and changed. I was hoping that the men would be gone when I came out. I did not want any more exchanges. To my relief they were gone. As I reached my sleeping quarters, the lights were already out and I stole quietly to my bunk. That night I let all the sweet sensations I had experienced with Marika wash over me again and again until I found myself floating in a gently rocking sea that carried me to the shores of a land I had not visited before.

"You look sleepy!" Ivan remarked teasingly when I arrived in the shop the next morning.

"Yes, I know, I didn't sleep well all night."

"What a pity!" he said with sincere concern in his voice. "Maybe you should work a little slower today. You have been working at a frantic pace in the past two weeks. No wonder!"

I thanked him profusely for his observation and suggestion. I almost felt guilty and deceptive because Ivan did not know the secret activities I was involved in. He would never know. But even that day with my less than full strength, I gave everything to him I had in me. Thoughts of the upcoming evening carried me through.

Though the day seemed long, the evening inevitably arrived. The practice session was exhilarating. Our subsequent love-making was more prolonged and more passionate than the night before. And so it would progress through the next few evenings. We were so insatiably thirsty after years of drought that we didn't seem to be able to imbibe enough each time we drank at that inexhaustible fountain. In those few nights until the performance, our happiness and our thrilling experiences seemed to know no end. We became reckless and threw all caution into the wind. Every night I stayed longer with Marika than the evening before. We had shrugged off all worries and lived just in those moments we were together. It sometimes crossed my mind that we needed to be more careful, more restrained. But then I quickly dismissed those thoughts.

On the third evening on my way to Marika's I did not feel concern when I met the Hungarians' doctor, Marika's superior, in the hallway of the infirmary. I thought I remembered him from the stargazing night. Stephen talked to me about him some time ago. I also remembered that his name was

Sándor. He was dressed in a doctor's smock and a stethoscope dangled from his neck. He said 'Hello' to me and threw me a quizzical look. He must have been surprised to see me in this hallway knowing that I was a German prisoner. I returned his acknowledgement likewise. We both rushed past each other. I do not really know, but he may have turned around to throw another glance at me. I however moved forward in great haste. I did not want to look back.

It happened at the same time the following night. I was again on my way to Marika's when Sándor popped through the infirmary door exactly as he had done the night before. Even then I was not worried. We said our 'Hellos' and hurried off in opposite directions. I did not tell Marika about my encounters with Sándor.

On the fifth, our last night before the performance, I was met by no one in the hallway. But even in my haste and excitement to get to Marika, I did take note that the hallway had been empty. I felt a sense of relief. And seconds later in the arms of Marika, my passion for her seemed endless.

That night she told me about her family and her childhood.

She was an only child and grew up in a loving home. Her father was a Hungarian doctor; her mother was a dancer and singer, and she was of gypsy descent on her mother's side. Marika remembered her mother and father loving each other very much. They hugged and touched each other a lot. Marika and her parents lived together in a comfortable apartment overlooking the river in the center of Budapest. Their lives were happy. Her parents entertained frequently, and her mother always sang for their guests and was accompanied by a couple of hired musicians. As a child, Marika would marvel at her mother's elegant but colorful clothes, different, more striking, than those the other ladies wore. She always appeared carefree, but was somewhat moody, temperamental, and even capricious at times. But her father admired her mother. His face was pale and he had red hair, whereas her mother had dark, wavy hair and striking green emerald eyes. Marika's idyllic home life, as she remembered it, changed drastically when Hungary became involved in the war. Her father was drafted into the Hungarian military as a field army doctor. The Hungarian military was loyal to the Germans at first. Marika was eighteen when her father left her and her mother. She very infrequently saw him after he was inducted. She continued living with her mother. She had started studying nursing at the medical college in Budapest. In the evenings she had begun to take dancing lessons, and she and her mother entertained themselves by singing and dancing together after the father had left. But her mother's health slowly declined physically and then mentally when life in Budapest became duller and bleaker as time went on. Two years later, Nazi officers came to her mother's apartment, Marika was twenty then, and took her mother away for interrogation. They sent her to a camp in Poland in which, Marika suspected, her mother perished, for she never heard from her again. During his rare returns to the apartment, Marika heard her father moan during the night as one in great pain. She knew it pained him greatly to have lost his beloved wife. He also drank heavily which she had never noticed before. He would drink Scotch whisky during their pre-war parties and sometimes in the evening, but never ever to excess. He loved Scotch whisky. Marika now fended mostly for herself. She was still attending nursing school, and earned her diploma a few months after her twentieth birthday. Her father's sister came to live with her since her husband was also gone. Marika and her aunt kept each other company in her parents' apartment until Marika was inducted into the Hungarian nursing corps to serve the war effort. After the Hungarians' switch of allegiance to the Russian side, Marika was sent against her will to Russia to serve the massive Russian war effort. She never had contact with her father again. At first she moved from field hospital to field hospital. She couldn't remember anymore in all the strange places she had been. Just when she thought that she might not survive her ordeal, she was transferred. She thought herself very lucky when she came to this Hungarian prison outpost a couple of years after the end of the war. She said she had lived a very easy life here in comparison to what had transpired before, but it was the loneliness and social ostracism that bothered her very much.

I felt touched and overcome with sadness by Marika's emotional account of her youth, her family life, her parents, her mother's and father's demise, and her own odyssey and hardships in a foreign and hostile land. All I could do was to hold her and stroke her gently until calmness came back to her. Marika knew my own story in detail. I had told it to her the night before.

"Somehow we will make a life for ourselves that will be the equivalent and perhaps even better than what we have lost," I promised her and added, "This prison will be closed soon. I feel it. It's now more than three years after the war ended."

She looked at me and smiled and nodded her head. She wanted to believe me desperately, I knew, and I held her for a long time.

The day of the festivity arrived. It was to start at seven. I left the workshop punctually at five, and never took more care in preparing myself than for this event. I had not seen Stephen since the day I searched for him during my lunch hour. Having been occupied as I was, I really did not think about him much anymore. Though I had forgiven him, once in a while I still felt a stab of pain in my heart because I thought he was my very good friend, but he did not once during the past two weeks come to see and talk to me. I knew I would see him briefly during the festivities. But our meetings would be short, superficial and marked by his kind of lightheartedness.

The night before the festivity, Marika had brought my performance costume to the practice session. It consisted of slim, black pants, black calf-high leather boots, a royal blue waistband, and a sumptuously detailed, white cotton shirt of the finest quality. I could have sworn the items were Hungarian made. I felt a sense of thrill when I changed into those clothes in our small dance studio. I went out to the washroom just to see myself in the mirror. I looked stunning in those theatrical clothes that fitted me perfectly. My face was clean-shaven, and my blond hair carefully combed. The deep blue of the waistband blended beautifully with the blue of my eyes. I was immensely pleased. And always in the back of my mind stood Marika's love and devotion for me. Even under my uncertain and precarious circumstances, I felt myself to be a very lucky man.

As I entered the dance studio again, Marika was already present, transformed into the incredibly beautiful dancer I had seen at the concert. She wore the second costume she owned, the one with the red, gold-embroidered bodice and the golden yellow, calf-length skirt. Her slender arms were bare and barely capped at the shoulders by the small, puffy sleeves of her white cotton blouse. She appeared stunningly beautiful. Her mass of red hair ringed the top of her head in a nest of braids, and on top sat a sparkling tiara. I wanted to rush over to her and embrace her, but I refrained. I was afraid I would crush and destroy her sparkling beauty. There would be no love making tonight, no feast of passion, just a feast for the senses of sight and sound.

A young man then entered the studio with a tray of caviar, chicken liver pate and golden wheat wafers, and a carafe of water. He offered these delicacies to us. It seemed like it was a feast just prepared for us on our special evening, as if it were our celebration alone. At the same time, I could not believe what my eyes saw and my mouth tasted. Leave it to the Hungarians, they will perform miracles, I thought to myself, and added quickly that I now knew what Stephen had been involved with. He must have set the whole universe in motion to procure these delicacies.

251

The concert began. Marika and I moved over to a space just off to the side of the slightly elevated stage the band stood on. We could watch through a curtain as the band played their incredibly fine renditions of popular Hungarian folk music. Then it happened like it had during the concert. Their music whipped up the audience into an emotional frenzy that always died away periodically as the music fell back into the slow pace as it had started. It became a waxing and waning of passion and abandonment to sentimental nostalgia. The music played on for about an hour.

Then it was Marika's and my turn. I was not quite sure about Marika's feelings, but I entered the room in extreme excitement. We stood in the same place where Marika had stood during the last concert. We must have made a fine appearance, for the crowd applauded, shouted, and stomped their feet even before we began. It took a while before we could start. We just stood there in anticipation of our performance and smiled, nodded our heads to the audience and then looked at each other in disbelief. To interrupt the audience's cajoling, whistling, and carrying on, the band began to play and the emotions simmered down. Then the music stopped abruptly and it remained silent in the hall. Marika and I took our positions and the music of the fast dance began. We performed even better than during the best practice nights. There could not have been more precision, harmony, exactness, and passionate abandonment between us. The audience felt it. They swayed back and forth and clapped rhythmically but gently so as not to drown out the music. It was magical. We performed both dances splendidly. The audience roared in delight. Among the clapping and whistling, the call for an encore became stronger and more demanding. We danced our dances two more times and still the audience demanded more. We felt elated and exhausted at the same time. As we bowed the third time, the lights were suddenly switched off. We stood in darkness, and that signaled the definite end of our performance. We were able to escape from the room then, and the audience was suddenly stunned into silence. When the hall lit up again, Stephen jumped up onto the podium and called for a fifteen-minute intermission.

It was then that I saw him again after his two-week absence. He came backstage and greeted us profusely. He embraced Marika first and thanked her for her "miracle work" as he called it, and the night's performance. He laughed his usual laugh and seemed very excited. Then he turned to me.

"What a miraculous transformation, Janos!" he cried. "From prisoner to performer par excellence!" He embraced me tightly then and held me for a long time it seemed.

"I knew you would make it a great success! Thank you for doing this for us." By then he had released me, but he still clasped my arms with his hands and held me like that at arm's length. "You are very talented, Janos, in more then a few areas," he said, I thought, slightly cryptically, and I wondered at the time what other areas he was referring to. I hoped he had no knowledge about everything we had done and my brief, seemingly accidental meetings with Sándor suddenly popped into my mind. It was a disturbing recollection.

"I should be thanking you, Stephen." I tried to keep my calm. "You made this wonderful experience possible for me. I feel immensely grateful to you."

"Oh, don't mention it. The gratitude is all on our side. What would this festivity have been without your and Marika's contribution? You two are really something. What a performance!" And he laughed a full-chested laugh this time as if to underscore the pleasure everyone had experienced. With an "Excuse me, friends, I need to see to the next details," he rushed out of the room.

The third part of the concert consisted of another performance by the band and a few vocals by Marika. In the end we all came together on stage and bowed while the audience hollered and applauded to their hearts' content. And then, unbelievably, they asked for one more dance. They insisted and insisted. We all looked at each other on stage, Marika and I raised up our shoulders and stretched out our arms with palms turned up as if to say, "What should we do?" Then the bandleader nodded to his musicians, and we danced our dances one more time.

It felt strange that I should stand in the receiving line next to Marika after the performance was finally finished and done. How everything had changed within a few weeks I marveled to myself, and I remembered how I had blushed in front of her just a short time ago. Now I was finally myself and in command.

We all parted shortly after midnight after consuming the leftover delicacies of cake and coffee, champagne and wine. We mingled with the audience. There seemed no end to their compliments. When Marika and I said our final good-byes, we held our hands standing in front of each other. She still looked radiant at the end of the night. She gave no sign of fatigue. I looked at her so intensely as if I wanted to imprint my inner self with a vision of her. I was speechless then for all my intent of taking her in.

"I'll see you soon. Thanks for a wonderful evening," she suddenly said. She pressed my hands very tightly then.

"Yes, yes, I thank you too," I replied with some confusion and feelings of unreality, for it seemed to me then suddenly as if I were speaking my last words, which I was certain that it could not be so. She departed quickly then. All evening she had never betrayed her true feelings. She had behaved properly and admirably, and I had taken the cue from her. As soon as she was gone, I went to the washroom and changed. I left my costume with Kálmán the bandleader and asked him to give it to Stephen.

As I tumbled down the stairs, Rilke's "Spanish Dancer" suddenly, out of the recesses of my mind, entered the forefront. In my elated mood I recited the poem to myself. With every new stanza a sudden excitement grew within me, and I knew I had found my Spanish Dancer:

A match is struck: the center blazes white
before the flame spreads out in all directions
and, all around, the orange tongues ignite.
The audience in a circle. All at once
she comes alive and flares into her dance

and suddenly the dancer is all fire.

The eyes flash once: she sets ablaze her hair
then in an instant, boldly, brilliantly
whirls her whole dress alight—and you can see
two angry arms extended from the flames
like writhing serpents, rattling and alarmed.

At last it is enough, for she can spare
exactly this much fire, nothing more.
She rakes it up to cast it, roaring, down
and watches as it blazes on the ground
her manner masterful and proud.

Serene in victory she lifts her head
and smiling sweetly in acknowledgement
she stamps her sturdy feet and leaves it dead.

32

Loss and Gain

That night my elation knew no end. I lay in my bunk for hours, letting the experience of the evening parade before my mind's eye again and again. It felt as if I had slipped into a wonderland where everything and anything was possible. Sleep did not come to me until the wee hours of the morning. I had not been worrying about my insomnia because the next day was Sunday. I could sleep as much as I wanted the following day. And that I did. I missed breakfast and lunch on that Sunday, something I had never ever done before since the beginning of my imprisonment. I did go to the dining room for dinner. But at the time of the evening meal, I hungered more for a word from Marika than for food. When the Hungarians came into the dining room as a group as always, I thought I would be able to attract Stephen's attention. I thought maybe I could sign to him, and he could talk to me after the evening meal was over. But Stephen never showed up. I wondered why he would miss this meal.

I became very restless and tossed myself onto my bunk right after the meal was finished. I closed my eyes to give an outward appearance of calmness in the hope that my fellow roommates would leave me alone, and they did. Despite my apparent calmness, a storm raged inside me. Thoughts flew by in rapid succession like gale-driven clouds in the night sky. My mood was dark. I suddenly thought that possibly I would never see Marika again. It seemed to me at the time as if she had disappeared. Even Stephen did not seem accessible anymore. A panic then gripped me that was exacerbated by my inability to move in my bunk let alone to take action. My chest felt constricted, my head ached, my temples pounded, and my limbs were trembling. It felt like I was on the verge of suffocation. Every time when I was about to scream to release the panic I felt, I got up to go to the washroom, just to find relief and to get out of the self-imposed, outward state of calmness. How I finally went to sleep that night, I cannot recall. It was probably pure exhaustion in the end. All of the calming techniques I tried, most of them Mei Chi's, did not work that night.

I was up the next morning just as the first faint rays of the sun streaked across the morning sky. I was much calmer then and wondered why I had panicked so badly the night before. Standing by the window with everyone still asleep in the room behind me, I tried to work up a feeling of faith and hope for the new dawning day. What I was sure of was: I would give my all to working with Ivan. I needed work more than anything else at that moment. Working myself into oblivion seemed the most desirable activity in the world then.

And, indeed, I was fine while I worked with Ivan. He lavished two hard-boiled eggs on me that day. I kept on chatting with him continuously all day while we worked. The more involved I was with talking, the less my own private thoughts were able to intrude.

Lunchtime I spent again under my tree, and I was hoping that Stephen would show up. But he did not come. By nightfall there was still no word from Marika or Stephen. He was not among his friends at dinnertime either. My unrest grew. I did not know what to make of Marika's silence and Stephen's mysterious absences. Marika could have gotten a note to me if she had wanted to. Then something happened inside me that I thought would not have been possible. I began to doubt Marika's sincerity. Could she have led me on with that warm, passionate, and giving manner just to make our performance a success? But I dismissed that thought almost as soon as it surfaced when, in the next moment, I recalled our wonderful, passionate evenings together. No one in the world could have faked those feelings, such complete giving of herself, not even the best actress. No, Marika had been real and sincere.

It was not until the third day after the festivity that I spied Stephen as he came through the gate in the fence. I watched him as he walked towards me, a different man, I thought, than I had known him. His usual springy gait was slow almost dragging as if he were reluctant to meet with me. His face was serious. Even when we made eye contact, his face remained somber. He never did flash his usual endearing smile as we greeted each other. He let himself down next to me so slowly that I thought he would not reach the ground before the lunch bell rang.

"Janos, I am sorry that you have not seen me during the past few days. I couldn't bring myself at first to come and see you, but I knew I had to. You must have been wondering why I would not communicate with you after that fine performance."

He had spoken very slowly and haltingly as if a heavy weight was constricting his chest.

"Don't worry, Stephen, it's fine. I am just very happy that you have come today. But tell me what has been going on these past two days," I asked him with an unveiled curiosity in my voice.

"I don't know whether I am really capable of telling you, for I am hurt and you will be hurt just as much, maybe even more than me. I always hated to be the bringer of bad news. I always only wanted to deal with good news," he said with sadness in his voice.

"I think I know you well enough, Stephen, that I understand. What's been happening to you that could make you this distraught? I thought I would never see you like this." He grabbed my hand then and pressed it hard.

"It is not me, Janos, it is Marika. I know you have grown very fond of her. That is why this is so hard," he said in a desperate tone as he pressed my hand even harder so that it pained me.

"Marika has been taken away," he suddenly spurted out rapidly without looking at me. "She is gone, vanished from this Godforsaken camp. Armed guards had been waiting in her room while she performed with you that night. As I understand it, they had already packed all her belongings by the time she came back, and she was whisked away in a military vehicle at gunpoint. Where to, we do not know. I wasn't present when they took her, but Ágoston was and he told me."

Even though the clarity of his words with which he recounted these happenings did not diminish, his voice did. It almost died, and his last few words were barely audible. With every word Stephen had spoken, little by little, everything went cold inside me as if a deep winter freeze had suddenly set in. And a numbness came over me that prevented me, I believe, from fully grasping the news he had brought. My face must have become a stone mask.

As I felt his eyes on me, he said, "I feel devastated and incredibly sad and sorry, Janos. I know you became very good friends. She was my friend, too. She was a friend to all of us. We are beside ourselves."

I still could not look at him or say anything; instead I stared off into the distance.

"Janos, please," he started up again; this time pleadingly, "Please don't take it this hard. I have already gone to see Leskov several times since her disappearance. He and I have become friends of sorts. He has helped us so much over the past year and has given us so much freedom that we are grateful to him. But in this case, he has remained very secretive and non-committal. Every time I have gone to see him, he has been steadfast in not divulging anything that concerns Marika. He simply won't budge. He says he doesn't know any details. Unfortunately, no information is forthcoming from him, except that he assures me that Marika would be very well taken care of. He asked me not to worry. But he won't even give me a reason why she was taken away this unexpectedly. We know, the prison administration will act and intervene in prisoner affairs oftentimes without prior warning. But in this case, we were stunned by the drastic and completely unexpected action. Then, during our last conversation, he completely dropped the subject of Marika. And as if to placate me, he told me then that we Hungarians would be released within fourteen days, perhaps sooner. I would have normally jumped for joy at hearing this news. God, we have been waiting for so long for our release! But in light of what has happened to one of us, I couldn't even get excited. In times like these, I can see the abyss that lies between the Russians and us that can sometimes not be bridged. This last act they shouldn't have committed. Oh, Christ, it felt like an act of last punishment before they will set us free." I had heard his words as from a great distance. My far-away gaze returned to him. He appeared very distraught when he was uttering the last few words, and he hung his head as if in defeat.

"I am more than devastated, Stephen. Marika means more than the world to me with all she has taught me. I don't know how I will be able to get over this or go on without her. Right now I am too numb to comprehend the full extent of this tragedy. I am very sorry and sad for all of you."

I would have loved to embrace Stephen, but I couldn't, not in full view of Ivan and my fellow shop workers. Instead tears now flowed out of my eyes spontaneously and rolled down my cheeks while my face otherwise did not betray the despair inside me from where these tears sprang.

At that moment the bell rang, and Stephen gathered himself up.

"I'm immensely sorry, Janos. I cannot express my feelings in words. I will see you soon. Take care and be strong, my friend."

With these words he left me while I quickly got up and turned my back to the shop so that I could wipe away my tears. Moments later I was back at work.

After a while Ivan commented, "How different your Hungarian friend had looked today!"

I knew then how closely I was always being watched, much closer than I had expected.

"It's because he brought bad and good news." I replied. " One of them has been taken away unexpectedly and at gunpoint. He expressed his sadness and dismay to me over this incident. At the same time, he brought the good news that they will be going home soon, all of them as a group."

"Ah, this explains the difference in his demeanor. I thought he might be ill. But don't you be distraught. This fellow prisoner of theirs, I can assure you, must have done something unforgivable. Otherwise they would not have removed him in that way." I well understood then that Ivan had infinitely more faith in his own people than we prisoners did.

I suffered through the days and nights one more week, and then something happened that has affected my life to such an overwhelming magnitude that I still, even now, after all those years, cannot comprehend why life or forces beyond life would deal me such disastrous and fortuitous cards, all at about the same time. Since the news of Marika's disappearance, I began to pray night after night to remove this latest misfortune from me. I did not know whom I prayed to: God, the Master of the Universe, the all-pervading Creative Spirit, or the One that goes by many names. But I felt such an urge to pray, as I had never felt before to ease my pain.

Then, out of seemingly nowhere or it could just as well have been a finely crafted act, a part of the grand design, Mikhail showed up in the shop one afternoon. He waved to me, but instead of coming over to me, he went to see Ivan. They talked quietly for awhile, and then I heard Ivan say, "Yes, of course, he can go right now and stay as long as he has to." After that, they both turned towards me and Mikhail said in an apparently friendly tone, "Janos, you are wanted in the administration. Please follow me."

If his tone had not sounded friendly, I would have been very worried. Ivan then added, "I have given you time off. Take it easy, Janos. And don't worry about work for once."

"Thanks, Ivan."

"Come with me then," Mikhail encouraged me and added after a short pause, "The official who is asking for you wants you to come right now."

"I am ready," I said with a great deal of concern in the back of my mind, for I could only think that it was now my to turn to be called on the carpet. What unfortunate fate could befall me now after all those years of getting by relatively unscathed were the only thoughts that crowded my imagination?

Mikhail and I rushed across the street, past the guard at the fence, and into the dining hall. We were headed for the door that I knew concealed the administrative offices. It was exactly where we had gone to meet with Director Leskov well over a year ago, on that fateful day that rescued me from the mining camp. Mikhail stayed steadily ahead of me even as we entered the hallway leading to the offices. Obviously, he did not want me to talk to him any further. His silence began to worry me. He used to be, even if a little reserved, quite friendly. He must have faked the initial friendly tone he struck in the shop in front of Ivan I thought. My heart began to sink.

Then, suddenly, Mikhail threw open an unmarked door and asked me to enter. He closed the door behind me very quickly. A fine slim figure, immaculately uniformed, stood by the window. His back was turned towards me. I could not imagine who it could be. I knew it was not Leskov. He did not have the fine appearance this person had. Then he turned around quickly, and I recognized him right away even through his impressively official facade. His suddenly standing in front of me took my breath away. I wanted to call out his name but remained strangely speechless.

"Janos," he called out and his face beamed. "Have you forgotten me already?"

I still stood very still and silent like one who had never heard or spoken a word before in his life.

"Janos," he called out again, "What have they done to you. I thought you had been treated well since you came to this section of the camp. I have been following your progress and received regular reports."

He then stepped very close to me until we were standing face to face. As I looked into his gently smiling eyes and felt his breath brush my cheek, I found my voice again.

"Andrei!" I cried out suddenly and with tears in my eyes. "Andrei, my friend, benefactor, and savior!" A feeling of happiness flooded my entire being almost instantaneously at the moment when I regained my speech.

Before I knew it, Andrei had wrapped his arms around me. While we stood there in a long embrace, he said, "You don't have to say anything, Janos, my friend. It seems a long time since Dom Sovieta. I know your seeing me here must be overwhelming to you."

He let me go then. Looking into my now happy face, he added. "I have been worried about you, but now that I see you, I am relieved. You look well. They must have treated you well, but you must have done your part too."

"I tried to very hard, Andrei. I don't know how to thank you. I had no idea it was you who saved my life."

"We are friends, aren't we?"

"Yes, we are. I always knew we were."

"Well, we are now and always have been. Listen very carefully, Janos, because our meeting will be short. I am on my way to Moscow. I have been promoted. I will no longer be involved with prison camps, but will have an assistant position in the foreign ministry, and I am determined to work my way up. I have been very fortunate. Shortly after you left Dom Sovieta, Bolkov, remember him, he was transferred and Bukarin recommended me to Moscow for Bolkov's position. They granted it. It prepared me for my new position in Moscow, and Bukarin's recommendations helped a lot, believe me. But what I really wanted to tell you was that Dom Sovieta will be closed down completely in two months. I was the first to leave that dreadful place. But the best news is for you. Keep it to yourself, please. This camp will be closed within six to eight months. Prisoners will be released slowly, in stages, until the camp will be emptied out."

He had whispered the last few sentences, and he continued in that vein. "This is absolutely confidential information. It's strictly between you and me. I wanted you to know to make sure that you will be hanging in there to the end. After it is all done and over with and you are back home, I hope you will consider working for a company that does business with Russia. So, you see, we will see each other in the future on equal terms. I can't wait for that to happen, and I'll do my best to make sure that it will. Believe me, I will keep tabs on you."

He laughed then a victorious laugh, I thought, if one could call it that. I suddenly laughed, too, and quite freely.

"Andrei, Andrei, you are just about the most wonderful person I have ever come across. Let's hope for a long friendship."

"I'll drink to that," he said and he lifted his arm with an imaginary glass inside his cupped hand.

"Yes, let's." And I lifted my imaginary glass as well.

Our meeting came to an end quickly. He took a note out of his pocket that he handed to me. On a scrap of paper he had written his full name: Andrei Barinov as well as his official Moscow address at the foreign ministry. "Just in case you come to Moscow before I can contact you in Germany! I want to be doubly safe that we will meet again. Tuck this note away so that no one can find it. It's best that you carry it on your body at all times. It would even be better if you committed the information to memory and destroyed the note."

"I will certainly do as you say. I am daring to get excited about the future right now."

"Let's make it a good one, better than our elders were capable of. Remember I love and respect you Janos Jablonsky."

Now I wanted to hug him, but he had already walked over to the door, and I followed him. I understood that our meeting needed to be brief and that he needed to be cautious. Suddenly he turned around once more, grabbed my arms, pulled me towards him, and kissed me lightly on the right and then on the left cheek in true Russian fashion. I let it happen with happiness in my heart. Our eyes met once more in a strong, steady, and determined gaze; and it seemed to me in that moment as if he was elevating me, the prisoner, to his absolute equal. He opened the door, and I left the room quickly for we had possibly tarried already too long.

As I walked back to the shop to continue working with Ivan for the rest of the day, I felt a lightness in my body that I hadn't known since I was a youngster. I felt incredibly blessed because of my friendship with Andrei. I suddenly knew that my intense prayers of the last few days had been heard and acted upon, however in a mysteriously and unfathomably different way than what I had been asking for, and I was ready in my heart to accept this precious gift by faith.

I had wanted to tell Andrei the story of Marika and me right there and then in that small, impersonal office and to ask for his help to find her. But some intuitive impulse prevented me from mentioning my loss and pain to him. I felt that I could and would ask for his help when we would meet again.

My stay at the prison camp was as Andrei had promised. Within seven months I was on the train riding across Russia to freedom. The Hungarians had left within two weeks of my painful meeting with Stephen. He came one more time to say good-bye. We held hands and reminisced about our friendship, but we did not speak of Marika again. I felt he wouldn't be able to do anything about her. And I sensed that his mind was already back in Hungary, I felt it strongly, surveying the opportunities that lay in store for him. I felt happy for his release.

When I finally left the camp seven months later, the only person who seemed crushed was Ivan. Sweet, stoic man!

"I have never met and will never meet an outstanding worker like you again, Janos. This time with you has been the best of my life." He moved me to tears.

"It was a very good time for me, too, Ivan. I will not forget you. Thanks for everything you have taught me and have done for me." We hugged for a seemingly long time. But when I broke away, I turned quickly for my emotions were boiling over and my tears ran freely. He was one of my saviors, too.

PART III
Epilogue

November 1, 1959

33

Parting

I awoke like out of a dream when he stopped talking. Could it really be that opposite me, across the table, sat my mysterious boss visibly exhausted? He had been talking tirelessly and animatedly all night, and I had hungrily absorbed the story of his incredible odyssey. I felt overwhelmed by his wanting to share these horrifying and elevating experiences with me. My heart and mind bulged with the images that had flooded them in an incessant stream until both seemed on the verge of bursting. They could hold no more. But what a gift I had been bestowed!

Outside, a first faint grayish light was rising in the east and settled softly over the park-like landscape of the immaculately kept garden. Ah yes, I remembered now, we were in Joachim Breitner's home, and memories of my farewell party came back to me. I looked over at Janos. He had raised his head and looked across the table at me with a wan smile. He seemed drained and speechless now. But what a firework and what feat of story telling he had displayed! I think he was just as overwhelmed as I was. I remembered now how he had started off the night before. He had grabbed my hands, held them tight for a while as his story, almost inadvertently, tumbled forth. It was like a fresh mountain stream after a snowmelt. Nothing could hem it in or dam it for it rushes with the urgency of nature unleashed down the mountainside. That's how Janos's story came rushing down on me. It must have been frozen for a long time. How and why the ice melted, I will never know. I did not probe into the reasons why, I just accepted the outpour as an incredibly precious gift. And yet I had questions that I was dying to ask. I was almost discouraged to ask them when I saw his tired and far away gaze. He was still immersed in the past. But I could not contain myself.

"What happened to Marika? Did you ever meet her again?"

To my surprise, Janos looked up at me and life returned to his eyes immediately.

"I haven't found her yet, but I am still searching with he help of Andrei. We see each other socially and on business every time I travel to Moscow. I think you know how well our business connection works. He now has a family, a lovely wife and two children. He invites me to his home, and we cherish the long and heated conversations we always have when we meet."

His face was illuminated by a satisfied smile as he contemplated the times he had spent with Andrei under the new conditions of his cherished freedom. And I thought to myself he is still looking for her. Steiner was right. He had mentioned to me some time ago that Janos was looking for a mystery woman every time he travels to Moscow. When Steiner brought it up in sort of a flippant way I dismissed it as pure gossip.

"Did you ever see Stephen again?"

"No, I lost track of him, and I did not make the effort to contact him though I cherish the fond memories of him. Maybe I am doing him an injustice but a nagging feeling that he knew more than he let on will not go away. God forgive me if I am wrong."

"And what about Walter? All these people I have never known now suddenly mean so much to me. It is as if I had been there and witnessed all your experiences."

"I must have told the story well, and I am glad you are taking such an interest. I knew you would. Now I am not so much of a mystery to you anymore. I will always remember how you looked at me sometimes, quizzically, with that question so obviously in your mind, 'Who are you?' Am I right? Say I'm right."

I blushed then. I felt my face turn crimson before his eyes. He did not need an answer. I was easily readable.

"Ah, yes, you asked about Walter. He made it home to his beloved wife and daughters. That much I know, but there was no sense in trying to renew our relationship because he would not be able to forgive me for being a traitor to the fatherland. I, myself, cherish the fondest memories of him. In my mind he remains a good, compassionate, and very gifted man."

As soon as Janos had finished his last sentence, Joachim's head popped through the sliding door, his hair unkempt, his face unshaven. He had obviously just woken up.

"What are you already doing here in the breakfast room all dressed up. I thought you had gone home. There won't be breakfast for a while."

"Sorry, Joachim, we haven't just come back, we have been here all night telling stories. Will you call a taxi please, I need to get Miss Werner home."

All of a sudden, the magic was gone. The morning, the new day, and another person had intruded.

A few minutes later, Janos accompanied me to the taxi that would whisk me away. He gave me a last hug so full of strength and feeling that I knew I would not be able to forget him and that his spirit would live with me forever.

As I sat in the taxi and turned my head to look at him once more, he stood there at the curb, bear-like and somewhat forlorn and solitary, like all the other times.

I would soon be off on my travels and would most likely never see or communicate with Janos again in my life.

Lament

Whom will you cry to, heart? More and more lonely,
your path struggles on through incomprehensible
mankind. All the more futile perhaps
for keeping to its direction,
keeping on toward the future,
toward what has been lost.

Once. You lamented? What was it? A fallen berry
of jubilation, unripe.
But now the whole tree of my jubilation
is breaking, in the storm it is breaking, my slow
tree of joy.
Loveliest in my invisible
landscape, you that made me more known
to the invisible angels.

Rainer Maria Rilke

Printed in the United States
68835LVS00003B/367-408

9 781424 109678